THE TALL SHIPS

JOHN JENNINGS

The Tall Ships

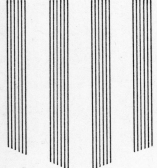

McGRAW-HILL BOOK COMPANY, INC.

NEW YORK   TORONTO   LONDON

FOR BERNIE

I must go down to the seas again,

　　To the lonely sea and the sky,

And all I ask is a tall ship

　　And a star to steer her by,

And the wheel's kick

　　And the wind's song

　　　And the white sails shaking,

And a gray mist on the sea's face

　　And a gray dawn breaking.

Sea Fever—JOHN MASEFIELD

PART **I** ☆

My Maryland

Friday, March 20, 1807.

I am not likely to forget the date. It was Nancy's sixteenth birthday and the Colonel gave a mighty party for her at Holly Hall. That evening the Colonel asked me to carry a load of oysters for him across the Bay to Annapolis in my bugeye on the morrow, and Nancy begged to go along.

In themselves these were small matters, but from them all the rest followed.

Holly Hall, our neighbor, was one of the larger plantations on the Neck. It sprawled across the widest part, from Chesapeake Bay on the west to the coves and inlets that notched the shore of Harris's Creek on the east. From north to south it was more than 3 miles long, and was split neatly down the middle by the oyster-shell road that crossed the Neck. West of the road the great fields where Colonel Savage raised his corn and tobacco and melons ran far down to the Bay. To the east a considerable stand of the virgin forest remained, and the little clearings here and there among the trees were used for the kitchen gardens and for pasture for his blooded horses and purebred cattle and sheep and swine and fowl.

The Hall itself stood aloof upon a knoll at the tip of one of the little finger peninsulas that jut into the creek. Its approach was a lane of gnarled water oaks, and it was surrounded by fine gardens enclosed in hedges of precisely trimmed boxwood. It was a large old house of mellowed yellow bricks with twin single-story wings and double chimneys and high white-pillared porticoes front and back. Before the wide veranda, a circle of shell and gravel served as a turnaround for carriages, and the lush lawns rolled down gently to the tree-fringed basin of Little Holly Cove. In the back, lawns less carefully groomed sloped down to the row of yellow-brick cabins which housed the Colonel's slaves. Beyond the cabins a single stout dock thrust a long finger toward the middle of Great Holly Cove, where the Colonel's sloop and cutter and clumsy big market schooner rocked in the sheltered anchorage.

Over on the west side, on the Bay, the Colonel had built a

long landing stage. Here a vessel might tie up to load or unload, if the sea were calm. But in all the length of his Bay-side acres there was no place where the Colonel's boats could lie untended and sheltered by so much as a point of marshland.

It was different with us. We had Forbes Landfall—so named to commemorate my father's retirement from the sea with the loss of his right arm after the War for Independence. Forbes Landfall was far less grand than Holly Hall. Ours was a white frame house, smaller than the Hall and without porticoes; only a flight of wide steps with gracefully curved balustrades led up to the front door. Our fields were fewer but more compact. We, too, looked out over sloping green lawns dotted with dogwood and laurel magnolia, sweet gum and wax myrtle. Below was our prized and envied possession, Forbes Inlet— one of the few protected coves to be found along that side of the Neck. Beyond its encircling arm of marshland stretched the broad reach of the Bay itself, blue and sparkling in the sunlight, boisterously forbidding in storm, past the low bulk of Poplar Island, to the distant green-crowned bluffs of the western shore.

All this was within our compass. So were our most important markets. From Forbes Inlet, Annapolis was no more than two or three hours' easy sail in good weather; Baltimore was no more than an hour beyond. But from Great Holly Cove it was the better part of a day's journey to either, for a vessel must run southward from Harris's Creek all the way down around the bottom of the Neck before turning northward up the Bay.

I thought little of it then, but there have been times since when I have wondered whether the Colonel did not have his eye on our inlet rather than on me.

A genial eye it was, as I think back, but there had never been any affection in it. The Colonel, for many years a widower, was a hard man with his money and his slaves and had an evil temper. 'Twas said that he loved no one but his daughter, and that too much. 'Twas also said, up and down the Neck, around Romancoke Bay, and as far south as Cambridge on the Choptank, that one day Nancy Savage and Ben Forbes would marry. Yet everyone knew that the Colonel intended Giles Penrose, of the Penrose Hundred estates, for Nancy. So much for gossip.

My family had always been politely cool toward the Colonel. We are not finer folk but we did not mistreat our slaves and, although poor enough, we were openhanded. The coolness did not, however, extend to the motherless Nancy. From the time when, escaping her nurse, she had trotted her pony down to our inlet and had fallen in, to be fished out by me, she was the darling of my father, mother, and sisters. From these easy conquests she had turned to me.

A boy already plagued with three sisters does not take kindly to a self-made fourth who seems to have nothing better to do than to dog him. But my sisters had always been nastily female, full of giggles and shrieks and unaccountable tears. The red-haired skinny brat from Holly Hall had not cried when I pulled her out of the inlet; she had only stared. The second time she came I was ordered to take her riding. That was not to my liking, and when we went out I kicked her shins. She did not run bawling to my mother. She thought for a moment, looking at me with her green stare, and unexpectedly returned the kick with good measure. After that we were much together, riding and fishing, crabbing and swimming. Sometimes I took her sailing, but not too often, because once when we were quarreling she called my precious bugeye a silly old tub. That was long ago, of course, and we remained friends and allies against the rest of the world. All the same, I could never be persuaded aboard the Colonel's sleek schooner which was the envy of my soul.

On the day of Nancy's party, folk who lived at a distance set out early for Holly Hall. All morning long we saw them coming, in carriages, on foot, in boats. For many who came by water it was convenient to moor at Forbes Inlet, permission for which was cordially granted, and they passed the time of day with us while our carriage and pony cart went back and forth, carrying the ladies to the Hall. My two elder sisters, married now, had arrived early, and there was such a female clatter in the house that I spent the day at the inlet among the boats. By the time I had dressed, the house was empty and I rode alone to Nancy's party.

It was dusk when I arrived and Holly Hall glowed brightly from the lights of a thousand candles. Old acquaintances seemed strangely unfamiliar in their silken and jeweled finery. I made out half a dozen Tilghmans. The family had been among the original grantees a hundred and fifty years ago, and the clan had spread out along the Eastern Shore so that one could scarcely move without stumbling over a Tilghman. I was hailed by Dick and Tom from Avalon and Fairbank on Tilghman's Island, warmly thumped by John from Sherwood Hall, given a nod by Lloyd of Rich Neck and a greeting by Dr. William Tilghman from Saint Michael's.

I saw the Clays, Tom and George, who'd come all the way

from Claylands, and the chattering Sears brothers, William and James, from Sears' Fancy down the Neck. There was Jacob Gibson who owned Sharp's Island and who so admired the bandit Bonaparte that he had named his four plantations Jena, Austerlitz, Marengo, and Friedland. And of course the Penrose family, of Penrose Hundred. Threading my way through the rustling silks of girls and women I knew, who tonight were transformed into grand ladies, I paid my respects and my apologies for latecoming to my mother and sisters. Mother arranged the ruffle at my throat in a way that made me afraid she would inquire whether I had washed my neck, and so I retreated to the veranda. There I came upon Giles Penrose. We exchanged a look but did not speak. The first time we met, many years ago, we had set upon each other for no reason but that we had to. Animals and boys know their enemies within their own kind.

"Ah, Ben, my boy." The Colonel advanced upon me, beaming. He was a little man, standing not above the bridge of my nose, and I no more than middle height. He was puffy and strutty as a bantam.

"Yes, yes," he said, anticipating me, "a happy occasion. Yes." He waved it away. "I've been watching for you. Let me speak of it before it slips my mind. The nigras brought in a cartload of oysters last night and we couldn't ship them today because of the ball. If I don't get them to market tomorrow morning they'll go bad."

And that, I thought, would be a painful loss to you, Colonel. But I didn't say it. I looked out at the broken, driven clouds in the evening sky and "felt" the weather as a sailing man does. The general drift of air was from the south but the clouds themselves were moving in from the east—a bad sign.

"Ben!"

Here was Nancy, holding out her hands in warm welcome. I hadn't seen her in a month, save for glimpses of her in our house where she had been in mysterious feminine consultation with my mother and my sister Wendy. It had annoyed me a little. Why should there be such a fuss over a party? Here was the reason—to produce a different Nancy from the one I had known. Her coppery hair was piled high. She seemed taller, and willowy. Taking her hands, I noted she was wearing a slender, high-waisted, yellow gown of a filmy stuff, trimmed with golden ribbons in the French manner so that they crossed between her breasts, making much of them. This was somehow confusing.

"Hello, Nan," I blurted. "Happy birthday!"

"So will you take them?" asked the Colonel.

"What? Oh, I beg your pardon, sir. The oysters."

"I'd pay, of course," he assured me hastily. "The usual."

I often did such chores for him and we had long since agreed upon the rate. He'd no call to be cutting me down to a paid errand boy before the new golden Mistress Savage and within the hearing of others. But I only said, "The weather is making up."

"Oh, come!" he scoffed. "You can't be afraid of a bit of a blow."

"Ben afraid?" Nancy looked at her father in astonishment. "Of course not! And I will go too, if he'll permit me. I have ever so many things to buy."

"There!" said the Colonel with fatuous pride. "Nancy wouldn't be afraid if the devil himself came up from out of the sea. She'll go along and see you through."

"Cato's beached," I said, "and the bugeye's hard to handle alone if we get any kind of sea."

"You can take my Tip," the Colonel offered.

I hesitated. I knew his Tip—a great, hulking blue-gum black from the lower Carolinas, good-natured, strong as a bull, and as clumsy. He was not to be compared with my lithe, tawny Cato, with whom I had grown up. But Cato had changed of late. He was surreptitiously lying with Cassiopeia, one of our house girls, and when he wasn't dreamy he was jumpy. He was no good to me or to anyone just now, except maybe Cassie.

"I'll have the boys fetch the cart to your dock an hour before dawn," said the Colonel, as if it were all settled. "Tip will have your cargo stowed away before you're ready to sail."

"And you *will* let me come, won't you, Ben?" Nancy was sweetly pleading. "It's my birthday, you know. You are not to deny me anything."

My father had quietly joined us. "Quite so," he said smiling. "There comes a time in every gentleman's life when he cannot and may not deny a lady."

I bowed formally. "It will be an honor to have the company of Mistress Savage."

"Perfectly! Perfectly!" said the Colonel in a way he had, blinking and nodding rapidly the while. "And Ben, you might fetch me back a few items. Nothing much. Tobacco and flour, a couple of pipes of wine, and a keg of powder and some shot. I'll send the list with Tip." He touched my father's empty sleeve where the elbow would be. "Captain, I have some choice drinking whisky...."

"I should be delighted to join you in a toast to the occasion,

Colonel," my father said, and they went off most amicably together.

The titles were purely courtesy. Father had held no more than a sailing master's rank in the Continental Navy, while the "Colonel" had mustered out of the Maryland Line, after Yorktown, a mere captain. But it was the custom and nobody minded—save only myself. To me an empty title was an empty sleeve. I had become impatient of my father's determination that I would one day serve in the fleet. I would as gladly have gone to sea in a merchantman as wait forever for a commission. For five years now I had been listed in the Navy's books a midshipman. But first had come the Peace Establishment Act, sharply limiting the numbers engaged and setting aside many good men at half pay; and then we had the unwarlike Mr. Jefferson with his little gunboat fleet. To be sure, we had fought a war in Barbary, but with small forces and I had not been chosen, so at seventeen I still stewed ashore or fiddled about the Bay in my bugeye, lonely and savage, yearning like some lovesick creature for a man's world.

Nancy said, "Well, Ben, aren't you going to kiss me?"

I looked at her and felt myself grow hot. "Here? Now?"

"Where else?" she said, all innocence. "You haven't given me a proper greeting. You kissed me on my fifteenth birthday, and on my fourteenth, and—no, on the thirteenth I scratched you—but it was all right on the twelfth, and you brought me a beautiful toad. And on the eleventh. . . ."

I seized her then, but she turned her head so that my lips slithered across her cheek, and with a supple twist she was out of my grasp, but not before I'd felt the warmth of her young body against mine. Her laugh, floating back, sounded wicked in my ears. I saw around me the amused faces of guests who had been watching us, and to escape them plunged after her into the house.

TWO

The Colonel called it a ball, but it was not so grand. Indeed, it was no more than the usual kind of sociable gathering of old friends and neighbors in a sprawling countryside where every possible event was made the most of.

A stand-up supper was served, since to seat so many was clearly not possible. There were oysters and crabs and all manner of roasts, fowl, game, and fish, and pies and fancy cakes and brandied fruits and wine and cider. Later the elders drank more potent stuff while the young were regaled with punch and fireworks on the south lawn above Little Holly Cove, and on the wide veranda five musicians played industriously.

For myself, after dining well and drinking perhaps too well, I permitted myself to be lured into one of the box-enclosed gardens by a Nancy who appeared to have something on her mind. Overhead the tattered clouds swept across the face of the moon. I sniffed the air. There was a promise of cold in it, and of wet.

"Please, Ben," said Nancy, "let me be of more consequence, tonight at least, than the weather."

I faced her in the patchwork pattern of shifting light and it came over me with a feeling of surprise that she was lovely! Her eyes shone like dark stars in the moonglow and her small pixie face was wistful. Why should she be sad? I had never seen her so.

"What is it, Nan?" I asked gently.

"I don't know. It's being grown, I think," she said gravely, as though she had weightily pondered it.

From my own superiority of one year and a half I could smile inwardly. But I felt a great tenderness for her and I knew that I did not want to hurt her as children do, as we had often heedlessly hurt each other. I said, "You must not be unhappy, Nan. You will fall in love, and he will be very tall and wonderfully handsome and marvelously rich, and he will worship you as you deserve."

"Yes, of course," she said matter-of-factly.

I did not like that and so I sniffed the weather again.

"Ben!"

I sighed, feeling much put upon.

"You were not kind to me when you arrived. And I was so happy to see you! I had been waiting and waiting for you."

Was it possible that she was going to cry? "Nancy!" I exclaimed. "Why, Nan, I didn't mean—I did want to. . . ."

She did not turn her face from me this time, and her mouth was soft and warm, and it was no child's kiss. Something had happened to the skinny little brat who had been all bones topped by a green stare and a tangle of red curls. It was a woman's body that filled my embrace, her arms about me, her disturbing breasts raising a frightening but delicious clamor in all my being.

Footsteps crunched on the gravel path. We started guiltily apart as Giles Penrose came upon us. For a long moment we three stood gaping at one another. Then, filled with a different kind of exaltation, I found my voice.

"You seem to have been misdirected, my friend," I said pleasantly. My meaning was plain enough. Holly Hall boasted two fine, spacious yellow-brick outhouses.

"I was sent by the Colonel to find Mistress Savage," Giles said icily.

Nancy hesitated. We waited, Giles and I. At last, with an odd little secret sort of smile, she gathered up her skirts in both hands and slipped away. We listened to her receding footsteps in the gravel and it came to me that Giles, searching for us, must have been walking for the most part upon the verge of lawn. It was like him, I thought; a landsman he was, not an open, honest seaman.

We eyed each other.

"All right, boy," he said with easy insolence.

It was his usual infuriating manner, inviting me to accept a thrashing. But in the instant I saw him as the lover I had foolishly promised Nancy, for he was tall—much taller than I—and heavily built, and women—my sister Wendy, for one— thought him handsome; and the Penrose estates were among the richest around. My old response toward his challenge had always been a bristling, yelling, doglike rage, and invariably I had been trounced. Now, however, I was possessed by a new, joyous passion so calm and purposeful that it might have been a song.

With his first blow I merely moved my head. It grazed my cheekbone. He had been careless.

Laughing aloud, I plunged my fist into his unguarded middle. With a grunt he doubled. I intended to end the matter then and there with a jolt to the jaw, but a cloud must have darkened the moon, or else my aim was poor. I hit nothing but the wind and, recovering my balance in time, told myself ironically, "Bad weather."

We moved like lively puppets, he flailing his fists and I dancing lightly out of their reach, now and then smartly rapping him about the head and body. At last, maddened, he rushed me. Once again he left himself open. This time my fist's short, vicious arc found his face and came away wet with his blood.

I looked down at him, stretched his full length on his face among the rosebushes by the side of the path, and felt the quiet satisfaction of a job well done. I was prepared to discuss the fight with him while flexing my hands, straightening my coat, and rearranging my neckcloth. "You've gone soft, Giles," I explained. "It's because you hate the water, hate even to get your feet wet."

A sound came from him but he did not get up, and so I left him there.

I looked for Nancy and found her on the veranda surrounded by admirers pleading for the next dance. She saw me. With that curious secret little smile she lifted her chin, turned, and moved off with a Tilghman. Putting on airs, was she? I thought her ridiculous, and retreated in search of better company.

At a pillar of the south portico, Alec Carmichael was holding forth against England and all things British. Jerry Pratt and bird-faced Oliver Ahrens were baiting him but he did not mind. Alec, a great, hulking lad from the upper end of the Neck, plodded on to an end and then said to me, "Your mouth is bleeding."

Unspoken questions filled the air as I swiped at myself with my handkerchief. "It was only . . ." I began, but at that moment Giles himself came stalking out of the dark. He was a sorry spectacle, even in our dim light, with leaves, dust, and dirt clinging to his coat and his hair all in disorder. With pleased interest I saw that his face was scratched, probably from the rose thorns, and he was dabbing at a thin stream of blood that trickled from his nose. I wondered fleetingly where he was bound for in such a state.

At sight of me he halted abruptly. "You struck me, sir!"

Bewilderment left me speechless.

Carmichael took command. "Did you strike him, Ben?"

"That I did, Alec," I said in no little indignation. "But his was the first blow, and it was a fair fight."

"Sir," Alec inquired of Giles, "was it a fair fight?"

Giles made no reply to the question. Instead he said, "Gentlemen, bear witness. I demand satisfaction."

I could scarcely believe I had heard him right. Dueling was a common enough way of settling differences in the big cities of Baltimore, Richmond, and Charleston, but along our Eastern Shore it was rarely invoked.

"Alec, he's gone mad!" I cried.

Jerry Pratt interposed. He was a long, gangling youth, pale of face and hair, scarcely prepossessing in appearance, but he had cousins in Baltimore and was known to have stood a second there in at least one duel, perhaps more. He said, "Forbes, you may not insult the—" he sought a word—"the proponent. There are rules that must be observed."

Oliver Ahrens, who was from Buckthorn over beyond Saint Michael's, laughed in a high, tittering kind of way. "Was it Nancy? What were they doing, Giles?"

"The rules, sir!" Pratt rebuked him.

Giles said, "I insist upon satisfaction."

"He insists," Pratt relayed to me, as if the rules did not permit me ears.

"Then he shall have it," I replied.

We stood for a moment in noble and dignified stance. "Well," I said, "what do we do now?"

"You and Giles choose your seconds, of course," said a new voice. Mordecai Wright, the sharp-eyed dandy from up Queenstown way, had joined us. "And then. . . ." He glanced back. On the veranda the music had stopped and several couples were coming down the stairs.

Hurriedly I chose Alec and Jerry Pratt for my seconds. Giles named Oliver Ahrens and Mordecai Wright. Ahrens proposed we go to the library, but Mordecai said the Colonel was there with the heavy drinkers among his guests.

"The study, then," I suggested. It was in the back of the house, overlooking the slave quarters. There the Colonel of a morning cast up his accounts and administered punishment to miscreant slaves.

As if by conspiratorial agreement, although nothing was said, we divided, three and three, each group going around the house in an opposite direction. We met as by a miracle of perfect timing before the door to the study. Pratt entered first and announced that all was well, the room was empty. We filed in. We stood about, resuming dignity. Giles, I saw, had in transit brushed his coat and smoothed his hair.

"Well?" I asked impatiently. "What now?"

"Sabers," Giles said grimly. "At dawn."

I had never held a saber in my hand but I was familiar enough with the cutlass and thought it might not be very different, and so I was ready to agree. But Jerry Pratt said sharply: "One moment, sir. It lies with Forbes, as the challenged, to name the time, the place, and the weapons."

Giles Penrose stared at him in unbelief. "Who says?" he demanded.

"Those are the *rules*," Pratt said firmly.

Giles looked at the others.

Oliver shrugged. "I don't know."

"We'll go by the rules," growled Alec Carmichael.

"I don't know too much about it," Mordecai admitted, "but I think that is correct, Giles. As I recall, that's how it was when Burke and Hempstead had it out in Gallows Field three years ago."

"Very well, then," said Giles.

All turned to me.

"Pistols," I said, remembering a book I had read. "Pistols. At ten paces."

"Pistols it is," said Pratt. "What about the time?"

"Dawn tomorrow," Giles cut in, forgetting the rules. "Why wait?"

"Agreed!" I said promptly. That too had been in the book. But then I suddenly remembered. "No! I'm sorry! I promised the Colonel to carry a load of oysters to Annapolis for him tomorrow. Do the rules say anything about oysters, Jerry? They can't wait, you know."

Giles said, "You might decide not to come back."

"I'll be back!" I said hotly.

"You'll have to accept his word," said Pratt. "This is a meeting of gentlemen, and a gentleman's word is not to be questioned."

"That's so," said Alec, adding, "The oysters come first, Giles. If you should kill or maim him he'd not be able to keep his promise to the Colonel, and he made that promise before ever this began."

The clear logic impressed even Jerry Pratt, who had been frowningly considering the question of the oysters. "All right," he said. "Day after tomorrow. It's settled."

But Oliver Ahrens spoke up. "That's the Sabbath, day after tomorrow, and I don't think we'd consider this God's work."

I liked him a little better for that.

Alec nodded agreement. "It will have to be Monday."

"Monday it is!" Pratt snapped conclusively. "Now, what about the place?"

Again they looked to me, and all at once I was filled with an unholy glee.

"The place?" I said musingly, as if casting about in my mind. "Ah, yes! The very place! Poplar Island, the far point behind James Sears' house."

The very thought of crossing an expanse of water made Giles look ill. "Poplar Island!" he cried. "Oh, see here now—"

"You challenged, didn't you?" Jerry Pratt said coldly, and Giles fell silent.

"The rest," Pratt said, "is up to the seconds. In fact, if it had been properly done you gentlemen would not have ex-changed a word after the challenge and its acceptance. It should have been done by note of hand. Well, there it is. The gentlemen may go now and leave the further details to their seconds."

"Who has the pistols?" Alec asked.

No one spoke. We all looked to Pratt as the acknowledged veteran of these encounters, but at this point he seemed as lost as the rest of us. Giles remained sullenly silent.

"I couldn't lay my hands on anything but a fowling piece," said Mordecai Wright.

"That would not do," Pratt said.

"Maybe the Colonel. . . ." Ahrens began timidly.

"Don't be an ass, Oliver!" Pratt told him.

"My father has a pair," I ventured.

"Will he let you have them?" Pratt asked.

"I think so," I said, but in honesty had to add that I was not certain.

"This is not in the rules," Pratt said reproachfully. "The weapons are always available."

I snorted. "Would Giles's sabers have been easier to find?"

Pratt looked at Giles and decided not to press the question. He frowned fiercely in concentration. "Forbes, your father may refuse. In that case, we should have some alternate."

I was tiring of the silly game. "Scythes or pitchforks will do," I said carelessly.

Even Alec was aghast at the suggestion, and Giles broke his silence. "This is a *gentleman's* quarrel," he protested.

"A quarrel's a quarrel whoever's involved, Penrose," I told him. "If there must be weapons, then we fight with whatever weapons come to hand. What does it matter, so long as the match is even? But I will try to secure the pistols."

I went to the door and was about to leave when I recollected my manners. "Sir!" I bowed to my challenger, holding the door for him.

He in turn bowed to our seconds, saying, "Thank you, gentlemen."

They bent low, and he left without a glance at me.

It occurred to me as I too bowed to the seconds, with my thanks, that we must all have read the same book.

As I closed the door, I heard: "We'll need a doctor. It's in the rules." That was Jerry Pratt. Our seconds were getting down to details.

THREE

The party was ending. Many who had far to go had already taken their leave. The usual disorder prevailed, with mothers rounding up their children, and wives their drinking husbands, and stern fathers their dancing daughters, for the fiddles still sawed away on the veranda, their sound mingling with the shouts for horses and carriages, and the private battles among the scurrying grooms, and the crunch of wheels and hooves on the gravel turnabout.

I had time for a cordial and, at her request, brought one to Nancy, who was being very gay with John Taylor. Alec Carmichael appeared at my elbow and drew me a little aside. "It's all settled, Ben. Doc Tilghman will attend. If you can't get the pistols it will be your choice of scythes or pitchforks in a 10-foot circle. First man to draw blood steps outside and. . . ."

I clapped a hand to my ear. What was a whisper to Alec shouted, it seemed to me, clear through my head and across the room. But then I thought myself mistaken, for Nancy appeared oblivious. She was radiant with John Taylor and poor John was as a man in a dream.

When I took my leave, Mistress Savage was so marvelously sweet that I found myself gaping, bemused. I wondered how many conquests she had made that night, and swore to myself she deserved every one of them and was not to be blamed if she lightly tossed them away.

"Tomorrow at dawn," I heard myself. "Pitchforks."

"Pitchforks, Ben?" I caught the secret smile in her eyes.

"I mean—breakfast. You'll breakfast with me at the Landfall?"

"My thanks. How very kind. *Dear* Ben."

I bowed low. "Your servant, ma'am."

She curtsied.

This fine formality I marred, however, as a thought came to me while joining the outward flow of the departing guests. "Nan!" I called back to her. "Be on time!"

FOUR

I handed my mother and Wendy into our carriage and saw them off. My father and I followed ahorse. Father rode on every pretext to show himself, or maybe God, that with one arm he was a better man than others with two, and I think he loved his black stallion the way the Colonel was said to love his daughter—more than anything or anyone in the world.

We rode the first quarter of a mile in silence while, as usual, he taught the great wilful beast who was master. My father was a lessoning kind of man, for his family as well as for his horses. But he never used his whip.

The stallion subdued, I spurred my mare to ride beside him, trying out in my mind various approaches regarding the pistols. Yet I knew it was a useless exercise. Father had never permitted wheedling or any manner of subtlety.

Before I could gather the courage to speak, he said, "I have talked with Jacob Gibson. He has seen Charlie Gordon. You remember Captain Gordon of Oxenhall?"

I did. Charles Gordon was somewhat better than a courtesy captain. He had retained his commission, which was that of a master commandant.

"The *Chesapeake* has been ordered out of ordinary to be refitted for sea duty. Gordon has been offered the command. I go to Oxford, Ben, to speak for you to Captain Gordon."

The *Chesapeake* was a man-o'-war and it was news of great moment that she was to sail again, but hundreds of able men would be clamoring for a berth. I saw no hope for me.

However, I blessed the *Chesapeake* and Jacob Gibson and Captain Gordon for having put my father in excellent humor, and my "Thank you, sir!" was so warm that father's hand reached down out of the jogging night to clap me on the shoulder.

And so, without any preliminary, I asked to borrow his dueling pistols.

The stallion plunged under his hand and whinnied in protest.

"Ben," said my father in the cold, lecturing manner I hated, "I have tried hard to make a man of a reckless, hot-headed boy, a man who would with honor carry on my name. The sea is no melon patch. There is no place on it for children."

Having thus delivered himself of the opinion that I was not a worthy son and in all likelihood would disgrace a naval commission, he said sharply, "What have you done now?"

Despairing, I said, "I have been called out, sir."

"Called out? Preposterous!"

He fell silent but I sensed his anger. After a moment I ventured, "It doesn't much matter, sir. If I cannot have the pistols we will fight with scythes or pitchforks."

"What!"

It had not occurred to me that my father would have strong feelings on this matter. Yet it appeared, from his hearty swearing—which I enjoyed much better than his hectoring—that all Maryland would be shamed in the sight of the Federal Union if, on its sacred soil, a duel were fought with scythes or pitchforks. The son of Allen Forbes could be no party to such a disreputable affair.

"But there is nothing in the rules...." I began.

"Who called you out?"

"Giles Penrose. Father, the rules say nothing. . . ."

"Penrose?" Again his mount suffered. "Penrose!"

His tone had changed entirely.

Years ago my father had, even as George Washington, left his five ancestral acres to go to war against George III. While he had fought at sea and lost an arm for independence, the then head of the Penrose family had sat at home amassing a fortune through the exploits of merchantmen turned privateers in which he had invested part ownership. To him my father, on his return, had been forced to sell his own rundown holdings. With the money he had purchased Forbes Landfall. This I knew from the slaves but nothing was said of it in our house.

Nothing had been said, and yet things unsaid may make a speaking silence. I wondered now how much of my hostility toward Giles Penrose had emanated from my father. But this was a thought too deep for me. It addled my brain and I shook it off.

"Was it—" my father said hopefully, "hum—er—did it concern a lady?"

In my heart I was doubtful. Giles and I had always fought on the occasions when we had met. Nancy or no, we would have fought this time, too, and it was only because Giles could not bear to be beaten that he had called me out.

Still, without lying I could say that it concerned a lady, and did so.

"Ben, you were not in the wrong?"

"No, sir!"

"When is this encounter to take place?"

"Monday morning."

"Where?"

"Well, sir, I—chose Poplar Island." He gave way to laughter. Father rarely laughed but when he did it seemed to rock the earth. His horse was having a bad time this night.

When he had recovered he said, "You may have the pistols."

"Thank you, sir."

"And, Ben."

"Yes, sir?"

"I only had to use them once. Do not dishonor them."

I did not see how there could be any honor in the affair. The guns would go off and frighten a lot of gulls and there would be a great deal of bowing before and after.

But I said, "Yes, sir."

Nancy was late. The black shadows had faded, and although the lights were still yellow in the kitchen and dining room and on the porch, it was no longer necessary to carry a lantern. For the fifth time I went down to the dock. The grass was wet. The air was wet, too, and a squall of rain was crossing the cove before me. Although the land wind was wild and blustery, out beyond a gray fog hung over the Bay, almost perceptibly thickening, hugging close to the water. We should have been on our way half an hour ago.

The Colonel's huge black boy was perched on the rail of the *Ladybug*, my bugeye. "Ready, Mist' Ben?" he said lazily.

I shook my head. He grinned.

Once again I considered setting off without waiting any longer for Nancy. Once again I reconsidered and went back to the house.

The dining room provided little comfort. What with Cato's air of mournful reproach, it was as sodden as the weather. It occurred to me only now that he had no right there. "Where's Cassie?" I demanded.

"That Cassy-opee, she done got a kin' of pleuritick fevuh this mawnin', Mist' Ben."

Pleuritic fever was a term for any mild malaise, but diligent Cassie had never sought to evade her duties. She must be with child.

"You'll be marrying Cassie," I remarked. "My mother will see to it. You know her."

"Ma'ied?" he said in alarm.

"Well, why not? People do get married, don't they?"

"Uh-huh. I reckon," he conceded. "But Mist' Ben, 'fore a man take a big step like that he got to know."

"Know what?"

"Man's got to know kin he live with a woman, an' how's he goin' to know that if he don' live with her firs'?"

I laughed. "Well, you ought to know by now."

"Hones' to Gawd, Mist' Ben," he said earnestly, "I don' know no more'n when I firs' started. One minute she sweeter'n cane candy, nex' thing she meaner'n a sheddin' snake."

I heard outside the light chair Nancy drove, and in duty went out to hand her down. "Good morning, Ben," she said with an attempt at brightness but it was an effort. She seemed half asleep. I took the cloth-covered basket she had brought.

"A change of clothing," she explained. "For Annapolis. I couldn't be seen there in this."

She yawned.

"This" was a blue dress of stout linsey-woolsey that I thought pretty but did not say so. Taking her elbow I propelled her firmly up the stairs. She stopped to examine herself in the hall mirror. Nancy had never in my presence or recollection troubled herself with mirrors. Maybe the mirror, I thought bitterly, was one of the deep problems of being grown —for a woman.

"Mawnin', Miss Nancy," Cato greeted her.

"Why, good morning, Cato," she returned sweetly with no effort at all. "I am delighted to see you up and around. Ben said last night you were poorly."

"Beached," I corrected her.

Cato sent me a heart-breaking look which I attempted to ignore. Our exchange appeared to give Nancy pleasure. "Men *will* quarrel," she said complacently and fell upon her breakfast with hearty appetite.

But the atmosphere grew heavy and over the coffee she said, "Ben, you haven't directed so much as a word to me. It's very rude."

"You promised to be on time," I said accusingly.

"I did not."

"You did."

Her green eyes flashed. "No! And you may not give me the lie, even if it were true, which it is not. And it was shameful of you to shout at me before all my guests."

"I did not shout."

"You did!"

Forced to a defensive position, I said, "I only reminded you not to be late. And you *are* late, you know you are."

"I overslept," she said.

Filled with my wrongs I did not deign to reply.

She said, "No lady could be expected to rise at such an hour the morning after a ball. Your mother and Wendy are still abed. And your father too, I'll warrant."

Rising, I said, "My mother and father and Wendy did not beg permission to accompany me to Annapolis."

"I did not beg."

"If you say so, ma'am," I replied.

"I *asked*."

With cold formality, I bowed.

"I won't go."

"Very well." Fuming, I left the house.

Under the stubby yellow spars of the *Ladybug* at the dock, I heard behind me a scurry of feet. Down the lane between the trees dripping with mist, flew Nancy, struggling with her basket. "Ben," she said appealingly as I took it from her, "don't be cross with me."

My mind was already on the problems that lay ahead. It might be wiser not to venture out. The Colonel's oysters would spoil, but what of that?

Nancy, her hand on my sleeve, looked at me inquiringly.

"The fog is thickening," I explained.

"Pooh! You could sail the *Ladybug* blindfolded. And any other ship, too."

The extravagant compliment made me smile, and yet, absurdly filled me with pride. Above us Tip, who had not moved, lumbered off the rail. "Ready, mistress!"

"Do hurry, Ben," said Nancy. "We're late."

PART 2 ☆

Ladybug—
Ladybug

ONE

Over the lead-slick waters of the cove the marshes of the Hook were blurred and indistinct, and when I glanced back the sharp angles of the house had taken on wraithlike contours. Filmy wisps of mist floated silently past. Overhead was without a sky.

Nancy ducked down the scuttle to my little cabin with her basket and the lunch hamper my mother had provided. I nodded to Tip, signaling him to cast off and hoist the jib. I let go the stern line and hauled on the mizzen sheet. The *Ladybug* moved off coyly, playing with the capricious land breezes. But before we were a dozen yards from the landing the wind settled and came steadily on our larboard quarter. When Nancy appeared on deck, grotesque but endearing in my musty canvas coat with her gleaming hair hidden beneath an oiled cap that tied tightly under her chin, we had cleared the inlet, and only the dim line of the marshes remained in sight to suggest that there was any land at all, anywhere. The house, the lawn, the tree-lined shore had all sunk into the mist entirely, and without my telling him Tip was already heaving away at the mainsheet.

By the time the main was up and drawing, we were in a small world all our own, shrouded in gray fog. The sleek, gray-green seas ran up astern, lifting us, slewing us half around, passing under the keel, and then plunging us down as if dropping us backward. Only the wake and the full-spread sails, set wing and wing, offered assurance we were making headway.

Annapolis lay almost due northwest from Forbes Inlet, but it was not possible to attempt a simple, straightaway run. Two obstacles stood in the course—the southernmost tip of Kent Island and the pointed underlip of the mouth of the Severn. I must first run northwest by west, then northwest by north, and finally northwest, to fetch the market dock at the foot of Fleet Street.

For the first time I admitted my father's wisdom in having installed a hooded binnacle just forward of the helm. It was a pretentious piece of equipment for a lowly bugeye. On the

Bay, where the shore was almost always in sight, even larger boats did not have one. At night the lights of the plantations were enough to steer by. But my father had insisted upon teaching me navigation. I had thought this a wholly unwarranted criticism of my seamanship, but now I had the good sense to be grateful.

In about an hour the first faint mutter of breakers sounded from almost directly ahead.

"Kent Point?" Nancy asked.

I nodded. "We will not see it today, unless we pile up on it."

"Well, don't!" she said.

I went off the compass, bearing a point more to the west in order to allow ample sea room. The grumbling of the surf pounding the rocks under the old fort grew louder, came close, slipped along to starboard, and finally died out astern.

Having passed the first danger point I felt more confident and decided to cut it finer for the second. The sound of the breakers would serve to guide me. Accordingly I set the new course at northwest a quarter north, and again ran wing and wing before the southeast breeze.

Tip puttered about amidships, faking down the ends of sheets and halyards. I kept an eye on him until he settled himself on the larboard rail, with his huge, bare, black feet braced against a convenient stanchion, and fell idly to tying a series of complicated knots in an old bit of rope's end.

Nancy remained beside me at the helm. In better weather I might have given her the wheel or even turned it over to Tip while she and I went forward. But this day, with the long green seas hissing up swiftly behind us, the little vessel tended to yaw and roll. The sails bellied full as we topped each wave and hung limp as we dropped into the trough; the compass card swung wildly; the rudder kicked to starboard with the surge of each following wave. It called for no little concentration to keep the *Ladybug* from veering off course.

I only half listened to Nancy chattering about the party. One of the Fothergills' nags had been lamed, she said, in the drive to Holly Hall and Fothergill had borrowed the Colonel's best team for the return journey. And Lily Loockerman had behaved most scandalously with Jacob Knapp, and poor Betty Knapp already seven months on the way! And Giles Penrose had been observed, from his appearance, to have been engaged in some vulgar brawl, likely having to do with a woman—a hussy, undoubtedly. And Sears, the one who yearly summered on Poplar Island, had spoken of nothing but its beauties; he would honeymoon there when he married.

"Poplar Island?" I looked at Nancy sharply. It was unlike her to be babbling in this fashion. And Poplar Island was in no way famed for beauty, and it was not possible that James Sears would think of carrying a bride to that hated exile.

Nancy's face under the big hat was demure.

"You needn't think," I said indignantly, "that Giles and I are fighting over *you!*"

All innocence she was. "Fighting? Over me? For shame, Ben!"

Devil take her! I was about to expostulate again when the secret little smile that had puzzled me the night before burgeoned before my eyes and burst into proud and radiant bloom. Nancy stood in my canvas coat and oiled hat a knowing, dazzling creature, one well worth a bullet through a brave man's heart. I struggled for breath.

"Nan!"

She said, almost shyly, "Some girls marry at fifteen."

My arm was around her. She lifted her chin.

Then all at once she stiffened. Her eyes widened in terror. A scream came from her distorted mouth.

I whirled around.

Out of the fog loomed a great black topsail schooner, like a ghost ship, but horridly real. Her swelling bow was already all but on us.

Thrusting Nancy forward, I flung the helm hard up to starboard and snatched for the jigger sheet, bawling, "Wear, Tip! Wear! Mind the boom!" From the schooner I heard the hoarse bellow of commands and a clatter of feet upon her deck.

The *Ladybug*, alway quick to respond, seemed to spin on her heel. I clung to the helm. Nancy, good sailor that she was, had understood in a flash what I intended and hugged the binnacle. Out of the corner of my eye I saw Tip flailing his arms for balance while the great main boom swooped down as we jibed.

In that same instant came a tremendous, crashing shock. The little ship leapt beneath my feet as if the seas under her had exploded violently.

My eyes swept around and up. The schooner's rail was sliding by. Thanks largely to the agility of my little bugeye she was not running us down. But spry as we were, there was no avoiding the grinding, rending, flank-to-flank collision. It snatched us up and rolled us over, nearly on our beam ends. Heavy timbers groaned, then screamed in wracked protest. I heard a line snap with a loud twang. I felt the masts rocking and shivering in their steps.

Above, hanging as if disembodied over the schooner's rail, I caught a swift, momentary glimpse of a man's dark, full face suffused with anger, and beside him, a woman—pale gold hair and great eyes of a blue that was the color of glory.

Our sails caught the wind and filled with a crash, and we rolled back, shouldered aside. The black schooner yawed off and swung away on the opposite tack. I caught a flashing glimpse of her name and home port pricked out in gold against the black transom stern: *Oriole,* Baltimore. A man's voice came drifting, faintly but furiously, "Damned chowderhead!"

Then she was gone.

T W O

The world of fog was silent and forbiddingly lonely. It had begun to drizzle, as if grudging even of tears.

"Nan?" I called.

She stared at me. Her face was very white but perfectly composed, as on the day I pulled her out of the inlet.

She was not harmed. More pressing matters demanded attention. The main boom hung far over to larboard, the great mainsail slatting in the wind.

"Tip!" I yelled. "Sheet home that boom! Tip!"

There was no movement, no reply.

"Ben, I think he's hurt," said Nancy.

Without a word I belayed the mizzen sheet so that the jib and spanker at least were drawing. Then I turned the wheel over to Nancy.

"Hold her as she goes," I told her, and I went amidships.

Tip—or what was left of him—lay sprawled on the larboard scuppers. He must have been flung headforemost from the rail directly into the path of the heavy, down-swinging boom, for his skull had been crushed like an eggshell and his neck had been broken. His head was skewed all around so that his sightless eyes stared up into the wet drizzle of fog while the rest of him lay breast and belly down against the planks. All around him, from scuttle to scupper, the deck was ugly with blood.

I stood for a stricken eternity. Then came a retching nausea. I fought it off, thankful that the mizzenmast and the tack and luff of the spanker blocked Nancy's view from both me and the dreadful remains of what had been, only minutes ago, a vigorous, full-bodied man.

A sudden flapping of the mainsail recalled me. Feverishly I took up the slack in the mainsheet until the sail was drawing and belayed it. Only then could I attend to poor Tip. I could not approach him until, with a few buckets of bay water, I had washed the blood into the scuppers and out through the holes.

Nancy called my name in a half whisper, "Ben?"

I wouldn't look at her, just shook my head.

There was nothing to be done for Tip—nothing that really mattered—but somehow it seemed to me important that he be made tidy and comfortable. Again fighting nausea, I straightened his head as best I could upon his shoulders. I tucked a tarpaulin around him and lashed his body snugly to the rail so that he would not roll with the vessel. Then, with a lesser kind of sorrow, I looked to my little bugeye.

I sounded the water in the bilges and was relieved to find that we were scarcely leaking. We had, in fact, suffered astonishingly little damage. One of the shrouds had been torn away and a section of the larboard rail smashed inboard—doubtless the blow that had sent poor Tip hurtling into the boom. No other damage was visible abovedeck. How she had fared overside I could not tell, for at the moment we were running heeled well over with the wind upon our starboard beam.

I made my way to the after cockpit. Nancy looked up at me. "Tip?"

"He's dead, Nan," I said gently.

She nodded. "I—I saw. I saw it happen."

I drew her close to comfort her and because I shared her grief. "He was a good boy," I said.

"Good boy!" she flared. "He was the best buck nigra we owned. I heard Daddy say he wouldn't take less than five hundred dollars at stud for him, and wouldn't sell him for under two thousand. He's going to be terribly angry!"

Stunned, I could only gape at her. Here was still another Nancy—the Colonel's daughter.

"Don't stand there like a—like a chowderhead! We'll never get to Annapolis on this tack. We'll fetch up somewhere near Matapeake."

I brought the *Ladybug* up into the wet wind, and as I dropped the main boom into the cradle and furled the big sail, Nancy held the little ship in irons. I took the wheel again and let her head fall off until she had the wind upon her quarter, then set her on a northwesterly course to run in toward where I thought Annapolis must be.

With the new tack lifting her larboard flank well out of water, and with Nancy again at the wheel, I leaned out far over the side. What I saw sickened me. For fully half her length the planking was ripped and scarred and splintered. Here and there great lengths of caulking trailed from the seams. Nowhere had the side actually been staved in, but clearly the planks had been scraped almost paper thin. I had to tell myself sternly that the *Ladybug* was not a human being, not blood and bones, only wood.

I took another sounding of the bilge. We were taking on water. Quite likely, I thought, one or more of the stout oaken knees joining the deck beams to the ribs of the hull and bracing the sides had been mashed, or at least sprung, but of this I could not be sure until the hold had been emptied. In any case, we were in no peril. I went forward to break out the pump.

"Ben," Nancy called, "is she hurt?"

Her concern cheered me somehow. "She'll hold," I said.

I pumped away for half an hour until I heard the sound of the seas breaking on the underlip of the Severn's mouth. Then I took another sounding. The level of the water had lowered by a few inches. We were not dry but all was well, or well enough. I took the helm. In silence I weathered the point and rounded into the river. Without difficulty I brought my little bugeye into the long, narrow throat of the market dock and moored alongside the stone quay.

When the lines were fast I helped Nancy out of the canvas wrap. "I must go see Callander," I said. Callander was the Colonel's agent. "I'll have my hands full here most of the day if we're to patch this hooker in time to get home."

"Oh, bother!" She was untying her hat. "I hoped you'd come uptown with me and help me with my shopping."

She pouted prettily but I paid her no heed. As I clambered up onto the quay, Nancy dropped into the cabin to change her dress.

The bustle and excitement of the water front and the big city held no charms for me this day. Walking to Andrew Callander's counting rooms at the foot of Dock Street, I noted that the fog was thinning. But the wind had shifted nearly due east—a bad sign, foretelling storm and rain, perhaps even, at this time of year, thick white squalls of driving snow. It was turning cold. Down toward the mouth of the river I could make out the misty forms of several vessels coming in to shelter.

Andrew Callander was a tall, lean Scot with a narrow face, red but blue-veined, and a mop of white hair as irascible as himself. For as long as I could remember he had represented the Eastern Shore families in the two major ports of Baltimore and Annapolis. If a planter had a crop of tobacco or corn for disposal and transshipment, Andrew Callander would see to it for him. If he had a lesser and more perishable harvest, such as oysters, fish, soft crabs, terrapin, melons, or berries for the local market, Callander would tend to that, too. If a man required something unobtainable in Cambridge or Oxford or Chestertown—a pipe or two of port, canary or madeira, or some niggerhead twist for his slaves, or even a new slave—Callander would send them over. If the planter's lady yearned for a bolt of some special silk or sheeting, Callander would find the right thing.

He was at his scarred and paper-strewn deal table, itemizing bills. He looked at me over the rims of his spectacles. "Ah, there, young Forbes."

"Good morning, Mr. Callander," I said civilly. "I've a load of oysters from Colonel Savage."

His hair bristled. "And I suppose you want me to get 'em to market right away."

"They'll spoil over the Sabbath."

"Why the devil couldn't you have brought 'em yesterday?"

I explained that I hadn't known of their existence until last night, and then, as he still scowled, I said bitterly, "Dump them into the Bay for aught I care."

His thrifty soul revolted at the thought. "Young man," he said with conviction, "mark me, you'll come to no good!"

The oysters thus obliquely accepted, I gave Callander the Colonel's long list. "And Colonel Savage asks you to make these purchases for him."

I well knew that Colonel Savage had had no such thought in mind. He had intended me to buy the stuff and Tip to stow it on board, in this way saving himself the cost of Callander's commission. But now there was no Tip, and I was in no mood to be concerned for the Colonel's pocket.

"I'll see to it," Callander said grumpily, and turned as if to dismiss me.

"I need carpenters," I said. "At once."

"Carpenters?" He rounded on me. "Good God, boy! And where would I be finding carpenters at this hour of a Saturday morning? You know well enough the best are busy at the boat works, and the others are tacking up their wives' hen coops or sleeping off their liquor."

I stood my ground.

"Why d'you need 'em for?"

"Repairs," I said shortly. "And then, sir, I require your advice on what to do about the body."

"The what!" he cried.

"The body, sir—a dead man."

The air crackled with oaths. Finally, expelling a long breath, he settled back to listen.

"Damned bad business!" he swore when I'd finished. "I've warned the Colonel—aye, and a dozen others, too—that something of this sort would happen if they kept on letting you young whippersnappers carry for them. I suppose you were way off course."

"No, sir," I replied stiffly. "I was exactly where I should have been—running northwest from Kent Point with the wind dead astern. If only we had started in time I'd have crossed safely a full half hour ahead of that fool schooner."

"What's that?" Callander demanded. "What d'you mean—if you'd started on time? Eh?"

"Miss Nancy was late," I said miserably.

"Miss Nancy?" He was startled. "Is Mistress Savage on board?"

"Yes, sir. She saw it happen to Tip."

He pulled at his hair. "So now we'll need a doctor, I suppose. Is she being looked after? Is she screaming? Swooned?"

"Not Miss Nancy!" I exclaimed.

"But she's only a wee girlie."

"Never was, sir—not that kind. And she had her sixteenth birthday yesterday."

He gave me an odd look. "Yes, yes, yes! Well now, what about this black boy. A common field hand, was he?"

"Tip? Oh, no, sir! He was one of the Colonel's best. Miss Nancy said her father would not take less than two thousand for him."

A calculating gleam brightened his pale eyes. "She did, did she? Yes, yes, yes! Well. We mustn't leave the poor child too long alone with the—ah—corpse. I'll take care of the matter and see to a proper burial. Two thousand. Hum. We must see to reimbursement. You're a sharp lad, young Forbes. Were you sharp enough to catch the schooner's name?"

"The *Oriole*, out of Baltimore."

He flung himself back in his chair, spectacles sliding to the tip of his nose.

"You know her, then?" I asked.

He nodded dolefully as he reached for his hat. "Know her? I'm afraid I do, lad, afraid I do. Happens I'm one of her owners." He sighed. "Ah, well. Let's be getting along then to have a look at what Captain Boyle has done this time."

THREE

The fog had lifted. We cut across the broad cobbled way and as we walked to the quay all was visible down to the point at the mouth of the river, but the skies overhead remained low and leaden and the river water looked cold and mean. White-caps danced in the harbor, whipped by the raw wet wind that had hauled around now to blow almost directly from the east. The sudden shift would be raising a nasty cross-chop out in the Bay, and with my bugeye damaged, I did not look forward to the homeward voyage.

I dropped to the deck and thumped the cabin roof. "Nancy! I've brought Mr. Callander."

Her muffled voice came back with the assurance that she would be with us shortly. Callander examined the swathed form of Tip, still lashed to the rail, then the battered planking overside and the broken shroud. He ran a practiced eye along the masts. "They're both sprung," he said, pointing out the newly opened cracks that followed them up from the deck. "Wouldn't you know it! They'll have to be replaced."

I had not noticed the cracks before, and even if I had, would probably not have understood their import. I had had no experience of sprung masts. But I did know that to replace them was no small matter. It would require time and money I could not spare.

"They'll have to wait," I said. "I promised the Colonel to have Mistress Savage home by nightfall."

"You'd be in a sorry fix if you lost 'em halfway over," he remarked. "But they brought you in. Might be they'll carry you." He pursed his mouth. "And might be they'll not."

A vessel was warping up the channel toward the berth just ahead of ours. But we were too engrossed to take note of her. Mr. Callander stamped his foot on the deck tentatively. "What damage below?" he asked.

"I've no way of telling, sir, until we have the cargo out. The hold is filled to the deck beams."

I stripped off the canvas cover of the cargo hatch. At the sight of the great oysters that filled the space below, he very nearly glowed. He dropped to his knees and reached down for a handful of the big bivalves. "Ah, yes, yes, yes! Prime!"

We heard Nancy's feet on the deck behind us, and Callander rose, dusting his fawn-colored knees fastidiously.

"Mistress Nancy, child!" he said most gallantly, "I understand you are to be congratulated."

"La, sir," Nancy replied, dropping a town curtsy, "'twas only a birthday." Her glance slipped past Mr. Callander's shoulder and her eyes grew large.

I turned. Andrew Callander turned.

The ship that had been moving into her berth had completed her mooring. Her bow, breast, and stern lines were already fast to the bollards ashore. She was so close that her wide transom overhung our dwarfed bowsprit. A young woman in a sky-blue traveling dress and a lace-trimmed bonnet, from beneath which peeped curls of pale-gold hair, leaned upon the after rail staring down at us; and under her feet, across the transom in large golden letters, were the words:

ORIOLE
BALTIMORE

"God bless my soul!" said Andrew Callander.

The girl in blue turned and spoke to someone hidden from our view. As she did so we moved forward, as if drawn by invisible threads from the schooner, until all three of us stood in a group upon the *Ladybug's* tiny forecastle.

The girl had turned back and she smiled at us with obvious relief. "Oh, you are safe, then!" she called. "I am so happy!"

She spoke with a faint accent, a pleasing, lilting inflection.

Two men appeared beside her. The one at her left was very tall, well over six feet, and thin. His face was strong, sunbrowned, and nearly square in shape, with a wide mouth and a nose beaked like an eagle's. Under bushy eyebrows, almost white, his eyes were as blue and striking as those of the girl beside him, and since he wore no hat I could see that his hair was thin, finespun, and sandy-bleached.

The second man was the same dark-faced, dark-browed individual I had glimpsed at the moment of collision. He was much shorter than the other, sturdily built and blocky, with heavy shoulders and a thick neck. He wore a black beaver hat, sober enough in itself but rakishly cocked, and his heavy, curly black hair came far down on either side of his round face to end in well-trimmed points. His nose was large, his mouth small and just saved from petulance by a quirk of humor at the corners. By his blue coat with brass buttons I knew him for the captain. Captain Boyle, it would be.

"Holy Mary!" his voice boomed down. "'Tis the old dev—'tis Mr. Callander himself! Bless me, sir, 'tis happy I am to see ye well and safe. I'd no notion yerself was aboard."

"I have only been here a few moments, Captain Boyle," Mr. Callander said dryly. "Fortunately, I was not on board when you had your recent—ah—misadventure. Mr. Forbes, here, has reported the matter to me."

"D'ye tell me so?" said Captain Boyle genially. "Why, then, it's happy I am to know ye were not shaken about. As for you, Captain Forbes—and yerself, ma'am—the sight of you, safe and hale, lifts a weight of worry from me heart, for it was certain we were that ye'd been lost with all hands. But was I wrong in thinkin' I saw three of ye?"

"You were not mistaken, Captain," Mr. Callander said curtly. "Three it was. The third lies now beneath yon canvas with a broken skull."

"Oh! Is he hurt?" cried the girl.

Andrew Callander bowed with courtly irony. "Madam," he replied, "he is dead."

FOUR

There was a sudden stillness. With startled horror the girl pressed her fingers to her mouth as if to stifle a cry. The tall man put his arm about her shoulders and looked somber. Captain Boyle tugged thoughtfully at his chin, and his dark eyes flicked over the knot of idlers that had gathered on the quay to observe what entertainment we might offer them.

"D'ye tell me so, indeed, Mr. Callander!" he said at length. "Then here's a sorry mess. Perhaps 'twould be best to talk in private, eh? If ye'd all care to step aboard . . . ?"

"I think that might be wise, Captain," said Callander.

Handing Nancy up the sloping gangway I observed that she had changed into a gown of russet silk and a tiny fur-trimmed bonnet which prettily set off her coppery hair and green eyes. She had changed more than her dress; subtly, in a way women have—I had seen it many times in my sisters—she had changed herself. Or perhaps the transformation dated to the moment she had seen the blue-eyed girl? Her head was high, her skirts swished, and there were hints of a supple body moving beneath the russet silk.

I suddenly felt myself a boor for the way I'd been treating her all day. "That's a handsome dress, Nancy," I said for her ear alone.

"I am astonished," she said coldly, "that you noticed it," and left me irritated with both myself and her.

The *Oriole* was large for an ocean-going topsail schooner. She was as long as most brigs but her lines were narrower and her flush deck lay lower to the water. She was built for speed, and because of her fore-and-aft rig would be easily handled by a small crew, more easily than a square-rigger. She was the largest and most beautiful vessel I had ever set foot upon. How smart she was! Her deck planks had been holystoned to the smooth, spotless whiteness of bone, and all ropes and lines that were not in use had been meticulously faked or flemished, according to their need and place. Without any confusion her men were furling and stopping down the sails. The brightwork glistened, even on that gloomy day, and not so much as a bubble showed upon her paint. Her masts fairly leapt at the sky. I leaned back and craned my neck to see to the top of them.

"They build 'em tall in Baltimore."

I came back with a start. Captain Boyle's dark eyes were amused.

"Captain Thomas Boyle," he presented himself. "Or better, Tom Boyle, of Baltimore. Yer servant, sir."

My bow and my civilities improved on his. I was not going to be outdone by a fool of an Irishman who had almost run me down. I presented my passenger in the most formal manner.

He made her an elegant leg. " 'Tis honored I am, Mistress Savage. I'd give me arm and all to have met in happier circumstances." He added handsomely, "I'll say the same for yerself, Captain Forbes."

I corrected him. "Not 'captain,' just plain Ben Forbes."

He somehow indicated in his bow that an ungrateful world was to blame for my want of title, and proceeded with introductions in fine style. "Mistress Savage—Mr. Forbes—Mr. Callander—'tis my honor to present Baron Carl Christian von Lund and his daughter, Mistress Charlotte Christina, of Copenhagen and the island of Saint Thomas."

There was a great deal more of bowing, but here I quite forgot my manners. Mistress Charlotte Christina's eyes were all that I could see, and as I stared they glinted with tiny, mischievous lights, like the sun dancing on blue waters. Yet there was no sun, so how could this be?

I heard Captain Boyle say, "Gentlemen, shall we step below? The ladies may prefer to remain on deck . . . ?"

"No, sir!" said Nancy. "That was one of my father's best nigras, and he'd expect me to be there when it came to an accounting."

"As ye wish, ma'am." Boyle stood aside to hold the companion door. Nancy swept by me and by Mistress Charlotte

Christina with her nose in the air, but she turned a sweet smile on Captain Boyle.

The captain's cabin was palatial and shipshape in the extreme. It stretched the full width of the vessel and was luxuriously, it seemed to me, furnished with a round table and four chairs, a sideboard holding firmly in wooden fiddles an array of decanters and glasses, a clothespress and a chest of drawers, a long cushioned settee and the captain's bunk with a telltale compass set between the beams directly over his pillow so that he might check his vessel's course simply by opening an eye. I had heard of this convenient instrument but had never seen one. Beside the bunk was a rack of well-worn books, and at the head a whale-oil lamp hung in gimbals. I gained a new respect for Captain Boyle, seeing him in my mind's eye lying of a night deep in a book on navigation, glancing up now and again at his compass.

When we were seated Captain Boyle said, "I daresay 'tis too early in the day to be offering refreshment, so there's naught left but to get down to business. I take it, Mr. Forbes, and you, Mistress Savage, ye hold me responsible for what happened out yonder?"

"How else would we feel?" I demanded. "You ran us down blindly."

He appeared offended.

"You know it, sir," I said.

"I know nothing of the sort, Mr. Forbes. I'll admit we made a kissing acquaintance in the Bay. But I think ye'll not deny ye were to windward of me, wing and wing, while I was on the starboard tack. If ye're familiar with the rules of the road, sir, ye'll know 'twas for yerself to keep clear."

Andrew Callander looked at me almost hopefully, I thought.

"I'll admit to that, Captain Boyle," I replied. "But you'll recall another rule of the road. It demands prudence and caution when navigating heavily traveled waters in thick weather. I know naught of your eyesight, sir. It may be keen enough to pierce the heaviest fog. My own is not, but had you been sailing with reasonable care, I would have seen you in time to stand off. As it was, you were no more than a cable's length away when you came racing down on us out of the fog with all sails set. Even then I tried to stand clear—Mistress Savage will witness. I luffed and risked broaching in those seas."

"But we did not see you, either, Mr. Forbes," the Baron interposed, "until it was too late. Then Captain Boyle also tried to sheer off."

"Your pardon, sir," I said to him, "but that is no excuse for sailing so recklessly. Through Captain Boyle's arrogant negligence. . . ."

"What!" cried the Captain. "What was that ye said of me?"

I had grown impatient of the show of manners. "I said, sir, you were arrogant and negligent!"

Unexpectedly the Captain grinned. "A tartar! A very tartar, and he knows all the words! And what else was it ye were about to be sayin', Mr. Forbes?"

"Only this, Captain. That because of your carelessness my ship has been badly mauled and a black boy lies dead on my deck."

"One of our best buck nigras," Nancy put in. "Daddy refused. . . ."

"Yes, yes, Miss Nancy," Callander said hastily. "Ben has told me."

"Well, somebody had better begin to think about paying for him," she said grimly.

"And there is still another rule you overlooked, Captain Boyle," I said. "Having run us down, you did not even take the trouble to put back and see how we fared and what help you might offer."

For the first time Captain Boyle looked angry. "Sir!" he began.

But the golden-haired Danish girl interrupted him impulsively. "Oh," she cried, "but that is not so! My father protested but Captain Boyle insisted upon turning back in search for you. He even sent out his boats, and when we did not find you in the fog we thought you must have been sinked—sunk."

"I thank ye, Miss Kirstie." Captain Boyle bowed to her. "Ye heard, Mr. Forbes?"

"In that case I owe you an apology, Captain."

Lightly he waved it away. "Think no more of it. Indeed, if Miss Kirstie had said naught, the fact that we came to port after yerself would suggest that we dawdled somewhere along the way."

"That's true," I admitted.

I glanced curiously at the Baron, wondering at his cold-blooded protest. Wherever ships sailed it was an unwritten law that all who could must go to the aid of a ship in distress. I saw that Andrew Callander and Nancy were also regarding the Baron with distaste.

Captain Boyle read our minds. "Baron von Lund," he said, "had reason for impatience. He goes to Washington on an urgent mission. That may explain to ye, Mr. Forbes, why I would risk carrying all sail in such weather. And I might be adding, Mr. Callander, that by reason of the premium he paid for a swift passage, he had some right to protest any delay. I think ye'll be none the loser."

"Ah, so?" Mr. Callander, whose face had been growing longer and longer, brightened considerably.

"You have not forgotten Tip, I hope?" Nancy put in sharply.

"Tip?" Captain Boyle looked puzzled. "Oh, yes, the blackamoor. No, ma'am. I've not forgotten. I cannot bring him back, poor lad. But I have made a profitable voyage. Very profitable."

"Daddy will insist. . . ." said Nancy.

I felt apologetic, wondering what Mistress von Lund must be thinking of this haggling over a dead man.

"All will be well, Miss Nancy." I thought Andrew Callander was somewhat irked with her. "Be sure I will settle the matter entirely to your father's satisfaction."

She did not even thank him.

"As for your ship, Mr. Forbes," Captain Boyle said, "I'd like to do what I can. If the loan of my carpenter and his mate will do aught of good, I'll send them over to ye, and ye're welcome to what we have in the way of pitch, oakum, cordage, and the like."

A great-hearted man, this Irishman of a captain! Gratefully and eagerly I accepted his offer, informing him of the extent of the damage. "Later, when I get her home, I've no doubt she'll have to be careened. But since I must be back by nightfall, I'll make do with temporary repairs."

"Think ye can make it?" he asked as one captain to another.

I laughed as one who knows his waters as a field hand his rows. "I think so."

We bowed the ladies out and then ourselves. Trust Andrew Callander! In the short distance between the cabin and the gangway he took complete charge of the von Lunds. He would send a boy to town immediately to engage the best available carriage for their journey to Washington. He recommended an inn—the Indian Queen on Pennsylvania Avenue. He would have their heavier luggage sent on after them. There was, of course, no mention of money but I knew the Scot well enough to be sure there would be a profit for him somewhere in his helpfulness.

Nancy's foot was already on the cleated plank of the gangway and I was making floundering adieus to the Danish girl, when Mr. Callander suggested that Nancy wait for the carriage and ride to town with the von Lunds.

"Honored," murmured the Baron.

"Oh, yes. Please!" said Mistress von Lund.

Nancy's reply was prim. "No, thank you. I can walk!"

I was bemused. There was no accounting for Nancy's uncommon rudeness. Still less was there any accounting for the strange breathlessness aroused in me by the Danish girl. Miss Kirstie. Lady of snows and sun. Taller than Nancy she was, and larger of bone, but somehow softer and with the easy grace of a princess and a dancing laughter in her eyes. Soon she would be on the road to Washington. And soon I would be sailing in the opposite direction. I saw the distance between us widening endlessly, and with this the river and the Bay became in my eyes a dreary waste, while under the slim, soaring schooner my *Ladybug* was the tub Nancy had once called her.

PART 3 ☆

Flyaway

ONE

I had scant time to moon, however. As I stepped aboard the bugeye, Andrew Callander's blackamoors came to take up the cargo and carry away the bundled remains of poor Tip. At the same time the *Oriole's* carpenters arrived. They set up a scaffold, and in the forenoon we worked over the sides, caulking and pitching the open seams we could reach. Chips borrowed a dinghy from the schooner and from below caulked those out of reach. To get at the seams below the waterline, we heaved her down with block and tackle rigged from a bollard ashore to the top of the mainmast. While we were straining at the tackle Chips pointed out that one of the sprung masts had bowed beneath the strain. But at the moment my attention was on the von Lunds whom I saw climbing into their carriage. I found myself yearning with all my soul after the trim figure of Miss Kirstie, and was rewarded by a wave of her handkerchief from the carriage window, and then in a rattle of wheels and a spatter of mud from a dockside puddle, they were gone.

There was nothing to be done about the mast, in any case. By midday we had replaced the torn caulking and stopped all the leaks we could find. I examined the *Ladybug's* flank and was grieved and alarmed to find that the heavy planking had been scraped thin as a shedder's shell. When I pressed my hand against it I thought I could feel it give ominously. Here was our weakest spot. I would do well to favor that flank as much as I could, for if it gave way, a half-dozen such pumps as I carried would not keep us afloat.

When the carpenters went to their dinner, I snatched a cold fowl and a bottle of wine for my own. There was no sign of Nancy. In the few peaceful moments alone, I found myself wondering what kind of a land was Denmark and what was the city of Copenhagen like.

When the carpenters returned, we set to work in the hold, bracing the sprung knees and ribs with heavy timbers. It was near midafternoon when we were done. Callander's boys brought the Colonel's supplies and stowed them. There was nothing now left to do. Waiting for Nancy, I swabbed the deck down twice and pumped out the bilges. When the pump sucked air it lacked only three hours until dusk. Grumbling at Nancy for a spoiled wench, I went aft and was standing in the cockpit testing the wind when she chose to appear. I did not see her as she came down the gangway; in fact, it was not until she spoke that I was aware of her.

"Ben, I'm back," she said half apologetically. "Do help me with my purchases."

"You should have been here an hour ago," I fumed. "Your father will skin me alive. . . ."

Whatever else I might have said died in my throat and was forgotten. The shock was too great, my surprise too complete. For the voice might be her own but this was not the Nancy I had seen a few short hours before.

She had again changed her dress. Gone was the russet silk I had admired; probably it was in one of the bundles that piled her arms. In its place was an excessively high-waisted, high-throated gown. It was dashingly styled for a traveling costume but its color, a kind of pinkish lavender, was hideous beyond belief. As I think back on it now, over a far greater acquaintance across the world, I cannot conceive of any woman who would have been flattered by it, unless, perhaps, some sloe-eyed, black-haired maiden of the South Seas. Above it Nancy's green eyes, usually so fine and clear, were almost bilious, and the chestnut hair was dead and wiglike.

The hair! The eyes! My fascinated gaze was drawn from the unbelievable gown to smaller but no less extraordinary items. A misguided hairdresser had worked long and hard, combing, frizzing, piling the hair high on top of his victim's head and lavishly applying pomade to fix the entire structure so that it rose, a sticky, polished mound, without a curl or softness, from a forehead that looked somehow indecently exposed. He must have been lavish, too, with coloring, for it had an orange glare. The eyes, outlined and accentuated with blacking pencil, seemed to belong to another face entirely. I made out rouge and rice powder, and a crescent-shaped beauty mark had been pasted by the side of the chin. Embracing the horrid vision was a long-billed capote, trimmed to profusion with purple violets.

"Good God!" I gasped.

Mistaking this for admiration, she pirouetted. "Isn't it elegant?"

I could not speak. She looked at me and what she saw in my face made her pitifully uncertain. "You don't like it?"

I managed to shake my head. In an instant she was all

aflame. "I saw you making a silly fool of yourself over that pop-eyed towhead. I saw you! Don't deny it!"

But by now I was laughing helplessly. The bundles slithered to the deck. A pointed shoe flashed out. My laughter changed to a yelp of pain, and I made for her. But before her heaving breast and throttled tears of chagrin and fury, I stopped short.

"If your father sees you like this, I don't want to be in the same county. He'll have my hide." I gathered up her bundles. "Now go below," I said, "and get into some decent gear."

"I will not!"

"I warn you, we'll be having rain, if not worse."

She did not reply and she turned her back on me. So without another word I cast off.

The wind was blowing straight out of the east and I had to tack several times before we were clear of the river mouth, running under only jib and jigger, which was as much canvas as I could handle alone in such narrow waters. When we had cleared the north point and stood into the Bay, I brought the *Ladybug's* bow up east-northeast, setting off on a long reach on the starboard tack for the upper end of Kent Island.

Nancy gave me a puzzled look and spoke in spite of herself. "What are you doing? This isn't the way home."

Long rollers swept up from the south and the east wind whipped up a cross sea that made us pitch and roll. Ordinarily we would have turned southeast on the larboard tack.

"If you had been back when you were supposed to be," I told her, "you'd know. The planks all along the larboard side are badly weakened and I'll take no chances. I'll hold her so, with the heavy seas to starboard, until we run into the shelter of the island. Then I can turn and run south almost all the way in the lee of the land." As I spoke the little vessel dipped her bows and then tossed her head. Green spray came hurtling back upon the wind. I could see it coming and had time to duck my head. But Nancy, standing broadside to it, received it full. It knocked her bonnet askew and drenched her face and hair and spread great wet splotches all down the side of the new gown, turning it to a dark purple wherever it touched.

"Oh!" Nancy screamed wrathfully. "You did that on purpose, Ben Forbes!"

She snatched at the helm, and I had to struggle to keep her from twisting it from my grip.

A second green sea came sweeping down upon us and this time drenched us both.

Nancy let go and fell back a step. "Oh! Oh! Now look at me!" she cried.

The wave had done its work thoroughly. Water dribbled from the violets. Black rivulets trickled down her cheeks. The mound of hair had collapsed and hung in drab strands. The new gown was soaked from top to bottom.

"That's better," I said, grinning at her. The Nancy I knew and could feel something for was reappearing.

"I—I hate you!" She fled, ducking into the little cabin and slamming the hatch doors behind her.

I hammered on the cabin roof. "Don't forget to wash your face. And hurry. I need you."

But it was a while before she rejoined me. In the meantime the bugeye labored in the heavy cross-chop, making slow headway. Since Nancy's help was not forthcoming, I braced the wheel and with all speed went forward to run up the mainsail. The weakened mast groaned and bent ominously as the big sail filled, but the added canvas steadied us and increased our speed. When I returned to the helm it was raining hard, so hard that I could not see the distant shore of Kent Island ahead nor yet the low line of the hills around Annapolis behind. All I could do was to hold her steady by the compass and hope the rain would thin enough to permit me to see the shore of the island in time.

That was one worry I might have spared myself, however. For hard as it rained and despite the occasional flurries of wet snow, the weather did not shut in as tightly as it had in the fog. Within a mile or so of the island I was well able to see its low bulk stretched out along the tumbling water ahead. Of far greater concern was the wind. From the time we had left Annapolis it had been veering slowly but steadily northward, forcing me, with each point of the compass that it shifted, to alter my course more and more toward the northerly tip of the island in the effort to stay on the starboard tack. But this could not go on much longer. If the wind continued to shift, soon I would be running directly up the Bay, or even heading back toward Baltimore. I must come about onto the larboard tack and risk our weakened flank against the seas.

I had reached the conclusion that the time had come to take that chance, when the companion doors flapped open. Nancy's white face peered out at me, and even in that moment of swift apprehension, I noticed she had washed her face and combed her wet hair and looked herself again.

"Ben, there's water down here!"

"Water?"

She nodded. "I thought it was just coming down from above,

but it isn't. It's welling up through the floor and under the bulkhead."

I turned away to conceal my alarm. If there was water in the cabin, there would be much more in the hold, which had been dry when we sailed. The pitching and wracking of my little bugeye must have reopened a seam. What we might do about that depended entirely upon how badly we were leaking.

"Have you changed into your old clothes?"

"Yes, Ben." Our quarrel was forgotten.

"Good! Then you'd best slip into my rain gear and take the wheel. I'll go forward."

She bobbed below for the canvas jacket and sou'wester. I looked toward the dark fringe of Kent Island. We were not more than a half-mile off shore. If I came about now on the larboard tack it would be but a brief run. Once under the lee of the island we could turn south and run free with the wind on our larboard quarter, keeping only a few rods off shore. We'd be fairly well sheltered, and if necessary, could run into Matapeake or one of the other plantation coves along the island.

Nancy came on deck and I thought she seemed subdued and a little contrite. As she stood at my elbow I brought the 'Bug about and put her on a reach southeastward so that, by a long diagonal, we would come in close under the island. The masts creaked and protested, but they held. When we were fairly on the new course, I explained it to Nancy and gave her the helm. Then I went forward and dropped the long, thin rod down the sounding well.

I was prepared for a shock, but not for one so grim. The rod revealed nearly a foot of water in the hold. This meant that the bilges were already full. As I unfastened the pump lashings, I calculated furiously. If she had begun to leak as soon as we left the Severn, and if the leak had not grown worse, the pump could deal with the trouble. On the other hand, if she had begun to take water during the last few minutes, we were in a bad way. That would mean the water was pouring in faster than the pump could carry it off.

The only way to find out was by pumping, and I lost no time in falling to. For a moment the pump wheezed. Then the nozzle gurgled and spat, and settled to a steady spouting of dank green water that splashed upon the deck and rolled away, flowing out the scuppers.

I pumped steadily for better than half an hour. When I sent down the rod again it was to find I had done little more than hold my own. The water was only half an inch lower. But it *was* lower. We should be able to make it, although it was obvious now that we would not be in before dark. Already it was growing dusk and the pale lights of Matapeake were winking through the mingled rain and snow that was falling steadily now. We could put in there and wait in comfort for the storm to blow over. Nancy could stay with friends while I beached the *'Bug* and searched out the trouble.

But the northeaster might blow for days, our families would worry, and I had an appointment for Monday morning.

I decided to put the choice to Nancy. Making my way aft I found her hunched over the wheel with her back to the storm and the rough collar of the canvas coat turned up about her ears. I put my mouth to her ear and over the howl of the gale explained the situation.

"What do you think?" she shouted.

"I think we can make it if I keep pumping," I yelled back. "But if you'd rather . . .?"

She shook her head violently, and I felt a rush of warmth for her. "You know what to do?" I shouted in her ear.

"I know. South until we pass Kent Point. Then I bear east-southeast until I pick up the Neck, then south again along the shore until we reach the cove."

I saluted her and saw her smile.

I went back to my haul and bend at the pump bar. As I pumped, rhythmically, steadily, I watched the darkening shore of the island slip swiftly by. Soon it would be night and then the visible world would be limited to the tiny pinpricks of light that marked the plantation houses. By the sound of the wind in the rigging, the storm appeared to be worsening.

An hour passed, and the better part of another. Darkness closed down. The fury of the storm behind us increased. But we were sheltered somewhat by the bulk of Kent Island, and still I could see the lights ashore, although at times they disappeared, leaving me straining anxiously until I saw a gleam again. Now and again I paused in my pumping to listen. At last, from somewhere up ahead and to larboard, I began to catch it—the faint grumble and mutter of the surf on the rocks at Kent Point. I slipped a temporary hitch about the pump bar and, fumbling with the deck plug, once more sounded the well.

Since I had no light, I felt along the rod to find the water mark. Standing the dip beside me, I was able to measure it with fair accuracy. I had gained little but had not lost. Apparently we were taking on water about as fast as I could pump it out. As long as I could maintain the pace, I felt we had nothing to fear. Another hour should see us into the Inlet.

I groped my way back to the cockpit. Nancy was shivering. I put my arm about her and held her close. "It won't be much longer. Hear the breakers? Hold her as she goes until the sound comes from astern. Then bring her up until you have the wind broad on the larboard beam, and sheet in the spanker till she takes. Use the cleat or you'll burn your hand. Can you do it?"

"Yes."

"When you start the turn, I'll handle the mainsheet. Don't get tangled in the lines."

She laughed. "I've been out before, you know."

I hugged her. I wouldn't have admitted it to anyone, but I rated her as good a sailor as myself.

I went back to the pump. The sound of the breakers swelled from a low muttering to a grumble. Gradually it rose to an angry roar. Finally it passed and fell behind. For several minutes we held steadily on our way.

Then, as we drove into open water, the storm grew suddenly furious. Driving rain and snow flew almost parallel with the deck; the howl of the wind in the rigging lifted to a wild shriek. The seas pounded at us from both sides at once.

Only then did it come home to me that in my eagerness to get into the lee of the Neck I had discounted—in my mind, overleapt—the wide, open mouth of Romancoke Sound, where the east wind would come screaming down upon us across the 15-mile sweep of open water. Nor had I taken thought of the tide, which was setting out strongly now, making for an ugly chop. Our sore side was exposed to a savage pitiless hammering.

In the frozen moment of realization I saw that Nancy had already spun the wheel and begun the turn.

As the deck swayed I sprang for the mainsheet, hauled the heavy boom inboard, and made the line fast. The *Ladybug* lunged far over to starboard. To counter the list I scrambled for the weather rail. But the full force of the gale descended upon me, solid as a wall. I leaned into it but couldn't move.

Then, as if annoyed at our resistance, the storm rose still higher to hurl upon us a brutal, smashing blow. The *'Bug* reeled and shuddered. At this instant a tremendous sea came snarling out of the night to burst upon our weakened flank.

Underfoot I felt as much as heard a dull shivering thump, like some distant muffled explosion. The bugeye stumbled, then staggered, like a running deer mortally wounded, in mid-air. From far above me I heard the savage, splintered, whining protest of twisting wood upon wood. There was a crash. A second followed so closely that it seemed an echo. Through them sounded a volley of smaller snaps and pops and cracklings. A rope's end slashed my cheek. And a wailing scream rent the terrible blackness:

"Ben! Oh, God! Ben!"

T W O

The cry was still ringing in my ears and heart when the night seemed to burst apart, showering down a welter of smothering canvas, frayed and whipped cordage, and jagged broken spars that battered me to my hands and knees and sent me slipping and rolling and clawing across the sloping deck. Why I didn't go over the side or how I escaped being felled by one of the flailing spars or wildly snapping blocks I have often wondered. The devil's own luck must have been riding on my shoulders that night. Something did hit me in the ribs so that I thought them caved in. The breath was knocked out of my lungs. A blanket of clammy wet canvas settled over my head. As I struggled, trailing wreckage and torn rigging caught at my limbs, dragging me toward the sea. Forward I sensed rather than saw the mainmast go by the board, taking the mizzen with it. My scrabbling fingers found solid hold in the scuppers, my feet lodged in the main chains, and there I hung on for dear life.

Relieved of the weight of her straining top hamper, the *Ladybug* rolled sluggishly back to a comparatively even keel, riding the waves with the dull placidity of a sodden raft. With her movement I freed my head from the smothering canvas. As I gulped the air a wave, breaking across the deck, slapped me full in the face and left me sputtering.

The chill and tingle of it revived me. In a burst of desperate energy I clawed my way out from under the tangled web of wreckage and felt my way aft to the cockpit.

Even in the dark I could make out the shambles. The mizzen had been snapped off clean and dragged forward, with the spanker and boom and all its rigging, by the heavy weight of the toppling main. Apparently its trailing ropes and tackles had swept across the cockpit, for the wheel was bent halfway round and doubled over, and the binnacle, torn from its bolts, lay half in and half out of the cockpit.

Nancy! Of her, no sign whatever!

Until this moment I had not had time to be frightened. Now I felt the cold clutch of panic.

I shouted her name.

The only reply was the howling of the wind and the roaring of the waves and the hollow gurgle and slap of water sloshing inside the hull.

"Nancy!" I cried again. "Nan!"

The wind snatched my voice away.

Had she been fouled in the lines and dragged overboard? I wrestled with a wild despair that urged me to plunge to certain death in search of her. Sobbing defiant curses into the storm I fought despair and thrust it from me. Life will not believe in death. Somewhere in the wreckage I would find my Nan.

Carefully I pawed my way through the tangle, feeling for her as I went. If Nancy was pinned under the wreckage, I must have a weapon to free her. I fumbled in the locker under the seat in the cockpit. My hand closed upon the ax. Gripping it, I clambered back up to the littered deck, groping and hacking forward along the broken starboard rail. And it seemed to me that I was the last man left alive in a black, malignant universe, a man alone with a hope that could die only with my last breath.

I inched with unsteady feet along a deck ripped and splintered. Heavy canvas lay in thick folds half in, half out of the water. There seemed no end to the piled wreckage. Never losing my grip upon the ax, I climbed, crawled, groped. My face brushed something smooth and soft, and my heart leapt as my free hand sought it out. It was a bare foot.

The miracle had occurred. Nancy was safe. But was she? Relief had left me weak. A driving fear succeeded it. Was she alive?

"Nancy!" I croaked.

There was no answer.

My hand went swiftly to the ankle, the leg, the knee. The knee was bent crooked between the overlap of the sail and the solid wood of the mast. I must know how she lay and what was holding her.

My trembling fingers worked up the length of her cold thigh to the roundness of the hips. Here the rough edge of the canvas, still secured by wooden hoops to the mast, checked me. I felt for her other knee. It was wedged between the mast and the boom. I worked around under the canvas. Most of her clothing had been ripped from her, and I blessed the fact for it enabled me to find the faint heartbeat and to feel an unmistakable rise and fall of breast. She was alive!

My impulse was to hurtle upon the welter of wreckage, hacking and slashing. Cool reason restrained me in time. I dared not lash out blindly for fear of maiming or even killing her. Nor could I use the ax which I still gripped. It was too dangerous. I must work more surely, deftly, than the ax would allow. There was not a moment to lose. Nancy lay with her head and shoulders hanging over the water. With the wallowing of the stricken bugeye, a hissing sea now and again broke over her head, so that although not in the water she was nevertheless in peril of drowning.

It cost me an effort to release my cramped hold on the ax and find instead the stout sheath knife which, like all sailors, I carried in my belt. In the blackness, with all my senses concentrated in my hands, I went to work cutting away the lashings until I was able to roll the sail back a little and ease myself into the narrow space between Nancy and the rail. I clasped her waist to draw her inboard, but something held her. I remembered that the mast and boom had her leg in a vise. I worked my shoulder under the stub of the mast and with all my strength lifted.

Luckily it was the mizzen, which is much lighter than the main. Yet for a terrible second it would not move. I knew it must, and strained with every muscle in my body. Slowly, reluctantly, it rose with me, and as it scraped cruelly down the length of my back, I drew out Nancy's leg.

She began to slide, slowly, headforemost, toward the sea. I flung myself upon her and felt a steady tug. Something was pulling her, something too strong for me to pull against.

In the wild, black night, this unseen, mysterious, persistent pull was terrifying. It was as if I were at a tug-of-war with some grisly monster of the deep. But my free hand, as if impelled by a calm intelligence all its own, sought and found the answer. Nancy's right arm was stretched taut over her head, the wrist in the grip of cordage which was part of the mess of canvas and debris that had gone overboard and was floating on the waves below.

Holding Nancy's body tightly, I wormed myself along the deck, searching a foothold to battle the pulling power from the sea. At last my knife hand touched the lines. Three times I slashed. The lines parted so suddenly that I dropped the knife and, only just in time, caught the rail. Painfully, with sobbing breath, I dragged Nancy and myself back on board. Then I half dragged, half carried her into the cockpit.

She was so cold. Frantically I set to slapping and kneading her. I put my hand to her heart, my ear to her mouth. Thank God, there was a breath, a heartbeat, still. Gently I went over her chilled body, feeling neck, arms, hips, ribs, legs, for broken bones. But if there were any, they had at least not pierced the flesh. There was nothing between her and utter nakedness but a few shreds of cloth. I stripped off my jacket and wrapped her in it. Wringing wet though it was, it did offer some protection against wind, rain, and snow.

Now I became fully, suddenly awake to every movement of my little boat, and knew in a moment that the *Ladybug*, slowly, steadily, was sinking. We dared not stay with the *'Bug;* wind and tide were carrying us out into the Bay as if having decided, in an evil compact, upon our burial place. Yet, in that sea, how long could I keep afloat with Nancy? I had a flash of murderous hatred for the Colonel and his insistence upon the oyster expedition. Let him balance his puny profits against the loss of his daughter!

Yet I could at least postpone the inevitable. I groped my way forward, found the ax, and chopped away as far as I could the wreckage that was dragging at the ship, helping to pull her down. The exercise warmed and heartened me, and I went back to the cockpit again and attempted to revive Nancy. Now and then I bellowed a useless "Halloooo!"

When Nancy seemed less chilled, I left her to resume my work. I managed a sea anchor of sorts simply by leaving a dangling headstay and one of the main shrouds uncut. Relieved of the weight of the wreckage that had dragged at her from the sea, my brave, pitiful *Ladybug* swung free to the end of the two remaining lines, where the tug of the sea-borne wreckage there brought her head around and into the gale while her stern swung down wind. Now the cockpit was better sheltered, and the smashing seas were parted by the bow before they reached us.

I scrambled aft once more. As I swung my leg over the coaming it seemed to me that Nancy stirred. I dropped to my knees beside her, fondling her hands and calling her name over and over. And at last there came a response, a low moan, and her hand moved in mine, and then she was still again. With a swift surge of hope and joy, I attempted once more to warm and revive her. Then a sudden lurch of the stricken bugeye confronted me anew with the hopelessness of the situation.

Had Nancy been spared, only to die a second time? The hull must be filled with water by this time. We would float for a little while longer while the hatches held, trapping a bubble of air inside. But when the pressure mounted, as it must, the hatches would give way, and then we would go down swiftly.

Listening for another sound from Nancy, I heard instead a faint, rhythmic whisper talking insistently in the teeth of the wind almost dead astern. I stiffened to concentration, and soon was certain. Somewhere in the blackness, and not far away, breakers were sounding their crashing fall—over a sandbar? Against a reef?

But where? I knew the Bay as I did my own dooryard, and could think of no land we might be driving upon—not here. I tried to recall our course, point by point, and the wind, and how far it might have taken us northward. Was it possible that we were close upon the northern tip of Poplar Island? More likely we were being blown toward the sandbars of Kent Island and would go aground there.

A slim hope lived in that prospect. If we hit there, the bugeye would hold momentarily. There would be solid bottom which I could touch occasionally, and so hold up Nancy's head and mine above water to the shore.

This hope roused me to action. In an instant I considered and rejected several expedients, then struck upon the most promising. The main hatch cover was still in place. This wooden frame, about 5 feet square, would make a raft. I worked my way forward, knocked away the battens, and stripped off the covering tarpaulin. As I raised the cover, the pent-up air in the hold rushed out in a mighty sigh, and the deck began to settle under my feet.

With all speed I laid Nancy face down on the hatch cover and lashed her limp body to the planks. Out of some deep dream of unconsciousness, she whimpered. I looped a bight of heavy rope around my waist, fastening the other end to the flush rim of the cover, so that we might not be separated in the water.

By now the seas were hissing along the rail and even bursting over us. The breakers sounded louder, a grumble of thunder warning that the sandbar was close by. The critical moment was upon us. Rallying all my strength, I hoisted the raft with its burden to the edge of the rail, holding it poised there until a heavy wave came under it, lifting. Then I gave the raft a mighty thrust and stepped off into the water after it.

THREE

I dropped down like a weighted stone. The water was ice-cold. A freezing hand clutched at my throat and locked the wind in my body so that I felt I could never again, in what life was left to me, breathe a warm breath. But my feet and arms struck out, flailing frantically, winning back to the surface. I gulped down air and water so chill that they rasped my lungs like a sharp file. Something kept pulling me down, and I realized that I had forgotten to kick off my boots. Clinging to the raft with one hand, I worked them off, then stripped off shirt and trousers. Naked, I was not only freer but less cold.

The bugeye, if still afloat, had disappeared into the blackness, and I could scarcely make out the shape of the raft at an arm's length. I had only the wind to guide me. Setting my back to it, I struck off to my left, calculating this to be east-southeast. Current and wind would drag me southwest, and between the two my general direction would be south, where the island ought to be.

Struggling with the waves, I tried to keep the raft snubbed close beside me. It was like holding a plunging, unruly horse by the bridle. I could not know whether I was making headway. I could only go on toward the land I prayed was there. Swells came from below and bore us up, and now and then a great wave mounted from behind to smash down upon us. When I felt one of these coming I swung my feet down under me, tilting the raft, in order to keep Nancy's head above water. There was as yet no sign of bottom.

At last—it might have been minutes since we had left the doomed bugeye, or hours—my feet came down hard against the sloping face of a sandbar. The relief I felt was short, for now I found myself pitted against new dangers. Sharp oyster shells cut my bare feet like knives (I still bear the scars). And because the water here was shallow, each wave was twice as high. The first tumbled me over, nearly smothering me in flying spume and spindrift. I fought to keep my grip on the raft, which bucked and battered at my chest.

But my hold upon the raft helped me to my feet again. Step by painful step I worked my way along the bar. The water grew shallower, I rose out of it inch by inch, and the seas dwindled to a lacework of wavelets that curled about my ankles. Now the bitter wind cut me, and the driving snow was as a million needle pricks. Ten, fifty, perhaps a hundred paces, mud mingled with sand, then tough swamp grass with shells, and at long last I staggered out upon a narrow shingle of beach. Here I summoned a final ounce of effort to drag up the raft.

I knelt to undo the knots by which I had fastened Nancy to the raft, and all at once remembered the time I had pulled her out of the inlet when we were children. At this grotesque memory I began to laugh, hearing my voice in my ears as an insane cackle, and then toppled over senseless on the soggy sand.

PART 4 ☆

Home

ONE

I must have shivered myself back into consciousness. It was some time before I realized that the uncontrollably shaking body and chattering teeth were my own. And then, like a dreary blur that clicks sharply into focus, I remembered the bugeye, the raft, fighting the water, reaching the sandbar, and Nancy. Nancy! The cold became frightening. Even in my unconscious state it must have warned me naggingly that it was cousin to death.

I reached out. The raft was beside me with its motionless burden. In attempting to warn Nancy I made my own blood flow, and a thousand aches I had not been aware of merged into agony. Shivering now with pain as well as cold, I had the devil's own time undoing the knots that bound Nancy to the hatch cover, and had to use my teeth as well as my fingers.

Meanwhile the grass I had lain upon and the shingle under my cut feet had registered the welcome fact that our haven was Poplar Island. Shelter, food, even warmth were at hand, if I had the strength to reach them. The small island was as familiar to me as my own barnyard. The Sears boys had permitted me the run of it for hunting, ducking, and trapping in return for help in moving their cattle here for summer pasturage. James Sears had shown me how to trip the secret latch on his back door.

On my knees I gathered Nancy into my arms, for I could not trust myself to bend without falling. Bracing my lacerated feet wide apart, I moved like some tormented, mishandled puppet toward the fringe of pine I knew must lie somewhere eastward. Small land noises of trees clattering in the wind fell upon my ears like a homely blessing. Nancy seemed to warm in my arms, and daring for a moment to bend my head, I felt on my cheek the soft touch of her breath. At last my feet were on the sandy track that led up to the house from the dock. I stumbled on, numbed now, feeling no pain whatever, and the house seemed to come out of the night to meet me. Letting Nancy down, holding her like a doll under one arm, I found, in the frame over the door, the loose board that lifted the latch. I dragged my burden to the bedroom, tumbled her on the soft feather bed, arranged her as if she were indeed a precious doll, and covered her with a blanket and a comforter. With jerky movements informed by long habit, I found the woodbin, the tinder in the box on the mantel, the snaphance that hung beside the fireplace. Upon the wide hearth I kindled a blaze. The dry fat-pine logs popped and crackled merrily. I knelt before the flame, unable for a moment to move. The light was like golden sunshine on a blind man's eyes. Never, it seemed to me, had I seen or felt anything so beautiful.

But I dared not delay. I lighted all the candles I could find. In a closet I found a pair of old linsey-woolsey breeches and a much-mended shirt with which I covered my nakedness, some rags for my tortured feet, and a pair of sea boots; and in the cupboard beside the fireplace, a brandy bottle half full. Fortified, I stumped out to the well and fetched two buckets of water, filled the blackened kettle and two pots, and swung the crane over the fire. The larder yielded tea and sugar, flour and cornmeal and salt. In the cold shed, my head reeled with the sight of riches—two hams and six flitches of smoked bacon hanging out of the reach of rats, and a keg of rum resting snugly in the crotch of a sawhorse.

With joy in my heart I went to Nancy. The sight of her brought me up sharply. For an eternity she had been a pale blob in the night, a fear of death and a hope of life, a weight upon my heart and body. Now the light of my candle illumined a face like death with sunken cheeks and dark hollows for eyes, and a trace of Annapolis rouge mocking the bloodless lips and the streaming coppery hair.

With a gasp of horror and dread I set down the candle and laid my cheek to Nancy's mouth. I could not detect a breath. Frantically I tore off the covers to listen for her heart, but here before my suddenly incredulous eyes lay a nude woman with full round breasts and softly rounded hips and thighs and the slim beauty of a young waist. At some time in the course of our perilous odyssey my coat, which I had tucked around her, had slipped off. My darting thoughts went back. Was it a naked Nancy I had lashed to the raft? To my near hysterical mind, it seemed somehow very important to know. The dashing waves had removed the last shreds of her garments. I had carried this unclad body from the beach to the house. Why, then, should it now be so astonishing?

This was nonsense! My concern was not with nudity but with a life. Yet, when I pressed my ear to her breast, I was acutely conscious of the pink nipple that brushed my cheek and could not hear her heart for the thudding of my own.

66

I flung back the covers even more hastily than I had removed them, and went for the brandy with such speed as to stumble in the clumsy sea boots, and was glad of the shooting stabs of pain from my poor feet. Mixing brandy, hot water, and sugar into a cracked cup, I returned and raised her, holding her gently in the crook of my arm. At my first attempt the liquor ran down her chin and neck. But then I thought she took a little. Suddenly she coughed, swallowed convulsively, and coughed again. Her eyes slowly opened and looked up at me unseeingly, then as slowly closed.

I sped to the cupboard and there thanked God and James Sears for having left behind a man's nightshirt, old but clean, and muslin sheeting. Although it was uncommonly difficult, I made it a point of honor not to stare at Nancy's nakedness even while I examined her body. She was cruelly cut, bruised, welted, and scraped, mostly down her right side, but I could find no broken bones. I washed the dried blood and brine from her cuts; it must have stung, for she whimpered. I slipped the nightshirt over her head, covered her, and again gave her brandy. This time she swallowed involuntarily and her pallor became less dreadful.

I thought of setting forth to brew a broth of sorts, of going to the shed for a ham, and to the well for more water. I actually thought I was occupied with the task, when it came over me that in actuality I had not moved from Nancy's bedside. Will and purpose had somehow been translated into a dream, and the resolute, tireless Ben Forbes of the dream seemed to stand apart, jeering at the spent body of the dreamer. This was very curious. I observed the phenomenon stupidly.

"Ben?"

Nancy's voice, no more than a whisper, brought me to my senses. Her eyes were strange and glittering in the gleam of the candle, but they knew me, they knew life. The small pinched face was like that of an old woman. It tore at my heart.

"I hurt," she said wonderingly. Then, having apparently stirred under her coverings, she gasped with pain, and flashed me an angrily accusing look. "I hurt!"

She moaned in protest as I held up her head, but I coaxed her to drink, and when she had finished she fell immediately to sleep.

With no small effort I tore myself away from the soft, inviting bed. I heaped more wood on the fire. Rain and snow slatted against the shutters; the wind screamed through the pines, the seas roared—at a safe distance now. But a dream fell upon me and once again I battled the waves, a very giant of a Ben Forbes, towing the *Ladybug* on a great raft while a naked laughing nymph swam easily at my side, now and again in evil sportiveness pushing me down into the green depths where oysters opened their shells to snap at me.

When I woke, I was lying on the settle by the hearth. The fire was a heap of gray ashes. A stripe of light slanted under the door. I started up, but fell back heavily with a grunt of pain. My sleep had stiffened me, and now from every part of my body came aches, twinges, and throbbing soreness. The soles of my feet seemed aflame, as if they had been bastinadoed.

On my hands and knees I remade the fire and then crawled to Nancy. She still slept and I was thankful for that. I cut away my blood-soaked rags, washed my feet, and rebound them with clean bandages, swigging rum to endure the torment. I could not wash my body. It was a mass of bruises from the makeshift raft, which had battered me mercilessly in the sea. I shuffled painfully outside. Day had come, a fitting partner of the night. Rain had won over the snow and all the world was soggy and dripping. The wind howled. The black branches of the trees writhed and tossed. The bay was shrouded in fog. There was no boat in the barn, only last summer's hay. Even if there had been a boat I could not have launched it, nor would I have dared to move Nancy. Still, its presence would have given me comfort. No matter. For the duration of the storm and the fog, we were marooned.

I prepared a breakfast of ham, cornmeal cakes, and tea. Nancy wakened when I came to her bed. She tried to sit up, but moaned and pressed her hand to her side. "Oh, Ben, it hurts so!"

I told her it was better than being dead, which she doubted, demanding querulously to be taken home. I explained that we were castaways, and only then did she inquire where we were and how we came to be there. Ordering her to lie very still, and spooning her hot tea laced with rum—she turned her head from the food—I began to give her an account of the wreck, but she stopped me, "Oh, Ben, you do go on so."

After a moment she said drowsily, "How elegant! Ben will be that surprised."

Her eyelashes fluttered. She slept.

Vaguely disquieted, I ate my own breakfast, then found myself retching it up. I cleaned up myself and the mess, puzzling over her words. Perhaps Nancy, like me, was too exhausted to eat, and she had been dreaming while awake, as I had done, but of shopping for a gown in Annapolis. That was all. Reassured, I wrapped myself in a blanket and slept a little. Rising with a renewal of pain, to which I was becoming reconciled, I split some wood, built up the fire, and replenished the kettle.

A scream rent the air. "No! No! Get out! Go away!"

I snatched up the poker and ran to the bedroom. Nancy was huddled in the far corner of the great bed, staring wildly at the closet door. Poker raised, I looked about cautiously. Then I opened the closet. Nothing. No one. Only the wavering shadows cast by the flickering candles.

"It's all right, Nan."

She whimpered in terror and took no notice of me. Her face was flushed and it was dry and hot to the touch.

"Nan!" I cried sharply.

"Ah!" She gave a great sigh. "He's gone now."

"Who?"

"Tip, it was. Our very best buck nigra, but he had no right in my room. Ben, you must strap him good."

My flesh crawled, but I promised I would beat the dust out of his hide.

"You will, truly?"

I put my arms around her and solemnly vowed I would, assuring her that Tip would soon be cursing the day he'd been born. But my voice choked in my grief for Tip and my fear for the burning, tormented creature in my arms. She clung to me tightly and wept. The tears did her good, and I was able to leave her for a moment to return with a brew of hot water, cornmeal, and sugar and rum. Soon she lay back and was asleep again.

The dreary day darkened imperceptibly into night. I remained beside Nancy, leaving her only for cold wet cloths to cool her face, and for tea, rum, and cornmeal potations for both of us, making hers very hot in the hope of breaking her fever with a sweat. I was dozing in my chair, when from out of some evil dream she began to babble shrilly. I quieted her. She begged me to stay so piteously that I kicked off my boots and lay down beside her, pillowing her head on my shoulder. We slept.

Something, perhaps a sixth sense, woke me. It was as if a presence had tapped me on the shoulder and said, "It is time, now." Immediately I was bright awake. Daylight was filtering through the chinks in the shutters, and it was not a watery daylight but clear at last. I thought I heard the murmur of voices. Carefully I disengaged my aching arm and shoulder, and eased myself out of the bed. Nancy muttered but went on sleeping.

Outside the sun was rising. I blinked and stretched. The world was clean and sparkling, and there were people in it. Again I blinked and rubbed my eyes to clear them. Up the wet path from the rickety little pier, where a little bay schooner bobbed, came a solemn procession of men. The sight of it made me laugh and laugh until I had to sit down on the step and lean weakly against the doorpost, still laughing.

Giles Penrose and company!

Fighting for my life and Nan's, I had forgotten the duel!

T W O

Giles Penrose, Oliver Ahrens, Mordecai Wright, and Doctor Tilghman fetched up and turned upon me a concerted stare of amazement.

Giles was the first to find his voice. "Ben Forbes," he said, in the tone of one righteously offended, "this is scarcely the occasion to play the clown."

I howled with mirth.

"Where are your seconds?" Mordecai demanded. "And the pistols?"

I could not speak.

Without a word Doctor Tilghman doused me with the contents of a bucket from the well. I sobered instantly and gaspingly thanked him, pleased to note that the others were almost as well splashed as myself, but they cursed the quiet doctor while I blessed him.

"Mr. Forbes," said Mordecai Wright in a declaiming style, "this is not mannerly conduct. Be good enough to explain yourself."

I was good enough. I gave an account of my adventure, cutting it short to inform Doctor Tilghman that Mistress Savage lay within, injured and feverish.

Giles was in a rage that appeared to me unaccountable. He seemed to feel that I had wrecked my beloved bugeye and imperiled two lives for no other purpose than to excuse myself from the duel. "The pistols! Where are the pistols?"

"Giles, please to shut your mouth," said Doctor Tilghman, and went into the house. The other three followed and I tottered after. All stood around the bed. The doctor seemed unaware of our presence. Already he had uncovered Nancy, who was still soundly asleep, or in some kind of coma, and was making his examination.

A soft snicker drew my worried eyes from him. Oliver Ahrens was pointing out my borrowed boots that stood on the floor, and the indentation in the soft bed where I had lain.

At this point Nancy stirred and the doctor turned and ordered us out of the room.

I went to the shed for an armload of logs and made up the fire. I filled the kettle and hung it on the crane. Then I tidied up the common room, for all the world like a housewife who finds callers unexpectedly trooping to her door. Despite exhaustion and worry for Nan, I felt somehow like a fool.

My callers meanwhile were sitting at the table with their heads together in the manner of conspirators. "A hundred to one," I heard Mordecai say, and felt myself flushing with anger.

The doctor came out to tell me what I already knew—that Nancy was badly battered and exhausted. To my great relief he said the fever had broken in the night, and inquired what I had done in the way of doctoring.

"Why, he slept with her, Doc," said Ahrens.

With one stride I lifted him out of his chair by a choking grip on his neckcloth and slapped him across the mouth.

He started for me, but Doctor Tilghman held him. He struggled furiously in the doctor's grasp. "God damn you, Forbes! I'll kill you for that."

"I shall be happy," I said, "to give you an opportunity, as soon as I've finished with Penrose."

Released, he stood livid, fingering his throat. "Gentlemen," he said in a voice trembling with rage and humiliation, "bear witness."

They bowed.

I turned to Mordecai Wright. "And you?"

He said most elegantly: "If by unfortunate chance you survive two encounters, Mr. Forbes, it will be my duty and pleasure to dispose of you."

We exchanged bows and laughter welled up in me. Three duels! Truly history was being made for Mistress Savage!

"Where are the pistols?" Giles demanded again. "What are we waiting for?"

"When we dock at the Landfall," I said, "I will fetch the pistols and we can have it out on the lawn."

"Would that be in the rules?" Giles asked.

Struggling yet again with laughter, I tottered.

"What's the matter with your feet?" said Doctor Tilghman.

I glanced down at them. Their rags were a shell of mud and dried blood. Here and there fresh blood was seeping through, making gay stains. The doctor seized me by the shoulder to set me by the fire. I winced under his touch and clenched my teeth as pain flooded over all my body.

He opened my shirt and gave a long, low whistle. "Great Christ on the foreyard! You look as if you'd been asleep under the hedge when the steeplechase came by."

His hand touched my left side and I yelped like a puppy. Through a haze of pain I heard Penrose declare me a circus ape, and steeled myself.

"Never saw such mischief," said Doctor Tilghman with professional interest. "You've three or four broken ribs there, my lad. Wonder they've not jabbed your guts and gizzard. Not spitting blood, are you?"

"No, sir," I said faintly.

"Well, since you've gone this long and lived, I dare say 'twill not harm you to wait a bit longer. I've dosed Mistress Savage, but we may not delay. She cannot be properly attended here. Nor you."

Instructing Penrose and his friends to knock together a litter of sorts, he made use of the top sheet of Nancy's bed and quickly bandaged me about the body. He cut the rags from my feet but after a glance said he could not tend them now. He wound them with strips from the torn sheet so neatly that I was able without difficulty to get into the boots.

Carefully he wrapped Nancy in the blankets, and under his sharp surveillance the disappointed duelist and his surly seconds carried her to the boat, and we set sail for the Neck and home.

THREE

The passage was smooth. These gentle winds, this generous sun, the innocent sky, and tranquil blue water, were ten thousand years away from the hell of seventy-two hours ago. Nancy slept. I sat by the rail, well away from the others, drinking in the peace.

A shadow fell upon me. I looked up wearily and here was the good doctor. He sat and talked quietly to me. I had saved Nancy's life, he said, and had grown overnight into a man. He said that he was proud to be my friend and much else that was soothing to my spirits. And then he said I had proved myself far beyond the necessity of fighting duels with young hotheads.

"Do you mean, Doctor," I asked caustically, "that I am to beg their pardon and propose a toast to shitepokery?"

"The Landfall is in sight," he said calmly. "I ask your permission to consult with the others in order to establish a general treaty of peace before we dock."

"Consult all you please. My terms demand an abject apology from each and every one of them."

Under a holiday sky on a millpond of a sea, we neared the inlet. As we ghosted into the sheltered cove, I saw with astonishment that the wide lawn sloping from my house to the water's edge swarmed with people. What were they doing there? They could scarcely have gathered to welcome us; our coming was unannounced. I cudgeled my brains for some grand family occasion I might have forgotten.

We were still a long cable's length from the dock when the small figure of Colonel Savage appeared at the very end of it. He seemed to be doing a sort of dance. Between cupped hands he bellowed: "Hullo-o-o-o, the schooner! Who's yon? Doctor?"

From the bow Doctor Tilghman shouted back: "All's well! Nancy's safe! And Ben Forbes!"

The Colonel was dancing again. "God damn Ben Forbes to hell!"

Other men joined him, some expostulating, and voices were angrily raised across the narrowing water. I saw my father, standing a little apart. I waved to him; he saw me and waved back. I sat quietly as we drew alongside the dock, bewildered by the hubbub ashore. My seconds, Jerry Pratt and Alec Carmichael, were there. That at least I could understand; they had arrived to accompany me to the dueling tryst. But all our neighbors were there, too—Jonas Welby, gaunt Major Caulk, the jovial Cap'n Hambleton, the Sears boys, Peter Denny, and many another. Above, in the middle of the lawn, the womenfolk were gathered, removed from male affairs by an unwritten law. Black faces peered from behind shrubs and trees and all the house servants had crowded to the door. It would seem that the alarm for Nancy and me had gone from house to house, and the first man to sight the sails of the homecoming boat, probably one of the Sears brothers, had sent out the word.

We bumped timber and there was a rush to board, the Colonel leading, but Doctor Tilghman, solid as an oak, stood them off. "Stand back, gentlemen. We have two patients." He turned to the Colonel and said gently, "I'm afraid, sir, your daughter has been rather painfully injured and is suffering from exposure."

The Colonel whitened and stood as one stunned. Penrose and Wright appeared from the cabin, carrying Nancy. "Make way! You, Forbes!" snapped Giles. But Nancy reached out and plucked at my sleeve so that they were compelled to pause. She looked so wan and peaked that tears started to my eyes. "Chowderhead," she said weakly.

They went down the gangway, and I hobbled after.

"Them's our blankets," I heard William Sears say flatly.

But here was my father, his hand held out to me, worry contorting his face. "All right, boy?" he said.

I might have fallen, blubbering, into his arms, but at that moment the Colonel, who had been hopping about Nancy in a rare state, pushed my father aside.

"You damned scoundrel! What have you done to my girl?" He fell upon me, clawing.

Agonizing pain surged through my body. I staggered and would have fallen but that my father's arm was about me. Through the blood-red cloud that threatened to engulf me, I saw that Doctor Tilghman had plucked the Colonel off. "Sir, have you gone mad? There's no call for such conduct."

"Them's my boots," James Sears intoned, but no one paid him any heed.

"No call?" cried the Colonel. "No call, you say? Then it's you that's mad, sir. Look at my girl! See what he's done to her!"

The doctor lost patience. "You fool! He saved her life. He fought through the worst storm this country has known within our memory and brought her safe to shore. He carried her to shelter, and there, while she lay stricken with fever, he gave no thought to his own hurts but fed and nursed and...."

"And kept her warm!"

Apparently the doctor's mediations aboard had failed, for the meaning of Ahrens's loud utterance was unmistakable. In the suddenly silent crowd someone sniggered.

"So!" said the Colonel. He expelled a long breath. And then, although his voice was now cool enough, and very unlike his usual popinjay style, he went mad indeed.

"Saved her, did you say, Doctor? Saved her! Ha! Yes! For his lust. Saved her—to have his use of her when she lay helpless. Saved her, sir—to spawn on her unconscious body a litter of his own whoreson breed."

My father's voice cut the envenomed air. "Sirrah! You are not yourself. Say no more."

I had never seen him so enraged, yet he contained himself. Not so Colonel Savage.

"No man will silence me," he said. "Bear witness, all. Oh, I have watched this son of yours with my daughter. I say he is a mongrel and a whelp of mongrels."

With this repetition of the unforgivable, I was as if miraculously freed from my pain. There was work to be done, and it must be done immediately, while I could yet stand. At some remote epoch a Forbes had been rumored to have acquired a leavening of Negro blood. It was to this the Colonel referred, and since he persisted in it before our friends and neighbors, there was no help for what must follow.

My father stepped forward, but I caught his sleeve. "Sir, this quarrel is mine."

With a wry and bitter look at the empty sleeve I held, he gave me leave.

And so I stepped out before all the world to go through the now familiar ritual, thinking rather bemusedly, as I said the words and heard the Colonel's and bowed and was bowed to, that once embarked upon this extraordinary course of dueling I appeared doomed to it for the rest of my life.

The arrangements were made even as my father went to the house to fetch the pistols. The four duels would be fought in proper order, beginning with Giles Penrose and ending, if I still lived, with the Colonel. I insisted upon having done with them all. Perhaps I was, by now, as demented as the Colonel. If so, no man present that morning was any saner, not even Doctor Tilghman.

"As a doctor," he said to me, "I order you to bed. As a man of honor, I ask only whether you can stand on your feet and take aim."

I replied in the affirmative to the man of honor.

FOUR

Details were still being thrashed out. Everyone seemed to have something to say in each and every matter. Feelings ran high.

There was a flurry of flying skirts and the men were forced to give way for my mother. She stopped as she looked at me and turned pale. Her hand flew to her lips. Then, to my horror, she opened her arms and came toward me.

"My baby! Oh, my poor baby!"

Retreating, I looked about wildly. If the earth could not swallow me, the inlet would.

My mother checked herself with visible effort. "I'm sorry, Ben. Forgive me."

She glanced from one grinning face to another. "Gentlemen," she said, "my son was lost, and I have been ill with anxiety. Now he is here and he is kept from me, and I find grown men fighting like children. Pray enlighten me."

The grins disappeared, and I breathed again.

It was Peter Denny who mustered up the courage to speak. He was a pompous, red-faced windbag who served, when occasion warranted, as constable and justice of the peace. "Mrs. Forbes," said he, "this is no place for lovely ladies. I regret to say that Colonel Savage has expressed himself in such a manner and with such words as to leave no doubt in the minds of all here present that the escutcheon of those who dwell on this estate—hem—namely, Forbes Landfall—has been sullied —hem—and with such a stain, Madam, as may be cleansed only with blood."

Well pleased with himself and the general approval, he mopped his face vigorously.

"Ben," said my mother, "what does he mean?"

"He means," I said wearily, "that Colonel Savage and I are to fight a duel."

"A duel? Nonsense!"

This feminine judgment on the situation was greeted with a grim silence.

"But, Ben," she said incredulously, "you're only a boy!" Hastily she corrected herself. "No, no. Again, forgive me. But Colonel Savage is old enough to be your father!"

"And if he'd been my son," said the Colonel bitterly, "I'd have brought him up at strap's end."

"As you brought up your daughter!" cried my mother with scorn. "Henry Savage, I credit you with better sense than to persist in this wicked quarrel with a mere child."

"Mother!" I began furiously.

She might not have heard me. "And that daughter you love so well, Henry Savage. She is plainly ill and you leave her lying there!"

Eyes turned to follow the sweeping gesture which brought us all into her angry contempt. The litter had been abandoned on the lawn. In the uproar of which Nancy was the unconscious cause, Nancy herself had been forgotten!

Doctor Tilghman started, and so, too, did I, and the Colonel. But my mother forestalled us by calling to the hovering servants, ordering them to carry Missy to the house. The Colonel objected but was silenced by Doctor Tilghman who, although red with embarrassment, said his patient must immediately be put to bed.

"And you, Doctor!" my mother stormed. "When you have quite done with all this manly nonsense, may we expect you? Surely the patient must not be left entirely to the inept care of women!"

The poor doctor winced, but he said with the dignity worthy of a great cause: "You may expect me, Mrs. Forbes—in due time."

"In due time," my mother repeated, with sudden fearfulness. She tried yet again. "Peter Denny, you are a constable of Talbot County. I believe dueling is not lawful. Where is your duty?"

The windbag had collapsed. He huffed and puffed to inflate himself enough to say, "The law's the law!" And collapsed again. "Mrs. Forbes, ma'am, it's an affair of honor. Why, I'd be hooted out of the county!"

My father appeared, carrying the rosewood case and attended by a wonderfully proud Cato entrusted with the powder flask and the shot pouch.

"Allen," said my mother desperately, "you cannot permit this. Surely. . . ."

He said quietly, "Go to the house, Martha. You have guests."

With rigid back and head high, she obeyed.

The spot chosen was the strip of level ground at the foot of the lawn by the water's edge. Argument arose among those who had no right to be present. Rules were quoted, tempers were snapping. My father, having ceremoniously delivered the rosewood case to my seconds, Pratt and Carmichael, cast a critical eye over the dueling ground.

"Gentlemen!" he exclaimed, and raised his voice. "Gentlemen! This is a private quarrel, and I wish you'd all go home. But if that is asking too much, for God's sake get up on the hill, out of the line of fire!"

They submitted, although with poor grace.

"Ben," said my father, hesitantly, "they say—four duels, is it, Ben?"

"Yes, sir."

"Four!" He seemed to sag.

"By the rules," I said quickly, "they must be taken in order. The Colonel is the last, and his insult to our house is the most important. I have no choice, sir."

"Quite so." He stood very straight and gave me a searching, steadying look. "Once before," he said, "as I told you, those pistols were used. I did not hit my man nor did he hit me. But honor was satisfied. They've never been blooded, Ben."

"Yes, sir."

We shook hands and he left me. I knew as certainly as if I were with him that he would close himself in the library and quietly wait there until all was over. And I knew, too, that within the house my mother and sister would be serving the ladies with a midmorning collation. The shots would fall upon their ears, and my mother would be determinedly discussing bonnets and babies with her guests, the wives and daughters of the men on the hill. And in a bedroom Cassie would be tending the unconscious Nancy.

I saw that Giles Penrose, stripped to his waistcoat, was moving toward the stick that the seconds had pegged down in the middle of the level strip. He seemed far away. I took one step, and an urgent whisper rose from the ground. Cato was kneeling before me; singularly, he was brushing my boots.

I was conscious of a vast loneliness. If anyone had asked me then for the name of my best and dearest friend, I would have replied, without hesitation, "Cato!"

"Mist' Ben, 'membuh when yo was knockin' the haids offen them sittin' ducks down the bay?"

I stared down at him, wondering.

"Well, yo do jes' like then, sah. Yo aims ra't at they haids an' yo git 'em eve'y time!"

"But, Cato," I said, "that was a rifle-gun."

"Make no diff'unce. Yo do like I say," he said sternly in the tone with which he used to admonish me when I was a boy.

I moved up to the stake, confused. For my father, I must miss my man. For Cato—and my life—I must kill.

Penrose and I met at the stake. Our seconds stood us back to back. Carmichael handed me the loaded weapon; Giles accepted his from Ahrens. Our seconds, falling back, began to count. We stepped off:

"One—two—three—four—five. Halt!"

I heard the lap and suck of the tide on the pilings and the mewing of the gulls. The sun was warm. It was a beautiful day for sailing.

"Turn!"

Turning, I looked across the ten paces into the eyes of Giles Penrose.

"Ready!"

In concert we raised our weapons, elbows crooked, so that the muzzles pointed to the sky.

"Take aim!"

I centered the tiny gold bead squarely between his eyes where his thick brows met, but in so doing saw in his face a dull bewilderment, which I knew with sudden insight was mirror to my own. I lowered my sights.

"Fire!"

I heard only one shot. We must have fired at exactly the

same instant. I saw two puffs of smoke. I waited; with a detached curiosity I waited to drop dead. I saw the gun fall from Giles's hand. He stumbled to his knees, bending forward slowly, clutching his stomach. The doctor was already beside him opening his bag and followed by Cato carrying a basin and sponges. And still I stood, waiting.

"Right!" said Jerry Pratt briskly, at my elbow. "Alec, go see what the damage is. And get that other pistol. They must be cleaned and reloaded."

Carmichael darted off and was back in a moment. "He'll do. He's gut-shot, but not bad. Doc will have to sew him up to keep his tripes in, but he'll heal. Judged it to a hair, you did, Ben."

A swift, overpowering wave of relief made me waver.

Pratt looked at me narrowly. "Are you all right?"

I nodded. I had not been touched.

"Are you satisfied?"

I looked at him stupidly.

"We have to ask that, you know—it's in the rules."

The dangerous laughter welled up within me and I fought it. "I'm satisfied," I said stiffly.

"Ahrens next," said Carmichael. "Might as well sit down, Ben, till we're ready."

I shook my head. If I sat it was not likely that I would be able to get up again.

Penrose was carried off the field of honor and Cato was sent to me with a glass of brandy. "I done tol' you aim at he head," he said reproachfully. "Howcum you to miss by so far?"

I flung the empty glass at him.

It seemed a long time, but at last I was stepping out to meet Oliver Ahrens. The narrow, sly face grew large, larger than life. For this vile creature I had nothing but hatred. At that moment I thought him not deserving of life. He contaminated the earth and the clean air.

We squared off back to back, measured the paces to the count, halted, and turned on the order, took aim. I had already blooded my father's pistols, and my purpose now was murderous. But in the hateful face of my opponent I read fear. Again, in the decisive moment before the final command, I lowered my sights.

"Fire!"

Two distinct shots. His bullet whizzed past my ear. I heard him cry out. He was holding his arm. Doctor Tilghman came smartly on the field with Cato. Pratt and Carmichael were reporting to me. My bullet had taken Ahrens just above the elbow. " 'Twill be a long time before he has the use of that arm," Carmichael exulted.

"Two down," said Pratt with suppressed excitement. "Wright is next."

The Sears brothers were acting seconds to Mordecai Wright, and their man was amiably conversing with them. The sky was blue as—as the Danish girl's eyes—and up on the hill the spectators had flung themselves down carelessly, wanting only picnic hampers to give them a festive air. I thought for a moment to send to Mordecai for the apology due me, and with that satisfy honor. After all, he had been drawn into the affray merely by way of supporting Ahrens. But I remembered the leering voice, "A hundred to one..." and knew the rest of that sentence, as I had known it then but had not believed: "A hundred to one he slept with her." All the same, I could not hate him.

Mordecai, small and dark and rather a dainty man, stepped out jauntily. When we came together in the middle of the field, he bowed. I doubted this courtesy was in the rules, but found myself liking him for it. Again I went through the puppetry. I pointed my weapon without taking aim. I had no intention of harming Mordecai Wright. I would fire wide, and so would he.

In one terrible flash, across the intervening space, I saw my error. The man facing me was no lad. In every line and feature he was formidable. He was a man, where Penrose and Ahrens were little more than boys. His eyes were keen, his arm was steady, his intent plain to see. I was as good as dead.

My hand jerked.

"Fire!"

The two shots rang out. I did not see or even hear the bullet that clipped my hair. All I knew was that I was still, incredibly, on my feet. I could not see Mordecai. Doctor Tilghman and the four seconds were kneeling where he had stood. Urgently I called to Cato, who came running with the decanter of brandy. Carmichael followed, and then Pratt. They said later that they had told me and that I had seemed to understand. But I did not, could not—not then. They said that I drank down a mighty dollop of brandy and stumped to the marker, bellowing hoarsely for Colonel Savage.

Jerry Pratt, giving me my weapon, asked, "Are you sure you want to go on?"

"Has the Colonel apologized to my mother, father, and

sister, and to his own daughter, and to me? Does he offer to do so?"

"No."

"Well, then?"

"You could put it off," Pratt said. "Maybe later...."

I stared at him. I said carefully, as if to a child, "You see, I am acting for my father and the honor of our house and all our kin. Why do you ask me to put it off, Jerry?"

"I just thought that—well—because of Mordecai...."

"Mordecai?" I frowned. "Mordecai who?"

All this they told me later, for I did not remember, not any of it.

"Mordecai Wright," they told me.

"Oh—from Queenstown. What is he doing here?"

"He's dead."

"He is?" I was quite pleasant, they say. "How did that happen?"

They hesitated. "Come," I said impatiently. "We must not keep the Colonel waiting."

And so they placed us and counted off the paces. They say I walked oddly, spraddle-legged, but responded correctly so that they could not cry halt to the encounter. I know I heard clearly the command "Ready!" and then, "Take aim!"

Smoke blossomed at the muzzle of the Colonel's pistol. I saw a bright stab of orange flame. I felt a sudden, smacking jolt, and staggered, but stubbornly kept on my feet, for by now it had become rooted within me that I must stand throughout eternity.

Then, to my stupefaction, came the order: "Fire!"

The Colonel, horror dawning in his face, dropped his pistol. He half-turned from me, stooping a little, and stood so. "Shoot! Shoot!" I heard his agonized cry. "In God's name, man! Shoot and have done!"

And I understood. The unfortunate man had committed the gravest of offenses against the code of honor: he had fired before the command had been given. He stood before the world hopelessly, shamefully dishonored—a criminal who, by the code, not only may but must be shot down in his tracks, if not by his wronged opponent then by his own seconds.

"Shoot, Ben!" he cried again, in that high-pitched, choking voice. "For God's sake—for mine!"

I cursed in my heart the ridiculously evil game, the laws, the rules, the code. Nancy's father, who should have been beside his daughter's bed, was begging me to kill him—and my own father, waiting for me up there in the house on the hill, would approve the senseless murder, the stupid demand of the code.

I did what I could. I fired wide, over the water. I said, "I am satisfied, Colonel Savage, if you are."

Then the sweet cool grass came up to take me to rest.

PART 5 ☆

Chesapeake

ONE

I struggled with shadows that drew me down into a hot black pit. I crawled on shores of slimy ooze, deep and black and stinking and all underlaid with oyster shells as sharp as knives. Now and again I knew myself on fire with pain, and fell back to begin again my battle with the dread shadows and the pit that was their home. Slowly I struggled upward into green fields and leafy woods, drifting weightlessly over dusty roads and blue-green waters. Taking on form and substance, I dwelt for a time in Paradise. It was very clear—a U-shaped bay, a white beach fringed with languorously stirring palms under lush green mountains, and I walked hand in hand on the soft sands with the loveliest of all women. But the skies lowered and a cold wind blew, and with heart-searing grief I left my love to go wandering once more in the darkness among the phantoms.

There came a day when I emerged into the sunlight. For a long time I lay very still, fearing it would leave me. I raised my eyes and saw a window, and it was night. It was night, and yet I felt the sun in all my being. Nevertheless, it was night and time to sleep. Obediently I slept.

When next I opened my eyes it was to a morning that had just been born. Dawn was past and it was now broad light, although the sun had not yet risen high enough to tip the trees with gold. I was safe in my own bed, in my own room.

A tousled head, a cinnamon-colored face set with great round eyes, popped up like a target in a tent show.

"Mist' Ben, is yo ...?" Cato stared, then his mouth curved in a jubilant grin. "Mist' Ben, yo is! Praise the good Lawd! Welcome back, Mist' Ben. Yo bin gone a lawng, fahr way."

I heard his feet slapping on the floor and I dozed off again.

When I woke my mother was sitting beside me, quietly weeping. I started up in alarm and fell back weakly. She kissed me. "Lie still, dear boy. You've been so ill, we were afraid for you." Gently she raised me and gave me to drink of a cup of steaming broth. "Skin and bones," she said so woefully that tears of self-pity stung my eyes.

"Ah, my baby! My poor baby!"

A dim memory was evoked. It scratched me with irritation like a sudden itch.

"Wendy's the baby," I protested.

"Wendy!" Mother vigorously blew her nose. "Indeed! What with Jerry Pratt and Alex Carmichael riding over every day, and now Nancy's cousin in attendance—I declare, that child has become so missish I much regret I never put her to the birch."

"Nancy?" I asked in bewilderment.

"At fifteen a woman grown, so she will have it," said my mother. "New dresses she must have, and ribbons, and laces...."

"Wendy?"

"... and ever reminding me that I was married at fifteen. Insolence!" But there was pride in her indignation. My mother had been a great beauty and was still, with some justice, "the enchanting Martha Forbes."

But I was confused. "Nancy is sixteen," I said. "Remember, Mother? She had a ball."

"Ah, the poor lamb," said my mother. "Ben, you must hurry. The English cousin is a handsome young man—of course, any man looks well in a uniform—and Nancy in bed is devastating."

Nancy in bed.... I remembered now a face like death. Devastating! I struggled to rise.

Concernedly my mother soothed me. Nancy, she said, lay in our house tended by our Cassie and her own Clytie who had been sent to her. She had contracted a fever which had touched her lungs. Here my mother maundered into harsh words against Doctor Tilghman, which in turn became an attack upon Colonel Savage. "Every door closed to him but ours, when he has used us so ill!"

It was too much for me and so I said I was hungry, which I was, and all smiles now she hurried out.

Cato fed me, and I ate with ravening appetite that was suddenly sated. Then it seemed to me that my room became a public promenade. People came and went. There were footsteps and voices. I paid them no heed, but pretended sleep when someone was about, and slept when there was no one. Now and again I opened my eyes to savor the early spring that was framed in my south window. Carefully, I did not turn my head to look out to westward, although my second window called me. But at last I could keep from it no longer.

Another day was dawning. I looked over the broad expanse of the bay to the distant, faint blue line on the horizon that marked the western shore. My reluctant eyes were drawn down. So clear was the early morning light that on the ragged little hump of land embedded in the bay, I could make out the sparse pines marching along the low, sandy ridge and the narrow spit of land at the northern end where, long ago, it seemed, I had stumbled ashore. Poplar Island.

Again a figure popped up, and I saw that Cato had a cot in the corner of my room. "Welcome home, Mist' Ben. Yo bin gawn...."

"You said that," I remarked testily.

"Yesttiday that was, Mist' Ben. An' I bin sayin' it ev'ry day fo' seven days. But yo ain't nevah heard me till yesttiday."

Seven days! A simple unit of time, but it seemed somehow difficult to relate it to myself.

"Mist' Ben," said Cato proudly, "we sho made ourself a rep'tation heah las' week."

"We did, Cato?" I said, absently.

"Yes, suh, Mist' Ben. What I mean, we is de kingpin o' de Eastuhn Sho'. Las' week we was jus' Cap'n Fo'bes's boy Ben. This week we's de man what come home half daid, an' tu'n raht eroun' an' fit fo' times, wif all de fixin's, like a gennelman. We's a fightin' man, we is, a reg'lar fire-eatin' man."

I had to laugh as I sent him out to fetch my breakfast. But when he had gone I turned again to the bay, and I knew that somewhere in those deep waters lay my *Ladybug*, gone from me forever. With deep sorrow I took my farewell of her and of a Ben Forbes who had died with her. A boy, and a boy's mistaken pride in his seamanship, had gone down with a boy's boat.

Without sails above me and a deck under my feet, what was I? A shadow without a body, a life without a soul.

Cato washed me, so far as my wrappings permitted, for I was trussed like a mummy; and he fed me, talking foolishly all the while of "our" greatness.

Then came my mother with a bit of embroidery to work while she sat beside me. She spoke of things long gone—of the mischiefs of her four children when we were very small. She recalled our tutors and how we had bedeviled them. She related how Patricia, my eldest sister, had played with baby Ben at Moses in the bulrushes, setting me afloat in a wicker basket that filled with water and very near ended my short life. And how in my fourth Christmas, Vixen, my second sister, had forced me into her long-discarded angel's costume and dragged me, winged and curled and howling, before a large company. And how little Wendy, violently refusing to be a redcoat prisoner, had been so well upheld by her sisters that I, Captain John Paul Jones, had been tumbled into the pigpen.

I had often thought that there are few worse fates any lad can suffer than that of being born into a clowder of sisters. From the very beginning he is outclassed, outmanned, out-gunned. His only salvation lies in nimble avoidance of the plaguey sex. I had been well pleased when Pat and then Vixen had married, taking far from me their giggles and storms and raptures. Wendy I could cope with largely by ignoring her.

My mother rambled on and dimly I perceived that she was clinging to a sheltered little world that was no more. It was as if, by evoking the safe and distant past, she could build walls according to her design to encompass the future. For I dozed and heard her still, speaking now of Nancy and our wedding. And although I had always known, it seemed, that Nancy and I would marry, I did not like being thus summarily ordered to the altar.

I roused to say a sharp word, and saw my father. He appeared unaccountably aged. There were lines in his face I had not marked before.

"Well, sir?" he said.

"Very well, sir," I replied.

We smiled at each other a little awkwardly, uncertain what to say.

He turned his smile on my mother. "You are tiring him, Martha."

"Ah, yes." She sighed and kissed me.

As they went out together I heard her say, "But there is so little time. . . ."

T W O

"Give Nancy my love," I said drowsily.

"Dear Benjy! How gallant of you!" This was another voice, and I had sent Nancy my love from out of a sleep; the sun in my window told me it was near midday. My sister Wendy was sitting beside me, and from her tone and the use of the nickname that irked me, I knew I must be prepared to defend myself.

"Who," she demanded, "is Kirstie?"

I was taken aback, and with a triumphant toss of her head she told me I looked like a gaffed fish. I called her a piggy and she returned the compliment with "Toad!" Our usual practice was to run swiftly and with telling effect through the more loathsome orders of the animal kingdom, but I found myself staring at her. Gone was the fat and rosy, tumbling, and squalling brat of torn bibs, pinafores, and smocks. In a week Wendy seemed to have grown a full two inches and to have diminished astonishingly in girth. True she was well rounded, but womanly. While informing me that I was a snake and a lizard, her gray eyes, which were very like my own, were purposeful.

She fell silent and we regarded one another, each as if seeing a new thing.

"Ben," she said at last, "you were talking through a fever of a Kirstie; and Nancy, too, babbled of this Kirstie, but not in the same way."

"What," I asked, "did Nancy say?"

"As if I'd tell!" she said scornfully. In the last year or so, she and Nancy had become close friends.

"Well, then, what did *I* say?"

Instantly I wished I had held my tongue, for Wendy began to pleat her lacy, purely ornamental apron in a manner that embarrassed me. "Go away," I said petulantly. "I'm ill and I'm hungry."

"You can't be both," she said.

"I can."

"You can't!"

I looked at the bay and yearned to be sailing on it in any kind of craft—bugeye, raft, or sieve.

"Ben, you said—oh, many things. And it was very wrong, because you and Nancy...."

I was making a show of examining the ceiling.

"You said—'Kirstie, don't you think we had better get dressed? We wouldn't want them to see us like this.'"

A sudden wave of heat rose from my toes to my head, and I looked at my sister in horrified dismay. She was scarlet.

"Wendy," I said quickly, "did anyone else...?"

"No. I was here alone with you. You see, when you'd begin about Kirstie I would send Cato out to guard the door, and when you were done I would fly to Nancy, and if she was a-Kirsting I would send Cassie and Clytie out. I swear that between the two of you I have near killed myself. So, Ben, you must tell me about this Kirstie."

I began to describe to her the brush of the *Oriole* with the *Ladybug*, but she said they knew all about it, having received word from Callander in Annapolis and an apology by note from Captain Boyle himself. "He wrote most handsomely, but father lays on him the blame for everything and will not send him so much as an acknowledgment."

"But, Wendy," I said, "the wreck was no man's fault but my own."

"No matter. This Boyle is a merchant captain, and it is better for father to blame Trade than to stripe your hide. You are not to argue with father. He's turned crotchety. Now, about Kirstie?"

"She is a Danish lady," I explained. "She was a passenger, with her father, on the *Oriole*. That's all."

"All?" Wendy looked at me and I felt myself growing hot again.

"It must have been a dream. I—yes, that was it—I must have been confused. You see, when I brought Nancy ashore she was—well, she had no clothes on."

Wendy said, "Oh, Ben! The Sears brothers were loud in claim of their property, including the nightshirt. There's not a family on the Eastern Shore doesn't know that Nancy was naked."

I seemed to hear an evil whisper: "A hundred to one...."

"Lie still," Wendy ordered.

"What's to be done?" I said miserably.

"I don't know," said Wendy, almost as miserable as myself. "Mother has it you must offer for Nancy at once, but father refuses to be related to Colonel Savage, and as for the Colonel...." She sighed rather like my mother. "Anyhow, Nancy may refuse you, what with this Kirstie and her own pride and her father's disgrace and all."

"Nancy refuse me?" The thought made me laugh.

She was angered in the old way. "You dolt! You—you chowderhead! Oh, Benjy thinks well of himself, he does. *Dear* Benjy! Men are wonderfully stupid!"

She flounced out and Cato promptly appeared with a heaped tray. To my surprise there was nothing wrong with my appetite. Having eaten I attempted to order my thoughts, but a slant of sun that lay across my bed held and distracted me. Once again I walked in Paradise, on a dazzling beach between mountains and the sea, and Kirstie came toward me, her golden hair loose in the soft wind, her eyes like stars. I opened my eyes and the dream was still clear within me. Mountains and palms. I had never in my life seen a mountain or a palm. What did it mean? Mistress von Lund was in Washington, and I had only exchanged a few words with her; and I must marry Nancy and would likely spend the rest of my dull days ashore in management of her father's acres, a husband, a landed gentleman of sorts, and, in due time, father of a brood of nasty redheaded little girls.

Ruefully smiling at myself, I turned on my side. Instantly I seemed to be standing in the cold dark of a moonless night on a high, windy place. I went down a rough, stony path, and a girl's hand, soft and warm, was in mine, and I knew that I loved the girl beside me with all my being. Down we went together and I could smell the salt sea air. All at once there was a rustle and scurrying, and there rose before me a huge black figure of a man and I knew that I confronted my enemy. I must hear his voice; I must see his face. How could I fight in the dark?

Someone was at the door.

Coming back, out of that second dream, was like running a long way and tumbling back into bed through the open window. Why the window? I do not know. In waking I seemed to hurry back from a far place and time, like a ghost driven swiftly across the bay. By way of the window I drifted to my bed and into my helpless body, as if in fear of being caught aroving.

My father came to me. "Ben, can you receive visitors?" he asked.

His tone was grim and I blinked at him, but said I could.

He ushered in Colonel Savage and a third man. The Colonel greeted me stiffly and inquired after my health, and I made civil reply. He bore himself more struttingly than ever, but the flesh of his face was sagging and his eyes were sunken and burning. He presented the stranger: "Lieutenant John Meade, of the Royal Navy, my nephew by marriage once removed."

The lieutenant bowed and said with easy politeness, "My honor, Mr. Forbes."

He was a tall dark man with a slightly arrogant and altogether aristocratic face. His nose was long but delicately shaped, his mouth full, somewhat sensuous, his dark eyes were faintly mocking under high-arched, proud, and thoroughly self-assured brows, and his chin was precisely cleft. He was, in short, as handsome a man as I had ever seen—and this was Nancy's English cousin!

I hated him at once, but not for being my rival. I hated him for his blue coat with its smart white facings and gold braid and the epaulet upon its left shoulder. I hated him for being but little older than myself and an officer in the greatest navy in the world—and I a nothing in a country with no navy worthy of the name. And I hated him for being British.

In the titanic struggle between Britain and Napoleon's France, Mr. Jefferson had declared himself and our country to be neutral. But few Americans were, in fact, neutralists, even here in our small world of the Eastern Shore. Not all of us, of course, were shipowners, or even shareholders in overseas ventures, but that did not matter. If a man's bottoms fell afoul of French privateers in the West Indies, he leaned to the Federalists who favored the English as against the French. If his ships and cargoes were molested by the British, he would become a Republican, all for Napoleon and the French. A few cried plague on both houses.

In the last few years, however, most seamen had turned against the British, for British warships had been stopping our merchantmen and with maddening impudence had been impressing their crews, declaring them British subjects, as if the United States were still a gaggle of British colonies. To this Mr. Jefferson had remained blind and deaf, so that there was any number of hot young men, like myself, and older men too, who were ready to set out in a barge, armed with squirrel guns or pitchforks, to decimate the British navy.

Yet, we were not at war with Britain—or so my father's warning eye reminded me—and Lieutenant John Meade was a guest in our house, and Nancy's kin.

"I had hoped," he said, "to call earlier upon my American relations, but the *Leo*'s only been on station three or four months and I have only now had the opportunity."

"The *Leo*?" I asked. I thought I knew the names of all the British blockading squadron that cruised between the Virginia and Delaware capes, ostensibly on the watch for French privateers and men-o'-war.

"His Majesty's frigate *Leopard,* fifty guns, Captain Salusbury Pryce Humphreys commanding, sir," he informed me. "We came to see if the French were still in hiding at Annapolis. My ship goes up to fresh water to be rid of her barnacles, and I was fortunate to obtain leave."

"And were they?" said my father belligerently.

I was pleased to see the grand lieutenant reduced to a startled boy. "Was who what, sir? I beg your pardon, sir?"

"The French—at Annapolis."

"Oh. Yes, sir. They could scarcely be elsewhere, could they, sir? We have them in a bottle. The only way out is through the neck—between the capes—and we hold the cork."

Three French frigates had been forced to take refuge in the bay during a hurricane in the summer past. They had been kept there by the British ever since and my father had never ceased to be infuriated by the situation.

"Is your commanding officer aware, sir," he demanded, "that these are neutral territorial waters, under the sole jurisdiction of the American flag?"

The Lieutenant seemed secretly amused but he said quite soberly: "I have not inquired, sir. It is not my place to question my superiors."

I was frankly curious. "Does your Captain Humphreys plan to try to cut them out? The French, I mean."

"In neutral waters, sir?" Deploring any such deviltry he raised an eyebrow, seeming to bring me into a small conspiracy as one who would understand. "We did nourish a hope that when the French saw the *Leo* sail on up the bay, they might make a dash for the open. In which case, of course, they would run straight into the *Melampus, Chichester, Triumph, Zenobia, Bellona,* and *Halifax*."

"In Lynnhaven Bay, I daresay!" said my father angrily.

The Lieutenant's eyes widened innocently. "Oh, no, sir. Outside the capes, sir. At least three miles out." Again he turned to me, confidingly. "Of course, it's an old trick, and in any case the French would far rather dance dandy at Annapolis or Baltimore than come out to fight. The frigates still lie anchored in the Severn."

I was suddenly very tired. They'd rot there, those French, and so would Mr. Jefferson in Washington, and I, too, in my bed.

The Colonel had been fidgeting at a window, and now without ceremony he attempted to hustle his kinsman out. But the Lieutenant contrived a proper leave-taking of me, wishing me well; and my father, recalled to his manners, escorted the two to Nancy's room.

I was left in a veritable sweat of anger, and the anger was directed against Nancy. That she should have such a cousin seemed to me little short of treason. Marry her? Why, I would not offer for Mistress Savage if she were the last woman on God's green earth!

Wendy tripped in and I groaned. Forbes Landfall was no house for a man to be sick in. She was wearing a gown that had once been my mother's, of a rich striped stuff, tasseled and ribboned. And she was in a feminine rapture, as I had often seen Pat and Vixen. "Oh, Ben, isn't he a love! I do like a dark man. I will confess that I had a fancy for Mordecai Wright and was quite certain that within a year I would have brought him to a declaration. I was vexed with you for killing him. Really, Ben, it was most thoughtless. . . ."

In this careless fashion was it revealed to me that I had killed a man. Doctor Tilghman arrived in good time to dose me with sleeping draughts.

THREE

In the next few days I became more fully aware of the consequences of my wholesale disaster.

Of these the casualties themselves were the least, and although it may seem strange to speak in such terms of the death of Mordecai Wright, yet so it was. The dead have no problems; that is reserved to the living.

Doctor Tilghman informed me that Giles Penrose had suffered no serious damage. "A bit uncomfortable," he said, "from the notch in his belly, but that will soon be over. In fact, you did him a favor. He's lost some ten pounds of fat he could well afford. When he can get back into his britches he'll find himself a trim lad in his militiaman's uniform."

"And Oliver Ahrens?" I asked.

"The bone in his upper arm was shattered. He is crippled with it for life."

"I'm sorry for that," I said.

"No doubt. No doubt," he returned, plainly indicating that he himself was not.

"You adhered to the code," said my father, who was present. "In each case the challenge was given, you met, and the issue was settled. Honor is satisfied."

"But Mordecai Wright," I said, "is. . . ."

"Dead," said the doctor quite cheerfully. "Dead as a mutton, and buried."

"Honor," my father repeated, "is satisfied."

I lay there, feeling sick in the stomach.

For the rest, Nancy had been dangerously ill but was rapidly recovering. My own injuries were healing. The Colonel's bullet had taken me in the left shoulder but the wound was clean and, said the doctor, "breathing well." The broken ribs were knitting; my feet were stiff but would soon be carrying me; and my bruises were taking the course of a garish, reluctantly fading sunset.

It seemed that Doctor Tilghman had taken a historical interest in the affair. "I have taken the trouble to look back through the records," he said, "and I find only one instance in which a multiple challenge has been issued and accepted.

A Midshipman Somers, of the *United States*, frigate, in 1800 challenged all of the commissioned officers on board to meet him one by one. The challenge was accepted, Mr. Decatur acting as Somers' second. But Somers met only three opponents. He was wounded by the first two, and insisted upon fighting the third from a sitting position, since he could not stand, supported by Mr. Decatur. That ended the affair. So far as I can discover, you are the only man who has faced four opponents and survived."

My father seemed to derive much satisfaction from this intelligence. He and the doctor endlessly discussed the duels, along with Jerry Pratt and Alec Carmichael who were daily visitors, as much for Wendy, whom they had newly discovered, as for myself.

What I learned was startling. Our neighbors were divided. To some I was a fire-eater and a killer, a danger to the community. To others I was the worthy son of a great gentleman. Among those against me fanciful rumors were being spread. It was said that Ben Forbes had a brace of nigra boys on whom he practiced sharpshooting; that he had studied ways of provoking a quarrel so that he would be in the position to name the terms; that he had a bottom streak of cold-blooded cruelty—that he was, in short, part rattlesnake, part alligator.

This extraordinary monster had been created by people who had known me all my life and had, until now, found me unremarkable. Between detractors and hot defenders, the news of me and my deeds had traveled through the county, around the bay, "north to Philadelphia," said Doctor Tilghman proudly, "and south, I don't know how far, but certainly to Norfolk."

After my sense of outrage had subsided, I might well have looked forward to a swaggering enjoyment of my new reputation. But there was another consideration that sobered me. Dueling was illegal. In the eyes of the law, a man who killed another in a duel was no better than a murderer. With my enemies pressing him hard to bring me to justice, Constable Peter Denny had fled to parts unknown on the trail of a nonexistent fugitive. Through a chain of Tilghmans—trusted messengers—he had sent to implore me to be gone from Talbot County before his return, which would be in a month's time. But I had no intention of fleeing. I had behaved honorably; of this my father constantly assured me. Come what might, I would not be driven from my home by evil minds. Besides, where would I go?

My mother and father had been quarreling. This I knew from Wendy and also from a look they had of strain and sorrow that did not wholly disappear with agreement. My mother, much indulged and, in turn, indulging, had never opposed her husband on any serious matter. But in the case of Nancy she stood firm, holding that the code of honor was designed to protect womenkind—and if ever a woman was in need of protection, said she, it was Nancy Savage.

Carefully, in a family conference held at my bedside, she explained the situation.

"Ben," she began, "it was very wrong of Nancy to have gone with you to Annapolis unaccompanied by another of her sex. If only Clytie had been with her!"

"But, Mother," I said in bewilderment, "Nancy and I have grown up together. She's been like one of my own sisters. Besides, we don't hold with formalities on the Eastern Shore."

"Yes," sighed my mother, "and there's the heart of the trouble. Because we are not given to punctilio, I have been lax. Nancy had no one but me to guide her, and so the fault is mine. You see, Ben, by her grand party Nancy entered the marriage lists with ceremony. If I had given thought to the matter, I would not have permitted her to go with you. But she was still to me a little girl and you my little boy. In any case, I was not even informed of the errand to Annapolis.

"No, no," she stopped the protest I was about to make. "I do not blame you. You and Nancy were merely going about in the old way, the way in which you were brought up. And it did not occur to me that the time had come to speak seriously to both of you, but in particular to Nancy. A motherless girl must be more circumspect than others more fortunate. If only the Colonel had been a proper father! But there! It is done. I accept my responsibility and you must accept yours."

"Mine?" I looked at my father, but he was staring gloomily through the window. I looked at Wendy, but she sat with eyes lowered carefully pleating her apron. I said slowly, "I accept my responsibility in the loss of my *Ladybug*. But what's the good of that? Nothing will bring her back."

My father burst out savagely: "God send Captain Boyle my way! I'll deal with him, I swear it!"

He and I would have embarked forthwith upon a furious argument, but my mother checked us. "Allen," she said warningly, and my father swung back to his dark contemplation of the bay. To me she said, "Ben, we are not concerned with a boat but with a woman."

"You mean Nancy?" I asked. It was somehow very hard to think of Nancy as a Woman. My mother's tone had put the word in capital letters. I had a picture of Nancy in that hideous costume she had purchased in Annapolis, the dribbling violets, the stiff and garish hair. I grinned.

My mother was displeased. "Very well," she said sternly. "I see that I must spell it out for you." She took a great deep breath. "It is no terrible thing that you saw and tended a young woman unclothed, that you saved her life and brought her out of the sea, both of you as naked as the day you were born. True, there would have been gossip, but all know us and very soon the foul tongues would have been stilled. Unfortunately, upon coming home you proceeded to fight four duels, each and every one of them over Nancy, and one with her own father! There it is, Ben. Nancy Savage left her home a highly marriageable young woman. She returns without prospects. Through no fault of her own she has become notorious. I daresay that sort of thing went down well in the days of Helen of Troy, but it is very different now. Her good name has gone. They may speak of her in the taverns, but not in a respectable home."

With growing astonishment I contemplated this new picture of Nancy as a Helen of Troy, misplaced in the nineteenth century in a small corner of the country of Maryland.

"Get on with it, Martha," said my father impatiently.

My mother obeyed. "Ben, you will marry her. You must declare yourself without further delay. It may beggar us, but we will have the grandest wedding the Eastern Shore has ever seen. It is the least we can do."

Wendy spoke for the first time. "I'm afraid she will refuse him, Mother."

I expected to hear from my mother an explosive "Nonsense!" But it came instead from my father, and thus was somehow the reverse of reassuring.

I said hotly, "She has no right to have an Englishman dancing attendance upon her. An Englishman, and in our house! I won't have it. I won't have her!"

Wendy rose to the defense of Lieutenant Meade. "He can't help it that he's English, you ninny. And he's a beautiful Englishman. Why, if I were Nancy I'd have him—if he offered, of course—and I'd go to live in England and I'd forget all about silly Ben Forbes, I would!"

This treason on the part of my own sister left me speechless.

"That will do," said my mother, silencing Wendy. But she added, "It would, in fact, be the very best thing for Nancy. But we cannot know the Lieutenant's intentions, and he may be already committed. In any case, Ben, your duty is plain and you will not fail us."

She left then, herding Wendy before her and escorted by my father who did not give me so much as a backward glance.

I lay in a turmoil. I reminded myself that I had always intended to marry Nancy, if only to spite Giles Penrose who was, or had been, her father's choice. But to be driven into marriage was quite a different matter. My boyhood enmity against Giles Penrose was gone. Giles had behaved well, and I had it from Cato that in the growing feud over Ben Forbes on the Eastern Shore the Penrose family, and Giles, were maintaining a strict neutrality.

Cleared of Giles, the question was: did I, or did I not, love Nancy Savage? Did I want her for my wife? Not a word had my mother uttered concerning love. I thought of the night of the party, Nancy's surprisingly soft and womanly body in my arms, her lips on mine; and I became confused. I raged inwardly against my foul-minded neighbors and wished that I had killed Oliver Ahrens on Poplar Island, choking the life out of him. I wished myself a thousand miles away, safe at sea amid the roar of cannon facing the *Leopard* and Lieutenant John Meade. I wished that I had never set eyes upon Nancy Savage, naked or clothed. I wished the Colonel's oysters at the bottom of the sea. I wished.... Well, no matter.

Whatever might come of it, I must go to Nancy and ask her to be mine.

That day I rose for the first time and with Cato's help tottered about my room, venting rage and despair upon my weakness and helplessness, and upon poor Cato.

FOUR

The next morning I was taking my first breakfast out of bed, sitting at the scarred and much-initialed table that had been my desk in the days of tutors who had attempted to pound into me Latin and Greek, the Roman Emperors, the Battle of Hastings, and Magna Carta. But never a word had they said of the French Revolution or of the great war between England and France now raging. They had informed me at length of triremes and galleons and the Spanish Armada, but would not be drawn on the subject of why we had no navy. For that, said they, was not history. History concerned matters and men long dead. It had nothing to do with yesterday or today.

Wendy shot into the room. "Ben," she said breathlessly, "I am to tell you that it must be today. Nancy insists upon going home. Mother is trying to dissuade her, but you know Nancy.

The Colonel refuses to be beholden to us any longer, and Nancy will go to him."

"Let her go, then," I said crossly. "She can't very well stay here forever, can she?"

"Idiot!" cried Wendy in exasperation. "You don't understand even now. Holly Hall is avoided like the plague, and the Colonel is drinking heavily, and Nancy will be alone with a handsome young man as her guest. Mother begs to be permitted to go with her and stay until he leaves, but Nancy will not have it. People will make the most of it. If she goes unbetrothed, and without mother to chaperon her—oh, Ben, what will become of her!"

"I don't know," I said. "How should I?"

Wendy looked to the ceiling as if imploring God to bear witness to the stupidity of all males and in particular of her brother. Receiving no reply from the plaster, she said in a tone of command, "You must get dressed and speak to her, and then we must prepare for the wedding. And then you will go into the Navy. There's so little time."

The Navy? What had she said?

"Wendy!" I roared after her. "Come back! What navy?"

"Father will tell you," she called from the hall. "Hurry, Ben!"

I had no time to think. The door banged again admitting Cato who carried my best clothes: ruffled shirt, fawn-colored breeches, buckled shoes, white-thread stockings, cravat, stock, and my father's embroidered dressing gown in lieu of coat, for my left arm was still in a sling. In the exhausting business of dressing, I plied Cato with questions concerning the Navy, but he could only say that my father had sent Virgil in the pinnace on an urgent errand fully a week ago. He had gone with a letter and with instructions to wait for a reply. Presumably, he was still waiting.

Supported by Cato I shuffled down the hall to Nancy's room, which had been Patricia's. Clytie opened to my knock. She was a muscular, handsome mulatto woman, very quiet and somewhat feared. It was said that she had a sixth sense and could read minds and, if she chose, perform marvels beyond ordinary powers. But this I did not believe, for surely Nancy would have told me of any marvels. She had been Nancy's nurse and all the mother she had had, besides my own.

She filled the doorway and her gaze made me feel very small and miscreant. "Miss Nancy's expecting you," she said.

I shook off Cato and walked alone to the bed, lowering myself carefully into the chair beside it.

Nancy was sitting up in a nest of pillows. She was all in white—lace and ruffles and satin ribbons—and there came from her a sweet scent, both exciting and cloying to my taste and troubled head. She appeared so frail that her coppery hair, streaming over her shoulders, seemed too heavy for her. Her eyes were very green, and they looked at me with a composure that was disconcerting.

"Hullo, Nan," I said lamely.

"Good morning, Ben. I am pleased to see you well."

There seemed to be a civil finality in the simple statement. I cast about for words and my eye fell upon Clytie standing with folded arms before the door. I appealed to Nancy. "Can't you send her away?"

"Certainly not," she said. "You are a man and I am a woman. Didn't you know? We must be properly chaperoned."

So that was it, I thought. My well-intentioned mother had done ill, talking to Nancy of conduct and chaperonage.

"Look, Nan," I said desperately, "you are you, and I am me. . . ."

She nodded. "Exactly. That's what I said."

I swore under my breath and began again.

"Nan. . . ."

"Yes, Ben."

Oh, she was amiable enough, but she was like glass, dangerously brittle, promising sharp, cutting splinters. What could I say to her? I must not speak of Lieutenant John Meade. Nor of the duels. Nor of her father. Nor of Poplar Island. . . .

"Well," I said at last, wretchedly, "I lost the *Ladybug*, Nan."

"You set her wrong," she declared. "I could have sailed her better myself, straight from Annapolis."

I was filled with indignation. "You could not!"

"I could so!" she flashed. "And *I* wouldn't have let a dirty old schooner run me down!"

"You were late," I said furiously. "If you hadn't been late . . . !"

"Chowderhead!" said Nancy.

We were silent, breathing hard and glaring at each other.

"Nancy Savage," I said in a rage, "will you marry me?"

"Why?"

The plain question seemed reasonable, yet it left me floundering. "Why?" I repeated.

"Yes. Why should I marry you? Tell me."

"Well, because—because you're a man and I'm a woman," I finished triumphantly.

She burst into laughter. "Oh Ben," she gasped, "it's the other way round. Oh! Oh!"

I grinned sheepishly but felt much better. Clytie brought her a glass of some milky liquid, and she sipped between weak giggles.

A thought occurred to me that would settle the matter. "You see, Nan, I may be going into the Navy. . . ."

She turned round eyes on me. "Ben! How wonderful! I'm so happy for you."

"So there it is," I said. "We'll be married before I go."

But she leaned back among the pillows. "I'm so tired. John is coming for me, and Clytie must arrange my hair."

"John!" I exclaimed, and anger brought me to my feet. "John, is it?"

"Why, yes. That's his name. John Meade." She gave me a sidewise glance. "You're not jealous, are you?"

"No. Of course not. How could I be?"

Her eyes closed. Clytie's strong hand was propelling me out. "Nan," I said, "I'll call on you. We'll have to talk about things. There's the wedding. . . ."

"Good-by, Ben," she murmured drowsily.

I went back to my room with a feeling of accomplishment. I had maneuvered well through tricky waters. The home port was in sight.

I woke with a start. My mother was beside me, her hands tightly clasped, holding an anxiety almost too great for her to bear. I had seen them so in the days before the weddings of Pat and of Vixen.

"Ben, did she accept you?"

"Who?" I asked sleepily.

"Did Nancy accept you?" she said urgently.

My well-being vanished. "Wait, Mother," I begged her. "Let me think."

I could almost hear her patience snap. "What is there to think about? Did you ask her?"

"Yes."

"Did she accept or refuse?"

I stared at her with slow, dawning surprise. "She didn't say no." I sat up suddenly: "But she didn't say yes!"

"Don't get up," said my mother. "She's gone now."

She pulled from me, word by word, what had passed between Nancy and me. When she was certain I had been emptied, she clasped her hands again in her lap and regarded them for a long while, and into her face, still young and lovely with the lightness of heart that had always been hers, came a look of stern sorrow.

"You will offer for her again."

I saw before me a vista of endless, dreary years. Feebly I protested. "If I join the Navy...."

"Before you go, you will offer again. And when you return. And again, and again. You will not accept a refusal. You will offer until she marries."

"But what if she never marries at all?" I cried.

"Until and unless she marries another, you are her only hope in this life. You are no longer a child. Do you understand?"

I did not, but I nodded, dumbly. And so she left me, walking heavily, as if carrying a burden.

Without Nancy the house seemed strangely empty. Until I felt her absence I had not known that I had felt her presence. Convalescence pressed down on me with leaden hours. I tossed and fretted, and when my father came I was not glad to see him but awaited some new blow. The Navy? What was the Navy but Mr. Jefferson's contemptible gunboat fleet? And in any case, I would be rejected. And I would go to prison for the murder of Mordecai Wright. Perhaps I would be hanged. That would be best. I nourished a grim satisfaction at the thought, and the vision of Ben Forbes nobly marching to the scaffold was so strong that I must have been quite pale with martyrdom, for my father inquired anxiously after my health.

Being reassured, he reminded me that when we were riding home from Nancy's party he had informed me that the *Chesapeake* was being readied for the Mediterranean. On the following morning he had looked for me to accompany him to Oxford in order to present me and my hopes to Captain Charles Gordon at Oxenhall. Although much annoyed at my absence—I was on the ill-fated voyage with Nancy to Annapolis—he had set out, nevertheless, and had been well received by his old friend.

"Charlie had just returned from Washington," said my father. "He had received his orders from Mr. Goldsborough. You know, of course, that they, Gordon and Goldsborough, are cup and can together?"

Excitement stirred in me. Mr. Goldsborough of our Eastern Shore was the Chief Clerk of the Navy and a power in Washington. He had thrice declined appointment as Secretary of the Navy, in which he had been wise. Secretaries came and went, but Mr. Goldsborough remained, and in his hands lay all the threads of navy administration. If Gordon decided to take one Ben Forbes aboard the *Chesapeake,* it was as good as done. The *Chesapeake!* She was no little gunboat. She was a great frigate of war.

From my father's face I made out nothing. Conversationally, he talked of James Barron, who had been named Commodore in command of the Mediterranean squadron to replace Campbell and would sail in the *Chesapeake* to carry himself and his flag to his station.

Impatiently I interrupted him. "Father, what did Captain Gordon say?"

"He was kind enough to remember you and to think well of you. He would, of course, have to go through the proper channels recommending you, but considered this a mere formality. He has, in fact, the privilege of naming at least half his own reefers, and I had come in good time. Only two had so far been taken. We were early comers; the word had not yet been passed."

"Then ...?"

"Then," said my father, "came the duels."

My heart sank.

"I sent Virgil in the pinnace with letters explaining the full circumstances. Charlie will be writing to Mr. Goldsborough. I have also written to my old friend Commodore Tingey, commandant of the Navy Yard, asking him to stand sponsor for you. Virgil is waiting for the replies. I am hopeful, Ben. We have in our favor the feud between the Army and the Navy regarding dueling. The Army is against it, the Navy condones it. I know Charlie Gordon. He will be happy to cock a snook at the Army by welcoming a blooded gentleman to his command. We can also rely upon Tingey. But what Mr. Goldsborough may think, we cannot know. So do not count on it."

I spent the rest of that day and all of the next not counting on it, rising and falling from fierce hope to black despair. My midway state was one of sulking, and I ordered Cato to exclude all visitors, even my family. With his support I stumbled and panted around my room, fell cursing into bed, ate hugely as if to strengthen and fatten myself like a fowl for the spit, and slept heavily. I gave up the pleasurable prospect of hanging and, deciding at last that Mr. Goldsborough had roared, "No! We want no Ben Forbes in our Navy!" I determined to tramp from Washington to Oxford seeking to sign aboard some merchant vessel out of Annapolis or Baltimore. I mourned the innocent years gone now forever. Cato managed to break through one of my savage moods, wailing that Cassie had done him a wrong by getting with child, and I turned on him with such a tongue-lashing regarding duty, responsibility, the code of honor, and the protection of helpless womenfolk that he backed and cowered, rolling his eyes, and finally fled.

I lay in bed moodily staring over the bay. Just as dusk was fading into darkness, I saw the slim shadow of the pinnace slipping into the cove below. I came alive then with all my senses throbbing. Virgil seemed to take an unconscionably long time at mooring. At last I saw his figure come up the path from the dock. He cut over the lawn in the direction of the lights in my father's study. I saw the yellow glow stab out into the night as the door opened, and closed behind him. I made myself lie back, telling myself my father would come to me. Surely he would not be so cruel as to delay until morning. With all my being I prayed and ordered and willed him to come.

He came, and in his hand was a packet of papers. He said, "Virgil had to wait at Washington while Mr. Goldsborough had your orders prepared."

I started out of bed. He laughed and flung me the documents. "You are to report for duty on board the frigate *Chesapeake,* now fitting in the Navy Yard at Washington, for service in the Mediterranean."

"When?"

"In a week or ten-days' time. Back your mains'l, son. They're not that hard pressed for reefers to tell 'em how to put things shipshape." With the same look that had steadied me on the field of honor, he held out his hand. "Good night, son."

I expelled a long breath. "Good night, sir. Thank you, sir."

I sat far into the night over the papers, and when I slept it was with words and lines running through my dreams like music: "Midshipmen's Full Dress: Coat of blue cloth, with lining and lapels of the same; lapels to be short, with six buttons; standing collar, with a diamond formed of gold lace on each side, not exceeding two inches square; a slash sleeve, with three small buttons; all buttonholes to be worked with gold thread. . . . A midshipman when he acts as a Lieutenant, by order of the Secretary of the Navy, will assume the uniform of a lieutenant. . . . Dirks will not be worn on shore by any officer. . . . A Commodore to have on each strap of his epaulets a silver star. . . ."

It must have rained that night, for it rained in my dreams —silver stars.

Doctor Tilghman took a professional pride in me. He could recall only one case of a more rapid recovery: that of a slave boy near *extremis* who had become well and whole in two days after being informed he was about to be sold to poor whites. I had many callers. Among them was Giles Penrose. We shook hands stiffly and exchanged a long look, and I was suddenly aware of a vast liking for him, landsman though he was. "Why, I might have killed you!" I cried.

He said that *he* could have killed *me*, but had chosen not to. I might have laughed him out of countenance but that he had none, for Wendy was present, and I marveled at how this little sister of mine, who was still to me more child than woman, could inflict such damage with a smile and an artful glance and stays and my mother's altered gowns. Having been nicked in the belly by me, Giles Penrose was now shot through the heart by Wendy.

My father took me to Baltimore, where his tailors, with no little ceremony, measured me and promised me two complete outfits in three-days' time. Then we went among the musty old shops, selecting sea hammock, bag, and chest, a chronometer and sextant, a sheath knife, a cocked hat and a tarred one, oilskins, and food and wine for a gentleman's friends on shipboard. Even the muslin kerchiefs and plain sturdy drawers were beautiful to me. We dined at the Indian Queen tavern on oysters and beefsteak and such quantities of ale and porter that I made the homeward journey in a state of fuzzily happy exhaustion.

In all this I had forgotten Nancy. It was my mother who reminded me of her. Nancy, she said, had closed herself within Holly Hall and would not admit her, nor even Wendy. Waving aside her own hurt, my mother said I must delay no longer in calling upon Nancy. But I refused to do so until my uniform had arrived. I sent her a note of my intentions.

At last, all decked out, and with Wendy's squeals of admiration in my ears, and in my vision the servants' bursting pride, and my father's quiet smile, and my mother's sweet tearfulness, I mounted my mare and rode to Holly Hall.

Save for two or three windows the great house was shuttered; the door, that had always been open, was closed. When I knocked the sound seemed to rebuke me, as it does in a house where someone lies sick to dying. Waiting, I removed my fine cocked hat and tucked it carefully under my arm. There was a noise of bolts and the door creaked a little in opening, as if wanting an oiling. Clytie greeted me. She had no word for my beautiful uniform. She said, "Master Forbes, Miss Nancy is not receiving."

I stared at her incredulously. "But it's me, Clytie."

She shook her head. I made to brush past her but she took one step and folded her arms, standing like a rock.

"Clytie," I argued, "we are as good as betrothed, Miss Nancy and I. And it is not proper for her to be closed in here with only John Meade to keep her company."

"Miss Nancy's a lady," said Clytie. "What's proper for her, is right."

She took another step and I had to give way. To be embroiled in a physical battle with Clytie was out of the question. Besides, I would probably be defeated.

I went down the steps in a raging fury to be gone. But below, the silence of the place fell upon me. The house had a desolate look. Save for Clytie still standing on the veranda, fiercely brooding down at me, there was no human face to be seen, no movement, no sound even. In the gravel under my feet, here and there green grasses were thrusting up, tentatively. I could almost hear them growing, crowding and pushing to reclaim the land.

I mounted my mare but reined her in. Before my eyes the house I knew so well became a vault, a tomb. It was a house of the dead and a spirited young girl was locked within, buried alive. A sickness overwhelmed me. Now at last I understood what my mother had attempted to tell me.

A small breeze stirred the curtain of an upstairs window. Or was somebody there? It was the curtain of Nancy's room. "Nan!" I called.

There was no reply.

"Nan," I shouted into the heavy silence, "listen to me. I'll be back for you. Do you hear? I'll be back, again and again."

Nothing. No one.

"Clytie," I said desperately, "tell her. In God's name, if you love her, tell her."

She nodded, and I let out my horse, kicking her with my heels, urging her on, fleeing from I knew not what.

FIVE

The morning dawned at last when, with my gear stowed on board the pinnace, I kissed my mother and Wendy, took farewell of Cato, Cassie, and the rest of the house servants, and with Virgil and my father stood across the bay for Baltimore. Scudding between Rattlesnake and Bodkin Point toward the mouth of the Patapsco, we passed the *Leopard* running southward under a mighty cloud of canvas.

"Damned insolence!" my father growled. "Mark her well,

boy. Soon you may be looking at her or her like through an open gun port."

But my only thought was that now John Meade would be leaving Holly Hall, and I cherished a hope that with his going Nancy would admit my mother. Then my mother would see to it that others came to that house and once more the door would stand open. It was a thought that gave me comfort.

In Baltimore I bade my father good-by. Each of us hid his emotion while Virgil, who was my father's boy, spoke for both of us by sniveling openly.

I boarded the stage wagon for Washington. It was a rough, sour-smelling, crowded vehicle. My place on the rearmost plank was between a Charleston lady and the lusty daughter of a New Englander. The Charleston lady said her actor husband had abandoned her in New York and she was now on her way home through the courtesy of kind friends who had advanced the money for her journey. She made a sadly appealing tale of it, yet not enough to make me empty my pockets for her. The New England lady punctuated the yarn with eloquent snorts indicating disbelief. Through that journey of more than twelve hours, I declare there was never a man so caught at and embraced and smothered in lace, perfume, and furbelows, as the two ladies attempted, across me, to do each other some sly damage.

Out of Baltimore we lurched and bumped and rolled and rattled over a muddy, rutted, much-traveled highroad through swampy swales and over high hills that were veritable mountains to my eye. Along the heights we raced at a gallop, our driver intent only on fetching down the northern mail to the nation's capital, while we within were tossed like jackstraws, clinging for dear life to straps and seats and one another. In the hollows were deep pits and puddles, and time and again we sank to the hubs in a quaking quagmire. I was thankful then to tumble out with the able-bodied men among the passengers to heave the bumbling conveyance out of the sticky trap. Each time I returned from this wholesome exercise the ladies shrank from the dank mud with which I was liberally spattered, and I had a little peace.

When darkness fell the ladies dozed and I entertained myself with the description of the *Chesapeake* which I had committed to memory. Built at Gosport Navy Yard, at Norfolk, only eight years before, she was 152 feet 6 inches long, with a 40-foot beam, and 13 feet 9 inches depth of hold, displacing 1,244 tons. She carried 340 men. Officially she was rated a 36, but she carried 28 long 18s in her main gun-deck battery, sixteen 32-pound carronades on her quarter-deck, and four 32-pound carronades on the fo'c'sle. I was eager to see the vessel these figures added up to.

At last we ground to a halt before Stelle's Hotel on Pennsylvania Avenue, and the Charleston lady sought to cling to me and load me with bundles. The New England lady ordered me to play the lackey for her, and no other. I left them exchanging abuse while I fled to the safety of a solitary chamber. The night being clear and the air balmy with spring, I would have been glad to see something of this city that was younger than I. But having a healthy mistrust of predatory females, I locked my door and went to bed.

In the morning after a quick breakfast, I paid my footing and was on my way, through rutted, unpaved ways, past scattered buildings and houses and open fields and patches of briers and woods, starting a covey of quail and a rabbit from under the hedges near the imposing capitol building on the Hill. Here and there servants were sweeping doorsteps and I paused, thinking to inquire after a Mistress von Lund. Surely in so small and new a city the presence of such a one would not be unmarked. But I remembered Nancy and was shamed. And so, after a struggle, I continued on down the slopes toward the cluster of masts and spars and warehouses at Anacostia Point and the mouth of the Eastern Branch that marked the Navy Yard.

At the gate I presented my orders to the marine on guard. He snapped to attention and gave me a punctilious salute, which in my pleasure I made haste to return.

"Two blocks over," he said, "turn right and go straight down to the quay. Can't miss her. She's the only ship preparin'. Ye'll find the *Essex* lyin' in the ordinary astern o' her."

"Thank you, Sergeant," I said.

"Corporal, sir," he replied with the hint of a grin.

"Thank you, Corporal," I corrected myself, flushing, and bent to pick up my sea bag and chest.

"Excuse me, sir!" His tone was shocked. " 'Tis against regulations for an officer to carry things save in the line of juty."

He turned to the guardroom. "Mahoney!" he bawled. "Bear a hand. Look alive, now!"

"Aye, aye!" An enormous marine lurched out, fastening his breeches. He pulled at his forelock and scooped up the dunnage.

I followed Mahoney past two rows of tall wooden warehouses—the corporal's "blocks." There we turned as the corporal had directed, and passing more warehouses, a ropewalk, an armory, and a sail loft, came out upon the quay.

I could see at once why the corporal had said I couldn't miss her. The *Essex* lay with her tops and spars sent down, her stubby masts dismantled, and her whole deck housed under a temporary, wooden, barnlike structure, so that she looked more like an ungainly ark than a man-o'-war. She was a good ship; Commodore Rodgers had come home in her after patching up the peace with Tunis. Why she should be squatting here with all the seas to roam in only Mr. Jefferson and Mr. Goldsborough knew.

While the *Essex* lay shamed, the *Chesapeake* leapt skyward with a whole new set of yellow masts and spars and a spidery network of golden rigging. Her new dress of snowy sails was smartly furled, even to the topmost royals and skys'ls. Her stout black flanks gleamed with new paint, and the broad white band, checkered with black gun-port lids and strakes, bore not a speck of dust. She was the grandest vessel I had ever clapped eyes on. My heart swelled with pride near to bursting as I followed Mahoney up the white-roped gangway and saluted the quarter-deck as my father had taught me.

I was received by a diminutive lieutenant to whom I announced myself precisely: "Midshipman Benjamin Forbes, sir, reporting for duty."

He grunted, seeming to inject a nasal New England twang even into that noncommittal sound, consulted a book, made a mark in it, and bawled, "Lucas!"

A marine stepped forward from the bulkhead.

"Conduct Mr. Forbes to Captain Gordon."

"Aye, aye, sir!"

To me the lieutenant said carelessly, "Your gear will go down to your quarters. That will be all, Mister."

"Aye, aye, sir!" I replied, saluting, and to me it was something so wonderful to hear those words on my lips that I could have wept with the joy of it.

On Lucas's heels I ducked into the companion, went down a brass-trimmed mahogany ladder, and found myself in the low-ceilinged wardroom, on either side of which stood the officers' cubbyhole cabins. There was just room enough to stand erect. Indeed, I ducked instinctively but unnecessarily for several transverse beams as I followed the marine aft through "officers' country."

Since we were to carry the flag and person of the Commodore, the great captain's cabin, usually occupying the full width of this after section, had been divided into three cabins by partitions. The largest of them would be the Commodore's, when he chose to come on board. Just now, however, the Captain was using it, and it was here that we found him, finishing his breakfast.

Captain Gordon glanced up and daubed at his mouth as the green baize curtain fell behind us. "Yes?" he inquired.

"Lieutenant Smith's respects, sir," said Lucas, "an' here's Mr. Midshipman Forbes reportin' for juty."

"Very good, Lucas. My compliments to Mr. Creighton, and ask him if he will step this way for a moment. Then return to your post."

"Aye, aye, sir!"

When he was gone, Captain Gordon flung his napkin on the table and rose. I knew him, although it had been many years since I had seen him at some family gathering of our Eastern Shore. He was a favored, genial man of moderate height who filled his breeches well without being too stout, and he had a Maryland look that warmed my heart. All the same there was a frosty air about him now that warned me to keep my distance. He was the captain, the king of this great domain, and I one of the lesser of his subjects.

"Forbes," he said as if to himself, then looked at me sharply. "I hear you've been setting the Shore afire, hey?"

"Hardly that, sir," I replied. "It was a case of damned if I don't and damned if I do."

"I'd not let any of it out in the reefers' mess," he warned me. "There's some in the Navy who encourage dueling, especially among the juniors. They argue it brings out a youngster's fighting qualities. I'm one of them—when ashore. But I'll have no dueling on my ship."

"No, sir," I said. "I mean—aye, aye, sir!"

He smiled then. "You'll tell me about it one day."

A dark, slender, fine-featured officer appeared, and I was passed to him like some packet for delivery. He was Fourth Lieutenant John Creighton, who, with Sidney Smith, the Fifth Lieutenant, and Mr. Hollabel, the Chaplain and Schoolmaster, was by way of being a wet nurse to the young gentlemen of the midship's mess. Leaving my order papers with the Captain, I followed Mr. Creighton to my quarters in what was called the steerage. It was on the berth deck, just below the main gun deck and next above the orlop.

The midshipmen's share of the steerage stretched the width of the ship, making a room some 40 feet long by 20 broad. In this space a score of us were to eat, sleep, and live for the two to three years of our service, and I must admit that at first sight it seemed to me a mean hole. It was dark and airless, for the berth deck was a little below the water line. The sole light came from the companionway and from the blue battle lanterns, only one of which happened, upon my advent, to be alight. Between the laterals I was just able to stand upright, but to pass forward or aft I had to stoop low because of the overhead timbers and the stout ring bolts set at spaced intervals for the hammocks. Stumbling about in the gloom I cracked my head four times. That I know because of voices that rose in triumphant count. Betting was going on. The two winners claimed me and it was between them that I slung my hammock. They were a Jack Crump of Georgia and Henry Broome of Richmond.

Lieutenant Creighton had duly presented me to my fellows but in the darkness they were no more than voices—lazy, laughing, jeering, drawling, twanging. Little by little they emerged: chubby, good-natured George Read, and the tall, saturnine Charles Morris, knot-muscled John Shubrick, and moody John Funck, and Matt Perry, a dull boy, outstanding only because at thirteen he was the youngest of us and brother of the famous Oliver Perry. Twelve reefers were already on board, and we should be nineteen by the time we sailed. But most of them I no longer remember.

It was extraordinary how soon I felt at home. Along the bulkheads, fore and aft, fiddles of 6-inch boards, exactly partitioned to the dimensions of a regulation-sized sea chest and bag, gave storage space. At night or when the day's routine required that the space be cleared, these were covered by the long benches which were our only seats in off or meal hours. The long tables, one for the larboard watch, one for the starboard, that split the cabin down the center on each side, could be swung up with legs folded under and lashed to the overhead timbers. This we did for inspection and also at night when they would otherwise block passage between the two rows of hammocks. Piped up at reveille in the morning, we rolled and lashed our hammocks in the bulwarks where, in an action, they would serve to protect against flying splinters and marksmen in an enemy's tops. At mealtimes and during off hours, the tables were brought down from above and secured to deck locks; the benches, which served as lids for the fiddles, were brought forward alongside the tables and similarly secured. After nightfall the tables were swayed up once more, benches returned to the bulkheads, hammocks brought down from the nettings and slung. The smoking lamp was doused at tattoo, and at taps every man, save those on deck duty, was expected to be asleep, or prepared to feign sleep for the Watch Officer's inspection when he passed perfunctorily down one ladder and up the other.

It was even more extraordinary how the space that was my home grew and grew in size. Every seaman, I think, has that experience. Any cramped hole in which one takes meals, sleep, and company, stretches day by day almost before one's eyes to comfortable and even grand dimensions. This remarkable phenomenon does not occur in any shelter ashore known to me. It is one of the mysteries of ships.

In the *Chesapeake* it was, perhaps, a matter of perspective. It was on the berth deck that the greater part of the ship's company was quartered. Forward, in the curve of the bows, was the sick bay. Aft of this, and extending nearly half the ship's length, was the fo'c'sle in which the foremast hands were quartered. Abaft, and still forward of the mainmast, was petty officers' country. Next, between the mainmast and mizzenmast, whose thick butts thrust down, was our own steerage country, given over to reefers and warrants, neither foremast hands nor full-fledged officers; and at the very stern, abaft the butt of the mizzen, were the marines' quarters.

Above us lived the lords of our little world: the commodore, the captain, the officers of the wardroom. Below were the holds, the shot and ammunition lockers, the bread locker and spirit locker, the slopshop, and carpenter's shop, and armory, and one yet lower form of life than ourselves: the chaplain-schoolmaster, the captain's clerk, the surgeon's mates, and their loblolly boys who, lumped together, shared like moles the stifling darkness of the cockpit.

Food and water for 340 men for several months at sea were being taken aboard and powder and shot for our batteries. Spare sails were jamming the *Chesapeake's* lockers and spare spars were being lashed on deck. Cordage and pitch, paint and oakum and turpentine were rolling up and being stowed; racks of muskets and chests of bayonets and cutlasses and pistols and boarding pikes for the armory; barrels of bread and biscuit for the bread locker; dried beef and pork for the hold; casks of rum and pipes of wine for the spirit locker; medical supplies for sick bay and cockpit; sand to sprinkle on bloody decks; cordwood and coal for the galley fires; kentledge for ballast, and yet more that never occurred to me until I saw it fetched on board: chickens and sheep and cattle and hogs that were penned on the spar deck midships, just before we sailed, so that we might have fresh eggs and milk and meat for as long as they might last.

In this busy world we reefers had little to do but to follow like eager pups the officers to whom we were assigned, learning the everyday ways of a ship's housekeeping. We'd have followed them into the privy in the head, such was our zeal; but we were a nuisance to them and often they snapped a dismissal, and time hung heavily on us as we yearned to be at sea.

My fellows were prankish, of course; midshipmen are expected to be and do their best for the tradition. Soon after my arrival they attempted hoary jests. I was ordered to ask the first lieutenant for the key to wind the ship's watch, to go ashore to purchase two hounds for the dogwatch, and to obtain from the commandant of the yard a box for the compass, and from the armorer a musket to "shoot Charlie Noble," and from the bo's'n the key to Davy Jones's locker.

To each of these commands I gave solemn answer. What, said I, did they not know that the Captain himself wound the ship's watch, using the carpenter's left foot for key? And did they not know that it was the Commodore's right to bring aboard the dogs? And surely everyone was acquainted with the custom of dressing the compass on Boxing Day! And Charlie Noble was shot only on St. John's Eve. And every first lieutenant on every ship in the world guarded the ship's key to Davy Jones's locker on a gold chain around his neck, holding it over his heart under his uniform.

I was voted a "fly one" and admitted into their fellowship to join in harassing each newcomer. We found that the schoolmaster, Mr. Hollabel, whose name we corrupted to Holy Hell, plagued well, and I led in persuading him to breach the storekeeper for a pea jacket to wear when he went forward to the head. And once when the cockpit was empty and the spirit-locker door stood open, as it often did in port for the fumes to escape, we added a gallon of good red vinegar to a pipe of the Commodore's best claret.

SIX

I came off duty at midday, after the morning watch, on the second Saturday after my arrival, to find George Read and Charlie Morris busily polishing their boots and putting a high shine on the buttons of their best dress uniforms.

Suspiciously I observed this unwonted activity. "Commodore Barron coming aboard?" I asked. The Commodore had been expected daily for more than a week, but if he were arriving today, I, as a member of the last watch on duty, would have known of it.

Morris held up a glistening boot to the dull light that came trickling down the companionway and examined it critically. "The Commodore? No," he said casually. "At least, not that we've heard. No, the President is entertaining at the Mansion —buffet supper with music to follow. All officers generally are invited. Nothing formal, of course. Aren't you going? You've left your cards, haven't you?"

Unschooled in matters of shoreside etiquette, I had taken pains to conceal my ignorance and was entirely in the dark about the social niceties expected of a junior naval officer on duty in the nation's capital. But I had at least known about the cards. Every officer of the Army or the Navy, when he came on station, paid his respects at the President's Mansion. Leaving cards was sufficient. One did not expect to be received, and was not.

So to Charlie I replied, "Of course. I did that last week." Read glanced up. "What about your official calls?"

"Official calls?" I said blankly.

Read's round, innocent face showed concern. "Don't you know? You're supposed to call on the commanding officer of your ship, the Commandant of the Navy Yard, and the Secretary of the Navy at their homes. Of course, the Old Man lives aboard, so your visit with him when you reported on board can pass for a call. And since Commodore Tingey was one of your sponsors, you can presume a little on friendship there and be forgiven the oversight. But you can't neglect the Secretary, Forbes. If you've been putting it off, I'd say don't hesitate another instant. Even now it may be too late. Marse Robert Smith's known for an ogre, and if he suspects for a second you've slighted him, you might live to be the Navy's oldest midshipman."

Morris, a cool and handsome sophisticate much looked up to, was equally concerned. "Why, Forbes, you can't show your face at the President's Mansion until you've made that call on the Secretary." With a troubled face he shook his head over me.

By this time several other of my messmates had come down and had quietly set to polishing boots and buttons.

I panicked. An hour later in my full dress uniform with the high, pointed collar trimmed in gold braid coming up almost to my cheekbones, with my buttons shining and my white gloves spotless, my cocked hat tucked under my arm, and my boots like dark mirrors, I stood at the top of the steps before the wide green door of the house in Georgetown occupied by the Honorable Robert Smith, Secretary of the Navy. With a feeling of vague unease I raised the big brass knocker.

Before I could let it fall the door swung open and I found myself confronting a large, florid man with a petulant mouth and light, impatient eyes. He wore a bottle-green coat and tight buff-colored doeskin trousers, soft-tasseled wellingtons and a gray cloak with black frogs and many capes. In the crook of his arm he held a shaggy, wide-crowned, dark-gray beaver. Clearly he was about to leave the house.

He seemed as confounded by me as I was by him. "Well?" he said gruffly.

I swallowed. If this were the Secretary, it could not be his day at home, although my shipmates had assured me it was.

"Excuse me, sir," I stammered. "I—er—Midshipman Forbes, sir, of the *Chesapeake*. I've come to call—to pay my respects, sir."

He started to speak and with dismay I knew that what he was about to say would not be agreeable. But then his glance slid over my shoulder. I turned a little and out of the corner of one eye caught sight of a quick, furtive movement among the bushes across the dusty way.

The stranger's eye was on me again, raking me fore and aft. "Come in," he said, stepping back and holding the door.

I entered a high-ceilinged reception hall with a broad curving stairway at the back. A lady was descending, wearing a plumed bonnet and a blue coat trimmed with fur, high-waisted in the French fashion that was much in vogue.

"I am Robert Smith," the man said to me curtly. "Have you a message for me?"

"Why—no—no, sir...."

"Then what the devil are you up to? Who are those fellows across the way?" He scowled ferociously.

A cold hand seemed to close on the pit of my stomach. It was plain now that my shipmates had sought to draw me on the shoal of shoreside etiquette, and I had swum into their net like a gullible herring. There they were, in the bushes, ready to greet me with a bellow of laughter when I was flung out. But what was the Secretary of the Navy to think? I saw my career wrecked by a mere joke.

"F-fellows, sir?" I gulped.

The lady had joined us. Her eyes were dark and bright, her face alive and intelligent, her lips smiling. "What is it, Robert?" she asked.

"This young scamp, my dear," he said with ill-suppressed

anger. "Some midshipman's prank, I daresay. They're all around the place. Come, sir! Out with it!"

"Now, Robert," she said soothingly, "remember your stomach."

"Damn my stomach!" he let out his fury in a full-blasted roar.

With all my heart I prayed for rescue, and Mrs. Smith, as if hearing my unuttered plea, smiled at me. I bowed low. "M-Midshipman Forbes, ma'am, of the *Chesapeake*, ma'am, your servant, ma'am."

"Now then," she said with a twinkle, "do explain yourself, Mr. Forbes."

"Ma'am, I hope you'll forgive me, ma'am," I said wildly. "I was told—I understood—respected—er, expected, ma'am, to pay my respects to you, ma'am, and the Secretary in person—and—and this was your day at home. . . ."

Astonishingly, she seemed delighted. "What a charming idea!" she exclaimed. "Don't you think so, Robert?"

Obviously he did not think so.

"You could set aside—say, one evening in each month," his wife pursued.

He was so red and choleric that I did indeed fear for his stomach, and my head as well. I babbled apologies, bowed and turned to flee.

I was checked by Mrs. Smith. "And those others outside?" she asked, not far from open laughter.

"Ma'am," I said despairingly, "the joke is on me. If you and Mr. Secretary Smith will be kind enough to forgive this intrusion, I will accept what is to come in a happier frame of mind."

She turned abruptly to her husband. "Robert! It's one against I know not how many, and I do love a joke. Robert, let us take him with us."

"Oh, no, ma'am!" I cried, fearing more than ever for her husband and myself.

She ignored me. "Robert, you always grumble about these pranks, and the grumbling has done you harm. Let us this time turn the laugh on the pranksters. Do. Please! What fun it will be!" Her hand on his arm, she coaxed prettily.

I protested feebly.

"Ha! Tush!" Mr. Smith silenced me. The dangerous color receded from his face. He began to smile, as if to himself.

I stood stiffly, scarcely daring to breathe, awaiting a softened dismissal.

Then, briskly he said, "Mr. Forbes, you will consider your-

self attached to my party—an equerry, shall we say? Yes, y
That is an order. Not a word more from you. I'll not have it.
Now then. Your first duty is to look outside to see if that
damned carriage has arrived."

"Aye, aye, sir!" I replied, not a little bewildered by the sudden change in my fortunes.

I opened the door just wide enough to peep out. The carriage
was there, a bright, shiny vehicle with black varnished body
and yellow wheels, looking very smart and incongruous in that
country place. I flung the door wide and stepped back. "It is
here, sir."

Mrs. Smith walked slowly down the steps and to the carriage, admiring the weather in high clear tones, Mr. Smith
most amiably agreeing and adding his opinion that never had
there been so remarkable a day. I brought up the rear. Across
the way the bushes quivered and rustled and shook as if
threshed by a storm all their own. But Mr. and Mrs. Smith
were exclaiming over the beauties of the sky, making much
of one small white cloud in it. I handed them up, first Mrs.
Smith and then the Secretary, and went around to take my
own place at their left. My eyes were drawn to the bushes,
but the Secretary in a tone of command said, "Kalorama, Mr.
Forbes."

"Kalorama," I relayed confidently (though I knew not what
the word signified) to the Negro on the box, whose shine
matched that of the carriage itself, and my buttons, and my
boots. I took my seat. He touched up his horses and away we
spun.

Mrs. Smith leaned back and began to laugh. Her husband
let out a veritable bellow of mirth. Soon the three of us were
convulsed.

It was a merry ride. The day was pleasantly warm and all
along the country roads the birds sang madly in the budding
trees, and I almost thought I could hear the cicadas announcing
the coming of summer in the fields.

Mrs. Smith, the kindest of women, chattered gaily. Kalorama, she informed me, was the home of Joel Barlow, who
kept open house all weekend, most informally. Mr. Barlow,
she said, was a wealthy man, a dilettante, a patron of art and
science. He had met Mr. Jefferson in Paris many years before
and they became fast friends. When Mr. Jefferson was first
elected, Barlow, taking up residence in Washington, built a
mansion overlooking Rock Creek. This was Kalorama, one
of the few great houses of the raw new capital, and here he
entertained lavishly. Robert Fulton, an inventor, was the lion

the moment. He was attempting to interest the Navy and
n indifferent Congress in a machine which he called an
"underwater torpedo."

From a distance I saw the huge Barlow mansion, Mrs.
Smith pointing it out to me rather unnecessarily, for it domi-
nated the landscape. It stood high above the deep cleft of Rock
Creek among parklike woods, gardens, and lawns. Other carriages were rolling toward it, some accompanied by gentlemen
ahorse; and in good company we swept up the broad curve of
the driveway.

We found our host on the vast sweep of lawn, bowing,
greeting, and hand-kissing away his gaggle of guests. He was
a small man with stringy, mousy hair which he wore in no
fashion at all, for he did not trouble to powder or club it but
permitted it to hang loosely on either side of his rather ascetic
face. He received me cordially, and in a moment discovered of
me that we were distantly related. His brother's wife's sister
was the mother of Betsy Patterson, who had married young
Jerome Bonaparte in a whirlwind romance and in defiance of
Jerome's mighty brother, Napoleon. These Pattersons of Baltimore were cousins of ours, cousins enough for us on the Eastern Shore to talk familiarly of "Buxom Betsy," although she
had little time for her poor relations across the bay.

Mr. Barlow presented me as a newly discovered relation to
his two daughters and his niece. All three were pretty and
vivacious and happy to have among the guests a young man
they could claim. They would have held me, and most willingly
would I have been held by them, but that Mrs. Smith whisked
me off.

I bowed to countless ladies and gentlemen, and soon wearied.
But Mrs. Smith was tireless. I began to suspect that the Secretary's wife, to whom I was so much in debt, was using me for
purposes of her own. A young man, even an innocent like
myself who has never been subjected to the machinations of
a matchmaker, quickly sniffs the breed as dog sniffs cat. My
bows to females became short, and I lingered before males,
hopelessly seeking shelter.

I recall the inventor Mr. Fulton, tall and bushy-haired. I
would have stayed with him, dogged him, for I was eager to
see the demonstration of his machine, but Mrs. Smith's hand
upon my arm might have been of steel. I found myself before
a gaunt, graying man in full dress uniform—Commodore
Tingey, Commandant of the Navy Yard.

"Forbes," he said musingly. "Ah, Forbes—then you'll be

Allen Forbes's boy, the fire-eater. How is your father? Well, I hope?"

"Yes, sir," I replied, much relieved to observe that Commodore Tingey found nothing remarkable in the presence of a mere midshipman at a social function he was honoring.

"Fire-eater?" Mrs. Smith said avidly.

"A mere matter of half a dozen duels," said Commodore Tingey lightly, and then he was claimed by Mr. Fulton. And now there was no possible escape from Mrs. Smith. Under the tall trees I moved with her, jerkily bowing and feeling increasingly disquieted.

I remember a Mr. Pedersen, the Danish chargé d'affaires: a moon-faced man he was, with straw-colored hair.

All at once, "Ah, my dear, my dear child!" cried Mrs. Smith, turning from Mr. Pedersen, and the clear, cooing tone warned me that my fate was at hand. I involuntarily stiffened to defend myself against the chosen female. The lady—a girl, rather—floated lightly toward us in a gown of summery stuff that might have been made of moonbeams. I saw the luminous blue eyes, the shimmering mass of spun gold crowning her lovely head.

I gasped.

"Kirstie!" I cried, as if I had called her that all my life.

She came with both hands outstretched, and when I took them in my own all the grand company and the broad landscaped acres of Kalorama blurred and faded. The babble of voices was a distant murmur, and I could have sworn that I heard the music of ripples on a serene and distant shore. Dimly I was aware of excited exclamations, of Mrs. Smith's triumphant delight, and of the quietly smiling Baron von Lund. Then somehow—I suppose Mrs. Smith contrived it—Mistress von Lund and I were alone.

We slipped away by a secluded path and found a tiny marble belvedere on a wooded point surrounded by white flowering dogwood and overlooking the ravine. There we sat and I talked and talked like one reborn who has a whole lifetime to recount, or like a knight who comes home to his lady with tales of high adventure and mortal peril, she hanging on his words, paling at his dangers, sorrowing for him, happy to have him safe again.

"And what of the angry little lady?" asked Kirstie. "Is she well?"

The everyday world came rushing back. I seemed to hear the echo of my own voice, full of childish bravado. Somehow

I had contrived to relate all that had passed without speaking once of Nancy, referring only to "a lady." Yet without Nancy there was scarcely any tale at all. Nancy. The pert face, the wilfulness, and heedless courage. Nancy smiling. Nancy grave. Nancy deathlike. Nancy's voice: "Chowderhead!" What was I doing here in a strange place with a strange girl, a golden beauty thrust upon me by the clever Mrs. Smith? It was Nancy I loved and to Nancy I had pledged myself—forever.

A coldness fell upon me. "Mistress Savage," I said, "has been very ill, but she is recovering."

Mistress von Lund shivered. "It is late," she said, and indeed the dying afternoon's shadows were filling the ravine. In formal style I apologized for having kept her so long and escorted her to the terrace, feeling myself a country bumpkin, a lout.

Commodore Tingey invited me to share his carriage, as he was driving to the Navy Yard on some business with Captain Gordon. I made my proper farewells, thanking Mrs. Smith with so little heart that she gave me a bright piercing look, which unaccountably made me redden. Firmly she brought me back to Mistress von Lund on the terrace. I bowed low before the Danish girl.

"Benje," she said softly, "shall we meet again?"

Her Benje was very unlike my sister's Benjie. I looked into the blue eyes and felt myself drowning. "Ah, Kirstie!" It was wrenched from me like a groan.

I heard Mrs. Smith behind me laugh a low conspiratorial laugh, a woman-to-woman sort of laugh.

I said, "You are very kind to a lowly sailor, Mistress von Lund. I am grateful. Your servant, ma'am."

A faint pink touched her cheeks, as if I had lightly slapped her. "Good-by, Mr. Forbes," she said.

Commodore Tingey in his carriage proved unexpectedly jocular. More than once he startled me by poking me in the ribs. I became aware he shared the joke the Smiths had played upon my messmates. Very like, his small business with the Captain was to impart it. How far away and long ago that joke was, how stale, how meaningless! It was an uncomfortable ride for me.

We whirled in at the Yard's gates, the sentries snapping to a smart present. We drove to the foot of the gangway, and I was happy to see my ship again, to be freed from shoreside affairs, petty intrigues, women. I followed the Commodore up the gangway, saluted the quarter-deck, and reported on board. Glazed stares greeted me. Not until then did I realize how singular it must have appeared for Midshipman Forbes to be delivered to his ship by no less a personage than the Commandant of the Navy Yard—Forbes who had been sent out on a ridiculous mission and who should have returned ingloriously.

Filled with anxiety, I went down to my quarters. Midshipmen are a close-bound company. I feared that I would be thenceforth treated like the thirteen-year-old Perry who, for presuming to own a great name, was the target of all.

At the bottom of the ladder, a slyly thrust-out boot brought me sprawling home. Over my luckless head rose an uproar of indignation. At last permitted to rise, I was forced to run the gantlet and was well and heartily thwacked. In final appeasement, and in accord with a sentence pronounced by a jury of my peers consisting of little Perry, Read, and Morris, I prostrated myself and bumped my forehead three times, declaring each time, "I am humble!"

All this I did with good grace, and so was once more admitted into the fellowship. And I was quite content, knowing as well as any that a surly pride has no place in brotherhood.

SEVEN

It was best not to think of Nancy or Kirstie. I gave myself wholly to a third lady, one that called more urgently and less confusedly for my devotion and concern.

For all her beauty in my eyes, the *Chesapeake* had a bad name. The old hands said she was unlucky. On her first voyage to the Mediterranean it had been discovered at Gibraltar that her mainmast and most of her spars were eaten half through with quick-rot. They had to be replaced at the Royal Dockyard, where her men writhed under the sneers and jibes of H. M.'s Mediterranean fleet which lost no opportunity to deride our "fir-built" frigates. Later still it was found that she had been improperly coppered, and she had to be hove down at Syracuse in Sicily to have the metal stripped, the teredo-infested timbers replaced, and be fitted with a new suit of copper sheathing.

Here in ordinary, in Washington, there was a grim feeling aboard. More rotten wood had been discovered. To the determination to make the ship perfect was allied a superstitious fear that fate was against her. From truck to keelson and from stem to stern she was overhauled. Ribs, timbers, planking, decking, knees and crosspieces, and posts and braces were being replaced, seams caulked and payed, her bottom cleaned and scraped. The banging of hammers and the thumping of caulking mallets could be heard all the way to Alexandria. The pace was feverish but there was no healthy joy in the work. Even to us, the light-hearted midshipmen, the feeling penetrated that the *Chesapeake* was beyond the best efforts of mere mortals—that she was accursed.

New masts were stepped, new spars sent up, and spare spars lashed below. New anchors came aboard and chain and cable. The painting and polishing seemed interminable. Temporary pens were built on the spar deck amidships to hold our livestock, which would be taken aboard at Hampton Roads.

Guns, ammunition, ballast, and the bulk of our supplies would be taken aboard at Hampton, when we dropped down the Bay; for we would be unable to work her over the bar at the mouth of the Potomac if we took them on at Washington. We could and did, however, make up and rig the gun carriages.

With my messmates I was very soon made acquainted with the discipline. To begin with, the ship's company was divided into watches. I was assigned to the second or larboard watch under the Second Lieutenant, Mr. Crane.

Next the station and quarter bills were drawn and posted. The station bill was concerned with the place and duties of each man of each watch in connection with the general handling of the ship. Thus some men were assigned to the tops, others to the braces, others to sheets, some to the forecastle, some to the waist, still others to the quarter-deck. Midshipmen were not given specific duties under this bill.

The quarter bill, however, concerned all hands, assigning every man to a battle station. Mr. Crane commanded the second division of great guns in the main battery on the gun deck. I was assigned to him here, too, and I took much pride in my post, for it meant that in the event of an engagement, should anything happen to Mr. Crane, the command of the ship's most vital battery would fall to me. I made up my mind to perfect myself in gunnery. Of course, no engagement was expected, but only an uneventful cruise. My messmates laughed at my zeal. Nonetheless, they applied themselves no less industriously to their separate duties, for among us in our steerage the prevailing superstition was translated into adventure: with the *Chesapeake,* anything might happen.

When the paper work and assigning were done, we were set to the drilling and exercising. It mattered not in the least that our decks were cluttered or that we had as yet no guns. The carriages were at the gun ports and we could scramble about and go through the motions of putting ourselves in readiness for battle. We learned to leap to our stations at the first tap of the drum. We were piped to quarters a dozen times a day, and at night, too, until every man jack of us could roll from his hammock and tumble up to his post in the dark, swiftly and precisely, still half asleep.

We were required to learn by heart the Navy Regulations of 1802. The first article under the heading of the duties of midshipmen stated: "No particular duties can be assigned to this class of officers." The second modified it considerably: "They are promptly and faithfully to execute all the orders, for the public service, of their commanding officers."

And who were we to protest that to race one another aloft to the topgallants and down again by the stays at the command of a junior lieutenant was scarcely "in the public service"? We midshipmen were ready—nay, eager—to sail the *Chesapeake* all by ourselves into the mouth of hell and out again, defying fate and the devil.

Such was our ardor that we even went back gaily to the schoolroom, there to wrack our heads over algebra and geometry, trigonometry and calculus, geography, astronomy, and navigation, submitting meekly to Mr. Hollabel who in his own department made free with his rod. And what tyrants we were, in our turn, when charged with a detail for loading and stowing, rigging, painting, or swabbing down!

Meantime, officers at rendezvous in Philadelphia and Norfolk were recruiting, for we had need of foremast hands: able and ordinary seamen and boys. Accordingly each week one or more drafts of new men were signed on board.

It was during my third week on board, as I recall, that a draft was sent from Norfolk by Lieutenant Sinclair, who was recruiting there. In it were three men who were received by us as heroes. They were William Ware, Daniel Martin, and John Strachan. Their story was that they had been impressed from American vessels by H.B.M. frigate *Melampus* and forced to serve in the Royal Navy. One night the *Melampus*, lying at Lynnhaven Roads and the ship's officers holding some sort of celebration in the wardroom, the three managed to steal the captain's gig, row to shore, and seek sanctuary with Mr. Sinclair.

The audacious escape made us passionately proud of our three new recruits. It apparently made the British just as passionately angry, for messages flew thick and fast. Demands were made upon Lieutenant Sinclair for the men's return. But he was an old hand at the game and he simply referred them to Washington. Exciting scuttlebutt rumors flowed about the fo'c'sle and down into steerage, carried, as tradition had it, by the ship's cat. It was said that Admiral Berkeley at Halifax, commanding His Majesty's force in American waters, was in a great rage, protesting that the three men were British and therefore deserters. But they were not British. Ware, a mulatto, and Strachan were natives of my Eastern Shore; I knew them by sight, and so did Captain Gordon. Daniel Martin was a coal-black Negro from Massachusetts, and I have yet to hear that there are any Negroes native to Great Britain!

About a week after the arrival of the famous three, all hands were piped on deck, and after a suitable interval for dignity's sake, during which we fidgeted, Commodore James Barron strutted up the gangway to the twitter of pipes and ruffle of drums. For all his glittering gold braid he was not impressive, being short and blocky with a paunch that made him almost pear-shaped in profile. He had a round chubby face with a surprisingly prominent, stubborn chin, and although his veined cheeks and nose were ruddy, he had a sallow look.

He glared wordlessly at the company and the cluttered deck, shook hands perfunctorily with Captain Gordon, and stumped below to his great cabin.

Almost immediately the parade of visitors began. Mr. Goldsborough came from the Navy Department. He was followed by an exquisite young man from the British Embassy, who was in turn succeeded by an only slightly less exquisite gentleman from the State Department. We began to fear for Ware, Martin, and Strachan, and were all ready to hate and despise our Commodore, and even our Navy, such as it was. The scuttlebutt cat was very busy.

At last it came down to us that the British Ambassador himself had made formal demand for the return of the deserters. Commodore Barron had slapped him back word that there were no Englishmen on board. That night we gave three cheers for our Commodore.

The exciting week ended in a round of highly critical inspections, after which the Commodore left us. By this time we were despairing of ever getting to sea.

He was scarcely gone when a new draft of recruits arrived from Lieutenant Sinclair, this time including among their number five deserters from the British sloop-of-war *Halifax*. While admiring Sinclair's reckless daring, we could not but be cool toward the five. In the first place, they were definitely Englishmen. In the second place, they had mutinied, threatening to murder the officer in charge before stealing the jolly boat. Finally, they showed contempt for our *Chesapeake* and for ourselves.

Sinclair paid for his indiscretion. No sooner had the English seamen collected the bounty that was offered to all recruits than four of them deserted. The bounty was stopped out of Lieutenant Sinclair's pay. Our indignation against the ingrates increased our hatred of the British. We were on an American frigate-of-war in a time of nominal peace. Among our company—certainly among the midshipmen—there was not one who was not, in his heart, at war with Great Britain. No greater curse could we midshipmen conceive of than inaction.

On the last day of the month, having received an invitation, I was given shore leave to attend a supper party at the home of Commodore Tingey. I was fearful—and hopeful—that Mistress von Lund would be there. She was.

Studiously I avoided her, and I was very gay with the Commodore's two daughters and with my new-found cousins, the daughters of Mr. Barlow. I was carefully attending one of my cousins at the stand-up supper, when suddenly she said, "Yes, she is very beautiful, isn't she?"

Covered with confusion, I realized that my eyes had been following Kirstie von Lund. Quickly I offered a compliment: "But you, too, are beautiful."

My pretty companion sighed. "Dear Ben," she said lightly, "you will never be a gallant. Perhaps that is why she is so taken with you." And then she laughed merrily. "See? What did I tell you? A gallant is not born to blush. Yes, I excuse you. Go."

As I moved toward Mistress von Lund she, although surrounded by admirers, somehow detached herself from them and came toward me. We stood together for a moment in silence. If before I had been overgifted with voice, now I was struck dumb.

"Benje," she said with gentle concern, "you have a great trouble."

I gazed at her raptly, and wretchedly, but not a word could I utter.

"If ever you need me," she said, "come to me, or send me word."

I managed a sound then; more like a frog's croak, it was. And then she was claimed by another. And as I stood apart, watching the glittering throng and the men on whom Mistress von Lund smiled, it seemed to me that every one of them was blessed. Envy and bitterness rose in me. Mistress von Lund, I told myself, was far too free with her favors. But what was it to me? There was a green-eyed, red-haired girl on the Eastern Shore who was waiting for me, whom I loved.

I made excuses and left early. That night I dreamed of Nancy—a Nancy with a fresh, young, inviting body and a death mask for a face. A monster!

Four days later, as the soft June dawn broke and the tide turned from the flood, all hands were tumbled out on deck by the rattle of the drums and the shrill pipes. Another drill? Standing at my post by the rail on the larboard quarter, I could not suppress a series of mighty yawns.

Midway through one of them I saw the gangplank lifted clear. I blinked and rubbed my eyes. Fore and aft the stout mooring lines were cast off from the massive iron bollards and came snaking swiftly inboard through the hawseholes. All was done soundlessly, save for the twittering of the bo's'ns' pipes and the patter of the seamen's bare feet, for the rule of silence in a man-o'-war was strictly observed.

With a thrill of elation I saw a watery gap widen between ship and quay. Forward, the jib rose and bellied; aloft, the topsails tumbled from the yards and filled. We gathered way. I caught the colorful flicker of skirts on the quayside between the grim, slab-walled buildings that slid slowly by. The Tingey daughters were there, and several others, waving kerchiefs. I made out a bright golden crown that set one apart from the others, and forgetting discipline I leapt upon the bulwark and waved madly. Behind me Mr. Crane barked a severe reprimand, and when I dropped down, his baleful glare indicated that I would hear more of this before the day was done. But for that I cared nothing at all; I hugged my happiness, and put it down to the now undoubted fact that the *Chesapeake* at long last was putting out to sea.

The great courses and the lower topsails, which was all the canvas she would wear as long as we were in the river, fell into place and filled, and we rounded into the stream, gathering speed as we crossed the bar and sailed into the broad Potomac. The yard behind us dwindled. I could no longer see the figures standing on the quay. The green hills closed in. In the rays of the morning sun the glinting windows and glistening slate roofs of Alexandria began to appear forward, off the starboard bow. To larboard rose the steep wooded bluffs of the dear Maryland shore. Astern, only the faint blue haze of wood smoke from the city's cooking fires among the folded hills marked the capital of Washington.

A miracle had occurred. A great ship was under way and I belonged to her.

EIGHT

But we were not yet at sea. We made a quick passage down the Bay and lay most of the night off Rock Point at the mouth of the Wicomico River, awaiting a favoring tide to help us up the narrow channel. The next day as we stood in under the Thimble Shoals and entered the wide mouth of the James, we could see far in the distance a number of vessels lying in Lynnhaven Roads in the shelter of Cape Henry. We guessed them to be a part of the British squadron blockading the entrance to the Bay against the escape of the three French frigates.

Inside the roadstead we avoided the long, shallow jut of Hampton Bar and came to anchor with good holding in six fathoms, close to Hampton Flats. Scarcely had our anchor settled in the mud when an eight-oared barge, flying the Commodore's flag, put out from behind Old Point Comfort. There was barely time to lower the accommodation ladder and muster all hands before it was alongside. Nonetheless, the marine guard stood stiffly at present, the correct number of side boys were at the gangway, the long command pendant broke smartly at the peak, the drums ruffled and the pipes twittered, and Commodore Barron was formally brought on board.

He glared as before and with Captain Gordon and the First Lieutenant at his heels set out upon an exacting inspection of the ship. We were much relieved when he went down to his cabin. He was gone again before midnight.

Next morning we weighed anchor and stood across to Gosport, where we fell to taking in the rest of our supplies. This was on the sixth of June.

For nearly two weeks an all but overwhelming deluge of material poured down upon us: guns and tackles and blocks, swabs and rammers and loggerheads, sand buckets, sand, tampions and fuses, cases of muskets, cutlasses, and pistols, powderhorns and flasks, axes, pikes, grapnels, barrels of powder, wads, smallshot and roundshot, grape and langrage, cable and chain, cordage and rigging, oakum and pitch and paint and turpentine.

And still it came: spare canvas in the raw bolt, slops and clothing for all weathers with buttons to match and needles and thread to sew them on. Boots there were, and spare sole leather, coal for the armorer's forge, mops, brooms, brushes, holystones, and whale oil for the lamps. There came coal and wood for the cook's fires, and even a spare smokestack for the galley, silver and china for cabin and wardroom, blankets and bedding, lumber and yet more lumber, casks of bread, biscuit, flour, and meal, salt pork and salt beef, limes and lemons. When the chickens, ducks, hogs, sheep, and cattle were in their pens, it seemed to me that Noah himself would be perfectly at home on our warship. We worked in shifts, stowing, packing, rigging, struggling to bring order out of a chaos that only appeared to grow more chaotic.

In the midst of the scurry and tangle, we were kept to our drills and exercises, and in every crack and crevice of time we scribbled letters. Mail had been waiting for us at Norfolk. I had a letter from my father, full of sonorous sentiment for the service and weighty and profound advice upon the duties and obligations of an officer and a gentleman—sadly out of date. A letter from my mother admonished me to dress warmly against the ocean winds and beware of the Mediterranean maidens who, she had heard, were not all they should be. I must be sure, she wrote, to change my clothes whenever I got wet and refrain from wiping my nose on my sleeve, thought to be a habit of midshipmen. Cato, she said, had grown sulky in my absence and did not speak save when spoken to.

From Wendy I had what news there was. On the day I left, the *Leopard* had come down and anchored offshore and fired a gun—she swore she had heard the whistle of the ball, but I doubted that!—and then sent a boat, "right into our cove, mind you!" and a la-de-da young fop of a midshipman had come ashore looking for John Meade, and had been sent off to Holly Hall for him. Father had been in a fine rage at having a British ship making free of Forbes Inlet. Nancy, she wrote, refused to be seen even by mother or herself, at which she, Wendy, was mad as a hornet. The Colonel, shunned by all, had taken to liquor. It was all very well, said Wendy, for him to drink himself into an early grave, but he seemed determined to take his slaves with him, for he was whipping them mercilessly, often with a leaded cat. Everyone was angry about it, for the bitterness of the nigras at Holly Hall was spreading to the hands at the other plantations, making them sullen and hard to manage. Giles Penrose—he had been calling often—had told her, secretly, that he had been ordered to keep the militia company in a state of strict readiness. A nigra uprising was feared.

There was a brief note from Mistress von Lund, slightly scented. She said it was Sally, the eldest of the Tingey girls, who had confided to her the date of the *Chesapeake's* sailing. She had spent the night at the Commandant's house in order to be at the quay in time to wave us good-by. They had all seen me leap on the rail to return their salute and felt much rewarded for their early rising. She wished me good fortune and ventured to express the hope that we would meet again, and signed herself, simply, "Kirstie."

Lack of word from Nancy troubled me. It was to her I wrote first of all. A hurried note it was, with reproaches, but determinedly I signed myself, "Your betrothed, Midshipman Benjamin Forbes."

To Wendy I replied that while I might possibly endure Giles Penrose as a brother-in-law, he was a pompous ass to go about frightening young girls in order to swagger in his militiaman's uniform. I wrote to my mother and to my father and even to Cato, but not to Mistress von Lund, although I treasured her letter and could not bring myself to throw it away.

On June 21, Commodore Barron condescended to return to his ship. The stream of supplies had ceased but we were still clearing and stowing and the decks were piled high. Now it was that our Commodore, who had seen fit to fritter away his time on shore, revealed himself.

To Captain Gordon he was chillingly polite. On the rest of us, from the seething little First Lieutenant Smith down to the lowliest powder monkey, he poured vials of wrath, swearing and ranting. He informed us that we were a lot of cunny-thumbed, lazy, slovenly, good-for-nothing sojers and nincompoops—that a left-handed sergeant of coast artillery, blind in one eye and paralyzed between the ears, could do better with half an awkward squad of infantry recruits than we had done —that he'd half a mind to call upon the Army, stationed at Old Point Comfort, to set things to rights and damned well would if it weren't that he might have to fumigate the ship when they had gone. He told us that we were already four months late in sailing, and had had ample time to get ready.

"You'll work around the clock," he snapped. "We sail on the morrow."

Breathing heavily, he favored the company with a final, malignant glare, turned on his heel and went below.

All hands set to, even we midshipmen being pressed into the "public service," where before we had merely volunteered. Fortunately there were cooler heads than the Commodore's in the wardroom and the work went by watches, with some men resting below while the others labored at accelerated pace. Sweating and grunting we pushed, hauled, rolled, carried, and had no breath for cursing. If the Commodore had had his way, the entire crew would have been ready to drop in their tracks by sailing time and there would have been none left to take her out.

We managed to clear the spar deck, and we rigged the carronades on the quarter-deck and fo'c'sle. But the *Chesapeake*, which had appeared to me so large, did not have stowage space for what she now carried. Cupboards, shelves, lockers, and partitions would have to be raised—where, I had no idea. We stowed much of the material that littered the gun deck into the cockpit, and we of the steerage were then forced to share our quarters with the "bilge mice," as the surgeon's mates, loblolly boys, parson, and clerk were called. But since the cockpit was important only in war, when it was a surgery and dressing station and hospital for the wounded, its emergency use as a hold was hailed by all hands as a stroke of genius.

When the cockpit was filled to its overhead deck beams, there still remained a bewildering clutter of lumber, boxes, barrels, cordage, rigging, spare sails, and oddments. Some we stowed between the guns and the rest we stacked neatly down the center of the deck, leaving space for passage on either side.

Then we turned our attention to the 28 long 18s of the three main gun-deck batteries, and managed to mount them all upon their carriages. Twelve of them, four to each battery, we were able to rig, ready for firing. Of the rest, half were partially rigged; the others we simply lashed down and secured. None of the equipment of the guns—the swabs, rammers, loggerheads, the powder horns for priming, or the wads for holding powder and shot in place in the barrels—was broken out. No powder barrels were broached, no shot laid by in the racks, no sand buckets filled, no sponges issued.

There was no time.

Yet, but for the Commodore, there was plenty of time. If we were already four months late, what did a few more days matter, or even another week? However, a commodore is no more gifted with prevision than other men, and it is always easy to know the pistol was loaded after one has shot away his toe. We were, after all, a warship of a nation at peace; there was no need to be prepared for action.

This, then, was the condition of the frigate *Chesapeake* at daybreak on June 22, when Commodore Barron came stamping down the ladder to the gun deck. We were pleased to observe his glowering ill humor give way to surprise and grudging approval. He sniffed loudly, coughed, then hawked and looked about for a sand bucket. But there was none, and he was too much the sailor to spit on the deck, so he gulped it down.

"Very well," he said. "That'll do! Captain Gordon, you will serve out an extra ration of grog all round. Have breakfast served up and then pipe all hands on deck and stand by to weigh and sail at seven bells."

"Aye, aye, sir!" said Captain Gordon woodenly.

In the next two hours of comparative ease, we midshipmen in our crowded quarters ate and drank ravenously. Now and again one of us groaned or swore, but for the most part we were silent from sheer exhaustion, and little Perry fell asleep at the table between bites.

I have often heard indignant talk about the disgraceful state of our decks when the *Chesapeake* put to sea, but in truth there was nothing unusual about us. We were, in fact, tidier than most ships that set out upon a long voyage, thanks to our evil-tempered Commodore.

We cleared from our anchorage promptly at seven bells and stood out through the channel between Willoughby Bank and the Horseshoe. A slack flood tide and sultry airs from the swamps to southward delayed us so that we were a long time getting down to the mouth of the Bay and breaking clear of the Capes. Overhead the sun was bright and blazing and the sky was blue and cloudless like a painted bowl. Behind us the bay and before us the sea held a deeper, more dazzling blue, and on the distant shores the wide sandy beaches were wavering stripes of gold between the water and the tall green pines.

Long before we reached Lynnhaven Roads, we made out the three British warships lying there. One of them, we noted idly, weighed and got under way—a large frigate, from the look of her. She picked up the sea wind and stood away to the nor'eastward on a course calculated to carry her well clear of Cape Charles and the Nautilus Shoals. Even at that distance her lines looked familiar to me.

As we came abreast of the Roads, I marked that the two remaining vessels were the line-of-battle ship *Bellona*, seventy-four guns, and the frigate *Melampus,* thirty-eight guns. We showed them the courtesies customary between ships of war of friendly nations. They responded but did not move. We picked up the sea breeze and heeled a little before it, gathering a white bone in our teeth and pointing our bows a little north of east, straight for Europe.

The sea's magic reached out, touched us. Temper and tension seemed to ooze away and an almost languorous peace and contentment took their place. Scowls vanished, weariness fell away. My shoreside problems, which had loomed large, dwindled to nothing: Nancy's silence, the troubles of Colonel Savage, the disquieting memory of Lieutenant John Meade, the prospect of Giles Penrose as a brother-in-law. . . . Let them be. They would settle themselves. Oddly, the image of Kirstie von Lund came to me, and no problem offered itself with her; not now. She belonged here, with the peace and the soaring joy of a white-sailed ship on blue waters.

On duty with the afternoon watch, my place was on the quarter-deck with the watch officer, Lieutenant Allen. In port I would have been set to oversee one or another detail of men, but now that we were at sea they were turned to under the bo's'n and his mates. I had nothing to do but to stand by for Mr. Allen's orders; and just now he had none for me.

My post was to leeward, on the larboard side. Filled with thoughts of Kirstie, I leaned on the rail midway between the after main brace and the mizzen shrouds, gazing idly at the graceful, proud-winged British frigate that had set sail before us out of Lynnhaven Roads. She stood some miles to the north and slightly east of us. As I watched she came about onto the starboard tack and began to run down southeastward. With awakening curiosity I realized that her course would very soon fetch her across our own.

The distance between us decreased; the two ships were converging rapidly, and all at once I recognized the Britisher.

"What the devil is she up to?"

Mr. Allen and Captain Hall of the marines were beside me. It was Hall who had spoken.

"Damned if I know!" said Lieutenant Allen with a puzzled frown.

"Who is she?" Hall asked.

Allen shook his head.

"Sir!" I ventured. "She's the *Leopard*, frigate, fifty guns, and her captain is Salusbury Pryce Humphrey."

Allen grinned at my obvious pride. "Snotty," he said—the term was often employed by lieutenants to midshipmen when there was no higher rank than their own about—"how do you happen to know that?"

"Sir, he's been in these waters for some time. He came up the Bay last spring, and one of his officers was visiting my— one of our neighbors."

"Mark how she runs," said Allen. "She looks like wanting to speak us."

After a moment he said, "Yes. I'll warrant that's it. But let's put her on trial."

He passed the order forward and we wore around so that we ran free before the light wind on a course that would carry us well clear of the Britisher. But the *Leopard* shifted her course correspondingly.

"So!" said Allen. "Mr. Forbes, inform Captain Gordon that the Englishman's bearing toward us."

"Aye, aye, sir!" I started for the companionway but at that moment the Captain himself stepped out on deck. "What is it, Mr. Allen?" he asked.

"Frigate *Leopard*, sir, fifty guns. Captain Salusbury Pryce Humphrey." Allen briskly appropriated my information. "I think she means to speak us, sir."

The *Leopard* was now not much more than a mile distant. Captain Gordon eyed her keenly and finally nodded. "Very likely," he said. He ordered his speaking trumpet and stood by.

All was quiet on board as the *Leopard* ranged alongside, not half a cable's length away, and smartly backed her main topsail—a gesture generally intended to signify that the commander wishes to pay a social call. She was so beautiful that I quite forgot she was British and that John Meade was aboard; there seemed no place at sea for hatred.

There came a hail from her deck: *"Chesapeake, ahoy!"*

"Aye, aye, *Leopard!*" Captain Gordon bellowed through his speaking trumpet.

"Captain Humphrey's compliments," came the reply, and Captain Gordon stiffened. The back of his neck reddened. "We have despatches. . . ."

Captain Gordon gestured toward our masthead where the Commodore's long pendant waved lazily, unmistakably. "This is Commodore Barron's ship!" he interrupted the Englishman.

There was a moment's hesitation, as if advice were being asked on the other deck. Then, "Sorry!" came the laconic apology. "Captain Humphrey's respects! We have despatches for you from Admiral Berkeley. May we come aboard?"

"Tell him yes, Captain." We all started at the new voice. So intent had we been on the exchange that none of us had heard the Commodore come on deck. I wondered if he had heard the earlier calls. Our long pendant was clearly visible and the other must have seen it, yet his choice of words—"compliments" instead of "respects"—had been those of a senior officer to a junior. The slur had been deliberate.

But Commodore Barron's expression revealed nothing. "You may heave to, Captain," he commanded. "I will receive the visitor in my cabin."

"Aye, aye, sir!" said Captain Gordon to the Commodore's back which was already disappearing down the companionway. Turning back to the rail the Captain raised his trumpet. "Send your boat," he called. "We will come up-wind and wait."

"Aye, aye," came the reply.

Captain Gordon issued his commands to Lieutenant Allen, who relayed them to the sailing master, who in turn passed them on to the helm and the waiting seamen. We wore around once more until we lay nearly head on to the wind, and there we hove to with our sails slatting gently as they alternately backed and filled.

The *Leopard* imitated the maneuver precisely. When it was done the two towering ships lay beam to beam, no more than a musket shot apart.

While the Englishman lowered away his boat, Lieutenant Allen fidgeted. This struck me as odd, because he was not a restless kind of man. Covertly, uneasily, I watched him.

"Beg pardon, sir," I heard him say to Captain Gordon, "but have you noticed his gun ports? They're triced up, ready for action."

"Hmmm?" replied Gordon. "So they are, Mr. Allen. Probably been exercising his great guns."

"No, sir," said Allen. "Begging your pardon, sir! I watched her sail from Lynnhaven. She's not fired a gun since."

"Airing the deck," Captain Gordon said indifferently. "Or else he intends to exercise 'em later."

"Yes, sir," but he did not seem reassured.

Captain Gordon caught his tone. "I agree with you, Mr. Allen. It's damned rude of him!"

The *Leopard's* boat was approaching and they moved toward the open gangway where the ladder had been let down. I think they expected Captain Humphrey himself, for they were greatly surprised when a mere lieutenant came over the side.

For my part, I was not at all surprised. Here, of all the British ships in American waters, was the *Leopard*. It followed that here. . . .

"Lieutenant Meade, sir," said the Englishman, saluting

smartly, "of His Majesty's ship *Leopard.* I carry despatches from Admiral Berkeley for Commodore Barron."

Admiral Berkeley was the British commander in American waters, stationed at Halifax.

Captain Gordon's face was a study in outrage. Yet he had no choice. Now that an official bearer of despatches was on board, he must be sent to the Commodore. He returned the salute perfunctorily and turned to me.

"Mr. Forbes, show Mr. Meade to the Commodore's cabin."

I understood. Ordinarily the duty, or honor, would have fallen to Mr. Allen, but in view of the insolence of sending a junior officer on such a mission, the only possible retort was to turn him over to one even more junior.

I led the way down the companion ladder, smiling to myself in the twilight of the deck below. "Well, sir," I said, as I turned toward the great cabin aft, "we seem to be meeting again sooner than either of us expected."

He made no reply, only stared grimly through me, as if I were not there. Angered, I said nothing more. When I announced him the Commodore was standing by his desk and I saw that he had changed his uniform. A decanter of sherry and glasses stood on the sideboard. As I came away I did not envy Lieutenant John Meade.

On the quarter-deck I found Lieutenant Allen gone and his place taken by Mr. Creighton. I thought I heard sounds of activity from the gun deck. My breath quickened. Yet what could happen here in our home waters, or anywhere, at a time of peace? Nothing, surely. No—anything! For I was part of the *Chesapeake,* and with the *Chesapeake* anything might happen!

For nearly half an hour the two ships lay side by side. Signs of restlessness appeared on board the *Leopard,* and I felt the subtle change to alert on the *Chesapeake.* I believe—but I cannot say for certain—that we too swung open our gun ports.

Suddenly the *Leopard* impatiently fired a gun to leeward, on the side away from us. At the same time a bright string of signal flags ran aloft to flutter from her main yard. The Captain sent word below by one of the marine orderlies.

In due time Commodore Barron reappeared on deck with Lieutenant Meade following correctly. The Commodore's pursy mouth was set in a thin line.

"I'll not detain you, sir," he said cuttingly, "since your captain appears to lack the patience for the ordinary decencies. You have my reply. You will deliver it immediately, and at the same time you will inform your captain that my instructions from my government expressly forbid it. And even if they did not, I could not permit the muster of my crew by any other than my own officers!"

John Meade saluted and dropped over the side to his waiting boat. The Commodore stepped to the open gangway and glowered at the *Leopard*.

A British demand to muster our crew for the purpose of taking off so-called Englishmen and deserters was not only insulting to our government but little short of a deliberate act of war. That the British had for some years engaged in such nefarious practices did not make the crime any the less damnable. How dared they make such a demand on our *Chesapeake*, on the Commodore's flagship! This was too much!

Commodore Barron for the first time became aware of the *Leopard's* state of readiness.

"Captain Gordon!"

The Captain jumped.

"Have all hands sent to quarters as quickly and quietly as possible."

"Aye, aye, sir! I have already passed the word to stand by."

I knew, then, what had become of Lieutenant Allen. He had been sent to his battle station as officer in charge of the third division. I debated leaping to my own battle station. The situation was confusing because the regulations were emphatic, and contradictory. When quarters were sounded, all hands must go to their stations. On the other hand, an officer on duty with the watch must remain at his post until relieved. In the presence of a fuming Commodore and at a time of crisis I dared not make a mistake.

"Very good, Captain," said the Commodore. "Pass the word, then. And mind! I'll have no noise. Have the guns loaded and charged with grape and cannister. At this range we must try to cut away her rigging and rake her decks."

"Aye, aye, sir!"

At once the group on the quarter-deck broke into fragments. Mr. Creighton went down to inform the officers. The marines scattered to see that the order was spread by word of mouth, but in spite of their caution one of the drummers apparently became confused. A few tentative taps of a drum sounded from below. Both Gordon and the Commodore whirled savagely.

"Dammit, I said silence!" Barron snarled. "Does that mean anything to you, Captain?"

Gordon took two angry steps toward the companionway, but

the drumming ceased as abruptly as it had begun. In the silence the creaking of the rigging overhead was loud. Below decks I could hear the pad and shuffle of bare feet as the men moved to their places. Once a snatch of words came up clearly, through an open scuttle:

"...goddam rammers! How th' bloody hell...?"

Fairly dancing with impatience and excitement, I waited for my relief. But no one came.

"She's coiled like a snake," said Commodore Barron grimly. "There's no doubt they mean business. Why the devil wasn't I informed that her ports were open and her tampions out?"

I did not hear Captain Gordon's reply, if he had any, for at that instant Harry Broome came from below, buckling on his cutlass, to assume his battle station on the quarter-deck. He grinned at me.

"Lucky hound!" he said out of the side of his mouth. "You've a choice view. It's bedlam below. Loggerheads cold, no powder nearer than the magazines, and that's yet to be broached. Even the powder flasks empty! And no one can find the matches! And not half of 'em have rammers. By the way, you're to stay here. Jack Crump's taking your place—Mr. Crane's orders."

Despairing, I turned to the rail. The *Leopard* hailed us, but I did not catch what was said. The ships had drifted somewhat apart.

"You have my answer, sir!" Commodore Barron bawled through the Captain's speaking trumpet. "I will permit no muster!"

A white mushroom bloomed on the *Leopard* fo'c'sle, stabbed through by a tongue of orange flame. A second later I heard the sharp, slamming crack of a single gun, but I did not hear the scream of ball. I saw a geyser spout from the sea a quarter of a mile beyond us, followed by a second still farther away as the ball ricocheted.

I stood rooted, incredulous. Despite all that had passed, I had not really believed that the Englishman would fire upon us. Bewildered, I found myself coolly reasoning, questioning. Why had the Englishman thrown that first shot across our bows? Such a shot is universally recognized as a warning to halt. But the *Chesapeake* was already halted; we lay hove to, right under the *Leopard's* guns. A sitting duck.

The Commodore spun upon Captain Gordon and the rest of us on the quarter-deck, his face working furiously, his lips quivering.

"You saw, Captain? Gentlemen? You heard? He has the brass-bound insolence.... By God! 'Tis a deliberate act of war! Captain Gordon, pass the order forward: commence firing by divisions. Thereafter, fire at will, as rapidly. . . ."

Not more than twenty seconds had passed since that opening shot. I heard the sailing master, Mr. Brooke, from his post by the helm, issuing his own commands restoring our main and topsail yards to their original trim, setting us under way once more in a proper condition for maneuvering. At the same instant Captain Gordon was relaying the order forward. In the waist the drums began to roll. Pipes twittered. Below decks I could hear the gunners' muffled voices picking up the command:

"Fire forward! First Division! Fire forward! Fire . . . !"

At that instant the whole side of the *Leopard* became a billowing wall of white cloud through which licked vicious tongues of flame. A mighty burst of thunder seemed to smash at us like an invisible fist and my head felt as if it had been hammered numb by one blow. Beneath my feet the ship jumped like a live thing and rolled, staggering, as if a sudden great wind had leapt upon her from nowhere. The air was full of angry, hellish noises—grinding, tearing, screaming, whining, roaring, battering—like a barrelful of rocks and rattling stones flung by a giant hand against the side of an empty barn, mingled with the swish as of dry peas thrown fanwise from a huge shovel across a taut stretched canvas.

I went down on one knee, clutching at a nearby brace. As I touched it the rope was taut, but even as my fingers closed upon it the brace went slack and I tumbled down. The roll of the ship sent me skidding across the deck to fetch up under the rack of belaying pins that circled the mizzenmast. There, high above, I saw a chunk of the mast free itself. It spun upward in lazy-seeming, end-over-end fashion until it thumped against the great sail. As I watched with mild interest, it came sliding down, gathering speed. It landed with a crash beside me, missing my head by little more than a hand's breadth. It was fully 6 feet long and tapered at one end to a jagged splinter. I reached out and patted it affectionately. God alone knows why.

Midships I saw one of our boats disintegrate into kindling. Great jagged holes gaped suddenly in sails that in the forepart of the selfsame instant had been whole and solid and bellying with wind.

I would have lain there, bemused but quite contented, but that I saw young Broome sprawled near me. I helped him up. He seemed unhurt, but my hand came away from him all red and sticky, and I saw then that the side of his jacket had been ripped and that blood was welling out. He laughed and said it was nothing.

We saw Captain Gordon running toward the open scuttle that led down to the gun deck. Commodore Barron still stood by the gangway, a little sheltered by the bulwarks and the hammocks in the nettings. He was bellowing furiously:

"Fire! Goddammit, forward there! Fire! Will ye stand like woolenheads while they cut ye down? Fire, I say! Fools!"

The smoke was drifting down and I could smell the acrid powder taint. The man at the helm was gone and a thick track of blood and entrails led from the wheel to a twisted heap of rags and flesh in the scuppers. Below, somewhere on the gun deck, a man was screaming on a note of agony that turned my throat dry: "Ai-eeee, ai-eeee, ai-eeeeee, ai-eeeee"—over and over again without ever seeming to pause for breath. The terrible sound pierced through the jumbled, shapeless clamor of men all shouting at once.

I saw Mr. Brooke take the helm and I swung toward him. But as I did so another quartermaster materialized and calmly relieved him. Somehow I had lost my friend, young Broome. I turned back toward the Commodore.

A second thunderous blast came at us. Again the ship reeled. This time I managed to keep my feet, although I ducked involuntarily, and no doubt quite uselessly. The smoke thickened and forward through the haze I saw someone fall. Then the Commodore loomed before me. He seemed dazed. He raised his left hand and looked at it. The sleeve from wrist to elbow was torn raggedly, the hand and forearm were covered with blood.

"You're hit, sir!" I said stupidly.

He stared at his hand as if he could not believe it. "Yes," he said. He let it fall. "No matter. Go forward, Mr. Forbes, and find out why we have not fired a single shot. Twice they've given us their full broadside and not one miserable goddamned gun have we loosed in return. Why? Why?"

I turned to obey and almost ran into Captain Gordon.

"Goddammit, Gordon!" the Commodore bellowed as I hesitated. "What's the matter with our gunners? Why the devil don't we fire?"

" 'Tis not the gunners' fault, sir," said Gordon. "There are no matches broken out—or wads, or rammers, or sponges. . . ."

"Then goddammit, use loggerheads! Wad with the men's shirts! Sponge with wet rags!"

"They're doing what they can, sir," Captain Gordon said—

almost gently, it seemed to me. "Some of the guns have been loaded but the loggerheads are cold."

"Fetch coals from the galley, then!" The Commodore was fairly sobbing in his frustration. "In the name of Christ, let us have one gun! One gun! Just one!"

It is a strange thing, but I seem to recall that seconds before I heard the thundering crash of the third broadside, I felt the crushing blow. One moment I was standing, listening to the exchange between my Commodore and my Captain, unsure what to do. The next moment I was picked up as by cruel fingers, turned in mid-air, and flung on the deck with savage force, so that I bounced and went all raggedy-hop, bumping and skittering, back again to my former place at the base of the mizzenmast under the rack of belaying pins. There I lay, quite comfortably, feeling no pain—only a vast numbness.

The deck leveled; the smoke thinned a little. I saw Harry Broome, near the wheel, and wondered why he was not lying beside me. As from another world I observed the Commodore and Captain Gordon, still standing, facing each other.

"One gun! Just one!" Barron cried like a man in unbearable pain.

Captain Gordon shook his head. It was as if a monument to grief had moved.

The Commodore sagged. His face was gray and he looked like an old, old man. "You may strike," he said. "Mr. Broome!"

Harry Broome turned to the halyards and I heard the blocks creak as the flag began to descend. From across the water a thin cheer rose, then stopped abruptly. And at that moment, from below, a single gun banged.

It was followed by a dull silence. Somewhere close at hand I heard a steady dripping. This seemed strange. The deck seemed to undulate beneath me; it was, I thought, the natural lift of the ship to the long, slow swells of the sea. It was pleasant.

From overside came the faint splash of oars. Then I heard the rattle of wood on wood and the clatter and creak of a rope ladder in use. A head appeared in the open gangway under a cocked hat, a handsome, aristocratic face, a sensuous, arrogant mouth. It came to me with absolute conviction that I had seen that face long before I had encountered its living image in my bedroom. I had seen it in some hell where I had wandered in my fever. It was the face of hate, the face of treachery!

As it rose it seemed to grow larger and larger and more and more evil. I knew I must warn them.

With a mighty effort I got my elbow under me and raised myself a little. I found my voice.

"May God damn your soul to hell, John Meade!"

For an instant I thought I saw an expression of surprise, even horror, cloud that handsome hated face.

Then a searing pain clutched at my throat and stabbed downward through guts and garbage into my vitals. Even today I can feel the bitter, metallic taste of it in my mouth. I dropped spinning, whirling, down and away into utter darkness.

PART **6** ☆

Calabasboom

ONE

I was unconscious of the passage of time, or of the snipping, the picking and probing, the cutting, lancing, bleeding, and bonesetting. When at last I opened my eyes I stared at a ceiling of dingy white plaster laid on lath, the regular pattern of which was visible through the rough troweling.

That there were others about I could tell from the murmur of voices and the sounds of movement, the curiously muffled whisper of footsteps and the rustle of clothing. I tried to move but could not. Somehow I knew that I was in bed, in a house safe ashore. And then, as if knowledge must be punished, the pain began.

Ah, the pain. The ghastly, inconceivable, ever-mounting pain! It coursed through my being, filling every crack and cranny of me, until I felt that I could hold no more but must scream it out or go mad with it.

I must have made some sound. An attendant leaned over me, an ancient pensioner clad in a filthy smock.

"Hey, ye comin' round, sonny?" He grinned at me with toothless gums. "I'll pass the word to Pullguts."

There was a wracked, interminable interval. A second face hung over me. It had a sharp, prominent nose and a long upper lip that gave its cheery smile the look of a benign V. Its owner beamed down at me.

"Ah!"—it was almost *Ach!*—"You are better. That is, you look better, but you feel worse, no? Here, drink."

He slipped an expert hand beneath my head and emptied the contents of a small vial down my throat.

When I awoke there was the toothless pensioner with a bowl of gruel. I could take little of it because the pain began again. Then came "Pullguts" with his precious vial. I slept, and woke to more gruel—sometimes it was broth—and Pullguts, whose little bottle seemed to beam as he did. My life settled around two faces, one of them having to do with nourishment, the other with surcease from pain; and for a long time I wanted nothing more.

For more than two months I lay in the narrow hospital bed, slowly taking in the world beyond its confines. Pullguts was, more properly, Dr. Lewis Heerman, Surgeon, U.S.N., in charge of the marine hospital as Gosport, to which I had been transported. A native of Hesse-Cassel, he was a young man—I think he was not yet thirty—who had already seen considerable action, having been with Decatur at the destruction of the *Philadelphia* before Tripoli. It was he and an older one, Dr. Cowdry, who brought me back from death to life, and they discussed me with no little pride in their workmanship.

I had caught a blast of grapeshot and had been laid by it under the mizzen, a shambles of tattered flesh, tangled guts, and splintered bone. If I had not called out, damning John Meade, I would have been left for dead.

As I slowly recovered, I learned from the cheery Dr. Heerman that my shoulder blade had been shattered and two ribs smashed beyond repair. The right lung had been punctured and the right arm, from above the elbow, badly mangled. There was still more damage, in great variety, and the doctors derived a singular pleasure in the recounting, leaving me lost in a maze of Latin and fearful I would be bedridden for the rest of my life. I marveled at Dr. Heerman's satisfaction in describing how he and Dr. Cowdry had worked over me: clipping, sewing, sawing, picking away the splinters and chips of lead and bone, literally replacing the living cartilage with delicately fastened, riveted strips and plates of silver, tying and suturing my punctures and lacerations with such a quantity of gut that I began to wonder if I were not more cat than man internally.

But it grew upon me, with bleak finality, that the gratification I had given to the good Dr. Heerman was the last I would give to anyone in this world. I wished to die; yet, to please him, I lived. Sometimes I had a fit of coughing and observed with little interest that when I took my towel from my mouth it was flecked with red.

One day the ancient attendant, whose name was Jemmy, took down the canvas screens that surrounded my bed. I found myself in a long room lined with cots. Faces, most of them heavily bearded, were turned toward me, smiling; hands waved at me, and one man raised and waggled a foot in greeting. Voices boomed at me. Some men were hobbling about and these were converging upon me when Jemmy reappeared and quickly set up the screens again.

"Visitors," he announced.

I closed my eyes. The mere sight of my fellow patients had wearied me to the soul. I asked only to be left in peace behind my narrow walls.

Silence fell. I heard a quick light step, a rustle of skirts.

But the voice that spoke was male. "Well, sir. Will you see us?"

It was kindly, almost loving.

My breath quickened, and I looked up into the compassionate face of the Baron von Lund. And beside him was Kirstie, tearfully smiling. She was dressed in a gray traveling costume trimmed in cherry-colored ribbon, and her gay little bonnet was daintily frothed with lace.

"I told you I would come," she said.

"I—I had forgotten."

All at once she was indignant. "Papa, did you hear? He had forgotten!"

Amused, the Baron tried to look grave. "That was very wrong of him, my dear. I would not forgive him."

Dismay dawned upon her. "You would not?"

He shook his head and said sternly, "Never."

"Not—not ever?"

"Well," he said thoughtfully, considering. "Perhaps...."

She glanced from him to me and found me smiling. "Oh! You—both of you! You are monsters to tease me so!"

I laughed then, and it seemed strange and wonderful to laugh. But it ended in coughing, and I turned my head away. I brought the towel down quickly under the bedclothes.

When I turned back to my dear visitors, Kirstie was sitting on the stool Jemmy had placed beside my bed. She leaned over me and I felt the touch of her lips on my forehead. They were so cool, so soft, and her fragrance was like that of some new flower born in the springtime of life.

"Now you must listen," said the Baron. "You must always listen when Kirstie speaks. Even I listen to her."

"Benje," she said, "why do you lie here?"

I could only stare at her.

"Dr. Heerman says you have scarcely moved." She seemed angry with me. "Yet look at you now."

I looked. Unconsciously, I had reached out my left hand to clasp hers, and I had turned upon my side. There was pain; but it was endurable.

After a moment I said fiercely, "Tell me the truth. Tell me —will I ever walk again?"

"Yes. If you wish it."

Her honesty was as pure and warm as the sun that shines on Forbes Inlet in the fresh young morning. I could not take my eyes from her. All was life and hope with this girl who was a woman, and who would always be both girl and woman.

"Benje, you are hurting me."

Horrified, I released her hand, and she smiled. "See, you

are strong. Sick, and with your left hand, you are stronger than you know. So it is very silly of you to be lying there. Now you must rest, and we shall see you tomorrow, but that is the last because we sail away to Saint John. And when you are ready you will come to us there. Do you understand?"

"Yes, Kirstie," I said meekly.

The Baron warmly shook my offending hand. "One always obeys her," he said with a boyishly confiding air.

"Always, sir?"

He nodded. "When we don't, we are very sorry later."

Before night fell I had risen from my bed and for one dizzying moment I stood on my feet.

In the morning I bedeviled Jemmy, demanding warm water, good soap, a mirror, comb and brush, a razor. But my bedmates, those of them who could walk, came to my aid. "Aaarh," said one of them, "that Jemmy, he'd be cuttin' yer throat, he would, and the little lady'd be that disappointed!" He was a big man but gaunt now and the flesh hung on his bones, and he looked himself a cutthroat, but he shaved my thin scraggly beard with a woman's touch. Little old Amos Fitch, late gunner's mate in the *Chesapeake*, examined my face with rough, scraping fingers, and when he pronounced the job well done, all were satisfied.

They washed my matted hair with cloths, liberally splashing themselves in the process; they brushed and combed it, and it was with difficulty that I dissuaded them from dousing me with a vile-smelling pomade called Elixir of Lilacs. They put me into a coarse but clean white shirt, and very gentle they were in their handling of me. Only then did they permit me to look into a mirror. I saw the face of a harrowed, suffering boy, a face absurdly young for a man of seventeen to be wearing. It was colorless, and it had no distinction that I could see, save for Wendy's clear gray eyes that stared back at me.

"Had a sister oncet like yer little lady," said a black-browed, one-armed man. "She was a one for waifs and strays. Allus bringin' home hurt cats and dogs and birds and such."

I dozed. When Jemmy came to put up the canvas screens, there was much bustle and scurrying. Everyone that morning had made a special toilet, and now each man hastened with the finishing touches, and the windows were opened wide to clear the air of foul tobacco smoke. At the sound of my visitors' footsteps a hush fell upon the room. There must have been an air of expectation, as of well-scrubbed boys in a classroom, for I heard the Baron say at once, "Good morning, gentlemen," and through the ragged chorus of replies came a hoarse whisper from one of my bedmates, "She smiled at me!"

And here they were, beside me. "Oh, Benje! How splendid you look!" cried Kirstie, and glory burst upon me with a light that seemed too much to bear. "But I rather liked the little beard," she added.

"How could you, Kirstie?" I said, making frantic gestures. She looked puzzled, like a kitten. But her father understood. "He is right, my dear," he said seriously, raising his voice a little. "There are beards and beards. I have observed some remarkable examples in this very room. No, Benjamin's beard would not do."

She said doubtfully, "It was truly not a good beard, Papa?"

"No, it was not."

"No, Kirstie," I said. "It was a very poor sort of beard."

Comprehending now she gave a little trill of laughter. "But of course, you are right! It was in truth the worst beard I have ever seen. Benje, when you have studied the others here, one day you will grow a better—no?"

Solemnly I promised that I would.

It was wonderful how light and laughter came with these two, father and daughter. They were very unlike Colonel Savage and Nancy. Their love was so strong and wholesome that they could play upon each other without hurt or the fear of hurting, and they took me into this beautiful game as if I were one of them, as if I belonged. It seemed to me that I had been, all my life, a sulky, selfish child. It was time to grow up, past time. When I went home I would not tease Wendy or Nancy, I would make them laugh. I would make Nancy gay and wholly lovely.

Nancy. . . .

"The doctor says you must not have a cold winter," Kirstie was saying, "not for some time. It is your lung, you know. So you must come to us at Calabasboom. That is the name of our plantation. It is funny, no? It is a Dutch name that means 'the Calabash Tree.' We have many Dutch names in the islands, and French and English and Spanish and Danish ones, too. We are all mixed together. It is very pretty, Benje, and the sun shines always. We would take you today if you could come."

"I must go home," I said.

"But of course," said the Baron. "Your family first, and then. . . ."

Wearily I shook my head. "There is more. But thank you, sir. I shall not forget your kindness."

Father and daughter exchanged a long look. The Baron said, "We tire him, my dear."

"No, Papa," said Kirstie. "He is so clear, one can see to his heart. It is his trouble that tires him. Benje, you will come."

I turned to cough into my towel. I felt her lips on my cheek. Then they were gone. On the bedclothes lay a piece of paper on which Kirstie had written: "Calabasboom Plantation, on the island of Saint John, De Dansk Vestindiske øer, by way of Amalienborg, Saint Thomas Island."

TWO

Because of my precarious state I had not been permitted other visitors. Dr. Heerman confided why he had sent me the Baron and Mistress von Lund. "I knew that little one," he said. "Such women are rare, although we have more of them in Europe than here. They are the great ones, the daughters of nature. Healers they are. I knew her, and see, I was right!"

It must have been so, for even while I grieved, and in secret even wept, for the girl I must never see again, she had left something behind. It made my inertia appear no more than a child's fear of the dark. Gone now was the terrible fear of a living death that had held me down. Slowly I began to strengthen.

All the talk in our room was of the affair between the *Chesapeake* and the *Leopard*. After his cowardly attack, Captain Humphreys had had the brazen effrontery to board us, muster our men, and search for deserters. He took Ware, Martin, and Strachan, and Ratford, of course, the English deserter from the *Halifax*, who had been found hiding in the paint locker. Refusing to accept the Commodore's sword in token of surrender—for that, I suppose, would have sealed the incident as one of open warfare—he had sailed back to his anchorage in our waters in Lynnhaven Road, as if nothing at all had occurred.

The *Chesapeake*, much damaged in her hull and spars and bearing three dead, eight gravely wounded—of whom I was counted one—and ten less seriously injured, limped back to Norfolk with pumps working and nearly 4 feet of water in her hold. There her wounded were removed to the marine hospital at Gosport. All the country round seethed in righteous fury. At Hampton and Norfolk the militia had to be called out to maintain order, and at Hampton a mob smashed some 200 casks the British had sent ashore for water. The British consul at Norfolk was forced to barricade himself within his house for fear of attack. Mr. Jefferson issued a proclamation ordering British warships from our waters, but he might as well have tried to whistle up a tree at midnight. Commodore Decatur fetched his gunboats down to the mouth of the river; but the three British warships complacently ignored them, as well they might.

Some of my fellows in the hospital were old shellbacks of the service, deep-water men who had sailed to the far-flung corners of the globe, fought the French in the West Indies and the Moorish pirates off the Barbary coasts. Others were merchant seamen, and some of these were old enough to have manned privateers in the War for Independence.

Wizened little Amos Fitch, who had been sailing before I was born, said passionately, "God give me a tall ship—not a big hulk, mind—just around 100 feet over-all and about 200 tons, carryin' ten to sixteen guns and 100 men. A topsail schooner, with a cloud of canvas for speed, lean and low in the water—a wet ship in a seaway. No cargo, only a letter of marque from Mister High-and-mighty Jefferson. Me and one tall ship, we'd raise holy hob with them British. They'd be runnin' all over the sea for me and never catch me. And when they wasn't lookin', there I'd be—bang! And I'd take prizes and I'd have gold to chink in my pockets when I stepped down the street."

I thought of my father, who damned privateers for a parcel of money-grubbing poltroons. "But that's plain piracy, Amos," I said. "It's cowardly."

There were a number of men sitting around my bed, smoking their pipes, whittling wooden whistles, or knotting belts and slip rings of hair and hemp. They froze at my remark.

"Have I said something wrong?" I asked hurriedly. "I didn't mean anything. But my father...." Eyebrows were raised. "No, he's no landsman," I protested. "At seventeen he was a sailing master in the Navy."

A snort came from Mick Shanahan, whose left leg had been crushed in a shipboard accident off Cape Hatteras. "Aaarr, Amos, ye windy booger, stow it. The lad's been raised up by wan o' thim gentlemen that came off the water brassbound between the ears."

"Ye damned Bristol man!" Amos Fitch retorted amiably. ("Bristol man" I knew to be the sailors' euphemism for a bastard, specifically, the offspring of an Irish thief and a Welsh whore.) "Now young sir," he said to me, "mark yonder mosquito on yer wrist. Ye slap at him, an' if ye're not quick he buzzes off laughin' an' he'll bite ye again. But if he just sat and let ye crush him, would ye say then, 'Pore, gallant, li'l varmint'? Hah! No, sir. Ye'd say, 'Serves him right, the fool! He sucked hisself so full of blood he hadn't the wit to fly.' And mind, if there be a lot of mosquitoes, all lively and with the common sense to fly off in time so's to come back to bite again, they'll drive ye near crazy. Them mosquitoes ain't no cowards, lad."

" 'Tis all so much piss in the ocean," said Mick Shanahan. "Mr. Jefferson'd be scared to say boo to the King's cat, and him warmin' his whiskers by the fire. Lubberly farmer, he is. Even most of the small frigates we've got he keeps laid up in ordinary, and he goes and orders up a God's mort of these damned little one-gun bumboats. God love us! Might as well send us out in bark canoes!"

Amos Fitch reverted to his first grievance. "Cowards, hey? Yer pa should have his arse kicked—saving your presence, sir. Would ye say John Barry was a coward? Or Silas Talbot? Or Josh Barney? Or Tom Truxton? Or John Rodgers, or Edward Preble, or Davy Porter, or Stephen Decatur—the old one, that is. Would ye call them cowards, young sir?"

"I'd not dream of it!" I said emphatically.

"Well, they all fought in privateers at one time or t'other, and proud of it, too."

"Mr. Jefferson or no," put in Eli Carey, a merchant seaman of Charleston, "we'll be fighting England one day, and with no Navy, so to speak. 'Tis privateers will win that war."

"They don't build ships like that nowadays," sighed Amos.

"You're a Yankee, Amos, so you don't know much," said Eli. "They make 'em better than that near where I come from. Schooner-rigged, clipper-built, they can walk away from a frigate as easy as skittering ducks across a millpond."

I thought of the *Oriole*. "He's right, Amos," I said proudly. "They build them tall in *my* country—in Baltimore."

A few days later my father came. At first sight I was chokingly happy to see him. I'd been miserably homesick. But to my bewilderment and hurt, he bore himself stiffly and appeared ill-pleased with me. Perhaps, I thought, he was affronted by finding me among common seamen. I regretted having mentioned him to my friends, for it was curious how I saw him as if through their eyes; and I squirmed within. He was like a high officer of the quarter-deck to whom commoners are sometimes useful but nonetheless insignificant. And indeed, had I come to this place, hale and fresh from the small world of our Eastern Shore, I, my father's son, would have shared his feeling. For among our gentry there were but two ranks or classes of people: ourselves and the others.

But my world had widened now. I held Amos Fitch and Mick Shanahan and their like among the finest of men, and I knew that a gulf had opened between my father and me.

He would not speak of the disaster. "Disgraceful!" he said angrily. "A disgraceful affair! We will not discuss it."

And so there seemed little to say. I inquired after my mother and Wendy. Curtly he replied that they were well. I ventured to hope that Colonel Savage was in good health. But there, too, he said, "Disgraceful!" and not another word.

After a strained silence he said he had learned that I would be discharged from the Navy as disabled.

This I had expected and I had resigned myself to a landsman's life. Yet now, because of my father's cold manner and his strange air of accusation, I said, "There are other ships."

"Merchantmen?" He was harsh, as in the days when he had administered discipline to a witless child. "I'll have no son of mine a merchant seaman. 'Tis no life for a gentleman."

Furiously I said, "Then I'll be no gentleman, sir!" and burst into such a fit of coughing that Dr. Heerman, who was passing, civilly but firmly ordered him out. He told me to send him word when I was ready to be taken home, and he left bristling, ignoring the rows of hostile eyes that followed his ramrod figure to the door.

It was mid-September before Dr. Heerman announced that I was free to go home. My father did not come for me but sent the pinnace with Cato and Virgil. These two old friends greeted me with unashamed tears of joy. We dawdled on the way. We stopped and fished for three whole days off Tangier Island. We crept in through Hopper's Strait and I tried my luck at ducks in Nanticoke Sound and shore birds in the marshes. But my wounds were not yet sufficiently healed for me to withstand the kick of the fowling piece, nor was I yet strong enough for the needful tramping, even with Cato and Virgil to go before and act as bird dogs, kicking out the game for me and retrieving when I had knocked one down. In truth we spent much of the time anchored in the shallows while I lay, stripped to the waist, soaking up the life-giving rays of the last warm suns of the autumn dog days.

Here and there I stopped to visit at one or another plantation. I found myself received with a mixture of curiosity and reserve. From angry words that burst through the bounds of hospitality, I became aware of a new current of feeling.

When the *Chesapeake* first returned to port, she had been everywhere seen as the victim of an unforgivable outrage, which indeed she was. But stories of her defenseless state began to circulate. They roused acrimonious criticism and, in time, took the form of outspoken censure of all her officers, and even of her crew. By her submission without the firing of one effective shot, she had wounded the nation's pride.

God knows that as a weak nation, slapped and insulted by the two great powers at war, we had small cause for pride. But irritation swells to anger and anger must have an outlet. The *Chesapeake,* a commodore's flagship which had bowed to the British in her own waters, became the scapegoat upon which was piled all the passion of long frustration and humiliation.

So I see it now, but even had I seen it then, which I did not, it would not have eased my growing bitterness. I felt like a good dog who, with every right to expect a kind word, receives instead a kick.

In Norfolk, Captain Gordon and Lieutenant Crane dueled with a Dr. Stark and a Mr. McConnico: an affair in which Stark was killed and both Gordon and McConnico wounded. And even among the officers themselves there was violent disagreement. Harry Broome and Jack Crump fought, and Crump was wounded in the thigh.

The storm shook Washington. Commodore Barron was relieved of his command. Later, he and Gordon, Captain Hall of the Marines, and chief gunner Hook, were tried by court martial and found guilty of negligence.

The Bay region was in a ferment. Every man who owned a bugeye or a barge seemed to feel that if he had been on the *Chesapeake* all would have been in readiness. Our decks would have been cleared for action, our battle lanterns slung, our matches alight, our guns mounted, loaded, and run out. We would have fought, giving as good as we received, and never never struck, but rather gone down with all hands in proof that true Americans refused to bend the knee to any cursed tyrant, least of all the Royal Navy!

Putting in along the Eastern Shore in the pinnace, I had only a small blast of this grapeshot of tongues, but it was enough to fill me with helpless fury. After four visits I sailed home as if the devil were at my heels. I sailed for shelter from a world gone mad.

I stepped ashore into the arms of my mother and Wendy, and was all but overwhelmed by a great wave of love for them, and for every blade of grass of the sweet-smelling lawn, and for every window and board and tile of the gracious house on the hill. Within, I walked about slowly, touching tables, chairs, curtains, vases, knickknacks, while my mother and sister chattered tearfully, pretending not to notice.

At dinner my father held forth, as often before, upon the rights and duties of a naval officer and the traditions of the service. I thought the subject in poor taste, but it was an old habit and so I paid no heed. My mother sent him warning glances but she only seemed to enrage him.

Suddenly he burst out, "Your ship was in a disgraceful condition."

"That she was, sir," I agreed. "But since we were, and presumably are, at peace...."

"There can be no justification," he said savagely, "for any man-o'-war to go to sea in such a condition. Even a common merchant would have more self-respect. The *Chesapeake* was little better than a floating pigpen manned by—vermin!"

"Sir," I said coldly, "she was no pigpen. And perhaps you forget that I was one of the—vermin."

"Allen, I beg you," said my mother, while Wendy whispered, "Ben, do be careful. He's so crotchety these days."

We eyed each other warily, my father and I, toying with our food.

"She was in no condition to fight," said my father. "You will admit that?"

"Certainly," I said. "We could not guess that we would be set upon by a damned bloody pirate."

"Guess?" he roared. "Who were you to guess? A man-o'-war has no right to go to sea in a state of unreadiness. Even so, you should have given a better account of yourself. Officers! A pack of cowardly, witless knaves!"

I flung down my napkin and rose. "Sir," I said, "I regret that I could not return to you a dead hero rather than a living son." Then the bubbling rose in me and I crawled up to my room to cough in peace.

THREE

My father and I patched up a truce of sorts. There was no more talk of the *Chesapeake* or of the Navy. But everything was changed between us, and I came to see him as a singularly narrow man—and pitiful. He had reared me for the Navy, as a long line of gentlemen Forbeses had been reared before a new nation was conceived in America. It was my father's misfortune that the young America had practically no navy.

From the beginning—that is, from the time of my birth—he had refused to accept that fact. He would have done better had he brought me up to oversee our acres and our small trade, to keep the ledgers, and to breed livestock. Being a gentleman, he was, it seems to me now, a little mad, in which he was not unlike many another old family of British ancestry and of traditions grown meaningless.

The affair of the *Chesapeake* had been a heavy blow to him. It had shattered his faith in what we had of navy. For all of that, he soon built up his idol again. He wrote letters. He wrote to Goldsborough and Smith, to Commodore Tingey, and even to Decatur, the younger, who had replaced Barron in command of the *Chesapeake*. He wrote to such good effect that instead of being discharged as disabled, I received an unlimited leave of absence. When I was fit, he said, he would arrange to have me assigned to one of Mr. Jefferson's gunboats.

I said nothing and let him go his own way. For I was filled with a very different concern. I had sent several messages to Holly Hall asking permission to call but had received no reply.

Wendy said of Nancy, "I saw her last in June. I was not welcome."

"But of course not," said my mother. "The Colonel intended her for Giles Penrose, and now Giles is in attendance upon you. He has not even called upon her. No one goes to Holly Hall."

"Have *you* gone, Mother?" I asked.

Her eyes filled with tears. "Yes, but she would not see me, and the Colonel is not fit to be seen. Nancy has her pride, and I honor her for it. She is ruined. Only you can save her, Ben. Or John Meade."

"Meade!" I cried. "I would see her in hell first!"

My mother said quietly, "That, Ben, is where you will find her now. And if she will not be taken from it by you, pray to God for John Meade."

From the servants and field hands I learned with some difficulty—for they preferred not to speak, which was a bad sign —that the feeling against Colonel Savage, of which Wendy had written, was not exaggerated. Two of his hands had died under the leaded cat he wielded in drunken rages. One was a mere boy, the other a woman with child.

On a brisk, fair morning I had Cato fetch Wendy's mare, as placid a nag as was to be found in the County Talbot. I let her take her own ambling pace to Holly Hall, fearful of what I would find. I turned reluctantly into the long, winding lane that led to the Hall.

There is not a great deal that needs to be done to a well-constructed, drained, graded, three-quarter-mile stretch of fairly level driveway ballasted with gravel and surfaced with crushed shell. Two field hands devoting to it only a day or so every month can keep it tidy. But the way to Holly Hall was unkempt. The weeds were high in it and on either side the brush and bramble were springing unchecked, to narrow it. I was shocked. The Colonel had always taken pride in his fine driveway.

But there was worse. As the drive curved to the house, I saw the lawns overgrown with tall, rank grass. It was a long time since the shrubs and rosebushes had been pruned. On the big yellow house the paint was peeling, chipping, streaking. A window had been broken and not replaced but merely boarded up. The silence was oppressive. The leisurely clop-clop of my nag seemed insolently loud, as in a graveyard.

I swung down stiffly from the saddle, looped the reins through the ring on the iron hitching post—a gesture familiar to me yet now somehow strange—and turned to the steps. Clytie was there, on the veranda.

"I will see her," I said.

She nodded and disappeared within.

Waiting, looking out into the sun, I heard a sharp sound, and I turned to see the Colonel slapping a whip on his boots.

"Good morning, sir," I said.

He made no reply. His eyes were red and deep-sunk, his mouth slack, his cheeks unshaven. His face seemed swollen and bloated. He, who had been something of a fop, was now in shirt sleeves. His shirt was open carelessly to his bulging belly, and he had availed himself of what we in the Navy called "a commodore's privilege," which is to say, he had neglected to truss up the points of his flap.

I stared at him in horror while his whip went slap-slap on his unpolished boots.

There was a rustle behind him but he did not take his eyes from me. "We have a visitor," he said. "I doubt 'tis worth seeing him. You are too fine for him, my girl."

"I will see him, Daddy."

He put up his whip then, bowed in a manner incongruously courtly, and went into the house.

Nancy stood in the doorway. She was thin and so still that only her eyes seemed alive. They were enormous and they shone with an uncanny green light. She seemed taller. Her gleaming red hair was piled high and it was faultless, as if newly arranged for a ball. She wore a stiff gown of a dark gold stuff trimmed with jet. It was no dress for a young girl to be wearing of a morning, or at any time. I had the conviction that she had been wearing this formal gown for a long time, that it was a part of her. Around her throat was a heavy gold circlet of old-fashioned style that had been her mother's. We had played with it once—how long ago?

In this Nancy there was little trace of the girl I had known so well. She was like the dread ghost of a great lady that magnificently haunts an empty house thronged with the shades of admirers, moving with spectral grace to the echo of fiddles long silenced.

She unfurled a black-and-gold fan. "Good morning," she said. "It is unseasonably warm."

I was chilled to the marrow. I wanted to fold her in my arms, to hold her close, comfort her. I wanted to take her up on my horse and ride away with her. But she was too grand, and too remote. I dared not.

"Nan. Nancy, my darling!" My voice caught.

Shimmering, she took two steps toward me, and flinched a little from a ray of sunlight that fell upon her white face. "You've been away," she said.

"Yes," I replied, puzzled. "You know that. Surely you received my letters. But you never wrote. Why?"

"Letters? Oh. There wasn't time. I have so much to do. The nigras are such a trouble, and I have had so many letters to write. John, you know...."

"John?"

She regarded me with sudden interest. "My kinsman, Lieutenant Meade. You must have seen him. He wrote to say he had seen you."

"Yes, Nan," I said grimly. "I saw him, the murdering, treacherous pirate!"

In an instant she was ablaze. "How dare you!"

"He was on the *Leopard*. He very likely commanded the gun that nearly killed me."

"Oh," she said, looking at me more closely. "Are you hurt? Yes, you are scarcely better than when I last saw you. How boring! Have you been arescuing again?"

With difficulty I suppressed a torrent of angry words, coughing into my handkerchief. Languidly she fanned herself, half in shadow, half in light.

"Nancy," I said, "this is madness. You cannot love a—an Englishman!"

With a coolly amused smile she said, "Love? Did I say I love him? No, I did not say so. But Ben, silly Ben, an Englishman is no less lovable, or hateful, than any other. Tell me, my stupid friend, who would you have me love?"

I said, slowly and carefully, "I would have you love me and no other man. But if another, of all in the world let it not be John Meade."

"La! How grown we are!" Her fan, her light tone, her mocking eyes, might have been her father's whip for the hurt they gave me.

"Nan," I cried, "love me or not, but come with me. Let me take you from this house!"

And now she was angrier than I had ever seen her, for it was not a hot anger but icily cold. "Keep your pity, sir! I will not again be rescued by you, to my shame. Oh, very fine it is to go arescuing, a brave and gallant knight, admired by all. But the lady will not have it, sir. God save me from a savior!"

Her fan snapped in dismissal. "I give you leave. I have much to do."

Regally she swept into the darkness of the house. The door closed behind her, and where she had stood the cold shadows seemed to gather round and thicken, thrusting me out into the sun.

I went heavily down the broad, dusty steps. I gathered my nag's reins from the hitching post. A dusky hand reached out to take them from me.

I looked up and saw Abner, the Colonel's stableboy. He had been somewhat like Tip, a huge, laughing buck with a happy, easy way about him. He was not laughing now. He was somber. He had loved gay kerchiefs and had dressed smartly. Now he was clad only in a pair of dirty white breeches.

"Mawnin', Mist' Ben," he said tonelessly.

I nodded. He held out his hand and helped me mount. Giving me the reins, he said, "Mist' Ben, won't do no good to come back. Ain't nothin' yo kin do noway."

"Abner," I begged him, "keep an eye on her. You and Clytie."

"I do that, Mist' Ben," he promised. "I won't let nothin' happen to Missy."

As I let out my mare, Abner turned to the stables and I caught sight of his back. In times past no one had ever lifted a finger to Abner. He had been one of the Colonel's pets and a valuable property. But now that broad black back was crossed and crisscrossed with old scars and torn with raw new red welts.

My mother and Wendy were waiting for me on my return,

but I went by them like a blind man and in my room wrapped myself in blankets and sat by the window in the sun. I could not get warm. They brought me a hot stone jug for my feet and tea with rum.

"What was she wearing?" Wendy asked.

"Gold," I said.

"It was green taffetas when I saw her in June," said Wendy. "In the afternoon—and with emeralds!"

She looked at me. "Oh, Benjie, I could almost hate her!"

"That would be wicked!" cried my mother.

"How can I hate her?" I groaned. "I want to love her!"

My mother kissed me.

Every day I rode to Holly Hall. Each time Clytie came out to shake her head. The door remained closed to me. Sometimes I paced the gravel turnabout. Sometimes I wandered in the fading gardens. Only a few dark figures moved in the fields. The Colonel's schooner lay idly at anchor. Sometimes I did not dismount but sat in the saddle, lost in apathy. Once I saw Nancy sitting at her window. She held a hand mirror and her heavy hair cascaded over her shoulders. Clytie was brushing it and I could almost hear it crackle. I called out. She spoke to Clytie and the shutter banged to. The vision remained with me for a long time: the burning hair framed in the window and the glimpse of a small white face in a hand mirror.

There were many visitors at Forbes Landfall. Old friends came to see me, and Wendy had a train of suitors, who in turn attracted avid mothers with marriageable daughters hopeful of catching a stray male.

One afternoon I was lazying on the lawn with Jerry Pratt, Alex Carmichael, and Giles Penrose. Jerry remarked that old Capt. Alexander Murray from Chesterton had taken the *Chesapeake* affair as a personal affront. "He's even been heard to say that if he had been in command instead of Barron, there'd have been a different story."

He broke off at the look on my face and the three exchanged glances.

"Is it true what they say?" Giles Penrose blurted, "that you had only four guns mounted when you went into action?"

"No," I replied shortly. "And we did not go into action. We were attacked."

"But you got away one shot," Alex put in.

"So we did," I said. "Mr. Allen brought a coal from the galley in his bare hands and dropped it in the touchhole of one lone gun, just as our flag came down."

Jerry Pratt's sense of propriety was shocked. "Do you mean to say you fired a shot after you had surrendered?"

I said, "I have already, on official request, sworn out my deposition for the Inquiry, describing to the best of my knowledge what occurred. Go to Washington and beg permission to read it. I have no intention of making out another for you."

They stared at me blankly and I left them, calling Cato to saddle the mare. The silence of Holly Hall was more agreeable than the curiosity of friends, or their games and laughter, or the coy flirtations that made the house and lawn a veritable battlefield of amours, as when Patty and Vixen were with us. In their time I had escaped in the *Ladybug*. Now I had only the pinnace, but she was not mine and I did not like to be constantly asking my father's permission to sail her.

It was growing cold. The days were chill and I spent much time in my room.

One evening we had a party in celebration of my eighteenth birthday. A poor host, I early excused myself and passed a restless night filled with memories of another party an eternity ago—Nancy's birthday.

The next morning was bright and crisp. I told myself that I must go down to breakfast, and then I would ride to Holly Hall, as usual. But I knew I would not, could not. It was such a beautiful day for sailing.

After breakfast I followed my father to his study. I asked him for the pinnace, saying I would go to Annapolis and would be gone for several days.

He nodded but did not dismiss me. "Ben," he said, "I could send you south—to Charleston or Savannah or New Orleans. I might be able to arrange shore duty there, which would pay your way. I would like to send you to take your ease at Jamaica or Barbados, but you know I am not a wealthy man."

"I know, sir," I said. "And Wendy will marry soon and must have a good dower. Thank you, sir, but Charleston, Savannah, and New Orleans are not noted for their weather, and an officer even on shore duty must live like a gentleman, and to keep a gentleman's state is costly. What with wines and tobaccos and small gifts for my messmates in Washington and my bedmates in the hospital, I have already set you back a pretty penny."

He glanced at a pile of bills on his table and sighed. "What is in your mind?"

I said, "If I can't go to sea in one way—with the Navy— then I must go another. I will go into the merchant service."

He clenched his fists. "You cannot. No son of mine. . . ."

"I was born to the sea," I said. "I will not rot here ashore."

"Merchant seaman," he said, and then exploded. "Rum-hounds, booze-battlers! Fair-weather floaters! Sharp traders! Petty thieves! Cunny-thumbed lubbers that don't know the difference between a Turk's-head and an Irish pendant! Whiners and snivelers who'll scream for the Navy's protection when a two-gun pirate shows hull down over the horizon, who'll run from your convoy and ignore your signals when they think the coast's clear! Water rats, like your friends in the hospital at Gosport!"

"No, sir!" I cried. "They were men!"

We glared at each other and then the fury receded from his face. "No matter," he said. "Given a year as a mid, you'd have gained enough experience to ship as an officer. As it is, you'll have to go before the mast. That's hard work, my boy. What merchant captain do you think will ship you as a foremast hand?"

"I don't know, sir," I said. "But I will go to Annapolis."

"Very well," he said. "But take Cato. The pinnace must return. I have need of it."

I was off that afternoon, leaving my mother and Wendy in tears.

It was a swift run across the Bay, and with a deck under my feet, my spirits rose.

"Wish't I was goin' with you, Mist' Ben," said Cato wistfully. "'At Cassie!"

"Count your blessings, Cato," I said with sententious good cheer as I leaped up on the quay.

FOUR

At Annapolis I found a situation that I had not foreseen. There were a number of West Indian traders lying off the mouth of the Severn, none of them ready to sail. One lone vessel lay in port readying for sea. She was the *Princess Anne*, a schooner. I paid her a visit, climbing on board on the heels of four men who had come over the little harbor from the other idle ships. As I came up the captain was regretfully turning them away.

"Sorry, mates, I've a full crew now, and no room to spare, even for a boy. Wish I did! Way things are now I could man a half-dozen ships and have my pick of able seamen. I've never seen it so easy. Half the sailormen in the country must be out scroungin' for a berth. Try Baltimer."

I followed the despondent men to a waterside tavern and

there learned what I might have known had I read the newspapers with more than half an eye or listened with more than half an ear to talk at my family's hospitable table.

Mr. Jefferson was threatening an embargo. "Ograbme," the seamen called it.

" 'Tis like this," they explained to me with kindly patience, leaving the details to one of their number whom they called the Perfesser. "The British, with their Orders in Council, say they've blockaded Napoleon and that nobody may trade with the French. So then Old Boney issues decrees in reply, sayin' all British waters are under blockade by *his* navy. We're in the middle, which means most of the coast of Europe would be closed to us if we agreed they'd such rights. It leaves only Denmark and Portugal free and open to us, and belike they'll not stay so long. One or t'other will gobble 'em up."

"Free ships, free goods," chanted a second man, half drunk.

The Perfesser gave him a withering look that sent his muzzle down into his wooden pot of rum.

"British and French," the Perfesser continued with his lesson, "take our merchants on the high seas when they can catch 'em, confiscate 'em, and send 'em into their own ports just as if they was prizes. Old Boney, he says he's doin' it for our own good, that he's pertectin' us against the perfidious English."

"Free goods, free ships," came from the rum-pot. "That's what Mr. Jefferson said afore he was elected."

A third man put in. "On the whole, things have been fair to middlin' good for us at sea. There's risks, aye. But profits have run high. And now—nothing."

"Nothing?" I exclaimed.

"Comes of being a writin' man, I reckon," said the Perfesser. "What with the British Orders in Council and the French decrees, Mr. Jefferson has a yearnin' to write something, too. An embargo. He'll lock our ships in our ports. If he goes through with his writin', no vessel of American registry will be permitted to sail from a home port for any foreign port. The only ships sailin' under the American flag will be those engaged in coastwise trade. So all the owners is waitin' to see which way the cat jumps. That is, to see what comes of Mr. Jefferson's fine writin'."

A burly man, he bowed to me from the waist and declaimed, "The pen is mightier'n the gun."

"But he can't do that!" I protested. "Why, it's like cutting off your nose to spite your face!"

"Aye," said the fourth man. " 'Twill improve his looks,

mayhap. We can all go to Monticello for to admire him. Sonny, there's many a land has a king without a head. Ours will be the first to have a president without a nose."

They laughed heartily at this, all but the rum-pot who chanted, "No nose, no ships; no ships, no nose."

That evening I went to see Andrew Callander at his home. He received me with more affection than I thought the man had in him.

"Ben Forbes, by all that's holy! Come in, lad. Come in, and tell me if ye can what manner of bedlam has burst loose over in your bailiwick yon across the bay. From the talk, ye'd think I'd near murdered Mistress Savage, and fouled her, too! me, Andrew Callander, as respectable a man as ever trod God's earth!"

And so I learned that the people of the Eastern Shore had a conscience of sorts. And a queer, twisted conscience it was. Feeling guilty about their neglect of Nancy and the Colonel's degeneration, and being held by honor from doing anything about it, they had shifted blame to Andrew Callander for all that had happened. For he had been part owner of the *Oriole* which had damaged the *Ladybug*. As for Captain Boyle, his name to the folk of the Eastern Shore was synonymous with Lucifer.

Callander ruefully shook his white thatch. "We had to let him go," he said, "and a better captain never sailed the seas. A leetle uncautious, o' course, but that's to be expected of an Irishman."

My heart sank at his news, for it was to find Captain Boyle that I had come to him.

"He has no ship, then?" I asked.

"No ship? Boyle?" Callander gave a snort of a laugh. "Many a captain there may be these days without a ship, but I'll be skewered if you'll find Tom Boyle among 'em. He'll have a ship, laddie, wherever he may be."

"Then you don't know where he might be?"

"No, that I don't."

He was kind and had me stay the night. We talked well past midnight, but he could not help me in my quest. The *Oriole*, under another captain, had come to port. Callander and his fellow owners had decided to hold her there until the situation cleared. They were apprehensive that the embargo might be declared while the ship was abroad, in which case they feared she might be forbidden reentry into a home port. I argued that surely, in the event of an embargo, the ports would be closed only to vessels outward bound, not to the incoming. But the Annapolis merchants were wary. "'Twould not do," Callander said, "to hazard a guess that might turn out wrong. Money is money, business business. I hear tell there be some in Baltimore ready to jump for it. But in Annapolis we've cooler heads."

He was kind, I have said, but he was more. For the next morning he took me to his office, and there he counted out the great sum of one hundred and fifty dollars, which he protested to be his share of the responsibility for the loss of the *Ladybug*. When I thanked him, he said gruffly, "I don't like your looks, laddie. Next thing ye know, the madmen in your country will have it I laid you in your grave, and then I'd be losin' a good part of the coastwise trade. Business is business."

I caught the stage wagon to Baltimore where I took lodgings at the old Fountain Inn, which was a favored meeting place of shipowners, merchants, and sea captains. There I began my search.

Baltimore port was far more active than Annapolis. It had always been to the fore in the West Indian trade. Indeed, I think that in normal times traffic with the Islands accounted for more than half of Baltimore's shipping.

Just now more than a hundred vessels lay along the quays or were anchored, some in the Basin, some in the Northwest Harbor off Fells Point. There were others as far down as Fort McHenry on Whetstone Point. Some, of course, were foreign. But more than two-thirds were of Baltimore registry, and of these I think well over half were frantically preparing to get to sea. The water-front streets were thronged with seamen; the warehouses were bulging; endless streams of blacks labored under piles of cargo and supplies.

In the crowded noisy taproom of the Fountain Inn, I learned that some owners and skippers were playing the same cautious, waiting game as those of Annapolis. But by far the majority took the view that there was time for at least one profitable voyage before the threatened embargo port-bound them. A few made no secret of the fact that, once they had cleared, they had no intention of returning until the threat was past or the embargo lifted. As long as they did not come home, they could continue to operate, carrying whatever cargoes they might find from one foreign port to another, and take their chances with the British and the French.

My spirits soared.

But the days passed and I found no work. I talked with owners. I went aboard the ships and applied to captains and mates. I offered myself as a cabin boy. With Callander's hundred and fifty dollars in my wallet, I even offered to pay my passage to any port of the West Indies where surely I could get a berth.

There was no room, not even for a deck passenger. Cargo space was at a premium; decks and even cabins were being piled high. As for a seaman's berth, nothing was available. Half the deck hands of the Atlantic seaboard seemed to be in Baltimore looking for work. From all the more timid ports, such as Annapolis and Alexandria and Chestertown, the crews had flocked to this city. There were a dozen able applicants for every berth, and my sickly appearance was against me. Skippers and mates eyed me up and down and shook their heads.

"Go back to the doctors," said one of them kindly. "Ye'll find none to run the risk o' ye these days. I'd not even have ye for a passenger. I'd not want to slacken sail for a buryin'."

My first days in Baltimore were cold and raw, lowering and windy. Then it began to rain, a faint, misting drizzle at first that increased to a slow, steady weeping from above. It was not enough to raise the level of Gwynn's Falls or Stony Run, but it made the town a muddy sponge. All week it rained, never enough to call for oilskins, but enough to keep a man's feet wet and his coat soaked over his shoulders, and to send dank fingers searching everywhere. Even into the beds. My cough worsened and the red spots appeared more and more often on my handkerchief.

Everywhere I asked after Captain Tom Boyle. Some knew him but could not tell me where he might be or what ship he had. Several ships were named, but when I went to their owners it began to appear as if Captain Boyle changed ships almost as frequently as a woman changes her dress.

In the taproom of the Fountain Inn a dusky old waiter told me it was useless to be looking for Tom Boyle. If he were in Baltimore, he'd be right there, no other place. I'd only to kick my heels by the fire and wait.

"How long?"

"Yo a sailin' mahn?" was his answer, implying that it was a silly question. But his look was almost like a pat on the head. Lesser inns might rely on wenches of dubious charm, but the Fountain Inn counted on good food and drink, and there was hardly a potboy in the house but was old enough to be my grandfather.

I dared not remain in Baltimore. It would not be gentlemanly to cough out my life here, not with two other men sharing my bed. They changed. Every night an old bedfellow was gone and a new one took his place. Few seamen looking for work could long afford the Fountain Inn. There were cheaper beds to be had.

And now it was Saturday, another hopeless day. Tomorrow, I decided, I must be gone. I returned to the inn late in the evening with the rain dripping from my hat and running down my spine. The long, smoky taproom was crowded, as usual, with shipowners and seafaring men. I stood about trying to make up my mind to climb up to my room in order to change into dry clothes before eating. The effort seemed too great.

My friend, the dusky waiter, tossed me a nod. "I done tol' yo!" he said triumphantly. I moved, by his direction, to a booth near the great, glowing fire. Only one man was there but he had laid claim to the second settle by the simple expedient of piling it with gear, and there was something in his manner that made it plain a newcomer would have to fight him for it. He was attacking an enormous beefsteak. It was surrounded by huge Chesapeake Bay oysters broiled in the shell, and a mug of hot rum toddy steamed at his elbow.

He was a dark, stocky man with dark-brown hair that took on a ruddy glint from the glow of the fire and the flickering lamps. His broad shoulders strained his neat, blue sea-captain's coat.

I stood beside him, holding my hat. Now that he was here before me I could not speak.

He glanced up and, his fork in mid-air, said with ironic politeness, "Ye wouldn't be wantin' to sit, would ye now?"

"Captain Boyle," I said desperately, "I would."

He looked startled. Plainly I was not worth a battle. Then he said, "Oh, then ye'll be the wan that's been askin' afther me. Now whatever would ye be wanting?"

I could not utter a word. His mouth full, he stared at me. "Devil take me now!" he said, when he had the space to say it. "Yer face is damned familiar. Bloody end to me if 'tis not. Now, 'twas not this week, for I've only just come down from Havre de Grace where I've been layin' in fresh water up the Susquehanna, clearin' the barnacles off me bottom. Now, would it be the week before?"

It was like a guessing game, and I smiled.

He slapped his hand on the table. "By the Lord, ye're the lad in the bugeye Annapolis-way! Ben ...?"

"Forbes," I told him. "Ben Forbes."

He rose, leaned across the table and swept his gear off the settle. A man promptly fell over it and swore mightily.

"Sit, and welcome, Ben Forbes!" cried Captain Boyle.

I sank gratefully onto the bench.

"Why, I've always remembered ye, for I liked the way ye stood up to me at first, when ye thought it all my fault, and then were man enough to apologize. And then there was the spittin' red-haired lady, and my own lady. I'm real fond of pretty ladies and a spot of romance, and there it was. Two pretty ladies and a stout young lad. No, I'm not like to forget it!"

The dusky waiter paused, smiling. "A steak," I said, "and oysters, like the Captain's there. And a hot rum, and another for the Captain."

"One fo *you*, sah?" said the waiter reprovingly.

"He's peaked!" Boyle defended me, and when the waiter had gone confided that he was the only man in the world that he, Captain Tom Boyle, was afraid of.

"Now!" said Boyle. "I was consarned for ye. But ye made the run, hey?"

"No," I said. "I sailed like a fool. I went down."

"Ye did? And the spittin' lady?"

"I saved her life," I said wretchedly. "Wish I'd lost my own."

"Oho?"

I found myself giving an account of my whole sad history. He hunched over the table, his dark-blue eyes widening. A better listener I could not have had.

When I'd finished, he let out a long breath. " 'Tis a tale close to me own heart. I'll have much to tell me little lady when I see her."

"No!" I cried. "You must say nothing to Kirstie. Promise!" And then I broke off, staring at him.

" 'Kirstie,' is it?" He chuckled.

"You—you'll see them—soon?" I managed to ask.

"Aye, so. If all goes as it should. We're lyin' now in the Middle Branch off the mouth of Gwynn's Falls taking aboard cornmeal for Saint Thomas. I thought to drop over to Saint John, for the Baron has sugar or muscovado or rum or bay oil to ship. . . . Why, damme, Ben, ye're shakin' like a leaf, and it fair roasting in here! Ye're sick, lad."

"Captain, take me with you!" It came in a rush. "In the name of God, let me ship with you. I'll go before the mast—or cabin boy—cook's helper—anything! Or I'll pay my passage." I took out my wallet and pressed it into his hands. "Look, I've lots of money. Take it all, every penny."

He stared at me in astonishment. "Ho, now! Hold on! God burn me britches!"

168

He called for a long-stemmed pipe and said nothing until it came, only eyed me—dubiously, I thought.

I huddled in my corner, trembling with excitement, trying vainly to contain myself. "I've been to every ship in port," I said. "They'll have none of me."

"Can't say I blame 'em," he remarked cheerily. "Sure ye look like death on a mopstick."

"I need only a breath of sea," I pleaded. "I won't die on you, Captain. I promise you that."

He tossed back my wallet. "I'll not take yer money."

The food I had downed seemed to turn to gall, the drink to hemlock. Inwardly I cursed myself for having dared to hope. "Thank you, Captain," I said dully. "I'm sorry to have troubled you. I'll say good night now, with your permission. I've a journey before me tomorrow."

But he ignored my outstretched hand. "Ye wouldn't be leavin' an old friend. Sit awhiles."

He called for more hot rum for us both and began to talk of his ship and how he had changed her name. She'd been the *Betsy-O,* he said. "And as you're most like aware, every fourth vessel betwixt Savannah and the Bay of Fundy's named the Betsy this or the Betsy that. I took her down a voyage to 'Statia and Saint Bart's and around the Grenadines, and when I got her back I told the owners I'd not sail her under that name. 'Twasn't fitting for Boyle to have a mere Betsy. They invited me, polite, to go to hell and call her what I liked. So I had the old lettering chipped off. I rechristened her the *True Love.*"

With an air of pride he awaited my comment.

"Well," I said tactfully, "it's very romantic."

He burst out laughing. "So 'tis. Ye've heard the old saw: the course of true love ne'er runs smooth? Well, damme, that's my ship! A crankier, more contrary, just plain ornery unhandy sailer never yet slid off the ways. Sometimes she wallows and sometimes she waddles, and I swear the master builder must of been drunk the day he laid her keel. She's a tendency to run off sidewise to larboard, like a lady with a sly way, a mincing lady."

I thought to myself that I wouldn't care if she pranced and bucked or performed a chicken-wing flutter in the middle of the sea, just as long as I was on her. I gave a sigh for my lost hope and lent myself to be as agreeable as I could.

"Then why do you keep her?" I asked.

"Ahaaa!" He leaned over and raised one eyebrow to impart his secret. "For all her idio—idion-synchist—damn me eyes!

—her cranky nonsense, she's the grace and speed of—of—damme, Ben! Who's the wench that rin the race, the Greek lassie?"

"Atalanta?"

"Aye, there's the one! He cheated with his damned golden apples or she'd of beat him."

"Then why didn't you call your ship the *Atalanta?*"

"Couldn't remember the girlie's name. Besides, she was a foreigner."

Atalanta! Despite my bitter disappointment, I was deeply stirred. An Atalanta of a schooner....

"She's a tall ship, then—the *True Love?*"

"Tallest ye'll find. She carries half again the canvas of the *Oriole*. When 'tis speed ye're wanting, I tell you, lad, she gets up on her heels and fair flies. There's not a ship that sails can touch her when she's a mind to run, and that's what's needed for trading to the Islands these days, mark me."

I was suddenly very tired. A vision had dawned before my eyes. I had seen for an instant a slender, soaring ship clouded with canvas. But she was not for me. She was gone. I sat in the smoke-filled taproom with Captain Boyle heartily sick of his friendliness and loquacity.

"Now, which wan of thim two pretty ladies takes yer heart? The red one or the gold?" I heard him say.

I said coldly, "I am pledged to Mistress Savage."

He would not be rebuffed but appeared to be relishing some private amusement. I was relieved, however, that he did not pursue the subject.

"How are ye with figures?" he asked casually. "Can ye keep books?"

"I suppose so," I replied wearily, longing for my bed. "My father lets me help him a little with his accounts."

"Ye wouldn't be knowing anything about trading, would ye now?"

"I've never done any to speak of," I told him. "Only what I could carry in the bugeye. Oysters and fish and farm stuff—corn, potatoes, melons, tobacco—now and again furs, ducks, terrapin, geese. Why?"

"How'd ye make out with it? Show a profit?"

"Not much, but I think it was as much as I could expect, considering the limited space."

"Tradin' a shipload's no different, only a matter of size," he remarked.

"Maybe so," I said.

Without warning his whole manner changed. He even

dropped his Irishness. "Very well, Mr. Forbes," he said briskly. "I'll take ye on. Ye'll sign articles to ship with me as supercargo."

FIVE

It was a very different Ben Forbes who next morning accompanied his benefactor on board the *True Love*. The rain had stopped at last and all the world was asparkle, and I was as joyous as a bridegroom on his wedding day. A portion of Tom Boyle's vigor had seeped into the marrow of my bones, even overnight, lifting high my spirits and my opinion of myself.

The schooner looked much like the *Oriole*. She had the same black hull and yellow inboard trim, the same flaring bows and graceful, overhanging stern. But she was larger by, perhaps, 40 gross tons; she was some 8 feet longer, and almost 2 feet broader in the beam. Her masts sprang from her deck like young forest trees, seeming to touch the sky, so that two men working aloft, swaying up a new foretopsail yard, were toylike. Her long slim bowsprit and jabbing jib boom, with their heavy dolphin striker, thrust forward like a rakish, tip-tilted snout, extending together nearly half again her full length on deck. Those spars were impressive, indicating the vast spread of canvas she would carry under full sail. In comparison with the frigate *Chesapeake* she was, of course, a small vessel, little more than an overgrown skipjack. But she was small enough to be loved, large enough to command respect, beautiful enough to be worshiped.

It was a Sunday and labor on the Sabbath is forbidden by state law in Maryland and by city ordinance in Baltimore. But on that Sunday the city fathers went to church and closed their eyes to the activity in port, and each seaman made his private peace with God. On the *True Love* officers and men were working together in complete harmony. And I mean all of them, from the mate down to the cook and the two boys. There was a lighter overside laden with sacked corn and meal. A human chain passed the sacks up and aboard and down into the hold. This was not sailors' work; it was ordinarily left to shoreside roustabouts. Yet here it was being done by sailors, swiftly, efficiently, cheerfully.

Captain Boyle presented me to the first mate. He was Archibald Hooper, a wiry little man with an enormous head sparsely covered with long stringy strands of finespun graying hair, a pugnacious jaw, and steel-gray eyes. He held a clip board and the tally sheets, and was keeping check, between the mainmast and the main hatch, while the second mate supervised the work on board the lighter, pitching in and helping with the sacks like any roustabout, encouraging the men by his example. I did not doubt that the third mate was down in the hold doing the same.

Mr. Hooper gave me the tally sheets and stood by to instruct me. "Supercargo!" he snorted. "Next thing you know, he'll be signing on a lady seamstress!" But he sent a little smile Boyle's way, a smile of affection.

Not many traders carried a supercargo. To take one was somewhat like putting on airs. Yet at this time, when all hands were needed to ready the ship, I was a valuable asset, relieving Captain Boyle and Mr. Hooper of the hated paper work. I was in charge of the tally sheets, manifests, and waybills. At night I worked to put the ship's papers in order so that they would be ready for immediate presentation to both shippers and customs as soon as our cargo was stowed. We would thus avoid the usual delay, inevitable when the captain turned from his deck work to complete the transcript.

It was Monday that I signed on. I then found myself in an argument with Tom Boyle. He appeared unduly proud of the distinction of having a supercargo, for he wanted to pay me a salary only little less than his own. I could only guess that his part in running down my bugeye and the series of misfortunes that plagued me afterwards weighed heavy on his conscience. I protested that this was too much; I would not have it. There must be a more businesslike way of determining the question, I said.

He began to look hurt. "Seems like I've taken on a—damme, Ben! What's that varmint that was in the bosom?"

"A viper?"

"Aye, viper." A thought struck him. "But that's a kind o' snake, ain't it? Your pardon, Ben, God strike me dead if I'd be callin' ye a snake!" He grieved over his blackness of heart.

Hastily I compared the scale of wages paid in the merchant service with that in the Navy. A supercargo on a merchant ship would be the equivalent of the purser and paymaster aboard a naval vessel, which was equal to that of a sailing master, which in turn was exactly that of a lieutenant. The *True Love,* I pointed out, carried a first, second, and third officer, who on a man-o'-war would be first, second, and third lieutenants. It followed that the salary of a supercargo would or should be about the same as that of the mates.

Captain Boyle promptly suggested I should receive the same pay as the first mate.

I pointed out that my lack of experience, assuming I were being ordered to serve as purser and paymaster in a man-o'-war, would rank me with the lowest lieutenant on board.

"Ye wouldn't be holdin' me to that," said Captain Boyle reproachfully. "Why, the Dutchman can't hardly sign his name. And you a book man knowin' Atalanta and the viper and such folk!" The Dutchman was Homer Aschenbrunner, the third mate; small wonder that he had difficulty signing his name.

We settled at last for the same salary as the second mate. At thirty-eight dollars per month and found, it was more than three times what I had received as a midshipman, and to my mind a princely sum.

I went back to my work marveling that Tom Boyle, with his great heart, his love for romance, and his impulsive but solid friendship, had managed to hold his own in the sharp business of trading.

The cargo now lading was for Saint Thomas, Saint Bartholomew, and Saint Eustatius. The three islands were the principal entrepôts of the West Indies: free, neutral ports to which vessels of all nations might bring their cargoes for deposit in bond, and where they might fill their holds with goods otherwise unobtainable. Nowhere else could Englishmen secure a cargo of fine French wines and brandies, much in demand in Britain, without payment of double duties. Nowhere else could Frenchmen gratify their tastes for British cottons and woolens, tea, and manufactured goods. An American trader had no difficulty in disposing there of grain, fish, lumber, tobacco, and naval stores, and in picking up French and British goods at minimum cost and maximum security.

Saint Thomas was Danish, 'Statia was Dutch, and Saint Bart's was Swedish. At least such was their status so far as we knew. At any moment, so uncertain were the times, one or another or all three might be gobbled up by France or Britain, even as we sat there talking about them, and we might not know of it until we arrived.

"'Tis one of the hazards of trade these days," said Boyle lightly, "and hazards make for high profit, and fun and games on the high seas."

By Tuesday afternoon our cargo was loaded, our holds were full. The hatches were covered and the battens hammered tight. That night I pored late over my forms and ledgers at the long table in the main cabin. By Wednesday morning I had the entries made, the manifests, waybills, bills of lading, and all the other papers prepared. Captain Boyle went ashore with them, taking also letters to post that I had written to

Nancy and to my family. Having left one set of our papers
with the owners, and a second at the customs house, he had
our own duly sealed and stamped. He was back well before
noon.

The clock in the belfry on Federal Hill was tolling midday
when the bo's'n bellowed and the men tumbled eagerly out on
deck. Half of them fell to at the capstan bars and walked up
our anchor with a lively chantey. Our ensign blossomed at the
halyards. The rest of the crew fell to the throat and peak
halyards, spreading our great white wings with yet another
chant.

I watched and listened with delight. It was a revelation to
me. Very different it was from the strict silence of getting a
man-o'-war under way, when the only sound had been the pipe
and twitter of the bo's'ns' whistles. Yet for all the hullabaloo,
the sing-song chanting, the bawling and shouting and relaying of orders which sometimes seemed to be at cross-
purposes, the maneuver was as smartly done on board the
True Love as on the mightiest, proudest, and most queenly
74-gun ship of the line.

We cleared and dropped swiftly down the bay. It was not
yet midafternoon when we passed the mouth of Forbes Inlet.
I caught a glimpse of our white house on its green knoll. The
gentle grief of nostalgia welled up in me and my eyes blurred.

Captain Boyle took the helm from Mr. Hooper. I had prided
myself on knowing these waters as well as I knew the way to
our backhouse, but Tom Boyle was fully my equal. He took a
short cut, threading his way through the shallows to the Choptank Channel by a series of pots and pits that I had thought
known only to a few crabbers and to me. I stood beside him so
filled with apprehension that I doubt I drew a breath until the
schooner sailed out into the main channel.

Once in the channel he cracked on sail, to my astonishment,
for I thought he had already hung out everything but "the
purser's pants." Besides the usual gaffs and stays'ls, jibs and
spinnaker and tops, he even put t'g'ans'ls and royals over his
tops, which is a thing I'd never seen anyone do, and I looked
to see him run the skys'ls over those. But it was enough, and
more than enough, even for him. The little schooner flew,
skimming over the surface like a flying fish. I'll swear she was
making close to 18 knots!

I laughed out loud from sheer exaltation and Boyle laughed
too. "I'm showin' her off for ye. Did I not tell ye she was fast?
Of course, we'd not dare this outside where we might run her

under in the swell. But here, where there's no sea to speak of, we can be puttin' her through her paces."

"I thought you said she was a crank."

"Oho! And don't ye go thinking she is not. So she is, with a stranger's hand to her helm. But I'm her master and she knows it, and she'll run through a needle's eye for me without scrapin' the paint of her sides."

Dusk found us off the mouth of the Potomac. It is about 90 miles from there to the Capes by the main channel, with some ticklish shoal water in between. Most skippers lie at anchor here, not caring to negotiate these waters in the hours of darkness. Not Tom Boyle. We shortened sail, of course, but we were still fully dressed as we slipped southward through the night at a good 8 knots, which is as fast as most ships at their best.

Somewhere below the Wolf Trap—I don't know just where, for I was sound asleep in my bunk—we made easting to slide over and run cheek by jowl along the Old Plantation Flats. Then we ran down southward again into the North Channel, between the Inner Middle Ground and Latimer Shoal. And at last, in the gauzy gray of dawn, we swung down around Fisherman Island and, avoiding the Nautilus Shoals, stood out to sea.

When I came on deck in the morning our bows were lifting to the long ocean swells. Lynnhaven Roads was already so far behind us that I could not tell if the *Leopard* was there, but I suspected she was not. There was a rumor that she had been recalled to Halifax.

It did not seem possible that I was well and truly embarked upon an ocean voyage. Events had conspired against me, and of my many frustrations that of the *Chesapeake* had seemed final and decisive. At this moment I could not believe in my good fortune.

Suddenly, to larboard, I saw a sail bearing down on us. A bitter coldness seized and shook me. It was all so like: the flat, wide ocean, ruffled only by the dawn breeze, the low loom of the Capes behind us, and the lone sail bearing down. I had a nightmare feeling. The affair of the *Chesapeake* was about to begin all over again.

Captain Boyle's hearty hand clapped me on the shoulder. "From her course," he said, "she's probably straight from European waters. We'll speak her and see if she's aught of news."

With his warm presence the nightmare passed and my sight

cleared. The stranger was a brig, a merchant vessel. I felt a fool. "I'm no good to you, Captain, or to anyone," I said shamefacedly. But he chose not to hear and turned to call orders.

We came up under her lee side and rounded to run starboard to larboard beside her while Boyle leaned over the rail with his speaking trumpet. She proved to be the *Falcon*, twenty-seven days out of Liverpool with a mixed cargo of manufactured goods, woolens, and cotton cloth.

"Ye're just under the wire," Boyle told them. "Congress is cryin' nonintercourse. That's certain to come, and a full embargo's likely. What's with the war?"

"Copenhagen's gone," came back the reply. "British come down without warnin'—blew half the city to bits, destroyed the Danish fleet. Roosians've declared against the English, there's already been skirmishin' in the Baltic. Boney's said to be massin' troops to invade Spain. Says there's too much tradin' with the British out of Spanish ports. 'Tis said he wants to strike through at Portugal and choke off the last neutral in Europe. 'Twill leave England with only a hangnail at Gibraltar on the Continent."

"What about the Swedes?" the Captain bawled.

"Still neutral, but maybe not for long. Boney means to lock the Continent tight as a Dutchman's barn."

Boyle waved his thanks and we sheered off.

In part from relief, and also through now being a "book man," I intoned, "There ariseth a little cloud out of the sea, like a man's hand."

Boyle looked startled and stared all around at the clean line of horizon. "Where away?" he demanded.

"Book of Kings, in the Old Testament."

"Oh! Well, now, I didn't think 'twas in the *Coast Pilot!* But 'tis the right word, Mr. Forbes." He was frowning, his face dark and troubled.

I realized that if the British had attacked Copenhagen, the Danes would probably declare for Napoleon. Their Caribbean islands might well be British captives by the time we reached them. Captain Boyle had to decide whether to change his plans, avoiding Saint Thomas and Saint John.

He looked at me, his eyes keen and searching. "Now, Mister Supercargo, let's know yer mind."

I weighed my own desires against the value of our cargo and of our beautiful ship. I said, "If I were a careful, cautious trader I'd give the Danish islands wide berth. If I were Tom Boyle. . . ."

"Well?"

"I'd go have a look for myself."

He laughed, but if he had then and there taken his decision, he did not make it known to me.

The days settled into a monotonous round. We were seventeen men, sixteen active and one idle. For there is little work at sea for a supercargo, and I'd have demeaned my position and Boyle's pride in it had I insisted upon an ordinary seaman's work. I envied even the two boys, pimply, rabbit-faced Dick Collier and chubby Oscar Mueller. I spent much time with the cook, for it was warm and dry in the galley. Moreover, I was always hungry and he attended to that. He was a tall saddle-colored mulatto with a broad smile and a mouthful of white teeth, and was known only as Bob. He lodged among his pots and pans and apparently followed Tom Boyle from ship to ship as devotedly as a dog that needs no leash. As a ship's cook he was something of an artist. I would not have been surprised had he turned out a delicious lobscouse from a pair of old discarded sea boots and a fistful of oakum. His plum duff was famous up and down the coast and throughout the Caribbean.

My cabin was a tiny cubby. There were six of them, three occupied by the mates. The remaining two were for the use of any passengers we might take on; or, by consent of the owners, if unoccupied they might be filled with cargo purchased by the Captain as a small venture on his own account. The Captain, the mates, and I ate together at a long table in the main cabin, which was the equivalent of a wardroom in a frigate. Almost a third of the entire living space abaft the mainmast was occupied by the Captain's Great Cabin which stretched the full width of the vessel over the fantail.

I became fond of the second mate, Abe Meyers, a tall, olive-skinned man with hollow cheeks, prominent jawbones, and a hooked eagle's beak of a nose. His deep-set dark eyes held a light of friendly interest. He had a gentle sense of irony and a mild good humor, qualities unusual in a man of his position. Second mates are generally blustering bullies whose most subtle notion of a joke is to see a man's skull split with a marlinspike. Abe Meyers had several books on navigation which I devoured. I ventured to ask him if Captain Boyle had read them. "Long ago, maybe, when he was in his cradle," Meyers said. "He's got sea water in his veins and his heart's a compass. It's a deep, dark secret but 'tis said he reads poetry to his ship in his cabin at night."

We were a happy ship, a company with complete trust in

and devotion to their captain. Sometimes, but not often, I was permitted to take the wheel. Mr. Meyers instructed me in the finer points of cargo stowage. Boyle would discuss the war with me: he was certain the United States would be driven into it in time. He liked to talk of ports great and small, trading, and legendary lassies who interested him. He thought well of the goddess Diana, stood in awe of Minerva, was positively savage against Helen of Troy, and was in love with Aphrodite. "Mistress von Lund's her kind," he said, looking at me sidewise to see me flush. The gods he dismissed as a pack of boogers, and while fascinated by the Argosy he insisted that Jason was an ass-brained sailor and Hercules no better than a village idiot.

We were, as I have said, a happy company—save for Ben Forbes. At long last I was at sea, but depression and anxiety still hung over me. I felt my uselessness. The weather did not help my state. It was sharp and chill; the seas were long, ponderous, and graybacked. Was it Amos Fitch who had said a Baltimore schooner was a wet ship? He'd said truly. With our long, low hull and tall, raking masts and great cloud of sail, we seemed to knife through the seas rather than ride them. More often than not our decks were ankle deep awash. There was no standing water anywhere inside that tight little hull but the damp penetrated everywhere. I was not surprised when I found that mildew had begun to show under the duslock joints of my sea chest.

I felt the cold considerably and my cough troubled me much. Several times I caught Boyle eying me anxiously.

Twice we were chased by British cruisers, malevolent frigates. One, thinking to intimidate us, summoned us to heave to with shots from her bow chasers. We paid no heed. We outran both the great ships with contemptuous ease.

Over the shallows outside the shoals about Cape Hatteras, the sea was a dark turgid green, capped with torn plumes of spindrift along the crests of the great rollers. It was here that I saw the *True Love* at her worst, for she fought her helm obstinately.

"Och, now!" said Tom Boyle with a grin. " 'Tis playin' with us she is!" He handled her as my father handled his black stallion.

One day, almost suddenly, we passed out of the green seas of the Northern Ocean into the dazzling blue of the Gulf Stream. It was like stepping from a dark room into a bright one. The seas changed. They lost their wind-whipped crests and became slow, surging swells of purest, clearest azure. And now, rather than driving through the waves we lifted and fell with them, as a sea bird will do. The winds warmed. We shed our watch coats and opened the scuttles and hatches to let the ship dry. The rigging, which had grown slack, tautened in the sun. Within twenty-four hours I ceased to cough, and Tom Boyle took the triumphant, happy air with me of one who has personally arranged the universe for my pleasure.

When the first school of flying fish leaped headlong into our sails to fall helplessly upon our deck, the men laughed to see my wonder and astonishment. I spent hours watching the porpoises and dolphins running and playing before our vessel, seeming always in imminent danger of being run down by the cutwater or crushed beneath the rigging of the jib boom; I saw then why that downthrust bar was called the "dolphin striker."

But still my depression persisted. Perhaps it was because the *True Love* was so feminine a ship, or perhaps because I had so little to do—but Nancy was with me night and day, a presence mocking, anguished, incomprehensible.

SIX

There came an evening when, after supper, Tom Boyle leaned back in his chair and asked me, ever so casually, if the ship's papers were in order. "Of course, Captain," I said and turned to the locker where the charts and log and such were kept.

He stopped me. "No need for 'em now. Tomorrow—maybe in the morning if the limesuckers're prowlin' the passage east of Culebra. We'll surely want 'em later, for we'll be in Saint Thomas by night."

My heart gave a leap.

"We'll be abreast the Cockroaches by sunup," he went on, "and through the Savana Passage before noon. We'll run straight across the Southwest Road and around Water Island. 'Tis a small bit shorter in through the Gregerie Channel, but ye lose time tackin'. We should be passing 'tween Hassel's Island and Muhlenfel's Point early afternoon. I'll be takin' ye ashore for supper, feed ye island lobster with a squeeze o' lime, and top off with soursop in cherry cordial. What d'ye think o' that, now?"

"You're joking!" I cried.

He chuckled. "Come along topside and I'll show ye."

On deck, forward, he swept his hand toward the southern horizon. "What d'ye see?" he demanded.

"Water," I said promptly.

"All right, then," he said patiently, "so 'tis only water. Now. Lift yer eyes but a bit and run 'em along above the edge of the water. Now tell me. D'ye see anything?"

I followed his instructions wondering if he were playing some game at my expense. "No," I said slowly, "unless you mean those few clouds."

" 'Tis not clouds they are. Islands."

I could not believe him. "Clouds," I insisted. "They'd be 100 miles or more away. Why, there's nothing under them, Tom— nothing joining them to the sea. If it were land, hull down. . . ."

He grinned. "Ye're right, lad. They're not land, for a fact. But then they're not clouds either."

"Then what?"

" 'Tis the reflection of the land," he said, "up against the sky. I've seen it often in these latitudes, and always at sundown. The sun strikes at just the right angle, it seems to throw the shadow o' the land against the sea, and that again is thrown up against the sky that's darkenin'. 'Tis a handy thing to know, for if ye're within 200 miles o' land, sometimes ye can tell it so. The long cloud, the one farthest to starboard, that's what the Spaniards call Puerto Rico. The one in the middle there—the short one—that's Culebra, the Rock. And the one stretchin' off to larboard—that's Saint Thomas and the rest o' the Virgins, all jumbled together. Mind the names I've given 'em. Ye'll see tomorrow."

And he was exactly right. When I went on deck in the morning we stood some 40 to 45 miles north by west of the Cockroaches and Dutchman's Cap, with Puerto Rico stretching away in a hazy blue serrated line to the southwest, the deep sparkling Culebra Passage almost due south, and the peaked bulk of Saint Thomas and the tumbled outlines of her sister Virgins looming southeast by south. Far down in the west Culebra Passage against the hazy gray-green of Vieques, there was a tiny white sail; but whether it was a British cruiser on patrol or a Spanish *guarda costa,* we could not know. Nor did it matter, since she was too far away to intercept us.

As Tom Boyle had predicted, by midday we were in the passage between Savana Island and the western tip of Saint Thomas, off Saltwater Money Rock. The very names were music to me. By midafternoon we swung round the tip of Hassel's Island, into the deep, cuplike harbor of Amalienborg. We dropped anchor off the *Kongevaerftet*—or King's Wharf.

In all this time Boyle was unconcerned about the British. "If they were about," he said, "I'd smell 'em."

I put to him then a matter that had been troubling me. "If

the British took these islands, what would happen to the von Lunds? Would they be in danger?"

"It all depends," he replied. "They leave most folk in peace, save for making 'em British subjects. Unless, of course, they fight. Then their lands're attainted and seized by the Crown. But what they'll be doin' about the von Lunds, I can't rightly say. That's one reason I've come—to take 'em off if they've a mind to go. Y'see, the Baron's a special kind o' man. He's served the Danish government often on special missions. Indeed, the only reason he's not governor is because he'd not take it. Fact is, he's an important man, so that might make a difference."

Seeing my dismay, he laid his hand on my arm. "I'm not sayin' it will, Ben, only that it might. In any case, ye've no need to fear they'll be cast into the dungeons or chained in the prison hulks. At worst they'd be removed to London or maybe Jamaica, where they'd be placed on parole and allowed the liberty of the town. But more like they'll only be told to stay home and behave."

The town of Saint Thomas, or *Amalienborg,* as the Danes call it, lies in a deep pocket on the southern side of the island, and is further sheltered from the open sea by the brush-clad hills of Hassel's and Water Islands, so that the harbor is well protected. The town spreads in a crescent about the harbor and sprawls in a riot of color over the flanks and knuckles of three steep hills, known to sailors as Fore, Main, and Mizzentop.

The British had not yet arrived, but were expected. The harbor was jammed with shipping. There were great, high-sided, bluff-bowed Danes and Dutchmen, Yankee brigs and barkentines, Baltimore schooners, island sloops, all furiously loading or unloading. Two smart Danish frigates lay at anchor under the flank of Hassel's Island near the harbor entrance.

Ashore, the Kongens Gade swarmed with life. There were sailors, planters, and government officials, stocky Portuguese and swart Spaniards, tall flaxen-haired Danes and moon-faced Dutchmen, sallow Frenchmen and apple-cheeked Yankees, and even a few English. Everyone seemed in the grip of a wild excitement—or did I see in them my own? In company with Tom Boyle, I chafed at the customs office on the King's Wharf, where at length we were permitted to show our papers and declare our cargo. Then we threaded our way through the throngs in the Kongens Gade, in search of the merchant to whom our cargo was consigned.

It was hot and dusty and whiffs of exotic smells filled the

streets from the open warehouses. Boyle was frequently hailed by one acquaintance or another and spoke a garble of languages. Of each acquaintance I begged him to ask after the von Lunds, but he only smiled and said, "Hold on, lad. Steady, now." I sweated with impatience and anxiety, uninterested in my first foreign port as such. I saw it as if it were remote: the tiny, bright red-brick fort, the green hills behind crowded with shacks and houses blue, pink, white, red, russet, gold, and yellow, and weathered brown, the brilliant splashes of bougainvillaea, hibiscus, oleander, and jacaranda, the flame trees and trumpet vines and cup-of-gold, the spreading tamarinds and whispering women's-tongues, and the rattling fronds of the coconut and banana palms. Some quiet place within me marked the green and flaming beauty of this little land while the rest of me leapt beyond, across the water, to the smaller sister island of Saint John and the home of Baron von Lund and his daughter.

We found our man at the spacious, stone-colonnaded Merchants' Exchange near Government House and the Residency. Nils Knud-Hansen was a huge man with a square face and a great mane of tawny yellow hair. Beside him Tom Boyle looked a rooster, while I felt myself a scrawny sparrow. He would have made three of me. From his great height he sighted Boyle and came plowing across the crowded hall to pump his hand. "Ah, Captain!" he beamed. "You come in the nicks of time."

Boyle presented me and he very nearly wrenched my arm off in greeting. "You wonder what is here to happen, no?" he said. "You have the news heard yet?"

"We'd a whiff of it," Boyle told him, "but no more than can be hollered across a ship's rail in passin'."

Knud-Hansen pounced upon the words apparently new to him. "Whiffs? Hollers? Ach, ya! Whiffs—shmellfuls, no? But 'hol-lers'?"

"Hollers." Tom scratched his head and prepared for laborious explanation.

I had no mind to spend the day in leisurely language lessons. "Hail," I said. "Call. Shout."

The Dane gave me a bow of thanks, but to himself he repeated pleasurably, "Hollers. Whiffs. Hollers."

But Tom prodded him with questions. Soberly our friend replied in a mixture of English, German, Danish, with a little French, but English on the whole, so that I followed what he said. King Frederik of Denmark had carefully striven to remain neutral, like Mr. Jefferson. "But something there is, I know not what, that must affright the English, for sudden

Admiral Gambier and Admiral Cathcart fall down on us. Half of Copenhagen they lay down in ashes yet. The fleet they destroy *toute entière*. Only remains the two *freggatten* here, and perhaps some small vessels on the African coast."

He spread his hands wide to suggest how powerless the Danes were to strike back.

Denmark, he said, had been thrust into the war on Napoleon's side, against the British. But the islands were far from the mother country. It had been decided, in the Governor's Council, to attempt to persuade a neutral country to accept and govern them and return them to Denmark when the war was ended.

"Last week departed our Commissioner to lay the plan before President Jefferson—and of course the Danish and English Ministers in Washington."

Tom Boyle shook his head. " 'Tis a slim chance."

Ruefully the Dane agreed. He was quite certain the islands would be taken by the British, but not alarmed at the prospect. Trade, he said, would continue.

"Perhaps," said Boyle. "But 'twill have to be carried in British bottoms. Or by Yankees like meself who won't go home if we have an embargo." He spoke almost to himself. "Tricky. We'll have to be careful not to carry what the British list as contraband. Or else turn smugglers for such as you—by British lights. Different sides, different meanings. 'Tis the magic o' words."

"So!" Knud-Hansen seemed lost in admiration of Tom Boyle and the homely philosophy of his utterance.

A suspicion had come to me. "Who," I asked, "is the Commissioner who has been sent to Washington?"

"Carl Christian, of course," said the Dane. "Who but else?"

"Carl Christian? Would that be the Baron von Lund?"

"Ja! You know him?"

I said I did, and he shook my hand, beaming. Under his kindly grip it seemed threatened with total destruction, but I did not mind. "And his daughter, Mistress von Lund?"

"Ja, ja, ja! The little Kirstie!" Again my hand suffered but Boyle intervened and we learned that Mistress von Lund had accompanied her father.

Not until then, I think, did I realize how heavily I had been counting on seeing Kirstie. We had probably passed in mid-ocean, all unknowing. Here I was in Saint Thomas, whence even with my one good lung I might puff enough wind on the *True Love's* sails to waft her to Saint John—but Kirstie was gone. And not gone to Denmark, to Africa, or halfway round the world to China—but gone back! Back to that very part of the world I had been so anxious to leave.

It was maddening.

During the long day and evening, Tom Boyle did not attempt to cheer me, and I was grateful to him for the depths of his understanding. I remember that Nils Knud-Hansen escorted us to the rambling Planter's Club, perched on Mizzentop. It had a wide, shaded veranda draped with boungainvillaea intertwined with fragrant jasmine, and within the big rooms black boys pulled rhythmically at long ropes that moved huge fans of palm fronds which cooled the air and drove about the swarms of flies, mosquitoes, and sand fleas. I had my first rum swizzle. I remember the strange, delectable dishes because, lost in my own yearning, I fancied Kirstie beside me, pleased as a child at my delight. There were papaya and the fresh meat of ripe coconuts, clear green turtle soup with a dash of madeira, delicate chicken lobsters in butter and lime juice, turtle steaks and Danish ham, yams and baked plantain, mangoes, soursops and sweetsops, and a fruit called a pineapple—not at all like an apple—that some planter had lately introduced from the Spanish island of Cuba.

It was nearly midnight when we rolled down to the Kongevaerftet and were rowed out to the *True Love*. I could not sleep but paced the deck. If the embargo was declared, the von Lunds would not be able to get back. They could not take an American ship. What foreign ships, I wondered, would be able to enter and clear our ports? I could not know, nor how effective or ineffective the embargo would be. On the other hand, if the Danish islands were taken by the British, it would be better if they didn't return at all. They would be safe in Washington. But then I would have no hope of seeing them. For I was on the *True Love* and we would not go home if there were an embargo, but must forever and ever sail the seas. There were so many incalculables. . . .

"Write a letter." Tom Boyle was beside me.

"Where? How will a letter reach her?"

"Ye're fuddled, that ye be, lad," said Boyle. "Write two letters, leave one here, in care o' Knud-Hansen. For t'other, look about ye. Dozens o' vessels, ye blind ijit! I'll lay ye odds there's at least ten bound for home ports—Charleston, Norfolk, Baltimore, New York, Boston, or where not? And ye'll find the same in 'Statia, and Saint Bart's."

"Tom Boyle," I said ruefully, "so much for book learning. You're worth six of any book men. How you put up with me I'm damned if I know!"

"'Tis a privilege," came his voice through the soft night, "to have a man that's in love with two lassies at the same time, 'twixt fire and water, so to speak, and heaven and hell. Takes a man with a fine grief to make a great sailor. Good night to ye, Ben."

I wrote that night far into the small hours, finding, curiously, that I could not write to Kirstie without first writing to Nancy. In the morning I found a schooner Norfolk-bound that took my letters.

On the *True Love*, Knud-Hansen's corn and tobacco were unloaded and we took on great quantities of dried cod that had been fetched from Gloucester in Boston and Salem bottoms. And so we sailed away to 'Statia.

In 'Statia, the Golden Rock, the excitement and activity were more fevered than in Saint Thomas. The Dutchmen of 'Statia were certain it was merely a matter of days before they would be occupied by the British. They told us that a strong fleet was being gathered under Admirals Lord Cochrane and Lord Brisbane, which would be augmented by the squadron from the Leeward Islands Station of Antigua, for the purpose of seizing all the remaining non-British possessions in the West Indies. Speedily we discharged such cargo as we had for that port, and taking on still more codfish, went on to Saint Bart's. Here we dropped what was left of our corn and tobacco and filled the chinks of our holds with more fish—and still more —until it seemed to me that we reeked like a bluenosed Fundyman.

Swedish Saint Bart's was busy but less hectic than Saint Thomas or 'Statia. We lay in its little port of Gustavia, waiting for news, I writing letters, eating and sleeping, swimming, soaking up the sun, or dangling a line over the schooner's side. It was well into December now, but who would know it with the benign tropical sun overhead and, below, a warm, translucent sea to rock a healing body and strengthen a soul to make a good sailor?

Presently we learned that Curaçao, the largest and most important of the Dutch islands, had fallen. Soon after, an ugly line of British men-o'-war hove into our sight. From the top of Saint Bart's we—and all the rest of the population with whatever we could find of spyglasses—watched their men swarm over the nearby islands of 'Statia and Saint Martin's. Countless patrol and despatch boats came and went between Saint Bart's and the English fleet, carrying supplies and mail, water and wine, eggs, chickens, fruit, to grace the tables of the admirals and captains and milords. The two heavy Swedish frigates in the harbor were ready for action, but Tom Boyle and the other captains of the vessels in the harbor counted more on distant "writin' men," the diplomats and statesmen in London, for the preservation of Sweden's neutrality.

There was nothing to do but wait. Boyle was much ashore; he had a ladylove. So also did the three mates. I doubt there was a female of the little island who, in this time, lacked for a lover.

Lying lazily at Saint Bart's, we learned of the abdication of Carlos IV of Spain, and of Napoleon's entry into that country from Bayonne, and of his army's march toward Portugal, which had refused Bonaparte's demand that she close her ports to the English. It was said the Portuguese royal family was preparing for flight. Some maintained—a little wildly, I thought—that they would go to Brazil.

Toward the end of the year we heard that the embargo had finally been declared.

Then came the news that the British had seized the Danish islands of Saint Thomas and Saint Croix. No one mentioned Saint John, but I knew it would be absurd to hope it had been overlooked. The von Lunds were probably in Washington, and there they would stay, prisoners both of the American embargo and the British occupation of their island home. Would I ever see them again? Or Nancy? Or my family?

One day the *True Love's* agent, Axel Froding, a lank, sorrowful-seeming man, came out to us in a small skiff. To my amazement, when he came over the side he was smiling from ear to ear, as one bearing great good tidings.

"Vell, Kaptin!" His command of English was not large and I had to listen carefully. "Iss gom! Der Franks und der Spaniens unter den Cheneral Chunot grossink der Spaniske frondeers py Alcantara und vers Lissbon marchink iss. Der Konig und family embarken und to Bahia oor Rio von Janeiro vill comen. I dink iss now areadty in der vater."

Tom Boyle turned to me. "Have ye got the manifests and clearances ready, Mr. Forbes?"

His manner was brisk, as on the night when he had said, "I'll take ye on, Mr. Forbes."

"Yes, Captain," I said smartly.

"Get 'em," he commanded. "And fill in as our destination: Brazil, port of Belem."

Within an hour Axel Froding brought us back our papers, signed and stamped. We fetched up our anchor and set sail —for Brazil.

Now I learned that as far back as Saint Thomas, Boyle had

been cannily planning. With the Caribbean practically a British sea, he had begun to load codfish thinking to trade with Lisbon. But Portugal had been taken. It was a stroke of good luck that the Portuguese royal family and the court were removing to Brazil. With their coming the Brazilian ports, which had been closed, would be opened. "For why?" Boyle echoed patiently in reply to my questions. "Because there aren't enough Portuguese vessels afloat and uncaptured by the French to keep 'em supplied, now that Brazil is the seat of their empire. And Ben, to be the first vessel into a Brazilian port with a cargo o' *bacaleu*—why, that stinkin' fish'll be near worth its weight in gold!"

"And then? If you're right?" I asked, excited despite the fact that we were sailing far from Saint John and Washington.

"Oho, I'm right, I am! Ye'll see! And then, why 'twill be cacao and Jesuit's bark for Funchal—and from Funchal we'll fetch back madeira for Jamaica, for it's not contraband and they'll be happy as lords to see us, as they'll not be gettin' port wine any more—and at Kingston in Jamaica we'll take on rice for Port-au-Prince, which is neutral and always starvin', neutral or not—and from there we'll find a cargo o' some kind for Saint Thomas. All around and back again. How'll that suit ye?"

"Fine!" I said, laughing. "If it works."

It did.

We arrived at Belem in the sultry, blistering heat of midsummer. Dom João and the Portuguese court had not yet reached Bahia, but were daily expected. Officially the Brazilian port was still closed to all but Portuguese ships, but what Tom Boyle had said turned out true, the scent of our codfish could not be resisted. We were the first foreign ship admitted and, our business done to Boyle's great satisfaction, set sail again.

The island of Madeira was closely guarded by the British, but our cacao and Jesuit's bark were not contraband, and they brought a tidy profit for our owners. It was the same in Jamaica back across the southern seas to the Caribbean. The short supply of port wine had sent the price of madeira soaring. In Kingston we took on yams and rice for Port-au-Prince.

It had been a long voyage of more than a year. We were often at sea for eight or ten weeks with nothing in sight but sky, water, and the horizon. Sometimes our stops in port were even longer. In Belem and Funchal we worked on our own, without benefit of an owners' agent. Haggling occupied much of our time and I became quite expert at it. At sea, although Boyle at first protested, I bore a hand with the crew at their watches. We tasted storms, and the *True Love* knifed through them gleefully soaking us, but never were they like the bitter gales of the northern seas. In the stickily hot ports Tom Boyle suffered and left much of the work to me. Time, lately a slack sail, bellied full for me.

We were crossing between Kingston and Port-au-Prince. I was in the Captain's cabin. Boyle had long since confided his dark secret to me (of which Abe Meyers had spoken) and we spent much time together, I reading aloud his tattered volumes of Homer's "Eyelid," as he called it, and the plays of Shakespeare. This evening after much discussion and argument we had agreed to condemn Hamlet for criminal negligence of Ophelia. But the young lady herself, we decided, was fair daft and would have made a poor wife and a worse mother.

I closed the book and yawned. Boyle was looking at me with affectionate pride.

"Ben," he said, "I'll tell ye. When we left home ye were invalid—only part livin'. Most o' ye was dead, and I'll say now there were times when I wondered if all o' ye might not be goin' the same way."

I smiled at him. "I promised I wouldn't die on you—remember?"

"Aye, so ye did. And ye're a man now a lassie'd be happy to see and proud to own."

I looked back in my mind over the seas and the ports and the months that had flowed like water. Through all time and all space, fixed within me was a vision of Nancy Savage—a cascade of metallic hair framed in a window, and features darkly seen in a hand mirror. Only that, and a falling house. Overlaying it, separate and yet a part of it, was a second face with sea-blue eyes, warm and smiling. "I will come when you need me," she said. And, "See, you are strong!"

Anguish filled me. Both were gone, Nancy and Kirstie. I was a sailor with only dreams and old tales of love and tragedy to fill a life that was hungry, ravenous for more substantial fare.

"Ye'll find her, Ben," Tom said.

"Which one?"

"The right one."

SEVEN

Port-au-Prince was the capital of the newly founded little country of Haiti which the Negroes had wrested from their

French overlords in a terrible, savage struggle. It had all taken place only five or six years ago, and more than one of our Chesapeake Bay neighbors had helped to evacuate refugees from Cap François at the time of its destruction.

As we approached Haiti from the southwest, the spine of the Tiburon peninsula shot up before us, a mighty wall clad in thick, green, tangled jungle. The dark capes and headlands jutted into the deep, blue seas like great claws. Tiny villages huddled between the sea and the forest. Never had I seen tropics so forbidding. Aboard our schooner voices were hushed.

We swept on around, into, and across the Bight of Leogane and up the dark, sweltering Gonaves Channel between the high, piled mountain ridges. At the head of the deep-cut bay the land flattened and reached back in a broad breathless plain, far and away into the shimmering heat haze. Where the lip of the plain touched the sullen edge of the brassy sea, we came upon the fetid, fantastic jumble of ruined grandeur and rickety squalor that was the city of Port-au-Prince.

Once it must have been a splendid city. There remained decaying remnants of palaces, fine houses, and public buildings that had been built by the French in the days before the black rebellion had ousted them from their prosperous colony. There were paneless windows and caved-in roofs, heaps of rubble, and many evidences of fire, hurricane, earthquake, and relentless war. Among the ruins and on every level space rose thatched hovels of crumbling native clay or thin-walled wooden structures, warped and tottering. The broken streets and makeshift market places were teeming with people, mostly black. At night the concatenate thumping of drums in the jungle thickets contributed an impending sense of doom that made my scalp prickle even as I lay safe aboard ship in the harbor.

This sense of ominous brooding grew upon us. This was a black man's country now, and the memory of past horror and cruelties was yet too hot and recent to be forgotten. Even though coming, as we did, with needed supplies of rice and yams, we were white men and thus only reservedly welcomed.

Earlier that year, and as a part of their vast West Indian campaign, the British, with their Spanish allies of the moment, had launched an attack on Saint Domingue in the east of the same island occupied by Haiti. It had sent the luckless French planters there scrambling for safety. Some had managed to escape to Guadeloupe or Martinique, some to the United States, and a few had been fortunate enough to find passage home to France. But many trapped on the island had fled in open boats or by rough trails over the mountains to the dubious asylum of Haiti.

It was these luckless souls that we found swarming in the black capital. Because of their presence, Haiti's air of bitter hostility and tension was sharpened to a raw, tingling edge, for these unfortunates were not only white but French. They lived here in constant dread of massacre. They came clamoring about the sides of every vessel that was not English or Spanish, begging for passage. But there were few such ships. Dutchmen, Danes, and Frenchmen found these waters too heavily patrolled by the British to risk venturing into them, and Swedes rarely came so far west. As for Americans, like ourselves, to accept a cargo of French refugees for any port was to court disaster. Of course, false papers might be prepared, to be shown if the vessel were halted by a British cruiser, but all the false papers in the world could not disguise a cargo of French refugees. The profits were high but the risk was great.

It was heartrending to listen to the desperate appeals of the refugees, all day long and day after day. In the streets, men and women darted out of their black holes to fall weeping at our feet, pleading for rescue. Some had babies and terrified children. Tom Boyle began to look grim and his jaw set at a fighting angle.

One day he came back from the city with a gaunt, grizzled Frenchman, emaciated and great-eyed from near starvation. He was a Monsieur Jules Bardon. I was surprised to learn he was not yet thirty; he looked near sixty.

Bardon had been a prosperous planter of Saint Domingue. With the coming of the English and the Spaniards, there had been an uprising of slaves in the interior. The Bardon plantation was sacked and burned. M. Bardon, with his wife, four small children, and his wife's aged parents had crossed the mountains to Haiti, destitute, and with only the clothes on their backs.

He was penniless. But his parents in France were wealthy, and he himself had large funds on deposit there. If we would put the *True Love* at his disposal, to carry him and his forlorn little family to—say, Bayonne—he would agree to any terms we might dictate. And if we wished, he would gather together a small group, each equally capable of paying well once they had arrived in France.

It was a familiar story.

"What d'ye say, Ben?" Tom asked me.

"Why, you want to take them," I replied. "You know you do."

Who could look at M. Bardon and the children, as Boyle had looked, and harden his heart? One would have to be British, or made of stone, and we were neither. But I was sadly torn. To rescue these people, and in so doing strike a small blow against the brutal, powerful British—here was a deed of which a man could be proud for the rest of his life. Surely the *True Love* was made for such greatness, and so was Tom Boyle.

But Saint John was near, and I had cherished the hope that, by some miracle, I might find Kirstie there. Many months had passed since the von Lunds had left for Washington. They might have returned. I had to find out.

Boyle and M. Bardon were watching me.

"I did promise ye," said Boyle, "that I'd get ye back to Saint Thomas or Saint John. And the northern climes'd not be good for ye."

My love for this man was so great that I could scarcely endure the thought of leaving him. Yet I said, "Leave me here, Tom. I'll find a sloop I can handle alone and run up along the islands."

"I thought ye'd say that. But ye'd never make it. 'Tis too far, and with the seas swarmin' with British cruisers and Spanish *guarda costas,* ye'd be certain to be taken. Or ye'd end up at the bottom o' the sea, for the island sloops are logy craft at best. I'll not have it."

He smiled at me. "I'm takin' ye to Saint John."

I argued that I could not let him take the added risk, but he refused to listen and he said to M. Bardon: "Done!" On the instant the man shed ten years. With difficulty he contained his emotion while Boyle arranged to carry him and his family and as many others as he could get, up to a total of thirty, to a French port in the Bay of Biscay. The astronomical price of one thousand dollars a head, payable on landing in France, was accepted by M. Bardon with grateful tears.

We sailed within the fortnight, crowded with French refugees—a silent, tragic lot who did not yet dare to hope. For ballast, and in the hope of some extra profit, Tom Boyle loaded Haitian mahogany and casks of Haitian rum which was much in demand in France. Over this cargo he laid a thick plank floor, leaving ample headroom, and had the space partitioned for the accommodation of his passengers. Provisioning had been a problem. Boyle had solved it by making a quick return to Jamaica for more rice and yams, penning a flock of goats on the fo'c'sle, and stowing fruits in the forepeak.

On his return from France—if he did return—Tom was to look for me at Saint John or Saint Thomas, and I would go on with him. It was agreed that if he was not back within six months, I was free to return to the mainland if I wished to do so and could find passage.

Boyle sent the *True Love* northeastward through the Westward Passage and Turks Island Channel and made a long sweep to the north before coming about on the larboard tack once again and standing southward over the Barracouta Banks, which would enable us to sweep in under Jost Van Dyke and behind Mingo, Congo, and Lovango Cays to the deeply indented northwest coast of Saint John. On the way we were twice sighted by British cruisers, one a frigate. Neither could come near enough even to throw a random shot after us. A little extra sail sent the *True Love* dancing away to lose them under the horizon astern.

On that roundabout, carefully plotted voyage, the total distance from Port-au-Prince to the cays just northward of Saint John logged nearly 800 miles. We covered it handily in four days' time. Much of the last day we crept along in precaution against possible observers on the hills of Saint Thomas or Jost Van Dyke. To suspicious eyes we made to appear a schooner from the Bahamas intent on feeling our way through the narrows between Saint John and Great Thatch for Road Town on Tortola, and we sailed, of course, under British colors. To heighten the deception, the *True Love's* foretopmast was sent down, giving her a stubby island look; the decks were deliberately lumbered to give a slovenly appearance, and we trailed the longboat astern—the islanders being too lazy to lift their boats inboard.

Boyle planned to come in behind Mingo Cay in the late afternoon. Creeping into the narrow passage, barely 200 feet wide, between Congo and Lovango Cays, we would be able to lie hidden in 27 fathoms until dusk, when we could slip out between Carvel Rock and Johnson's Reef across the Windward Channel into von Lund's Bay. There I would be dropped ashore and the *True Love* would be in a position to wheel swiftly, run across the mouth of the Narrows and around the tip of Great Thatch Island, out through the broad passage between Jost Van Dyke and Tortola to the open ocean, and stand away for France.

On that final day all was going as planned. But I did not

trust our luck. Even as the sun rose tension mounted in me. At dawn we stood well to northward of Saint Thomas within sight of the hazy blue shores of the great island. The wind was contrary. We had hoped for a westerly or northwesterly breeze, but the steady northeast trades had set in. It would not handicap us in working up to von Lund's Bay, but it meant that in passing out, the schooner would have to beat into its eye. I glanced at Tom Boyle as we made a note of it.

"Belike we'll be chased," he said. "So long as we're not hemmed in against Congo and Lovango and the rocks and forced to run southward across Pillsbury Sound to the main Anegada Passage, where the patrols'll likely be thick as flies, ye need have no fear for us. Even there I can lose 'em under the Fat Virgin. So set yer mind easy, lad."

The prospect of real danger had changed him. He was alight, almost like a child who plots some wonderful mischief against the grown-ups. His feeling was reflected among all the ship's company, who before this time had seemed more concerned with seeing that our passengers bathed and rid themselves of fleas, with fattening them, and sneaking off to dandle babies, than with perils of the sea and the British.

Midday found us near enough Saint Thomas to make out the folds of the hills, the palms at the head of the deeply indented bays, the cane fields along her lower flanks, and here and there a white dot of house or a red speck of roof. Away to east of south spread the 40-mile width of the Culebra Passage, and far down its throat a pile of white marked the towering sails of a ship—probably a British man-o'-war on patrol. Tom Boyle studied her a long time through his spyglass, hooking an arm about one of the mainstays to brace himself against the steady lift and fall of the schooner to the long, unbroken swells. After a while he lowered the glass and handed it to me.

"Frigate," he said shortly. "British. No doubt she's seen us, but she'll not be knowin' if we're comin' on down toward her or headin' to pass back o' the island."

The spyglass framed a great black ship with yellow spars and the broad black-and-white checkerboard line along her strakes and over her gun ports that marked her British. I guessed her from her size to be rated at about fifty guns.

"Will she chase us, do you think?" I asked.

"Not her," he said. "She's on station, with her eye out for bigger game. What's more, she's too big for these waters. She'll signal ashore and send out a smaller patrol to investigate us—that is, if she's interested, which I doubt."

We continued the general direction of our course, bearing almost imperceptibly to the eastward. By early afternoon the Cockroaches and Dutchman's Cap, and Outer and Inner Brass Islands hid us from searching eyes upon the distant frigate's deck. Then we turned and bore eastward, parallel to Saint Thomas, in the general direction of Tortola—so far as any observer could tell, nothing more than a sloven island schooner bound for Road Town. My excitement mounted. Amidships the French refugees kept down under the open hatch. Babies and children were hushed. The rules of this game had been laid down and reiterated before ever we left Port-au-Prince.

A little past midafternoon we slid in between Congo and Lovango Cays and let go our anchor. Dead ahead, through the cleft between the high, black-pinnacled rocks, I could see the distant bulk of massive Mary's Point, the round Whistling Cay, and the brush-covered slopes of Great Thatch Island rising between us and Tortola.

Later, with Abe Meyers and Dick Collier I went ashore on Lovango. We scrambled through the brush and catch-and-keep to the top of its highest hill. Some 250 feet below, where the sheer black rocks fell away to a bed of jagged black needles at the base of the cliff, we could see the entire expanse of Pillsbury Sound to the southwest, and the larger, unnamed island-fringed sound that lay to the north between Congo Cay and Jost Van Dyke. Nowhere in all that expanse was there sign of a sail. Straight before me, so close that I could almost feel its cool shadow, rose the wooded mountain flank of Saint John. It rose almost sheer from the blue sea and a lazy creaming surf surged around its rocky points. If necessary, I thought as I looked at it, I could swim to it from here. And in fact it would be best for all on the *True Love* if I did.

From the top of Lovango I carefully studied Saint John. On what I could memorize now I would have to depend in finding my way among the many coves and islets along the shore. I could examine it closely over almost an entire quadrant, from the bleak, brush-covered Durloo Cays to the south, to the high-shouldered bluff of Mary's Point on the east. Abe Meyers gave me the names of the places. Swinging from Durloo's east, the first land on the island itself was the long sharp-tipped Hognest Point. Next, the deep indentation of Hognest Bay, with its strip of fine, white-coral sand. A ruined chimney, overgrown with vines, marked where a fine plantation house had once stood; and the ruins of a stout wind-mill tower stood high on the shoulder of the hill on the eastern side. Beyond was the blunt claw of Denis Point, marking the end of Camelberg Mountain's hunched shoulder, and then Denis Bay itself, and a succession of smaller points and indentations. I could see Trunk Bay and its cay scored with tiny, rocky coves, and the heights of Cinnamon Point, and the mouths of several small bays beyond—one of which was von Lund's Bay.

"Whoo-hooo!" little Dick Collier half hummed, half whistled. "Betcha there's good fishin' in them coves."

Abe Meyers smiled rather grimly. "Swimming too. Barracuda bigger than you are, Dickie!"

I looked at him sharply. "Barracuda?"

"Common down here," Abe said. "Run from 5 to 7 feet big. The niggers that dive for lobsters, pearls, and sponges tell me they do lots more damage than sharks. Teeth bigger'n a dog's and sharp as a cat's claws. And they'll tackle anything that moves. I've heard tales of men having their hands snapped off just trailing them in the water. Thinking of swimming, Ben?"

"Abe," I said, "this is no time to be joking. Why, you and I have been in over the *True Love's* side a dozen times, in Saint Thomas and Saint Bart's and 'Statia...."

"Sure," he said, "but that was in port, close to the shore, over a sand bottom. It's out here around the rocks and reefs and deep water you'll find the barracuda. And they don't have to take much of you, because, you see, once you start bleeding in the water, that draws the sharks. The barracuda begin it; the sharks finish you off."

"Well," I said, not entirely believing him, "it's a chance I may have to take."

"Let's settle accounts, then," he said. "Didn't you borrow a couple of quid from me in Jamaica?"

I grinned at him. If there had been any borrowing done, it had been the other way round. Abe was always short after three days in port. He owed everybody, even the cook.

"You'll have to claim it from my estate," I told him and we laughed.

When we returned to the *True Love* the sun had dropped behind Saint Thomas. The gut between Congo and Lovango was in deep shadow. Dark fingers were creeping out from the ridges on Saint John, too, bringing the mountain backbone and buttressing ribs into sharp relief. The slopes, green and wooded in the sunlight, were turning gray and purple. Here and there the blue smoke of a charcoal-burner's fire rose sharp and clear in the evening air. The waters were purple now and looked restless.

Tom Boyle greeted us. "See anythin'?"

"Nothing," I said. "Tom, why go on? Let me swim for it."

He shook his head. "Barracuda. It'd be murder."

He signaled forward. Silently the crew at the capstan walked up the anchor. With the anchor dripping but hanging free, ready to be dropped when it came time to send me off in the boat, we crept forward slowly under a single jib and reefed mainsail. As we cleared the Cays and nosed out into the Passage beyond Carvel Rock, some of the Frenchmen came on deck and joined the crew in searching the seas for the least sign of a sail. But the only movement anywhere seemed to be our own slow crawl eastward through the gloaming, the long gentle heave of the sea, and the slow, white bursting of the surf against the distant rocky headlands. Already I had tossed my scanty gear into the longboat. I had stepped its mast, for I judged it would be quicker to go in under sail than with the oars. She was a good-sized boat and would handle easily under tiller and canvas.

Twenty minutes' ghosting through the deepening dusk brought us across the Channel and past Johnson's Reef. Here we dipped a little south of east to pass Trunk Bay and Cinnamon Point. I could see the white beaches at the head of Trunk Bay. All eyes were on the shore now, watching. Presently Tom Boyle, standing by the starboard rail, pointed with his chin toward a deep, high-sided cove. "There ye are," he said. "Von Lund's Bay!"

"I don't see any light," I said.

"Can't tell. The house is well up—half a mile or so. Better draw up the boat and get ready. I'll fetch the schooner up into the wind and anchor."

I dragged the longboat up along the starboard flank. My sea chest and bag were already stowed away in her thwarts. The *True Love* began to swing, pointing her nose out toward the tip of Jost Van Dyke. Nobody was bothering to keep a lookout now. When, through the quiet dusk, came the deep thundering boom of a cannon, it lifted each one of us, I think, a good 6 inches from the deck!

Our heads jerked up. Our faces turned, east and north, in the direction of the sound. I could hear the scream of the round shot as it crossed our bows. From the sea rose a tower of water as the ball struck. I watched successive geysers spout as the shot skipped, then heard it crash in the bush against the flank of Cinnamon Point.

Slowly my eyes found the source. A small, ship-rigged vessel, black-hulled with the familiar black-and-white checkered pattern of the Royal Navy, was standing down toward us out of the Narrows between Mary's Point and Thatch Island through the narrow gut between Saint John and Whistling Cay. She must have been coming up the Narrows from Road Town, hugging the bluffs on the far side of Mary's Point so that she had been invisible. Nor could she have seen us until she came opposite that gut. Then the fact that our attention was centered ashore had worked in her favor. She had been able to come about on her heel and come down before the wind straight for us. If she had not fired that warning shot, we would still be unaware of her.

Even in the deepening dusk I saw that her gun ports were open and her guns run out, tampions removed. I could make out the blue glow of her battle lanterns and the red glow of the slow matches poised ready over the touchholes. Ten long 9s to a side she carried, and two 18-pound bow chasers on the fo'c'sle. The *True Love* was trapped against the shore of Cinnamon Point and a single broadside would lay her in splinters all across the bay.

EIGHT

I could feel my shuddering heart for at least three full beats. I could hear my half-sobbing sigh of despair among those around me: "Aaaah—no, God! No!"

Swiftly, calmly, Boyle sent the Frenchmen below. What did it matter, I thought with hopeless bitterness. They were doomed, and we with them, merely because a fool of a Ben Forbes had to be carried to Saint John in the hope of finding there his true love.

The enemy came on. I could see her name now in bold gilded letters: *Recruit*. I remembered then how Boyle had rubbed our own lettering with lampblack. He had taken every possible precaution—in vain.

The *Recruit* came down under shortened sail, picking her way slowly and carefully, for though she was small for a warship she was yet large for these tricky waters. In any case, there was no hurry. We could not escape her. If we so much as moved she had only to throw over her helm and mash us with a broadside.

About three-quarters of a mile of reef-filled waters separated us. Even coming slowly as she was, she would be alongside in less than an hour. At sea that would be more than ample time to cut and run. But here, caught standing as we were, as long as her attention was fixed upon us there was not the faintest chance. Even as we watched we could see her swing out her barge and lower away. A half score of sailors tumbled down her sides to man the oars, followed by as many armed marines and an officer in the all too familiar gold-laced blue coat and white breeches and cocked hat. He wore his sidearms. We could see that, even from this distance, and each sailor carried a cutlass at his belt. The marines, of course, had muskets. The barge would travel faster than her mother ship. That meant they would be boarding us in less than half an hour—twenty minutes, probably.

The thought stirred my numbed brain. Twenty minutes. It was a world of time! The whole engagement between the *Leopard* and the *Chesapeake* had scarcely lasted that long.

I examined the barge as she shoved off from the *Recruit*. She was bigger and broader than my long boat, clumsier, not as maneuverable. The attention of those on board the *Recruit* would be divided now—half on the barge, half on us. If it could be turned, all at once, to the barge, and the barge alone...? So little time was needed. Night was falling.

"Tom," I whispered urgently.

"Aarrh!" His reply was a growl of helpless rage. For Tom Boyle to be trapped and taken at the very outset of his great adventure, and with so many trusting souls aboard regarding him as a kind of god! If it was hard for me, it was even worse for him.

Quickly, concisely, I outlined my plan. With a slap on my back and an exclamation, "God's great white horse!" he accepted it. It was a slim chance but the only one that offered.

Orders were whispered and passed along. A man stepped to the signal halyards and fumbled with the lines, deliberately clumsy. By jigging the ensign up and down we were pretending fright, attempting to call attention to our British colors. The act might confuse them, make them hesitate to open fire.

Meantime, moving like shadows, some of the men edged in to be ready to get up the foresail and headsail and stand by to shake the reefs out of the mainsail. My plan was to distract attention by jumping over the rail into the longboat and cutting her adrift. Tom would run to the rail, cursing, ordering the deserter back. The barge might not catch me, but even if she did she'd only have one man in a longboat. The *True Love* could be off and away.

"They'll be firin' at ye," said Boyle, troubled.

"What of it?" I snapped. "Now!"

I began to run. Tom came after me. I leaped back, and he caught at me. I squirmed and twisted. Shouts rose from the crew who watched, grinning. On the barge and on the *Recruit*, they would dimly see and more clearly hear the sounds of struggle.

"Good luck, lad!" said Tom in my ear.

"God bless you, Tom!"

I jerked free and leapt for the rail. He made a lunge for me and caught me by the sleeve. Those of the crew who were not on other duties were running about heavily, stamping their feet.

I twisted free and slid down the painter to the waiting boat, cut the painter, and with an oar fended off and out from the schooner's side.

"All right, lad?" came Tom's low voice from above. And then he bawled deafeningly, "Come back, ye damned, bloody, mutinous barstid! Come back, I say, or I'll come down and get ye!"

I laughed exultantly. "To hell with ye!" I yelled. "Ye damned limesucker! Ye'll not catch me now! Devil take the lot o' ye!"

There was more angry shouting from the men, and Boyle's curses were new and remarkable, even for the Irish sea captain he was. The echoes of our voices bounced down off the hills. They'd all have to be deaf on the barge not to hear us.

On the longboat my sail was unfurled, the snaps fastened. I had only to haul on the halyards to run up the simple sloop rig. I cleated the lines and kicked over the tiller, swinging the little boat's head away from the schooner and across the bows of the barge.

In the barge they were caught aback. Even the men at the oars had forgotten to row. They sat in the broad thwarts with oars poised and dripping, half-turned, as one man, staring, watching the little drama unfold. The officer in the stern sheets seemed glued to his seat. Not a single marine had yet thought to level his musket.

At the same time, from the direction of the *Recruit*, I heard the clatter of running feet and excited voices raised in conflicting commands.

As my sail filled and my tiny craft heeled far over to starboard, I flung a quick glance back at the *True Love*. The confusion on her decks, the bellowing of orders and counterorders, the running hither and yon were superb. But so far not a hand had been laid to the lines. I trusted Boyle; the timing had to be perfect.

Then the men in the barge came abruptly to life. The officer bawled; the oars dropped. The heavy boat leaped forward, closing the gap between us slightly. I saw the officer tug at the tiller ropes. The boat's head swung, as if to intercept me. At that I laughed aloud. For if he had kept to his orders, which were undoubtedly to board the schooner, my plan would have been useless.

I was running more swiftly now. But so, too, was the barge. Her men were putting their backs into it. The distance between us was narrowing perceptibly. In a moment I would have to change course in order to escape cleanly.

But now I saw a second boat splash down from the *Recruit*. Plainly she intended to leave the barge to deal with me while the second boat went on to the schooner. This would not do.

With a wild, exultant shout I ran directly toward the barge with all the speed I could summon. I had no plan in mind as I did so, but even as I centered her over my bows, I knew what I would do. It was mad. But in that very madness lay its chance of success. Who would dream that a lone, desperately fleeing man in a longboat would turn and attack the heavy barge of a man-o'-war? The second boat would turn to her rescue.

My mind worked furiously. I could not ram the barge directly. She was too heavy and my longboat was too light. But I remembered my brush with the *Oriole*. The only difference between that and this was—I might be shot.

As the space between us narrowed, I could see the marines on the thwarts nervously fingering their weapons. It was too dark now to make out their features but their figures were plain enough. I crouched low along the gunwale and tensed.

Then still another thought struck me. With luck I might even be able to forestall their fire. There were not more than 50 yards between us now.

I sang out, "Ahoy, the barge!"

There was an instant's silence, broken only by the rushing gurgle of the water as I drove through it and the faint hum of the wind in the rigging.

Then, from the barge, came a startled voice, "Ahoy! Who's there? You, in the boat! Heave to or we'll fire."

I laughed quietly at that, for I could plainly see over the edge of the gunwale that they were not ready to fire. To be sure, one marine was holding his musket up at a high slope, as if ready to clap the butt to his shoulder. But I was willing to gamble that it was not yet cocked. If I knew aught of their ways and discipline, no British marine would be ready to fire until and unless he had the order to present and aim, or to fire at will.

It seemed to me I knew the voice of the answering hail. That puzzled me. But this was no time for random thoughts.

"Wait!" I yelled. "Wait now! Hold on!"

Incredibly, they did.

They merely sat as I came down upon them. In the dusk their figures loomed 10 feet tall. I saw the sheen of twilight on the sailors' tarred hats and the white crossed belts of the marines, even the gilt buttons and gold lace of the officer in the stern sheets. The oars hung outboard, instinctively feathered, poised for the back-sweep.

They may have been yelling, I don't know. I glimpsed the officer in the stern get to his feet as my prow knifed into their wake not 8 feet behind them. Some of the starboard oarsmen and marines were already ducking for my flying boom, which must pass over them not just once but twice—first from this angle, and then as I swept forward alongside.

I flung the tiller over and braced my feet against it while with my hands I paid out the sheet and let the boom swing wide. The little longboat reared under me like a frightened animal and spun to take her new course. It seemed to take forever, but at last I felt her swing around before the wind. I took my foot from the tiller bar and let the rudder, of itself, swing back amidships. Righted, my little boat went scudding in a string-straight line toward the outthrust oars. My boom swung wide, my sail filled. I took a quick turn of the cleat with the bight of the sheets, and scrambled to brace myself and also to prepare to repel boarders with my fists.

As the boom swung, the spar thudded sharply against the officer of the barge. He went over backwards, landing in the laps of the marines and sailors of the first thwart—a most undignified position for an officer of His Majesty's fleet. But he bounced up as the boom passed over him. For the space of three ticks of a turnip we stood face to face, not 5 feet apart.

I heard him clearly. "Forbes! Great God! Ben Forbes!"

It was John Meade.

My move was entirely instinctive. I seized my stout tiller bar, snatching it from its socket, and lashed out with it.

His arm flung up and I have no doubt it saved him a broken skull. I heard my weapon thud against his elbow and the crack of bone. He staggered and grunted. His gold-laced cocked hat went spinning away. His arms flailed in the effort to help him regain his balance. Then almost slowly he went over the side, arms and legs widespread, to land with a fine splash in the now inky waters of the Caribbean.

Without a hand at her tiller or her rudder, my longboat surged forward. The long sweeps of the barge crunched and snapped under her keel. Their men were knocked sprawling. My sail, filled with wind, drew the scraping boom after it along the full length of the barge, tumbling the rest of the men. I stood upright. The interior of the barge was a thrashing tangle of arms, legs, and muskets. One musket went off with a thundering bang, but I doubt it was aimed at me; I never heard the whine of the ball.

In the next moment my longboat was past and beyond the barge and was beginning to yaw. Quickly I fitted the tiller bar back into its socket. I fetched my little craft back before the wind, running for dear life.

Far off, toward Whistling Cay, eyes on board the *Recruit* had evidently been watching. For now, as I sprinted clear and raced toward the shelter of Cinnamon Point, a gun boomed aboard the ship—then another—and a third. But they might as well have been throwing stones at a mosquito.

I looked back at the *True Love* and shouted with joy. The schooner was already well across the channel with every stitch of canvas set, skittering toward the western tip of Jost Van Dyke. At that moment the *Recruit* became aware of her. Her yards slatted around and the warship's head began to swing in that direction. But the *True Love* had already passed beyond the effective angle of fire. The *Recruit* would have to come well up into the wind before she could again bring her broadside to bear. By that time the schooner would be well out of range. Apparently the warship's commander felt some indecision, for she seemed to hang, hesitating. Then white smoke bloomed at her bows, and I heard the thunder of her two 18-pound bow chasers. Spouts of water, rising like fountains from the dark surface of the sea, showed where one shot fell well astern of the schooner; and the other went far wide.

In my absorption with the action I forgot to watch the barge. The negligence cost me dear, for of a sudden a blast of shot plucked me from the stern thwart and hurled me forward, slamming me against the starboard inboard gunwale. Numbed by the shock of the blow, I lay between the thwarts, knowing I had been hit but feeling nothing. Two more shots sounded from astern. One ball punched a hole in the taut canvas of my sail; the other I heard thud on the larboard gunwale.

I struggled to my feet. With relief I found I was not disabled. As long as I could move, I thought, I'd better be at it.

There would be time enough later to find out where I had been hurt and how badly. Every second that I could work without pain was precious.

The tiller bar had gone crashing when I had. The mainsheet, loosed from my restraining grip, had let go by the run and had only been prevented from flying entirely free of the blocks by the Turk's-head stopper knot that someone had thoughtfully reeved at the end of the rope. The boom was swinging wide and the little boat yawed crazily, threatening to overset.

I found the tiller bar in the bottom of the boat and, stumbling aft to the stern thwart, fitted it into the rudderpost again. The numbness began to wear off. My back and left shoulder felt as if someone were holding a red-hot iron against them. But I could feel no ends of bone grating, and although it hurt horribly, I was able to move my shoulder and use my arm and hand. So no vital spot had been touched.

It was nearly dark now. The barge was a black hulk against the heaving waters which faintly mirrored the fading twilight of the sky. Either they had fished John Meade out of the sea or someone else had taken command. The rowers had resumed their places, and half the oars had been passed across and fitted to the larboard tholepins. My longboat lay some 50 yards to seaward, broadside to the wind, with its boom hanging outboard and the sail flapping loosely. The barge was floundering in my direction. A musket cracked. The searching ball splashed in the water behind me, flinging a spatter of drops over me. It was high time to be off.

Fumbling, I found the sheet and hauled in upon it, swinging the boom toward me. As the sail caught the wind, the little craft heeled and leapt ahead. I took a turn of the cleat and a firm grip on the tiller bar, holding the rudder steady against the kick of the water, and let her run.

I was headed straight for von Lund's Bay. Then the folly in such a course came to me. If I went ashore there, in sight of the barge, I might as well hang a sign on my back saying whither I was bound. I must not endanger the von Lunds—if they were there.

I fetched the tiller hard up and brought my boat around once more. The gray sail flapped once, then filled away before the wind. My bow lifted. Almost at once the stumbling barge seemed to fall away, dwindling. With only half their oars they could not hope to keep pace with me.

Beyond the barge, the *Recruit's* second boat was coming up rapidly to join the first. Behind it, strung out like knots on a string, were three more. The man-o'-war herself was sweeping out under a cloud of canvas in pursuit of the schooner.

But I had no fear for the *True Love*. I could see her. Boyle had somehow managed to sway up his foretopmast, even as he ran, and already the schooner was carrying tops and t'gan's'ls. Nothing could stop her now. She would run clear across the ocean—to France.

Laughing, I waved her godspeed, but the movement sent a stab of excruciating pain down my arm. My wound, wherever it might be, was rapidly stiffening. I had been bleeding heavily. Under me the thwart was wet and slippery with blood. And I was being chased by five British boats. As my course now lay, in a few moments I would pass beyond the jut of Cinnamon Point. After that I would be hidden from their sight if I stayed close in against the shore. But they were sure to see where I had gone, for the barges lay low upon the water while the sail of the longboat rose high and her hull was white.

I was growing dizzy and I knew I was weakening. I slid around the tip of Cinnamon Point and into Trunk Bay. All was dark and still here. Suddenly a black bulk loomed. Instinctively I flung the tiller over, wrenching open my wound as I did so. I slid past a tall black spire of rock, so close that I could almost have touched it. For a moment I was bewildered.

Then all at once I remembered Trunk Cay. This must be it. The rocky, brush-covered islet lay only about 100 yards from Saint John. I had seen it clearly from the top of Lovango—a tiny islet deeply chopped and chewed by coves and gullies.

I recalled the deep indentation I had marked on the southeast corner of the islet. It was made by four deep-cut bays that faced the beach on Saint John. Their surface was broken by a veritable forest of jagged, black, volcanic rocks that screened their mouths from a passing boat, and the tortuous channels between were brush-choked. The cove at the southeasternmost channel was ideal for my purpose, for behind its rocky screen it was larger than the others; with short, narrow arms not more than 15 or 20 feet deep and 6 or 8 feet across, it formed a sort of cross.

Urgency lent me speed and strength. I ghosted southward along the islet until I came to what seemed a likely gap in the rocks. I slid into it. There was no wind here. I stopped the boat by holding to an upthrust rock, released the halyards, and dragged down the big sail. The ungreased sheaves at the masthead squealed—shrilly enough, I thought, to wake the gulls and echo to Tortola. I held my breath, poised and listening.

But apart from the thudding of my heart, the only other sound was the lapping gurgle of the water.

More quietly, then, I released the snaps that held the stays to the ringbolts on the prow and gunwales. I eased down the mast upon the canvas of the sail. At some time, this night still or in the morning, they would come in search of me; they must not see my boat. Ignoring my hurts, I pulled out the tiller bar. Having no boat hook, I caught up an oar and proceeded to pole my way in.

Finding my way among those rocks in the Stygian dark was like groping blindfolded through a maze. After countless turns I came into what seemed to be slightly more open waters, with a small space on one side and a sheer rock wall rising on the other. Pushing the boat along beside the rock wall, I came to a narrow opening that seemed to drive straight back.

I knew then where I was. This was the northern arm of the cross that I had seen from the top of Lovango. Quickly I eased the boat into the crevice. Something brushed my cheek. I was so startled that I almost fell overboard. But when I lifted my hand I found that it was only a streamer of foliage. I pulled. A mass of brush and streamers came away in my hand, a tiny cascade of pebbles and small stones rattled down from high above and splashed into the water. In my ears they sounded like thunder. I stood listening, scarcely breathing. Boats as fully manned and oared as those that followed me were bound to make some sound. But I heard nothing. The stillness was absolute.

I worked swiftly then. Feeling about, I dragged down brush, branches, and leaves, covering the boat from stem to stern. At last I could do no more. I wormed down into the mess. If they discovered me now, I felt, nothing short of magic doors in the living rock, or some such strange contraption as Mr. Fulton's underwater torpedo, could save me.

I lay in my nest, listening. As I waited I found I had not dragged down brush alone. Ants and other creeping things were sharing my bed. Spiders? Scorpions? Centipedes?

I heard the first boat come creeping along the island shore just outside my screen of rocks. There had been no need for me to strain my ears. I heard the oars swing, creak, dip, men coughing or snuffling, wavelets slapping against the strakes. Several times I could hear the boat hook or a musket butt rattle on the floor boards.

"See anything ahead there, sergeant?" a voice called.

"Black as th' inside o' me mother's belly, sor!" was the response.

Someone snickered.

"Quiet!" snapped the first. "Hold close to the rocks. Keep a sharp eye out. He can't hide a boat."

"Aye, aye, sor!"

Having breathed in an ant, I almost strangled.

The boat was almost at the mouth of my bay. I heard the cautious slapping of a second, moving more rapidly. The first boat halted, and there was utter silence. Tensely I waited.

Suddenly its officer called sharply, "Who goes there?"

There was a second of abrupt silence from the newcomer. Then, "Tortola!" came the reply. "Smead here. Who's yon?"

So "Tortola" was the watchword! I thanked them for the information. It might come in handy before the night was done.

"Damn you, Smead! Quiet! How d'you know we're not the very man you're after? You'll have to learn to be more careful if you expect to last long in this navy!"

"Recognized your voice, sir—Mr. Hilary," was the bland reply. "Uh. . . ."

For a moment I thought Smead was going to ask how Hilary had known that *he* was not the one they were after, but discretion won, or perhaps Mr. Smead's sergeant had nudged him. Clearly Mr. Midshipman Smead commanded one boat and Fourth or Fifth Lieutenant Hilary the other. Hilary was too pompous to be a First, too patronizing to be other than one recently elevated from the reefers' ranks.

I heard Hilary say hastily, "See anything on the other side?"

"I'd a sung out if I had—sir!"

There was a long silence. I could imagine the sailors and marines struggling with their snickers. Mr. Hilary was not popular.

"Well," said Mr. Hilary at length, "where are the others?"

Before Smead could reply a third boat came up. The word "Tortola" was passed.

"Ahoy! Hilary?" I stiffened. That was John Meade's voice.

"Aye, sir, and Mr. Midshipman Smead," came the reply. "Glad to hear you, sir. Are you all right?"

"Wet," said Meade shortly. "And I'm afraid he's broken my arm. Blast that Forbes!"

"You know him, sir?" Hilary asked.

"Aye, I know him," Meade said grimly. "He was on the *Chesapeake* when I was on the *Leopard*."

"Oh?" Hilary sounded as though he would have liked a fuller explanation, but Meade did not oblige him. "Well, sir, that ought to make him easier to find if he slips through our fingers tonight. He can't get far. We can just go around and look in on all his friends."

"I wouldn't know who his friends might be down here," said Meade. "He's from Maryland. I can't understand why he was here at all—unless. . . ."

"Yes, sir?" Hilary prompted him.

"Oh, unless he was looking for me," replied Meade, astonishingly.

"Looking for you, sir?"

"Forget it!" said Meade. "We've better work to do than gabble like maiden aunts. I've sent Caswell and Pocock to patrol between Limetree and Cabrita Points. But I suspect he's gone to ground somewhere between here and Hognest Bay. Have you searched this cay, Hilary?"

"Yes, sir. Not a sign."

"Very well," said Meade. "We can take it he's past this point. Hilary, you go over to Lovango and Congo. Smead, follow a zigzag course to Jumbie Point and wait for me there. I'll search alongshore. Fire two guns if you stumble on him. This may take all night. If the *Recruit* is not back by noon tomorrow, we're to go to Saint Thomas and wait for her."

"Aye, aye, sir!"

I heard the boats move off. One. Two. I waited.

"All right, lads," said Meade to his own men. "We'll begin at the end of Trunk Bay Beach. Work in as close as possible and follow the shore south."

They pulled away. Not until I was certain they were gone did I crawl out and start scratching my bites.

I dared not stay here. My hiding place seemed all too insecure. My pursuers would return. I could not know how well I had disguised my boat, and the shining tropical night might pick me out as clearly even as full daylight. In my weakening state I had not a moment to lose in a dash to the main island where, unhampered by my boat, I would find a better place of concealment.

To rid the boat of all the brush and trash I had pulled down upon it was more difficult than I had imagined. In covering it, I had only had to pull the stuff down. Now I had to lift. It was a long, painful task. Many times I had to stop and rest. By the time it was done, the rising moon, brilliantly clear, had climbed well above the shoulder of Saint John. Restepping the mast, I could feel the fresh warm blood from my reopened wound trickling down my back. Then in my haste, I confused the stays and snapped them to the wrong ringbolts and had to untangle them and reset them properly. I tore my hands and nails wrestling with the wet, heavy canvas of the sail. By that time I doubted I would be strong or clear-headed enough to raise the sail once I brought the boat away from the islet.

I took up my oar and began to pole out. Now everything seemed to work against me. The Lord had taken me in easily enough, but He did not seem to want me to leave. The boat kept getting wedged between the rocks and obstinately refused to turn the corners. I was in despair when, at last, I found myself in open water. Moon and stars informed me that I had taken two hours for a distance I had covered in less than twenty minutes.

The moon was silver bright upon the water. I rocked in my little boat, struggling with an almost overwhelming desire to sink to rest, but studying the shore and the waters to the south, I could see no sign of my pursuers. Satisfied at last, I pushed out into Trunk Bay and with some difficulty hauled up the sail. Beating back around Cinnamon Point I had to tack several times. Then, standing in toward the shore, I could not decide which of the small bays and coves that lay before me was von Lund's, which I must avoid. But I had no time. Choosing one at random, I drove for it, ghosting along on the starboard tack.

The shore loomed. In another moment I must abandon my boat and swim for it. I remembered Abe Meyers' remarks about barracuda and sharks. Would they come so near to shore? I was bleeding freely. I eyed the dark water hesitantly as I drove in closer to the land. It might be better to go ashore boat and all than be slashed and picked to the bone by carrion fish.

But the decision was taken out of my hands. I heard a shot and jerked around in time to catch the flash of the second shot. It was distant—over across the Windward Channel, beyond Cinnamon Point, under Lovango. That meant Hilary. For an instant I hoped he had mistaken something else for his quarry. But I realized that I was brightly outlined in the moonlight. The two shots were repeated, a little nearer this time.

Without further hesitation I dropped over the side. I doubt that any man ever swam 100 yards more swiftly. At every moment I expected to feel the snap of sharp teeth. I drove through the water like a scared porpoise and stumbled with gasping sobs on the rocks in the low water. I felt my way among them, finding footing in the shallows. At last I had to rest, crouching low in the lapping shore sea. Before me was an overhanging bank, dripping with creepers and overgrown with tall ferns. It leveled off into a moldy jungle glade.

Slipping out of the water, I crept up under the bank, keeping as far as I could to the rocks to avoid leaving a trail. In the blackness under the overhanging bush, my frantic fingers found a dank crevice. I squeezed into it, dropped onto my stomach, and peered out through the vines and the wavering leaves that screened me.

In the path of the moon, the longboat yawed crazily, its sail flapping loosely. At that moment the barge came around the point. It bore down swiftly and pulled alongside my boat.

I heard a seaman exclaim: "Cor! Must o' bin a full-blooded barsturd!"

"Aye," said another. "But where'd 'e get ter, hoi?"

From the direction of the point came a hail from a second boat. "Got him?"

Hilary's voice replied. "Caswell? We've got his boat but not the man. From the look of it I'd say he'd been badly hit. There's blood over everything. He may be at the bottom of the sea. Where's Mr. Meade?"

"Back at Limetree." Caswell's boat was closer now. "His arm's troubling him. Sure our man didn't get ashore?"

"Not likely," Hilary returned. "He'd have opened the sea cocks and taken his gear if he'd been able to do that much."

Caswell's boat joined Hilary's. "Well, they'll be sending out a search party along shore tomorrow, just in case."

They talked a while, interminably dawdling, it seemed to me. But at last they moved off, one barge towing the empty longboat. I watched them over the moonlit waters until they disappeared around Cinnamon Point. I must not stay. Tomorrow there would be a search party. Tomorrow....

I dropped my head on my arms and knew no more that night.

NINE

When I opened my eyes it was broad day. Birds were twittering and from somewhere far off I could hear the mournful coo of doves. I was lying on my back, looking up into a deep blue sky in which floated white clouds that looked solid enough to lie upon. I became aware that I was lying upon something far less comfortable, a tangled and knotted mat of ferns and sea grape. What was more, I was entirely exposed to any eye that might chance to alight upon me from the hills and ridges roundabout. My senses were jarred alert. By the sun, it was midmorning. The British would have begun their search for me at dawn, surely. Even now they might be just around the point.

I started up, and at once felt as though I had been slashed across the back with a cat-o'-nine tails. My shirt, dried and stuck to my wound, had jerked loose with agonizing results. I sat quietly for some minutes. A small animal scampered away with what seemed to me the crashing tread of an elephant. For the space of an indrawn breath I had visions of an entire company of British marines closing in on me. With difficulty I got to my hands and knees and, so crouched, scuttled sideways like an ungainly crab into the underbrush and the shelter of the overhanging leaves which I had abandoned in my sleep.

I took stock of my surroundings. To my left I could see how the green hillside came tumbling down steeply to the narrow level of the little flat on which I crouched. To seaward the shoulder of that hill butted into the greenish water in a skitter of rocks. To my right lay the deep blue throat of a bay, perhaps 200 yards across. At its far end I could see a dazzling white beach backed by tall coconut palms. Its nearer end was hidden from my view by the shoulder of the hill and the shelf on which I stood. That beach, I somehow knew, formed a perfect crescent. So great was its attraction that I seemed to feel its call, its invitation: Here is peace, here is safety, here is rest; here are delights beyond imagining.

It was a strange, an eerie, almost a frightening feeling. But I could not resist it. I edged my way down from my shelf and climbed over the rocks. I found myself not on the beach itself but on what had been a sort of quay or landing stage, all overgrown with vines and brush. Gingerly—for it was full of sharp thorns—I pushed my way through the tangle and was confronted by the crumbling wall of a stone building. To my left wild jasmine draped and softened what remained of a tall stone chimney, and before me a gaping hole marked what had once been a window. Through it I could see that the roof had long since tumbled in and a few ponderous pieces of rusty machinery lay in the rubble. A mill, it had been—probably for grinding sugar cane. But it offered no hiding place.

I moved around the building. At the corner I paused. I was well hidden there by the brush, the ruined walls on two sides, and a spreading breadfruit tree. Brush covered the "made" ground between the old mill and the outer wall of the quay. Two great tamarinds spread an umbrella of shade and partially blocked my view.

Far out toward the mouth of the bay, two white birds that might have been pelicans bobbed on the wavelets. I could see no other sign of life.

Cautiously I moved out from under the breadfruit tree and, passing between the tamarinds, came almost to the edge of the quay's wall. There I again paused, scanning the far side of the bay for any sign of a searching party.

I heard a light splash. It could have been the rippling flutter of a shoal of minnows breaking water in flight from my shadow, or a startled water bird. It came from the beach. I turned toward it quickly, half prepared to drop down out of sight—and promptly froze.

A naked woman was on the beach, knee deep in the limpid water. Her sun-bronzed body, between sea, sand, and sky, was more beautiful than anything I had seen, or could have hoped to see, in my life. Her golden hair was caught up in little girl's pigtails. I could see the little ribbons by which they were tied to the sculptured head. Half-turned in my direction, she moved into the crystal sea, her long shapely legs and rounded hips seeming to dance and waver slightly, undulating, as the water eddied and shimmered around her. Her hands and arms were lifted, palms daintily turned out, elbows high, raising her young breasts. She plunged. The water, clear and transparent as the air I scarcely breathed, closed over her. She was swimming in my direction.

I stood rooted, robbed of speech or movement.

She came on, scarcely stirring the loving sea, a goddess serenely bathing as in the waters of a private shrine. I made some sound, for the next moment she saw me. Startled, she floated, instinctively crossing her left hand to her right shoulder and raising her right, so that wrist and arm and hand covered her breasts. Her gaze was locked with mine, and I could have sworn that I saw myself in her wide eyes as in a mirror—bedraggled, blood-stained, dirty, stubbled.

I prayed to God to blot me forever from the earth. "Kirstie!" I groaned.

Her face changed. "Benje?" she cried. Then, "Benje! Oh! Wait! Please—there wait!"

She turned away abruptly and struck out, swimming with long swift strokes to the part of the beach where I had first seen her entering the water. I sank down in the brush with my head in my hands. All was confusion within me—the incredible vision, the miracle of having found her—and desolation, anguish. A torment. Just so, all unknowing, had I shamed Nancy. I saw the lecherous smiles of my neighbors of the

Eastern Shore, heard the sniggering. Kirstie doomed, like Nancy. Once again I had fouled purity by innocently gazing upon it. I had despoiled a shrine with my eyes. I was accursed.

"Wait!" she had said. How could I wait for the evil that must come? Yet I was powerless to move. "Wait!" In darkness of soul, in sick despair, I must wait.

I heard her coming and rose. She wore a loose gown of white textured silk stuff. Her hair, shaken out, flowed and rippled in the sunlight. Her hands were outstretched, her great blue eyes welcoming. A joyous little smile curved her mouth. I stared stupidly. It was all there, exactly as I had dreamed it long ago—the golden girl, the tall palms, the blue bay, the crescent white beach. Paradise!

The next moment she was in my arms.

After a while I said, firmly, "Now I must go."

She stirred and looked up at me, but she did not appear to have heard me. "You smell of the woods and the sea," she said dreamily. "And you have grown. Did you know?" Her hand caressed my unshaven cheek, and she gave a delicious little laugh. "It will be a fine beard. Even Papa will admire it."

"Dear heart," I said. "Listen. There is danger. In many ways I am a danger to you. I must go. At once."

"I had begun to be afraid," she said, "it has been so long. But I knew you would come. I knew it!"

How could I tear myself from this loveliness and from the delight that surged in me at the touch of her hand, the sweet scent of her hair, the marvel of the exquisite body in my arms that had so long been empty?

I stared about wildly, and suddenly saw—my tormenters and my salvation. Far away, at the tip of Cinnamon Point, high above the water's edge, a little string of red dots stood out clearly, pinpointed against the dark green foliage. Even as I saw them, several of the dots detached themselves and dropped down through the brush to the rocky shore. They began to move back methodically, covering the space between their comrades above and the very end of the Point.

They would comb the shoreline thoroughly, with typical British military precision. At that rate it would take them a long time. But there might be other search parties, nearer, hidden from me.

Kirstie had turned to follow my concentrated gaze. "British," she said, and with sudden comprehension looked from them to me.

I said urgently, "Forgive me. I did not mean to come here,

to bring trouble upon you. Later—if I escape them.... But now there is no time."

But she had seen my state. "You are hurt!"

"Kirstie," I said desperately, "for yourself, for your father, I must go."

I turned blindly to run—where, I did not know—but stumbled and fell upon one knee. I struggled to rise but my limbs were leaden. I was crawling, shaking the dizziness from my head.

Kirstie's arm raised me. I heard her voice as I moved helplessly under her guidance. She was scolding me in a foreign tongue. A goddess, scolding—in Danish. I began to laugh.

"There," she said. "That is better."

"Kirstie," I protested, "think of your father, if not of yourself."

"But yes," she said. "He will be so pleased. Come. It is not much more to go."

We were following a path that gradually climbed. It opened suddenly upon a compound of beaten earth shaded by spreading baobab, silk, cotton, banyan, and mango trees. In the center, half-screened by a row of shiny-leaved lime trees, stood a large, low plantation house. As I stumbled up the steps to the broad veranda, a lean figure in a fine loose shirt and white trousers rose from a hammock, leaving it indolently swinging behind him. Even in my pain and exhaustion, I observed that the Baron von Lund looked a different man here. He seemed younger, almost boyish. His bearing had been formal, even slightly formidable. Now he revealed a long-limbed, easy grace. I saw for the first time how much he resembled his daughter.

With mild interest, but without recognition, he regarded the ragged waif his daughter had brought him.

"Papa," said Kirstie reproachfully, "you do not know him? How is it possible!"

"Good heavens!" he exclaimed. "It is young Forbes!" Smiling and as if greeting a fine gentleman, a long-awaited guest, he shook my hand warmly.

"Sir," I protested, "it is all wrong. You do not understand. I tried not to come. I should not be here. I saw...." I must get it over with and be turned away, a despicable creature, an outcast. "I saw Kirstie...."

But I could not say it, and I knew from my flooding warmth that I was crimson.

He gave me a fleetingly puzzled glance. But Kirstie was speaking to him in their own tongue.

"So!" he said to me. "It was you, then, in the little boat."

"You saw?" I asked, surprised.

He gestured, and I understood. On the veranda, which ran all around the building, a man, himself in shadow and invisible from far, could look out through the screen of lime trees as through a green slot down to the sandy strip of beach and the deep bay, out to the blue ocean and the hazy fringe of islands as far as the tiny white beaches of Jost Van Dyke. No vessel could cross that sound or maneuver in those waters without being seen from here.

"I watched," said the Baron, "while it was yet light. Later we heard the shooting. Was it Captain Boyle in the schooner? Did he escape?"

"Yes," I said. "We had French refugees on board from Saint Domingue. That was why we had to do it the way we did."

I could not be certain of the Baron's political bent. Now that the Danish islanders were British by capture, he might be loyal, or perhaps honor-bound, to them. It was even possible that what I, as an American, conceived to be a misfortune of war might be good fortune to the inhabitants of a small island far from a weak mother country and rejected by the neutral United States. No matter. Surely the Baron would not wish to jeopardize himself, his daughter, and his island home by sheltering Ben Forbes!

I began to tell him so.

He listened with a polite, rather absent, courtesy.

"My bedroom?" Kirstie said to him.

"Hmm!" The Baron was quizzical. "It might not be such a bad plan. Sometimes these English—well—and sometimes, not! It will have to be the *orkanshullet*."

They exchanged some look of communication. Then without further ado they led me, one on each side—supported and propelled me, rather—into the house and across a long, high-ceilinged room that stretched its full width. It had tall, jalousied windows and furniture of carved and inlaid woods with silk and damask coverings. Its far wall was lined with bookshelves and it was here they brought me. The Baron reached for a book, and for a bewildered moment I thought he intended to show me his library. But the volume did not come away in his grasp. Instead, an entire section of the shelves moved forward smoothly on rollers and swung out like a door, revealing a closetlike opening and a flight of stairs leading down into blackness.

From a box nailed to the wall near the head of the stairs,

Kirstie took out a candle, lighting it from a snaphance that hung from a string beside it. The Baron, carefully but urgently, led me down into a stone-lined room, actually a cellar.

"Hurry, Papa," said Kirstie, who had preceded us with the flickering light. He nodded and left us.

"*Orkanshullet*," Kirstie explained, holding the candle high. "That is Danish for the hurricane hole. We have sometimes bad hurricanes, so we have hurricane cellars for safety. It was Papa's idea to build the bookshelves to cover the opening. There were too many doors in this wall, he said; it spoiled the look of the room. We thought it a great joke when it was done, and I often played here. But now it is very useful, no?"

"Yes," I agreed. "But Kirstie, if all have hurricane cellars, won't they look for yours and be suspicious if they do not find one?"

She did not reply but quickly showed me my refuge. It was a room some 20 feet square with shelves at both ends on which were neatly arranged supplies to outlast any storm: canisters and jars of food, casks of wine and water, blankets, and books. Couches ranged along each side, and there were canvas-bundled hammocks to accommodate many people if need be. There were no windows, of course, and no natural light. Ventilation, Kirstie showed me, was provided by rectangular vents in the brick columns. Their openings, she said, were in the baseboard of the room above, well concealed.

"There, you see?" she said. "You will be quite comfortable, no? In fact, you would be able to stay here a long time if necessary and no one would ever know."

There was no help for it, then, whatever the consequences. "I am your prisoner," I said.

She was suddenly grave. "Never that, Benje! You are free to follow your heart."

I had hurt her—why, I could not, dared not, understand. "My heart?" I said dazedly.

"But you are wounded and very tired," she said with sudden concern. She set the candle in a wall sconce. "I will return to attend you, if there is time. When they come you will hear them, and then you must snuff out the candle quickly. They may smell the tallow smoke."

She was gone. I sank down on a couch, overwhelmed by weariness and with pain that was more than physical. I was hungry, yet the thought of food sickened me. I sat hopelessly in the cool gloom, staring at the candle, remembering the candle I had carried to Nancy in the house on Poplar Island. I saw the bed, and the deathlike face, and the ripe young body.

But now the hair that streamed over the pillow was golden. I felt cold.

There was a light tap of heels in the room above. A glimmer of light came down the stairs, to be closed off with the clicking of the secret door. "Benje, can you help me?"

The brief but vivid nightmare was blotted out. Kirstie was on the stairs, struggling with a large pitcher of hot water and, under her arm, a rolled bundle. I came to her aid. "Sshh!" she warned me, and whispered, "They are near. Papa is watching. We must hurry."

She brought a basin from some hiding place, poured water into it, and opened her bundle. Wetting cloths with warm water, she worked deftly and with a light touch, soaking the dried blood that caked my back and pulling my shirt from it. She cleaned and bound the wound, describing it to me. The ball had caught me a little above the small of my back and striking like a glancing fist had ranged upward, ripping a ragged, uneven cut. It had done no serious damage, not touching bone, but Kirstie clucked and crooned over me so that I had to laugh at her.

When she had done, I got into the fresh shirt she had brought me. It was a snug fit and Kirstie smothered giggles as one button popped. "Oh dear. You are so much more across the shoulders than Papa. We must find you clothes. But now you must eat something."

She gave me biscuits and a curious gourd bowl filled with a mixture of wine and water. I found myself wholesomely hungry and thirsty.

Suddenly she snuffed the candle. "They are here," she whispered. In the blackness she sat beside me on the couch.

I heard from above the scrape of feet upon the steps of the house, the heavy tread of several men on the veranda, the thud of musket butts as they came to a halt. Every sound came clearly through the vents.

"Good morning, gentlemen," I heard the Baron, and was faintly surprised. In the blackness of the cellar I had forgotten that it was still morning above.

"Good morning, Baron von Lund." I started. John Meade's voice sounded as if it were in my ear. Kirstie's hand stole softly into mine and I was still.

"There is something you wish?" said the Baron pleasantly.

"You have a visitor, sir?" It was as much a statement as a question.

"A visitor?" The Baron's tone was admirably puzzled. "But, of course. Yourself, Lieutenant."

"No other?" Meade's voice was suspicious.

The Baron either shook his head or looked blank, for Meade continued. "Have you been expecting visitors, Baron?"

"No-o-o," said the Baron slowly.

"No?" said Meade sharply. "There was a schooner in the bay last night. Who was she? What was her business here?"

"Schooner? In the bay?"

"Come, sir. Surely you heard the shooting!" snapped Meade with some asperity.

"Your pardon, Lieutenant," said the Baron coldly. "I am a Dane. I am an enemy alien in my own land. You will excuse me if I see nothing—know nothing—of what does not concern me."

"You were not expecting her, then?" Meade persisted.

"No."

"But they were preparing to come ashore, obviously."

"I know nothing of it."

"How do you explain this, then?" Meade demanded.

There was a long silence. I could feel Kirstie's curiosity and apprehension mount along with my own.

At last the Baron said, "Yes, that is the name of this place —Calabasboom—and the address. It is my daughter's handwriting."

"Your daughter?" Meade exclaimed. "You have a daughter?"

"Yes," said the Baron. "Is that so strange?"

There was a curious pause. Then the Baron asked, "How did you come by this?"

"It was in his chest!" Meade seemed unaccountably excited.

"His chest? Whose? You speak in riddles, sir."

"Ben Forbes's chest!"

"Forbes?" Clearly the Baron refused to be startled.

"Sir, do you know a Ben Forbes?" Meade demanded.

"But of course."

I held my breath at the admission but realized in an instant the Baron's mind was far ahead of my own. In the face of that damning bit of evidence which they had found when they searched the longboat and my gear, he could not deny that he knew me.

He went on, casually. "He is an American. My daughter and I met him in Baltimore and again at Washington, and at Norfolk in the naval hospital. He had been wounded on board the *Chesapeake,* in an encounter with one of your own ships, I believe."

"Yes, the *Leopard*. I was there," Meade remarked.

"So!" I would not have wished to be in Meade's shoes at that moment. "I do not understand you English. You were not at war with Denmark, yet you attacked Copenhagen. You are not at war with the United States, yet you attacked one of her warships. In the same manner you appear to be waging war against this Ben Forbes. Why?"

"He was trying to come ashore here last night," Meade said defensively.

"And what of that? Is it a crime—for a neutral to pay a visit?"

"Oh! You admit it?" said Meade triumphantly.

"I admit that when we last saw Mr. Forbes we invited him to visit us any time he might be in these waters," the Baron replied. "If he was here, I doubt not that he attempted to do so. I see nothing suspicious in that."

"Perhaps not. But there were certain highly suspicious movements in connection with the attempt. The schooner did not wait for our boarding party. . . ."

"My friend," said the Baron almost kindly, "if you were an American captain I do not think you would welcome a British boarding party. Consider the English taste for American seamen."

There was another silence marked by a clearing of throats. My pursuers were plainly uncomfortable.

The Baron said sharply, "But what has happened to my would-be guest?"

"Sir," said Meade, "there was a scuffle. . . ."

"Yes, I see!" I could picture Meade's arm in a sling.

"My men fired on him," Meade continued, "and—well, sir, if he was only bent on a social call he got more than he bargained for. We found his boat. There was blood in it. And we have found no sign of his having come ashore. If he is not here, I am afraid that he is dead."

When the Baron spoke again, after a long moment of silence, he sounded so shocked that I felt shocked myself.

"Oh, no! Dead? My dear man, you don't mean that!"

"Yes, sir!" Meade's voice crisp, defiant.

"Ach!" the Baron exclaimed. "I am sorry. Kirstie—that is my daughter, sir—she will be sorry, too. Very sorry, I fear. You see, she was very fond of him."

"Your daughter—fond of him! Oh, now, damme, that is awkward!" Astonishingly, Meade seemed genuinely distressed. "It would have been the solution. So much better than this."

"Eh? What do you mean?" The Baron was startled.

Kirstie's lips were close to my ear. "What does he mean, Benje?"

"I don't know," I whispered to her, completely mystified.

"Nothing, sir," Meade was saying. "You see, I knew him too. If only.... Well, it doesn't really matter now, does it?"

"It does not matter?" said the Baron with cold anger. "It does not matter that a young man is dead?"

There was another silence. Then Meade spoke again, formally. "I shall have to search the house, Baron. You'll forgive me, I hope. I have my orders."

"I cannot stop you, Lieutenant," replied the Baron with frosty indifference.

We heard them tramping about overhead. Kirstie's hand grew hot in mine. I was gripping it tightly. After a time the footsteps passed out onto the veranda again and down the stairs. Kirstie gave a long sigh of released tension.

"Shall we go up now?" I whispered.

"Wait. Papa will let us know."

Her taut body relaxed. My arm was about her waist, her head lay on my shoulder. A great peace descended upon me. Wordlessly, blissfully, we waited.

TEN

Sunlit days and starry nights followed one upon the other. Calabasboom seemed a perfect retreat, secluded and remote. The plantation house was built of a sort of dun-yellow brick made of native tabby that blended well with the surrounding hills. The usual red tile of the roof had been thatched over thickly with coconut palms, which made it even more a part of the surrounding country. Ancient trees reached out over it and the rest of the compound, spreading a leafy green umbrella over all and keeping it cool even on the hottest days. Low buildings were scattered about the main house—workshop, storehouses, a row of slaves' quarters, the inevitable picturesque windmill in a circular stone tower, a stable, an overseer's house, a separate kitchen. They formed a complete little community sufficient unto itself.

Near the steps of the main house a tall white flagpole soared high above the sheltering trees. If there had been a flag there, it would have marked the spot plainly from the bay.

"We cannot fly the Danebrog," Kirstie explained to me, "so long as the English hold the island, and Papa refuses to raise the British flag."

I wondered then if the Baron might perhaps be engaging

in secret activities against the British. He was a gracious host but, it seemed to me, an unaccountably careless parent. Sometimes he was gone for several days at a time, leaving Kirstie alone with me. I could not but recall my mother's fear for Nancy when John Meade was at Holly Hall. And although the Baron gave every appearance of pleasurable indolence, there were nights when, from my great Danish four-poster bed, I could see through my jalousied window a late-shining light cast upon the trees from his bedroom.

But Kirstie was untroubled. She did not even appear to notice how I kept myself a little apart from her.

For I was restless and uneasy, like a hunted animal that sniffs the air, all senses alert, for danger. I was alarmed when the Baron went off and returned with clothes for me. He could not have procured them without having brought others into the secret that he had a guest.

Then I saw myself a fool. There was no secret, could not be. Saint John was a small island. I had no doubt that the Baron's slaves and house servants had long since passed the word, if it had not got around by other means. There could scarcely be a man, woman, or child on this island—and perhaps on neighboring Saint Thomas as well—who did not know that Ben Forbes, an American sought by the British, was to be found under the roof of the Baron von Lund's plantation house.

That much, surely, they would know—and how much more? I wondered. The thought sickened me. It seemed to me suddenly that there were eyes everywhere and evil tongues. There could be no escape from Saint John or from the consequences of my first meeting with Kirstie.

A sense of impending doom hung over me.

I'm afraid I was a poor guest, moody and irritable. I kept for the most part close to the house. Several times a day, however, an explosive force within me drove me down to the bay. But there was nothing to be seen. Sometimes Kirstie was on the path to meet me when I came back.

From the disused quay to the plantation house was a longer distance than I realized that first day. The once confused pattern of the landscape resolved itself into groves of coconut and banana palms, stands of limes and mango trees, papayas, star apples, sapodillas, sweetsop and soursop, alligator pears, and other exotic fruits in lush profusion. Here and there were small fields of pineapples and leafy-topped yams and some struggling corn.

"It is not much here," Kirstie told me. "Over on the Coral

Bay side, on the old Carolina plantation, is where we grow the cane. Here we have only what we use for ourselves, and a little more that we send to the market in Saint Thomas. Once all this was sugar cane—all across the bottom and halfway up the hills on each side. But after the black rebellion it went back again to the wild, and we have only reclaimed this much."

"The rebellion?" I asked.

"That was almost a hundred years ago," she said. "There is nothing now to fear." She gave me a searching look. "Nothing, Benje."

Disquieted, I examined a great tree beside the path. It had a thick, gnarled, gray trunk and a leafy head that was like a huge burst of green smoke shot with gray branches and the leathery brown undersides of the leaves. It was hung with a curious fruit which grew singly, close to the trunk and branches, like green, perfectly round cannon balls.

"That is our calabasboom," said Kirstie. "It is the biggest calabash tree in all these islands, and I think the oldest. See how big are the calabashes."

"Can you eat them?" I asked.

"No. They are nothing inside, only mushy and seeds. We ' scoop them out and when they are dried we use the shells for many things. Dishes and cups and bowls and dippers. Even cooking pots. Nature is good. She is a woman—useful and honest and giving."

"Kirstie," I said teasingly, "do you describe yourself?"

She laughed. "Do you find me so?"

I looked at her and my breath caught. I could hear the pounding of my heart.

From above, from the house, came the sound of the dinner gong, played on brass sugar molds by a dignified, white-coated, barefooted servitor.

"Come," said Kirstie. "We are late."

And so the dazzling moment passed, leaving me agitated by its intensity. How could I live in her presence without breaking under my forced restraint and silence? As my wound healed, my darkness of soul seemed to increase. It was as though I had a second, secret wound, steadily deepening, bleeding.

Kirstie said I was growing pale and would become ill. Determinedly, serene in her ignorance and innocence, she made me go with her to explore the little bays and beaches and to picnic in the glades and glens. She showed me how her father's holdings spread up and over the crest of the ridge and tumbled

221

down on the other side to the broad cane fields above Coral
Bay. Together we poked through the ruins of old plantation
houses that had dotted the island before the rising almost a
hundred years before, and she told me stories of those times.
We fished and rode and hunted up to the very tops of the
mountains in the center of the island, and there were times
when I almost forgot Nancy Savage—Nancy waiting in the
tomb of Holly Hall.

One afternoon we wandered over the ridge and past the
wide beach at Trunk Bay and came upon the tiny white strip of
coral sand that fringed the sheltered crescent of Dennis Bay.
The little beach here is warm and intimate, not more than 100
yards at the utmost from tip to tip. At its widest it is some 30
feet from the water's edge, where the little waves wash up
with a whispering swish upon the sand to the tangled, shading
thicket of sea grape that bounds it. On the one hand a low
headland shelters it from the wind; on the other it runs out to
a tumble of rocks. Between these points the bay is fairly deep
and crystal clear, with a rocky bottom out beyond the sand in
three or four fathoms. Over the rocks the water shades from
light to emerald green, and out beyond, where the sound
stretches away to Jost Van Dyke, it turns a deep ultramarine
blue. The sun beats upon the white sand but under the shade
of the sea grapes all is cool and still.

We came down and across the leafy flat at the head of the
cove, and dropped to the soft-packed sand under the overhanging canopy of sea grape. We sat in silence, taking in the in-
comparable beauty of the scene. Soon we would make our way
back to Calabasboom along the shore.

I said without thinking, "I dreamed it, Kirstie, long before
I came here. Perhaps I am dreaming still."

She was scooping and piling sand, absorbed, like a little
girl. "What did you dream, Benje?"

"The palms, the beach, and you. Not here, but von Lund's
Bay. I dreamed our meeting, Kirstie."

She glanced at me. "All of it?" She was quite pink.

"No, no," I said hurriedly. "Not—not the beginning."

"Benje," she said shyly, her eyes cast down on her sand
castle, "is it that I was not—nice? Did you find me ugly?"

"Kirstie!" My voice was almost a shout of shocked indignation. "How can you say such a thing! You are more beautiful
than any woman that ever lived! You are ... !"

Her eyes were looking into mine and their sweetness robbed
me of speech. My arms went out and I crushed her to me. Our
lips met, and it was as if the soft blue sea had come up to take

222

us, to cradle and rock us in a misty warmth, safe from black storms far above, safe forever in joy unutterable.

She stirred and gently pushed me away. Her eyes were starry, both laughing and tearful. "There," she said as upon another occasion, but breathlessly now. "That is better."

In a tumult of emotions I cried out, "Ah, no! Kirstie, forgive me. It is wrong."

She said, "I knew it would be so—like this—from the first, when I looked down from the big black schooner in the fog and saw you on your little boat, staring up at me, with your mouth open, angry and surprised. You were funny, Benje, but I knew it then. See, my dear one, you have broken the sand house I was building for us. But that is not so wrong because we shall build another, a better one, together. No? Now tell me, where is the wrong?"

And so I told her again of the shipwreck and the duels, but this time without bravado, and I did not spare myself but put Nancy into the story where she belonged, from the kiss in the garden on the night of her party to her nakedness on Poplar Island which had caused three of the four duels.

A little sound came from Kirstie. She was laughing! At me? I stared at her incredulously.

"I am so sorry, Benje," she said at last, "but they are very funny in your home place with codes of honor and false pride. A young man, quite by accident, sees a young woman un-clothed. . . . Oh!" She looked at me, her eyes very wide. "You saw me and you were afraid, and ashamed too, because of the shameful thing they made of it there. Poor Benje. But here, you see, it is not terrible. It was an agreeable accident, no? And as for me, I am very happy to be beautiful for you."

I reached for her, and punished her forwardness with kisses until she begged me to give her space to breathe. With flutter-ing fingers she struggled in vain to tuck back loosened curls, and I could not take my eyes from her. The slightest of her movements was a delight, an enchantment.

"She was very pretty, the little red-haired Nancy," said Kirstie. "She will be lovely one day. Benje, I asked once after her and you became strange—do you remember? It was in Washington at Mr. Barlow's."

"Dear heart," I said, suddenly saddened, "I remember."

"So there is more," she said gravely. "There is real trouble."

I told her then, dully, of the Colonel's grim solace of drink and violence, the desolation of Holly Hall, and of Nancy's fate, and how only I could deliver her, if she would let me.

Kirstie gave a little shiver. She rose and stepped out from

our darkening shade into the rays of the declining sun. Her loose classic dress—sea green, it was—flowed with her body. Her hair seemed to carry a nimbus.

"Do you love her?" she asked.

"Nancy?" I was startled at the question, which seemed to me irrelevant. "No!" I said. "It is you I love, Kirstie. You know it; you have always known it. For Nancy, I feel only pity."

She nodded. "It must be hard for a very proud lady to know herself pitied." Sighing, she said, "We must go home now, Benje."

We walked back silently along the shore, my arm around her waist. I was lightened. No longer did I carry the guilt and shame with which I had tainted the sweet-scented air. The ache in my heart was a clean, honest sorrow.

We came to our beach of von Lund's Bay, and paused where I had seen my beloved, a sea-nymph happy to be beautiful for the man she loved—although how she could love Ben Forbes, I could not understand. I felt humble.

"Out there it was, where you last saw Captain Boyle, Benje?" she remarked.

"Running like a deer for the western tip of the island," I told her, "and the open ocean. And from what Lieutenant Meade said to your father, he gained it with room to spare."

"How long do you think it will be?" she asked. "Before he comes back again, I mean."

I frowned thoughtfully. "He will need four weeks to go, at least, and four more to return. And he will probably be another four in port, collecting his payment from his passengers, and then he will be trying to find a cargo for the return voyage. With luck, we may have—say, four months."

"Four! And we are already ending the second."

I looked down into her lovely troubled face and the ache within me became an agony. "I will stay, Kirstie. I cannot go, not now. We will be married here, at once. To leave you would be like dying. You are my life!"

We clung together and her face was wet with tears. Kirstie crying! I could not bear it. I held her close, murmuring into her ears, kissing her hair and her eyes, comforting her and myself as well.

Then she shook herself free and with a laugh that was part sob, she said, "Now you see how bad I am. I laugh when I should not, and I cry when it is very wrong. You will go, my Benje. You must go, because we could never be happy. She would haunt us. She would give us no peace, waiting there, moldering in that dreadful house. We shall be happy while we can. And then—why, then we will pray that God will bring us together in His own good time."

"Ah, Kirstie," I groaned, "if I must marry her, I—I will hate her!"

She put her finger on my lips. "No. You are kind and good. You will not hate her, my Benje."

Slowly, bound together in our love and pain, we went back to the house.

The next morning I determined to make a clean breast of it to the Baron. He was sitting on the veranda looking out at the bay through a spyglass. When I began, hesitantly, he cut me short. "Kirstie has told me," he said. "Now I will have some peace."

Bewildered, I said, "Sir, I do not understand."

"Ben," he explained, "it is better for a woman to know that the man she loves is well and truly in love with her—far better than to fear that he is not. I have seen my Kirstie's suffering and grieved for her. I told her that if a man locks himself away, he may perhaps have nothing within worth the trouble of unlocking. But this she would not believe of you, and she was right. Always she is right, that little one. As her husband you will sometimes find it a trial. But I hope she will be wise enough to be wrong, now and then."

"Her husband?" I faltered. "But sir, I must go back and perhaps marry the other."

He cocked a thoughtful eye at me. "Perhaps," he said. "But it has been more than a year since you left that other—Mistress Savage, is it? I recall her well. So concerned she was for the money value of the slave that was killed on your boat. Such a furious young lady. I dare to hope that she will not be sitting in that house, as you left her, without anyone to scratch, to rake, to burn. Tell me, Ben, was there no other man, none at all?"

"There was her English kinsman," I said. "You have met him. He was here."

"Here? In this house?"

I told him of John Meade. "But she cannot marry an Englishman," I said.

"No? Why not?"

"Why, because—because he is English!"

He laughed. "You are still a boy. We Danes are at war with England but we do not make war on the love between a man and a woman. Now, think, Ben. You do not know whether he was in love with Mistress Savage?"

"No, sir."

"But he was truly agitated when he learned I had a daughter who was fond of you. Excited, in a manner most unmilitary. And he said it would have been the solution. The solution to what? And he knew—must have known—that we had a hurricane cellar, but did not ask to see it, to search it. Why? Think, Ben!"

I thought, but nothing came.

"Well," said the Baron at length, "we cannot know. And there are no ships by which to send a letter and receive a reply. So we must wait." He clapped me on the shoulder. "At dinner I will bring out the goldwasser and aquavit and kirsch. We celebrate your tentative betrothal, and we will all three be happy while we can. And I will very carefully inquire to see if I can find John Meade."

But the Baron did not find Meade. He went to Saint Thomas and returned with the news that the *Recruit* had gone and Meade with her. She had been replaced by the brig *Lancer*.

ELEVEN

The days, the weeks sped by. Christmas came and went and we turned into the New Year, but there were no wet snows or weeping skies. Every day was summer in Saint John, and Calabasboom was an Eden made for Kirstie and me. We took to swimming unclothed in the clear waters off our favorite beaches. It seemed simple and natural and right to do so. There was no shame and no lust. Had either of us, at such times, been overwhelmed by passion, I think the other would have yielded—joyfully. Yet we did not. Some day, we hoped, we would lie in each other's arms and enjoy the full rapture of our being. But now the specter of Nancy Savage stood between us, stilling the clamorous demands of the flesh—a little —enough. Perhaps we were fools not to take our joy as simply and naturally as we slipped into the sea. Some would say so. They who do cannot know and will never know Kirstie.

One morning Kirstie and I were swimming in Dennis Bay. It was Kirstie who first caught sight of the ship standing down between Jost Van Dyke and Tortola. She exclaimed, and following her gaze I saw the vessel with her sails bellying in the wind and the white seas creaming under her black forefoot. The *True Love!*

Every day I had watched for her, and Kirstie, too, each of us rather elaborately pretending to be doing no more than admiring the seascape. And the Baron, too, had been watching for her. It had been a long time since he had left Calabasboom on any of his small, mysterious errands.

I had begun to fear for Tom Boyle. And without knowing it, I had also begun to fear that I was marooned on Saint John for the rest of my life. For Paradise was not enough. It was a half-life we had been living, Kirstie and I. A little longer, and it would have become unendurable to both of us, despite our love—or more truthfully, because of our love. We were not children, to play forever in an enchanted Eden. The uncertainties must be resolved.

The world changed in an instant. There was purpose and urgency in it. I must see if Tom could smuggle me to our home shores, embargo or no, as he had brought me to Saint John.

I swam to the beach, Kirstie following. I snatched up my clothes, and the next instant dropped them. Kirstie was in my arms. Our wet bodies strained together, desperately. "Oh, Benje! I suppose it had to be—sometime!" She was close to tears and I myself was not far from them.

But I glanced again at the *True Love*. She was bearing in toward Cinnamon Point and von Lund's Bay. If we hurried, we could reach Calabasboom before her boat put in.

"Dear heart," I said gently, smiling at our nakedness. "We had better get dressed. We wouldn't want them to see us like this."

We were dressed and swinging back over the shoulder of the point and down to the old stone quay, when what I had said came back to me like an echo, clear and ringing and a little frightening. I seized Kirstie's arm in a grip that made her cry out. "What is it? Benje! What has happened?"

" 'We had better get dressed,' " I repeated slowly. " 'We wouldn't want them to see us like this.' Kirstie, I said it once before, in a dream."

Absently she rubbed her arm, staring at me. "Benje, you spoke of a dream—remember?—of meeting me here. Now tell me again."

When I had done she said, almost as if to herself, "I too dreamed of our meeting here. But that was different. It was wishing, as a little girl wishes very hard for the skies to rain flowers or the stars to come down and be played with. It was not real, not like yours."

"What does it mean, Kirstie?"

"Do not be afraid, dear one. It was given to you to see, a little—to know, long ago, that I would be here for you, and that you must come, and that we loved. What else was given? What more did you dream, Benje? Can you remember?"

Looking into her wondrous blue eyes, I remembered then, and I told her the dream of the cold high place, the black night, the downward path, and beside me my dearest dear, her hand in mine—and at the bottom, sudden peril. It came back to me with a thrill of fear.

"Benje!" To my amazement she was aglow with happiness. "Don't you see? That too will happen. Why else should it be so clear?"

"But there was danger, my darling. And how will it end?"

"It does not matter. No! Benje, I am there. I am there beside you, whatever else may come. We are together again. You see? You will go now and I will not grieve too much, for we know it is not the end for us."

We were beside the calabash tree, and there we stood, in close embrace, daring to believe in a dream.

Tom Boyle was as happy to see me as I was to see him, for he had not known how I had fared after leaving the *True Love* any more than I could know what might be happening to him on his far and dangerous voyage. We shook hands. We embraced, French style—Tom demonstrating, to begin with, and calling it a fine, romantic custom, very handsome—for the French. Then we took to slapping each other about, in hearty American affection, until the Baron threatened to lock us in the *orkanshullet* until we recovered from our transports.

Looking down from the veranda over the bay, I saw the little boat which had taken Boyle ashore bobbing back to the schooner. I was surprised, for I had expected that Abe Meyers would have orders to stand off and on, in case the British patrol vessel came into view. And I had expected the *True Love* to slip in at dusk, disguised as before, but there she was in broad daylight, bold and saucy, her lettering clear and bright.

Tom laughed at me. " 'Tis all right, Ben," he assured me. "We've nary a Frenchman aboard this time, and I've a warrant from the commander of His Majesty's forces at Saint Kitts to be gatherin' forage for the British fleet, so we've naught to worry about from them."

The Baron and Kirstie and I pressed him to tell us how this had come about, but he would do so only in his own time. So we sat down to dinner, and Tom raised his glass to toast Mistress von Lund with a grand speech which I will swear he must have practiced all the way over to France and back again. It was part Shakespeare, part Homer, and part—the best part —Tom Boyle. Long before he had finished he knew, probably from the looks exchanged between Kirstie and me, how it was with us, for he ended, "Miss Kirsten, ma'am, and me friend Ben Forbes, may God bless ye and bring ye back together."

With emotion he attacked his dinner and it was a little time before we could get another word from him.

Boyle had had clear sailing all the way to the Bay of Biscay. Even when he came into French waters his luck held. There had been thick fog along the coast and he had been able to slip unseen through the British blockade and run in to the port of Bayonne.

But here, to his consternation, it seemed that he had escaped the jaws of the British lion only to fall under the claws of the French tiger. Scarcely had they passed their lines about the bollards on the quay when they were boarded by an officer and a squad of armed guards bearing warrants for the libel and seizure of the vessel. It appeared that early in the year at that very port of Bayonne, Bonaparte had issued another of his decrees—this one evidently in retaliation for the embargo. It ordered the seizure of American ships touching at the ports of France, Italy, and the Hanseatic cities on the grounds that since American vessels were confined to their home waters any claiming to be such must be English, sailing with forged papers and masquerading under false colors!

Tom Boyle had had the foresight to include in his articles of agreement a statement to the effect that the American schooner *True Love*, Captain Thomas Boyle, had been engaged by the French refugees specifically for the purpose of conveying them to France, and binding them jointly and severally to stand responsible for the vessel, to the full extent of her value in addition to the cost of their passage, during such time as she was within French jurisdiction. Each of the refugees had signed. But even this might not have saved his beloved ship. It was his great good fortune that Jules Bardon turned out to be a man of considerable influence. Weeks went by before the matter was arranged to the satisfaction of all, but arranged it was.

With his money boxes full of French gold, and under the floor boards of his hatches half a cargo of fine French wines and brandies for the thirsty West Indian market, Tom once more ran the British blockade. From Bayonne he ran around to Teneriffe in the Canaries and there declared that he had been chased in by Barbary pirates. So sympathetic were the British that they did not even search the schooner. He completed his lading with sack and canary, and what was more, obtained clearance, all shipshape and proper, for Saint Kitts. At that island, while quietly disposing of his French wines and spirits at fantastic prices, he had persuaded the English admiral to license him for purposes of forage and supply, thus securing the freedom to come and go among the British-held islands.

Here was a tale of unparalleled triumphs, and Tom related it with such gusto that we were spellbound.

He had other news for us. Tucked away in Calabasboom, we knew nothing of the outside world. At home Jefferson had ended his second term as President, and in his place was James Madison, who had been Secretary of State and was well known to the Baron von Lund. But most important of all—the embargo had been lifted. Tom was going back to Baltimore. We were in May, five months and seventeen days from the night he and I had unceremoniously parted company, but more than two years since Tom and I had walked up Light Street together. He must return to settle accounts with the anxious owners of the *True Love*—a final triumph—and reaffirm his reputation as the greatest of the captains of tall ships.

"Now, by the Lord!" I cried out. Tom was shocked, and I hastily begged Kirstie's pardon. But she laughed, and said to her father, "It is right, Papa, no?—'by the Lord!' See, all is being arranged for us. Benje will quickly go home, and then we will know."

A thought had struck me. It seemed simple and brilliant. "Sir," I said to the Baron, "we could all go together. You and Kirstie might stay for a while in Washington, and I would rejoin you there, and Kirstie and I would be married. . . ."

My voice trailed off. I could not know if I would be free for Kirstie. There had been the dream, and so deeply had I shared her faith in it that I had forgotten it had been only a dream.

The Baron smiled at me sympathetically. I said eagerly, "But would it not be better, sir, for you and Kirstie to be away from here, in neutral territory?"

He shook his head. "There are some things that you forget. We are Danes, and this island is held by the English, with whom we are at war. You may be sure that they know something of the role I have played here. They know that I have served my sovereign and my country, and serve them still, although there is little enough that can be done. For us, you have served a good purpose, Ben. We who live here know and trust one another better. You see, you have not been betrayed."

"I have been stupid!" I exclaimed. "All this time you have been in danger through me. And now that I go, it will make no difference. There is still danger. I beg you, Baron, to come with us."

I looked at Kirstie and from the wistful and loving sadness in her face, knew that they would not come.

"The British know us," said the Baron quietly. "They have not yet troubled us and it is not likely that they will. I have been very careful, for my Kirstin."

"Then let *her* go!" I cried. "Kirstie . . . !"

She put her hand on her father's arm. "You may not ask that of me, Benje. Not yet."

"Then I will stay," I said wildly. "I will write a letter to Mistress Savage. Tom will carry it."

"Ben," said the Baron, "you cannot rescue a lady from a dungeon—self-imprisoned though she is—by letter."

Tom Boyle had been looking from face to face during this interchange. " 'Tis none of my business," he said in the silence and with delicacy, "but 'tis best that persons here know what a fourth, which is here, which at this moment he shouldn't be, thinks of the matter." He began again, rather desperately. "Ye're leavin' the gold for the red, Ben me lad?"

When he received no reply he said hastily, " 'Tis none of my business."

"Dear Captain Boyle," Kirstie said sweetly, "Benje will tell you later. He has my leave to do so. We have no better friend than you."

Dropping a quick curtsy, she fled to her room. And I too shot off, in the opposite direction, down the stairs and out into the coconut groves. We could endure no more for this time.

Tom Boyle sailed in the *True Love* to Saint Thomas to unload his supplies for the British and obtain the necessary clearances for the United States. He went without me to avoid any possible trouble, for while Saint John was safe enough, he learned from the Baron, who had it from Nils Knud-Hansen and other friends, that not all the folk on Saint Thomas were trustworthy. I watched him go with the hope that formalities would delay him. Alas! Had I been eager to go he would doubtless have cooled his heels for a month in Saint Thomas, waiting on the ponderous machinery of officialdom. But as it was, because Kirstie and I counted the hours, officials who perhaps yesterday would have balked at any urge to haste today were fired with zeal. Within forty-eight hours he was back.

The Baron meanwhile permitted me to help him with a cargo of sugar, bay rum, and limes that Boyle would take aboard. Then I fell into my duties of supercargo for the *True Love*.

I went ashore at last for the farewells. They were too quickly done. We were brave, Kirstie and I. We were confident. From each other we hid our anguish. But aboard the *True Love* I went quickly down to my little cubby and remained there long after I felt under me the swelling of the open sea.

In due time I was able to confide our secret to Tom Boyle. I must go home to see if Nancy would have me, while hoping and praying she would not, or, better still, that she had miraculously been rescued by another.

Tom was deeply moved. " 'Tis the course o' true love," he said. He slapped the schooner's rail, half affectionately, half in anger. "But don't ye fret, lad. She comes through, that she does."

PART 7 ☆

The Lizard

ONE

Summer comes to the Chesapeake in early June. Drab winter and wet spring lie behind, and the dusty heat of July and August has yet to press its heavy hand down upon the earth. All the world is fresh and light and sparkling. The wind drifts lightly from the land. You can smell it on the sea, soft with the breath of the warm loam, fresh-turned, redolent of the pines, scented with honeysuckle and myrtle, and tasting of the tang of the tide. The blue-green sheen of the sea, combed by the hinder crests of the breakers, sweeps up to the beaches north and south, and the hazy green pompadour of pines rises to the skies. Within the Bay the water shades from blue to green over the shallows. To the west brick-red bluffs glow with color, and on the east the green of the water blends with the deeper lush green of the peninsula.

It is a happy time of year, and in the old days I had frolicked through it with Nancy and the *Ladybug*. But it was very different now. If only Kirstie were here beside me, my bride, coming home with me to the ecstatic welcome of Forbes Landfall. Ben married, and with such a wife! I could hear my mother: "How beautiful she is! But, Ben, how could you—when you know we do so love a wedding!"

The voyage had been uneventful, and swift—only a fortnight, with fair winds all the way and not so much as a chance-met sail to delay us for an exchange of news. As we stood at last into the familiar waters close to home, past the reed-girt shores of Poplar Island, and turned in toward Forbes Inlet, I belatedly remembered my manners and invited Tom Boyle up to the house with me.

"No, no, lad!" he replied. "I thank ye for the courtesy, but I'm thinking 'twill be no moment for outsiders. No, no! Tend to yer homecomin' without me, and when ye've a day or so to spare come over to Baltimore and tell me about it—if ye've a mind to. 'Twill be six or eight weeks at the least before we start south again. Ye'll find me at the Fountain or the Mermaid. I'll send ye word of aught that transpires."

"You'll not go without me?" I cried, suddenly apprehensive.

For Tom would be going back to Saint John and I dared to hope I would be with him, a free man.

"Not unless I hear from ye that ye're not comin'," he said.

"You promise?" I insisted.

"Ye've me word and me hand on it!" he said solemnly.

Towheaded Homer Aschenbrenner set me ashore in the dinghy, and I felt alone and lonely as I stood on the dock at Forbes Landfall, watching him pulling back to the waiting schooner.

It was not yet midmorning. The sun had scarcely risen above the tops of the tall pines that crowned the low hill behind the house. It was very quiet. But as I walked slowly up the wide sweep of green lawn I remembered that this was the quietest hour of the day, for the field hands had long since gone to their work, while the family and household staff were not yet fully occupied with the domestic chores.

Why, then, did I feel a twinge of apprehension? After all, I must not expect them to come tumbling out to greet me when they had had no word of my coming. The lawn was as green and precisely groomed as ever. The trees and shrubs were trimmed and pruned. The gravel and crushed-shell path was raked and cared for. No weeds grew in the garden borders and the house itself had been painted at least once while I was gone.

But somehow the whole place seemed to me to be wearing an indefinable air of mourning. It was too neat, too still. Nothing stirred. Not even a bird flew across the lawn and behind the sightless windows not a curtain fluttered. I would have given much to see Cato's smiling face appear suddenly around the corner of the house.

As I climbed the path I saw that a little wisp of blue smoke curled from one of the chimneys. The sight swept away my vague fears. I laughed at myself. All was well with the Forbeses of Forbes Landfall.

I was approaching the door when it opened. A tawny wench, her head wrapped in a dust towel, stepped out half-dragging, half-carrying a long broom and a roll of carpet.

Spring cleaning, of course! A little late, but there it was.

"Good morning, Cassie," I said.

She whirled. Her eyes grew so round that I could see their whites. Her mouth formed a great, fat-ringed "O." Her color drained away, leaving her face a dirty, muddy gray, like the underbelly of a yellow river cat.

"IIIeeeeeoo-oo-oo!"

It was a scream, a banshee wail, that went through me like a knife. Her eyes rolled. The broom fell rattling, the rug dropped with a soft thump. Cassie crumpled and sank down, slowly, as a sail will do when the wind is spilled and the halyards let go by the run. She had fainted dead away.

I stared stupidly at the formless heap. I heard a footfall and glanced up to see my sister in the doorway.

"Wendy, thank God!" I cried. "Here! Give me a hand. I can't think what the devil ails the wench! All I did was say...."

My voice trailed off. For an instant I thought that Wendy was going to duplicate Cassie's strange behavior. Her eyes, too, flew wide, her mouth fell open, her freckles stood out like a spattering of measles against her pallor. But she uttered a gasping cry, stepped over the fallen Cassie, and flew to me. She caught me by the arms so tightly that I could feel her nails through the cloth of my coat. "Ben? Is it you? Benjie! It's— it's really—you!"

"Of course it's me," I said irritably. "What's the matter with everyone?"

She began to laugh at that, hysterically, so that I was frightened. I took her by the shoulders and shook her roughly.

"Oh, Ben!" she gasped. "Yes! Yes, I'll stop!" The color came surging back into her face, and smiling with bright, tearful joy she caught my face between her hands and kissed me so warmly that I was dumbfounded.

From within a door had opened. There was a slow step. We turned, still embraced. My father stood with his hand on the knob, blinking a little, for the sun was bright now. My eyes blurred at the sight of him. He had aged so! But it was only two years since I had gone—less than that.

"Daddy!" Wendy called to him joyously. "Look! Look, Daddy!"

He hesitated, glancing at me, frowning, and then looking away. He came out, stepping very carefully over the recumbent Cassie, as if the task required all his concentration. Haggard-seeming, and with his eyes now on my face and in them the same careful concentration, he came to us.

"Daddy, it's Ben!" Wendy said.

He came without speaking and stopped a pace away.

I held out my hand awkwardly. "Hello, Father," I said. It did not seem to meet the situation, but I did not know what else to say.

He took my hand gingerly, tentatively. Then his grasp tightened to an iron grip. "Ben?" His voice was little more than a hoarse whisper.

"It's all right, Father," I said.

He startled me then, for he stepped forward and caught me in his good arm and hugged me to him. Yet he was not a demonstrative man. Even as a child I could not remember his doing anything like that. His face against mine was wet.

A moan from the doorstep aroused us. Cassie was sitting up, rubbing her elbows, staring fearfully. I went to help her up but she recoiled from me.

"Wendy," I said helplessly, "do something. Take her inside. And if this is going to happen to Mother, for God's sake prepare her." A frightening thought struck me. "Is Mother all right?"

"She's well," said Wendy gaily. "And she's going to be very well indeed. She sleeps late now, or she would have been down. I'll see to it."

Scolding, she trundled Cassie into the house.

"Well," said my father, wonderfully recovered, "you're here, son. You're home. Won't you come in?"

I followed him to the study. The old familiar, paneled room was comforting, reassuring. Father poured out brandy and we drank, smiling at each other. He was still a little pale.

There was a scurry of feet, and there was my mother in a dark, hastily donned morning dress, her hair flying. She flung herself upon me crying and laughing, hugging and kissing me, and was finally torn off by Wendy who firmly applied smelling salts. Cato came, and Cassie again, and the other servants, and at last I was permitted to sink down exhaustedly, my mother beside me, holding my hand and now and then reaching up to pat my cheek; and the door was closed against further intrusion. I think it was the first time my mother had ever sat in that room. It was reserved for males.

"So you thought me dead," I began. "But why were you so certain of it?"

Wendy and my mother looked to my father. "You tell him, Daddy," Wendy said.

He nodded. "I can do better than that." Opening a cabinet under the bookshelves by the fireplace, he dragged out a brass-bound wooden sea chest. It was weather-stained and, as my father silently pointed out, stained with something else as well that looked like rust but was not. I gaped at the familiar box I had carried so long, all the way to Rio and back, and had abandoned in the longboat.

"It arrived about two months ago," said my father. "There was a letter with it told you had left a schooner off Saint John, fallen in with a British patrol, been fired upon. There was blood in the boat when they found it and the chest was there, but no other sign of you. It was assumed that you had been mortally wounded and fallen overboard. The evidence seemed conclusive. Regrets and condolences were expressed. The letter had been written by some English officer, but the signature was illegible."

"John Meade, it would be," I said. "That was decent of him."

"Meade?" said my mother sharply. "Nancy's cousin? He was there?"

"Oh, yes," I said wearily, "he was there, and he was on the *Leopard,* and he was here, and at Holly Hall, and God knows where else we'll be meeting. In hell, maybe!"

"Benjamin," my mother reproved me. "You must not use language in the presence of ladies. That's what comes of rough living."

I had to laugh and kiss her. Then I told them something of the goodness and hospitality of the Baron von Lund and his daughter, but not all. Wendy, however, guessed much more than I thought. "Was it Kirstie, Benjie," she asked excitedly, "and was she . . . ?"

But my eyes were on my father, who was looking at me accusingly. Defensively I said, "The embargo. I couldn't get word to you."

"The embargo was raised six months ago—in January."

I felt a little ill at the unnecessary prolongation of their grief; and guilty, too, recalling the idyllic, thoughtless days with Kirstie. "I did not know," I explained. "We had no news at Calabasboom. We knew nothing until Captain Boyle arrived to take me off. I wrote regularly, all along the way, until the embargo. Didn't you receive my letters?"

"We did," said my mother. "Ben, dear, your handwriting is shocking. You do not cross your *t*'s. I declare, after all your tutoring, and we had only the best of tutors, the very best!"

But she could not prevent my father from exploding. "Of all the captains in Baltimore, my son had to sail with Tom Boyle who caused all the trouble here by running down the bugeye! And now it has ended in murder!"

"Murder?" I said wonderingly. "But I wasn't murdered. I'm perfectly well." And then, with no little heat, "There's not a captain on the seas—no, and no one anywhere—that's a better man than Tom Boyle! You'll excuse me now. I've no time. I'll be off to Holly Hall to call on Nancy."

Suddenly silent, they exchanged glances. "Benjie," said Wendy brightly, "wait until tomorrow at least. I've so much to tell you. There's my wedding to Giles—we've put it off—because of mourning, you know. And now everything is wonderful, and we'll be so happy."

But she did not look at all happy as I kissed and congratulated her. Instead, she burst into tears.

"It's Nancy," she sobbed. "Oh, Ben, Nancy ...!"

My mother took the smelling salts from her and tended her daughter as she herself had been tended by her. "Your father will tell you, Ben," she said to me and led my sister to the door.

There she paused. "Ben," she said, "perhaps it was Lieutenant Meade who sent your chest, but we had it from Nancy. It came to her first and she sent it over from Holly Hall. But you cannot call on her. There is no one at Holly Hall. Nancy is gone."

"Gone?" I cried.

But with an arm around the still weeping Wendy, she left the room.

My father took out the glasses again and the decanter. I had never before seen him take drink in the morning, but what he had to tell me was so dreadful that my own need for stimulant more than matched his.

Colonel Savage had become increasingly violent, something of a madman. In proportion the slaves on all the plantations of the Eastern Shore, and perhaps farther, had grown increasingly restive. Among the planters there had been talk of sending a deputation to warn the Colonel to mend his ways. "You know, Ben," said my father, "it is not our way—anybody's way around here—to mistreat our blacks. They're part of the place. You paint your house—you feed your hands."

"Did the Colonel hurt Nancy?" I asked quickly.

"Not so far as we know. She was the only one who could do anything with him, and that was not much, it seems."

"What happened when the deputation warned him?"

"They didn't. It never came to that. The problem was solved for us in another way."

It was difficult for him to go on. But at last he got it out.

The Colonel, finding Holly Hall insupportable, had taken to going over to Salisbury and beyond. Sometimes he stayed away for days. And one day his body was found in the road near Sinepuxent, on the ocean side.

"But surely none of his blacks could get away over there without anyone's knowing about it!" I cried.

"No one knows who committed the crime," said my father. "But there wasn't much question why. He was—flayed!"

Overwhelmed by horror, I heard my father's grim voice lighten a little. The worst, then, had been told.

"Of course there was a great furor. Some were for going in a body to Holly Hall and hanging all its blacks. A few hotheads did try, but Nancy came down with a shotgun and had them running like rabbits. Good girl!"

"Did you see her?" I asked.

"Your mother and Wendy tried but she wouldn't let them in, just called through the door to tell them to go away."

"Where is she?"

My father shook his head and continued in his own way. After some time, he said, things had quieted on the Eastern Shore, and then Nancy sent all her people away except Clytie. Sold them, perhaps. She stayed on in the empty house. Clytie had brought the chest in the Colonel's cart, but would give no reply to questions. After my family's first grief for my supposed death, my mother and Wendy had gone once more to Holly Hall. Nancy and Clytie had disappeared. The next anyone knew, a lawyer from Philadelphia went through Holly Hall in company with our local constable, so that all was proper. He went off and sent down a caretaker. And nothing more was known, except that the house was still Nancy's property and that the caretaker was a morose, unfriendly man named Otis Farrell.

I rode that very afternoon to Holly Hall. The once well-kept driveway was a veritable forest of weeds that spread into the gardens, choking them. The house looked strange, almost drunken, in its neglect. Broken shutters hung at angles, more windows were boarded, and there was a wide crack in the bottom stair. No smoke showed at any of the tall chimneys; no dog barked. There were no cattle in the fields or chickens near the slave quarters.

I was sitting on my horse, staring at the desolation. The voice came so unexpectedly—sharp and harsh—that I jerked in the saddle, and my nag reared.

"Lookin' for somethin'?"

I saw no one.

"Up here, mister."

He was on the roof, in the shadow of a gable. He was tall and skinny and stood looking down on me with perfect composure, a hammer in one hand and a split shingle in the other.

Craning my neck I called, "You're Otis Farrell?"

He studied me carefully and spat a brown stream in a long arc to the ground.

"Yuh," he said then.

"I'm Forbes," I said, "from over the way. I'm looking for Mistress Savage. Can you tell me where I can find her?"

He glowered down at me, apparently weighing his answer. "Nope," he said finally.

I eased my neck, considering what little I had ever heard concerning the ways of Philadelphians. "Mr. Farrell," I said, "if you yourself don't know, perhaps you do know someone who can tell me?"

"Could be," he conceded.

I considered again and another brown stream came from above.

"Well, who is it?" I demanded. "Who can tell me?"

He pondered the question for a long moment while I tried to figure out how to climb to the roof in order to take him by his scrawny neck and kick the answer from him.

But at last he said, "Ed Burns. Tell ye 'f anyone kin." With deliberation he turned and began to fit the shingle into place.

"Who's Ed Burns?" I cried. "Where would I find him?"

"Lawyer," he tossed over his shoulder. "Philadelphey." He began to wield his hammer.

"Mr. Farrell," I shouted desperately, "it's a big place. Whereabouts in Philadelphia?"

Through the banging of the hammer I heard, "Pewter Platter Alley. Nigh Front Street."

With that I went home, but I had to spend another day with my family before I could persuade them to let me go, as go I must.

I sailed in the pinnace to Annapolis, as before, and there took the stage wagon to Baltimore where I sought out Tom Boyle. In a silence more emotional than "Burn me britches!" or the like, he listened to my tale. He gripped my hand across the table, the same table where we had sat two years ago. Then he blew his nose vigorously and cleared his throat, and blew his nose again.

"Why, then," he said, sighing heavily, "if there's the way of it, ye'd best be goin'."

I asked him how long he could wait for me.

"I'm runnin' up to fresh water above Havre de Grace to be cleanin' the barnacles off her bottom. She's overlong due for a full overhaul at the yard—that'll come next. Then there'll be cargo to gather and stow. 'Twill be September, likely, after the first harvests're fetched in, before we'll be off."

"That should be time enough," I said.

"Aye. But there's no tellin' for sure with the kind of a chase ye're settin' yerself. 'Tis a long, weary way it could be takin' ye. 'Tis in me mind I gave ye me word, and Ben, 'twould be a grievin' thing to me to be havin' to go back on it. . . ."

I assured him that it would grieve me even more, if I could not return in time, to think of him sitting there in Baltimore waiting for me, the cargo rotting and the *True Love's* owners in a rage, seeking another captain.

"Aye," he agreed dolorously, "that's the way of it."

I entrusted him with a letter for Kirstie. He would find a ship, island-bound, that would carry it.

"Never fear, Tom," I told him as I said good-by. "I'll be back."

It was four days to Philadelphia, a jolting, stifling journey on hard benches over execrable roads deep in hot red dust. It seemed endless. But it ended at last. Once in the city I had no difficulty in finding Pewter Platter Alley, and was there directed to the chambers of Lawyer Burns. But Mr. Burns proved elusive. It was three days before his clerk, whom I haunted day and night, grudgingly informed me that he was out of town. He returned at last but he was remarkably nimble. It was three days more before I was able to corner him, which I did by sitting unmovably on his landing for half of one day and a good part of another.

He was a paunchy little man with a cold, colorless eye, and I verily believe that when he was born he was suspicious of his mother's milk. He questioned me as to who I was and by what circumstances I had come into existence, and seemed to doubt that I had any right to be walking the earth.

Restraining myself with difficulty, I assured him that I had no claim on Mistress Savage, and no designs upon her; but that we had been, in a sense, betrothed.

"Oho!" he pounced.

"Oho to you!" I retorted. "We are not pledged, but she believes me dead, and it is possible that she may be happy to know I am not."

Lawyer Burns at this point wanted to know why I was not dead. After some altercation he ordered me out, saying he must have time to consider the situation. It was a very serious matter, very serious indeed. I might return tomorrow afternoon.

I thought then that Nancy must be there, in Philadelphia, and I spent hours walking the streets, hoping to come upon her. The next afternoon Lawyer Burns informed me that he was still considering the situation. The following day it was the same. Rising to go, I looked at the little mean-souled man with the cold eyes and the locked mouth, and I had the sudden conviction that he was enjoying his easy power to keep me dangling—as Nancy, perhaps, had been enjoying hers. The next moment my hands were around his throat in a merciless grip. Taken by surprise, he struggled and flopped like a gaffed fish.

My grip tightened. My rage was cold as his treatment of me. "By God, I'll squeeze it out of you!" I said grimly.

He pulled and clawed at my hands while his face swelled and his eyes popped. I raised him clean from the floor and smashed him down in his chair. "Now!" I said, standing over him.

He breathed hoarsely and felt of his throat, and his face and body were flabby with terror. But then he weakly flailed out with his arms.

I reached for him again.

He gasped out an address in New York.

The road north was better, the coach a little less uncomfortable, but we had a long ferry from Perth Amboy and I regretted that I had not made the entire journey by water.

The address in New York took me to a house in Greenwich, its folk friends of Colonel Savage. But Nancy was not there. She had left them some time since, they told me. She had gone to Newport to stay with relatives. At Newport once again she was gone—to Boston, they said, to visit with a spinster lady who had been a friend of her mother's.

I took post chaise to Boston, and there found the house of the spinster Mistress Leach in Brookline. It was a residence of red brick which, with its door of solid mahogany and its gleaming brass knocker in the form of a fish, contrived to look both prim and elegant. A white maid servant of scrubbed and starched appearance grudgingly admitted me when I demanded to speak with Mistress Leach on a matter of urgency. She left me in a parlor so crowded with furniture and knickknacks, so polished and shining, finical and mincing, that I felt large and clumsy, a country lout. I sat gingerly on the edge of a French settee and waited, staring at my boots which seemed shamefully dirty; yet I had had them polished only that morning.

I became aware of a heady perfume. The next instant I heard a sound, as of a sharply indrawn breath, and I rose slowly so as not to disturb the room, the house.

A lady stood in the doorway. She wore a flowing white muslin dress, very high waisted, in the height of fashion. Her startling hair was artfully drawn into a Grecian knot bound with a gold fillet. She looked like one of the porcelains in that parlor—something to be admired but not touched. Her hands were clasped to her breast, her face was very white.

I knew her, of course; and yet I could almost have sworn that I had never seen her before. She seemed a very fine lady —one of those who spend the day abed with megrims and the vapors to emerge at night, a languishing beauty surrounded by attendants and worshipers.

For a long moment we stared at each other.

"You—you're not dead?" Her voice was scarcely more than a whisper.

"Don't be frightened, Nan," I said. "I'm not a ghost. See? I'm real." I took a step toward her. A small table rocked and a vase on it teetered. I clutched at it and saved it, but an Indian ivory clattered to the floor.

Nancy laughed shakily. "Yes, I see," she said. "It *is* you, it is indeed!"

She came to me with outstretched hands. "Ben, I'm so glad!"

Deeply moved, I kissed her—but gently, carefully, as the house and she herself seemed to demand.

She patted my cheek. "Dear Ben," she murmured, and her green eyes were softer than I had ever seen them.

I was pierced with a terrible grief as by the sharp, clean thrust of a sword. In that moment I said good-by to my own dearest love—to Kirstie. This strange, drooping Nancy would be my wife, to go no more awandering but to reign at Holly Hall with a dutiful husband. But would the duty be so hard, after all? Her hands in mine were cold; I would warm them. Her delicate pallor recalled to me all her suffering; I would comfort her. Ah, dear God, if only I had never known Kirstie von Lund!

"Nancy," I began with desperate determination, "I have come a long way...."

"From the grave itself," she said soberly. "Ben, you must tell me everything."

And so I told her of my escape from the British and of having been befriended by the Baron von Lund on the island of Saint John. Too soon I found myself in difficulties. There had been a time when I could not speak to Kirstie of Nancy Savage; now I dared not speak to Nancy of Kirstie. Nancy plied me with questions about the plantation with the queer name of Calabasboom. I faltered and stammered as she persisted. Luckily, she did not appear to notice. At last she fell silent and looked at me thoughtfully.

"Nancy," I began again, "I have come to ask. . . ."

And again she interrupted me. "So you were hidden in the hurricane cellar," she said. "And John made no search for it?"

"It had a secret entrance," I reminded her.

"But John Meade is no fool," she said. "Ben, if it had been you who led the patrol, and John who was in hiding—Ben, would *you* have been satisfied to neglect attics or cellars, secret or not?"

"Nan," I said impatiently, "I am not Lieutenant Meade and it was the other way round."

But she paid no attention. "Think, Ben!" she demanded. "Would you?"

It seemed to me a curious question, but fixed by her entreating gaze I tried to put myself in John Meade's place—a British officer with orders to hunt down a fugitive who might be a dangerous enemy. Orders. And I was British, and I hated the Americans—and above all, one Ben Forbes. . . . I said slowly, "I would have had that house down rather than leave any corner of it unexplored."

A long sigh came from Nancy and she changed before my very eyes. Color came into her face. She seemed to put on flesh-and-blood substance. Her eyes fairly dazzled me with their brilliance. "No rescuer," she said softly, as if to herself, "but a true man."

I blinked, utterly confounded.

She glanced at me and burst into laughter. "Oh, Ben," she said, "you look so funny!"

I was offended, but I said doggedly, "Mistress Savage, I have come to ask if you will be my wife."

She did not reply. She drifted—danced, rather—across the room to the window which was hung with starched cobwebs of lace. "The carriage is late," she remarked, "and so, too, is Mistress Leach. She is being dressed. We are driving out with friends. Come tomorrow, Ben. Oh, I had almost forgotten! No, not tomorrow. I've so much to do, you cannot imagine! Next week. Come Monday next, Ben."

Reminded of Lawyer Burns of Philadelphia, I wanted to shake her until her teeth rattled and squeeze an honest answer from the white throat. But there lay between us a dangerous field of dainty tables and slim pedestals, vases, bowls, miniatures, figurines, countless objects, among which there was no path for a blundering male. And all at once it seemed to me that there lay between us a different sort of field, equally cluttered but even more dangerous—filled with brittle misunderstandings.

As frantically as I had clutched at the teetering vase, I clutched at my resolution. "Nancy," I said, "I'll not come back tomorrow or Monday next. I'll have my answer now!"

"Answer?" she said, staring at me in a puzzled way across the spinsterish parlor. "To what?"

Exasperated, I bellowed, "I asked you to marry me!"

"Oh." All innocent sweetness she was. "Why?"

"Because I gave you my word."

"I never asked for it," she said. "I don't want it."

"But I ruined your life!"

"Very nearly," she said. "But that's over and done with now. Go away."

"What!" I cried.

"Ben Forbes," she said coolly and clearly, "I do not love you. I do not want you. I do not need you. Go away! Go to your silly Danish angel! Go—go to the devil!"

I reeled as if she had struck me with a whip. The blood mounted to my head and I was shaken by a murderous fury. Nancy cried out in fear. I fought with myself, staring at her, and slowly the red mists cleared. I saw a woman I did not know and did not wish to know. A stranger.

Without another word I went to the door, wrenched it open, and banged it behind me. I took deep draughts of air and smelled the sea, and my soul expanded. I strode down the street like a lord of creation. Every step away from the fine lady in the cluttered and oppressive parlor was a step nearer to Kirstie. I wanted to shout, to sing. I was a free man!

TWO

It was now well into September and I was fearful that Tom Boyle would be forced to sail without me. I traveled night and day, and some two or three days out of Baltimore, when the stage wagon broke down, purchased a nag. She was elderly and somewhat bony, but willing. She dropped in her tracks on the outskirts of Baltimore and I left the noble beast lying in the road while I went on, running, a strong, good-natured oaf I'd hired on the spot loping beside me with my sea bag. I was only just in time. Boyle had held off his owners for a week and could have waited no longer.

We were two weeks on the voyage. Boyle held the *True Love* to Saint Thomas until the morning when the islands hove into view. Port regulations and our papers required us to make for Saint Thomas, of course; to put in first at Saint John was a violation of our articles of voyage. But what were papers to

Captain Boyle? He altered course slightly, bearing east-south-east, so that we fetched around the western tip of Jost Van Dyke and then cut directly across the sound to Cinnamon Point and von Lund's Bay. We had scarcely dropped anchor, and the crew were only beginning to furl the sails along the spars when the dinghy was swung out and lowered, and Tom was hurrying me to the side.

"Over ye go," said he.

I hesitated with a leg over the rail. "You're not coming with me?"

"Comin' with ye, at a time like this?" He was quite shocked. "D'ye think I've no delicacy at all. Get on with ye! Don't keep the lady waitin'. When ye've said yer say, give me a shout and I'll come ashore. Better, fetch her aboard and I'll marry ye meself."

"Would you do that, Tom?" I said, grinning.

"Nothin' I'd like more, me lad. 'Tis an affair close to me heart."

Dropping down to the dinghy, I rowed to the same strip of beach where I had first seen her. How long ago had it been? Scarcely a year! It surprised me to remember. Kirstie! My heart was soaring as I beached the dinghy and made it fast by the painter to the bole of a coconut palm.

I became aware of the stillness. The little waves still washed, swishing, up the white beach, and then swished back to meet the next oncoming wave. The tall palms hung silent, motionless. Somewhere deep in the grove a dove sang mournfully, a few short notes, and then it too fell silent. I was reminded of my last homecoming, when I had sensed that something was wrong at Forbes Landfall. I could not shake off a feeling of uneasiness. Surely, from above, the Baron or Kirstie or the house servants—surely, someone must have seen the white sails in the little bay? Kirstie should be flying to meet me.

But perhaps she was. At this very moment she might be coming. Why was I standing here like a dolt?

I hurried up the long path through the green tunnel I had so often walked with her, expecting at every moment to see her slender figure, fleet as a nymph, glowing with beauty and happiness.

But no sound came. Dust rose in little puffs around my feet. At the foot of the little hillock I paused to catch my breath and again I heard the dove.

They were asleep, I told myself. It was the siesta hour. We had slipped in unawares, and I would surprise them. Had I not dreamed of doing just that all the way from Boston? They would be napping, the Baron on the veranda and Kirstie under the mosquito bar in her bedroom, and they would be awakened by my joyous shout, and I would pretend to be apologetic for disturbing their siesta and they would laugh at me.

I hurried on along the zigzag path, climbing the rise. Here at last was the compound with the great trees over it. I saw the outlines of the house through the shady patches and felt a sudden relief. Somehow I had half expected that it would not be there, that perhaps it had never been there and I was in my old dream—only without Kirstie.

I called out, "Ahoy! Ahoy the house!"

There was no reply. In the stillness I heard from behind the mournful dove cry.

With lagging steps I approached the house.

There was no hammock on the veranda sagging beneath the Baron's long form, nor tables, nor chairs. Nothing but dust. The windows were shuttered, the doors closed and barred. I went all around the building, calling out with a dry throat, banging frantically on shutters and doors. I tried the outbuildings. They too were closed, and there was no one about, not anywhere.

I told myself that they had gone to Saint Thomas for a visit. But if so, was it likely that they would have done such a thorough job of it? The thought swooped at me as a bat goes flitting through the dusk, but I ducked away, avoiding it, refusing to see it, as one shields his soul from the hairy evil omen. They had gone to Saint Thomas—on business, perhaps, on a long business matter. Yes, that was it. I refused to admit to myself that there was anything at all ominous in the absence of even a caretaker. They had left one, surely, but he had a sweetheart in a plantation across the island; I conjured him up and, cursing him savagely for negligence, ran all the way down to the beach with the damned dove burbling in my ears like a misguided owl. I hurled the little boat into the sea and rowed back to the *True Love* with jerky strokes.

Boyle's face set in hard lines when I told him Calabasboom was deserted. "They'll be in Saint Thomas," I said.

"Aye," he said, with an attempt at reassurance. "Or maybe Saint Croix. Sure now, they'll be visitin' with friends. Nils Knud-Hansen'll have the word for us."

I said, "They'll be there, Tom. They will!"

"Aye," he said, and turned away to bawl orders.

It was near dusk when we threaded our way through the

channel to Saint Thomas, and once in port there were all the formalities to go through: manifests to show, pratique to be obtained, and destination certificates to be displayed. Fortunately the patrol had not seen us in von Lund's Bay and we had cargo enough for Saint Thomas to insure the courtesy of indifference at least. But it all took us more than two hours, and only when it was done could Tom and I go ashore.

We hastened up the Kongens Gade to Nils Knud-Hansen's counting rooms. The big Dane was there, poring late over his accounts in the yellow light of the dangling whale-oil lamp. He came forward to give us the painfully affectionate greeting of his warm, friendly strength. "Ach! At last are you kommen! Tom Boyle and mynheer Forbes, ja! For you I have been waiting!"

"Where is she?" I cried.

But it was wrong to hurry him. He was a slow man. "Who?" he asked.

"Please," I begged him. And then, "Goddammit, sir! You know who I mean! Where is Kirstie von Lund? Where have they gone? We stopped at Saint John. They were not there."

"Ach!" he said with concern. "That was a pity!" Perhaps in his mind's eye he was seeing the closed house, seeing me beating vainly against its emptiness. "But the letter will say all."

"Letter? What letter?"

"Why, the letter," he beamed. "Did I not say of it? How is this? I thought, and I did it, no?" He considered the phenomenon of thought unspoken, while Tom held me, begging me to be patient.

"Well," said Knud-Hansen at last, "perhaps yet I did not the letter mention."

I restrained myself while he rummaged in his desk, explaining how very strange it was that the instant he had seen me he had thought "Letter," and now it appeared he had not spoken it. "But no matter." He brought it out, a paper sealed and faintly scented. "Read first, and I with the Captain will talk, and after that...." He bowed deeply, touching his forehead in a sort of salute that said, "I will be at your service." He moved away with Boyle, leaving me his desk.

I sat down and stared at Kirstie's strong careful script: "Mr. B. Forves, par main de C ... Ani, Sant Tomas, De Dansk Vestindiske øer." I opened it carefully. It was dated not three weeks after I had left.

"Benje, my dearest own heart. Why is it that these things must happen to us? In Norfolk, had we been honest with ourselves, we would have admitted our love then, and perhaps all would have been different. But who can say?"

There was a blot here, as if a tear had fallen. And there were others among the words of love. It had been written in a great hurry. The gist of it was that someone on Saint Thomas, or perhaps even on Saint John, had betrayed the Baron. The von Lunds had been visited by a patrol of British marines, who came demanding the American, Ben Forbes. When he was not found, they were accused—idiotically—of having conspired with him to give the islands to the United States. Their lieutenant reminded the Baron that when Denmark *chose to align herself with England's enemies*—"Imagine, Benje, darling" (Kirstie here indignantly wrote), "he dared to say that, when all know that it was because the English attacked Copenhagen that we were driven to join Napoleon's system!"—the Baron had gone to Washington with the express purpose of turning these islands over to the Americans. It followed, in the British mind, that the Baron had secreted an American for purposes of conspiracy. The letter continued:

"'What else would the American be doing here?' Papa looked at me and said, 'What else indeed?'

"Benje, my dearest, we had to laugh, really we did!"

And so the British went away. But they came back, this time with orders from someone on high. They gave the Baron and Kirstie a few days to get ready—"And now they take us away, as prisoners. But where they do not say. We are not permitted to write to anyone, but they cannot be by my bed at night. Tomorrow I will find a way to give this to our overseer who will take it to Nils for when you come. If you do come, Benje. But you will, I know you will. Good-by! Good-by, my own love! We shall meet again—remember?"

A fool! An accursed fool! I raged inwardly at myself. What did I care for Nancy Savage? What dark, twisted strain of damnable chivalry mixed with self-deceit had sent me from Kirstie and, earlier, had made me fight four duels, one of them fatal and another even worse in its consequences! I seemed to hear Kirstie's voice: "How funny they are in your home place, Benje." I must be mad. I must have been mad to leave Kirstie.

I don't remember getting back to the ship. Tom Boyle said later, with some pride, that I had been a handful even for Nils Knud-Hansen, struggling and shouting curses against the King of England, the King of Denmark, Napoleon, and even the President of the United States, to say nothing of my family, one and severally, and all the friends and neighbors of the

Eastern Shore in Talbot County, Maryland. I was as one raving drunk. Tom got me to my cubby and detailed the ship's carpenter to hold me down, which he did by sitting upon me, until I fell into a sleep of exhaustion.

But I remember none of it. I only know that when I awoke the schooner was standing out to sea and that I was drained of all emotion. Too soon the pain began. It never settled into grief. There would have been quiet in that, and soon or late, the peace of resignation. It was a torment, like a raging thirst or a hunger, that gave me no rest.

We went around the hump of South America to Rio de Janeiro, and I worked with the crew at every task that offered. We came back with coffee, Jesuit bark, and a sort of turpentine drawn from trees called gum rubber from far up the Amazon.

We stopped at Saint Thomas.

Nils Knud-Hansen looked up and shook his head when I entered his counting house. "No word, mynheer."

"Nothing yet, Nils?" I said urgently.

"Nothing."

"Oh," I said. And then heard myself repeating, "Nothing. Nothing."

Back aboard the schooner I gave way. "Tom! Tom! In the name of God, Tom! What shall I do? I can't go on cruising with you forever, sailing up and down the seas."

"I'll load cargo for England," he said.

A voyage to England was risky and not so profitable. "And they might be anywhere," I said.

"Aye," he agreed. "And might be, even, they've escaped by now—to France, say, or back to Copenhagen. But I'll load for England, hey?"

His goodness brought tears to my eyes. "No," I said. "Cleave to your course. I'll go back to Forbes Landfall. There might be a letter. Or one might come if I wait there. Go on without me, Tom."

And so I came home again. I came in time for Wendy's wedding to Giles Penrose. It was a grand occasion on the Eastern Shore. Forbes Landfall was crowded to the very attics with guests for long before and long after, including my two older sisters with their husbands and their children. Giles Penrose was handsome and manly; I scarcely recognized in him my boyhood enemy. Wendy was radiant. On all sides it was said of her, "A beauty. After her first, she'll be more beautiful than her mother."

No one spoke of Nancy Savage, and at Holly Hall the morose

Otis Farrell still hammered shingles or otherwise kept himself occupied.

But there was no letter from Kirstie von Lund.

THREE

The Baron had been known, loved, and respected in Washington. I went there to see if someone might know where he had been taken. But everything was indefinably different. As Secretary of the Navy, Robert Smith had been cordial. As Secretary of State, he was guarded and also choleric. I should not blame him, for I plagued him and he could not recollect me. Nor did he try to understand why a Ben Forbes should be begging him for news of the Baron von Lund and his daughter, whom he remembered only vaguely. A Mr. Monroe kept appearing with a pointed nose and an officious manner. And there was a hovering New Englander by the name of Adams, a short, wizened, bald-headed man whose only mission in life, so far as I could see, was to complain endlessly about the mud in the streets of Washington and the cooking at his boarding-house. I tried to see Mr. Murray, the English envoy, but he refused to be seen. I bombarded him with notes and attempted to waylay him—in vain.

And so I went away. First to Baltimore. Tom Boyle was about to set sail for Rio again with corn and naval stores, and wanted to take me on. But I refused. I would go home. Kirstie might be sending a letter to me there. I did not want to go to Rio. It was too far from her.

"Far from her?" Tom Boyle repeated. "Then ye'll be knowin' where she is?"

I shook my head hopelessly, and Tom Boyle swore to himself for a while. "One day I'll blockade England for ye, Ben. That I will!"

"I'd not be surprised, Tom," I said, laughing against my mood. "All by yourself, too."

Life was very quiet at Forbes Landfall without Wendy. My mother fluttered about me and nagged at me, begging me to confide in her. And so I told her about Kirstie. She was delighted at the prospect of another wedding and embarked forthwith upon plans. Ben and his wife would live at Forbes Landfall, filling the house with laughter, quarrels, and grandchildren. There would be wonderful parties. . . .

One morning my father called me into his study. "Ben," he said rather hesitantly, "do you have your heart set on going to sea on a merchantman?"

All the dreary days ashore at Forbes Landfall pressed down on me, a leaden weight. To feel a ship under my feet, see the winged sails above me, look out to the far horizon—all my being yearned for it. Better far to sail forever than to be forever anchored.

I said, "I mean to go to sea in any way I can, Father. But I'll go!"

My father was pleased. "Then you'll rejoin the Navy," he said. "John Rodgers is to take out the *Constitution*. I have arranged to have you signed aboard. I've the papers here. You have only to sign and send them."

I agreed with such warmth that he said apologetically, " 'Twill be only a local cruise between the Capes, Cape Cod, and the Bermudas. A patrol. Something has to be done to stop this damnable impressment of our seamen."

"It doesn't matter," I said. "Thank you, sir."

My orders came, giving me the commission of a fifth lieutenant, and instructing me to join my ship at Annapolis.

I left early in June, running down to Annapolis in the pinnace. The *Constitution* lay off the mouth of the Severn, and a more disgraceful ship I had never seen, with green mold in her rigging, patches on her sails, rotten spots in her hold, and God alone knows what tons of growth on her bottom. When I came aboard, the officer of the deck saluted me perfunctorily. Yet I knew him and he knew me. He was my old messmate of the *Chesapeake*, Charles Morris. He never cracked a smile but sent me below to report to the executive officer. Captain Rodgers was not aboard. He was at his home in Havre de Gras.

Some days later Lieutenant Morris condescended to unbend to me a little in the wardroom. "We're beginning to get a good ship's company here, Mr. Forbes," he said. "But the old man doesn't like her. Yonder lies the *President*. He'll get her, mark my words."

John Rodgers did get the *President*, and he took her on the mission that had been assigned to the *Constitution*. Captain Isaac Hull came to us by way of exchange. A little roly-poly, cheery man he was, who could make a sailor "kiss the gunner's daughter" and still be loved by all hands, including the sailor. Sometimes among ourselves we called him Ike, and sometimes Bubble Pants because he split his breeches every time he got excited, and the ship's tailor was always busy repairing the seams.

Captain Hull took our stinking ship up into the Susquehanna, where we dropped some of the barnacles. Then we went back down to the Potomac and ran up to Washington, where we rerigged and refitted, victualed, and took on naval stores and ammunition. We worked hard and long to make the *Constitution* clean and taut. At Washington we learned that we would carry Mr. Joel Barlow, our new envoy to France, and in our strongbox the interest on the Dutch loan. We were to touch, it was said, at Portsmouth and Cherbourg. We sailed at the beginning of August in the fateful year 1811.

It was the year of Simcoe's plot to separate us from the West. It was the year of the Warhawks and of Free Trade and Sailors' Rights. It was the year of growing restiveness, bitterness, and political yammering. It was the year of the encounter at sea of our American frigate *President* with the British twenty-gun *Little Belt*. We knew of that event before we sailed.

And so the feeling aboard the *Constitution* was very different from what it had been on the *Chesapeake*. It was grim and businesslike, and the round form of our little captain was deceptive, for within he was hard metal. We were not a ship to be trifled with.

We sailed again to Annapolis, and there Mr. Barlow, with his wife and his niece, Miss Baldwin, were ferried out to us in the commodore's barge, bringing with them a mountain of luggage. On August 5 we dropped down the James River with the tide, rounded the Horsetail, squared away our yards above Lynnhaven Bay, and stood out to sea.

I regretted the old days. The huge frigate was as different from the *True Love* as a hut from a manor. My small experience in the *Chesapeake* was of little help to me. The whole routine of shipboard life was new and strange—stiff, formal, often meaningless. Save for matters of duty, each officer held himself aloof from his inferiors in rank, and I, a lowly fifth lieutenant, was the least of them. The wardroom and much of the officers' country was turned over to our distinguished passengers, and I was among the officers dispossessed, relegated to the steerage. The frigate fairly reeked with protocol. This state of things seemed to suit the others and it could fairly be said that we were a happy ship, save only for myself, coming as I did from the easy ways of a small trading schooner and Tom Boyle's warm friendship. I had a sense of having been tossed into a dark closet. Had it been possible, I would have crawled down to the bilges and come up for air only at night, keeping company with the ship's cat.

It was as if in taking on a fighting spirit we had been forced to borrow English manners. In addition, with two ladies aboard we were on our best behavior. The frigate seemed to swell with gallantry until it was a wonder the pitch did not ooze from her seams.

One morning—a fine day it was, halfway to the Bermudas —I was on the watch, standing a little abaft the helmsman, keeping an eye on the course. Mr. Barlow came up through the scuttle. He was alone.

"Good morning, sir," I ventured. "You're early topside."

He smiled as a man does at a lackey or at a humble acquaintance who must be kept at his proper distance. But he replied, "It's far too fine a morning to lie abed. How is our course and our rate, Lieutenant? You can tell me, I presume?"

"Certainly, sir," I said briskly, and gave him our bearing and the number of miles we had covered during the last twenty-four hours.

"But that is astonishing!" he exclaimed. "At that rate we should be in European waters in no time at all."

"Hardly that, sir," I said. "With the best of winds it will take us three or four weeks."

"Humph!" For a moment it seemed that he would challenge my statement. He dropped his nose and looked at me over the top of his spectacles. But then he said, "Ah, well. However wild the tempest, yet we must bide our time. Eh?"

"Yes, sir," I said. "It is not the same as at Kalorama."

He looked startled. "Kalorama?"

"Yes, sir." I explained, "You were kind enough to receive me once. Some years ago it was, when Mr. Fulton was your guest. You may remember, sir. We learned that we were distantly related through Buxom Betsy—Madame Jerome Bonaparte, that is."

He gave a sudden snort of laughter. "Buxom Betsy. Is that what you call her? Good! Good!"

The ice having been broken, we talked a little, renewing our slim acquaintance, and at last I dared to inquire if he had any word of the whereabouts of the Baron von Lund and his daughter. "I ask, sir, because I am betrothed to Mistress von Lund and have been unable to find her since she and her father were taken prisoners by the British."

He looked concerned. "Dear, dear," he said, regarding me owlishly. "Why ever in the world would they do that?"

I told him of the contents of Kirstie's letter, of how the British believed the Baron was plotting to turn over the Danish islands to the United States rather than see them remain in British hands.

"Ah, yes," he said thoughtfully. "I can understand why they might arrive at such a conclusion. Nonsense, of course, but not entirely illogical. I believe there was some French scheme at one point, was there not?"

"I cannot say, sir. I do know that the islanders hoped to place those islands in neutral trust for the duration of the current hostilities, but apparently we would not have them."

"Quite so," he remarked. "Should we have accepted them, do you think?"

I understood that in some way I was being tested. "Well, sir," I said, "without ships, without a proper navy to protect the islands, we might as well have taken the moon under neutral trust."

He nodded. "And you have no idea where the von Lunds may have been taken?"

"No, sir," I said despairingly. "I was in hopes that you might have heard."

"Unfortunate," he muttered. "Most unfortunate. If I am to bring about a settlement between the British and the King of Denmark, I could use the Baron von Lund. It all depends upon how fast the British hold him. If he is merely on parole in London, they may well release him for a diplomatic mission, for I've little doubt that the British themselves would welcome a cessation of hostilities in one small corner of the world. It has been in my mind that if we could be the instrument, it would be a feather in our cap. And we have need of feathers, Lieutenant. Our cap is somewhat threadbare."

"Sir," I cried, "you are bound for France. Send me to London to seek out the Baron von Lund! If he is there, I'll find him."

But he looked at me and he saw only a fifth lieutenant with a wild eye, and he was the American envoy to France.

"Thank you, Lieutenant," he said formally, "but the matter will go through the proper diplomatic channels. Undoubtedly there will be a Danish legation in Paris and in London."

More kindly, he added, "My secretary will take down your address, where you can be reached, you know. If I find the Baron I will inform you. You have my promise and I do not forget. Good morning to you, Lieutenant. I must attend my ladies."

With that he was gone and I had no further opportunity to approach him.

FOUR

We were less than halfway across when the plague suddenly broke out among the crew. It spread rapidly throughout the vessel. Gallantry went by the boards, for the passengers kept to their cabins, but protocol was heightened rather than lessened throughout the terror. It was as if, by rigid correctness of behavior, we could ward off death. Yet perhaps there was merit in this cold orderliness imposed by a captain whom we knew very well to be as warm-hearted and human as any that ever sailed the seas. When you see a shipmate at one moment hale and hearty beside you, and in the next, groaning in the scuppers, struck down by an invisible force, fear might well make you a gibbering idiot—if you gave way to it. The cold eye of a superior with its threat of a reprimand steadied many who might, perhaps, have broken. All the same it occurred to me, at such times as I hurried to help a stricken man, who all by himself was trying to crawl down to the improvised morgue in the sailmaker's locker, where he was likely to be lying dead in an hour or less, that it would be better to die in a ship captained by Tom Boyle without any protocol whatever.

At one point Captain Hull and Lieutenant Morris considered routing out all hands and fumigating the entire ship with sulfur candles. But we were in the midst of the equinoctial gales of late summer. Sulfurous quarters would be uninhabitable for some time, and the men could not sleep on the storm-swept decks. And so the plague took its toll. The sailmaker and tailor were kept working night and day to make canvas shrouds, and in the black night the bodies were lowered to their grave in the sea. Out of a crew of some four hundred men, officers, and boys, we lost nearly a hundred. Our passengers escaped unscathed. For my own part I went through the horror without a thought for myself. Kirstie had given me a faith that nothing could shake: "We will meet again."

The plague was well behind us and it was blowing a whole gale when we came in sight of France, the coast rising out of a blustery fog like the dripping back of a great gray whale. Five days of cold, labored sailing had wearied us. We were bearing north-northeast, no more than 10 or 12 miles from the tip of the Cotentin Peninsula, in whose shelter lies the French seaport and fortified naval base of Cherbourg, when a huge shape loomed out of the fog before us and stood across our course.

I happened to be on watch at this time of our first encounter with the British blockade of the French coast. For an instant I thought I was seeing one of the ghost ships that sail through the old sea yarns—the *Flying Dutchman* or the *Blanche Nef*. But then I made out the familiar checkerboard strake on the towering black hull, and I could see the open frames of gun ports, yellow spars, and a billowing cloud of canvas above. There was no mistaking her for aught but a British ship of the line, at least a 74 by my guess. Since these big warships on blockade never hunted singly, there would be one or more of the same rate in the neighborhood and, beyond doubt, anywhere from three to a dozen frigates as powerful as the *Constitution.* I glanced at the signal flags she was flying, and my stomach rolled slightly to the heave of the ship. For I had seen that signal once before, when the *Leopard* bore down on the *Chesapeake.*

I turned to the marine who stood duty beside the helmsman. "My respects to Captain Hull, and inform him we are being signaled by a British man-o'-war."

"Aye, aye, sir," he snapped, and was off.

The marine had scarcely disappeared down the scuttle when Captain Hull was beside me with Morris at his heels. Nevertheless, even in that brief time, so thick was the weather that we had slipped past the Englishman. The ship had disappeared in the misty wrack.

"What is it, mister?" said the Captain sharply.

"British first-rate battleship, sir. Couldn't make out her name, sir, in this weather. We're only some ten seconds past her. I think she wanted a better look at us, for she had signals flying."

"Hah! Did she so? Could you read them, mister?"

"As nearly as I could see, sir, it was a command to lie to."

"Was it? Damn my soul! And would you have obeyed, mister, had the weather been clear?"

"No, sir," I replied, with some surprise. "Not without an order from you."

"You were on the *Chesapeake,* were you not, Mr. Forbes?"

"Yes, sir."

"Then you'll understand me when I say you'll wait till hell freezes before you'll ever get such an order from me. I've no intention of being taken in the same box as Barron."

"Yes, sir."

Somewhere far astern a gun thumped. No doubt the Englishman was angrily trying to lash out across our bows. "Hope he hits one of his own damn ships," remarked Captain Hull. "Well, if he wants me, let him find me first. Mr. Morris, shift course two points to larboard. Mr. Forbes, you will have all hands piped to quarters and the vessel cleared for action. If he wants a show, he shall have it."

"Aye, aye, sir," I replied happily, and jumped for the bo's'n.

But if the Englishman was looking for us, he did not find us.

Late that same afternoon, with the city of Cherbourg in sight only a few miles away, we encountered four British frigates sailing in company before the entrance to the port. The weather had cleared somewhat. There was no chance to avoid them, nor did Captain Hull attempt to do so. He continued toward the harbor. The same signal which had been flown by the ship of the line snapped to the halyards of the lead frigate, the 50-gun *Phoebe*, and she with her consorts came about and bore down toward us.

Captain Hull ignored the signal.

When it became apparent that we had no intention of heaving to, the *Phoebe* hauled her wind and ran up close alongside.

"Ahoy, the frigate!" came the call. "Don't you see my signals, sir?"

"I see your signals, sir," Captain Hull blared.

The terse reply apparently took the Englishman aback, for there was a long silence. Finally came the call, "Then why the devil don't you obey? What ship *is* that?"

"The United States frigate *Constitution*," replied Captain Hull, "with the United States representative to France on board. My orders are to put into Cherbourg and I intend to do so. If your commander has anything to say to me, I will be pleased to entertain him or his representative on board. If he is unwilling to follow such procedure, then you may say to him, sir, that he detains me at his peril."

After another silence the Englishman hailed, "Will you be so good as to back your topsail and lie to? We are sending a messenger on board."

In due time an English lieutenant came over the side and was escorted by the marine on duty to Captain Hull's cabin. He came out again shortly looking very red in the face, descended to his waiting boat, and returned to his ship.

Five minutes later Captain Hull was on the quarter-deck. "You may proceed, Mr. Wadsworth," he said to the officer of the deck.

But now a new set of signals was displayed by the Englishman. I heard Alec Wadsworth report, "Englishman requests entry to Cherbourg be delayed until permission is received from his superiors, Captain."

"He does, does he?" Hull growled. "Ignore his order, bend

on the reply that I shall proceed as soon as weather permits."

And so, by heaven, we did!

The following morning when the seas had moderated and the tide was favorable, we passed into the harbor through the British lines without so much as a nod in their direction, saluting the fort with fifteen guns as we entered and receiving a like number in return.

At Cherbourg Mr. Barlow and his party left us. I watched them go with a faint hope stirring in my heart. Mr. Barlow was an important man and he was going to be a very busy one, engaged upon matters of high moment in the French capital. But had he not said that he did not forget a promise?

FIVE

The English Channel is notorious for its evil, tricky weather. Often when it might be assumed that the day will be fine, the Channel kicks up a blow as dirty as a hog-farmer's bucket. We sailed from Cherbourg with a favorable wind and tide and set our course northward for Flushing and Texel, where we were to deliver the $28,000 of interest on the American debt to Holland, which we carried in gold in our strongbox. I observed that on the way out of the port the British blockaders scarcely deigned to notice us. American belligerence was as yet too new a phenomenon. The British were not certain what to do about it.

The wind was out of the southwest from the Bay of Biscay: an evil omen in those waters. Captain Hull sailed with the hope that it would hold until he had cleared the Narrows and could run for the shallow Dutch roads of Texel. But when the tide turned, the wind hauled around and came tearing down on us, piling up mountainous rollers that smashed at us with the force of battering rams. We ran to shelter at Deal, on the Kentish coast.

There we lay for several days, but no one was permitted ashore, for we might sail at any moment with a break in the weather. I stared at England from the ship's rail, and England lay blankly under my eyes, with never a sign for me. Yet the more I stared the more certain I became that somewhere in London I would find Kirstie. I felt myself a prisoner on the *Constitution*.

We crossed to Dutch waters, where we were jostled, elbowed, and treated with scant respect by the British men-o'-

war prowling that area, yet with no overt act of hostility. We returned again to Deal, for what purpose I do not know save that we took on a passenger for Cherbourg. Crossing to France we were fired upon by an English third-rate, to whom Isaac Hull gave a proper dressing down without firing a gun.

On entering the harbor of Cherbourg, we were again crowded by the British blockaders. Captain Hull, who was by this time in a temper that kept his tailor very busy, would not fly the secret, prearranged signal that would identify him to the French. He would give nothing away to the British, damn their eyes! So we entered with bare halyards. The French batteries, seeing an unidentified man-o'-war standing in, opened fire upon us. Most of the shots went wild, but a few whistled through the sails and one smashed a longboat. Another lodged in the nettings. A third carried away the leg of a seaman passing along the gun deck.

The French were vehemently apologetic, but Captain Hull graciously admitted that they had acted properly.

We went to Spithead, where we figured in a rather comic interchange of deserters: one man from the *Constitution* swimming across to the British battleship *Havannah*, whence, on the following night, a seaman from the *Havannah* deserted and duplicated the performance in reverse.

At Portsmouth Captain Hull left Charlie Morris in command while he went to London to deliver despatches and credentials to the American Minister and the Navy agents. With other officers I was permitted ashore, and it was here that I seriously contemplated desertion. All my training, all my father's precepts, were against it, but I was on English soil and London was not far, and in London, mayhap, I would find Kirstie.

But what would Kirstie think of a deserter?

All the same, I might have made a dash for it, but that feeling ran high in Portsmouth. We were baited and insulted on shore and could not stay long, having been strictly forbidden brawling, which might easily have resulted in a battle royal and deaths. Pride in my ship and my country kept me from a step I would have regretted all my life. It was heightened by the behavior of the English frigates *Hotspur* and the famous *Daedalus*—the second popularly known in all seas as the "Dead Louse"—which crowded in so close upon us and our anchorage as to threaten to foul our yards.

Morris extricated us with consummate skill and moved us to another anchorage. The two frigates followed, but now they anchored at a respectable distance.

When Captain Hull returned, I waited upon him and asked

permission to resign, explaining to him my personal situation. He was kind but firm. He told me that by the regulations it was considered that all hands had signed on for the duration of the voyage; resignations were permitted only on return to the United States. He did not say that I should have known this, but it was a hangdog fifth lieutenant who went back to his duties.

As we raised anchor, spread our sails, and stood down through St. Helens Road, the *Hotspur* and the *Daedalus* both made sail, to come after us. Even before we cleared the port we had been called to battle stations. The blue-burning battle lamps were lit, gun ports were opened and tampions out. Gunners stood by with lighted linstocks. Quietly the word was passed along the gun deck from Captain Hull:

"Will you fight, boys, if it comes to it?"

And the word came back from the gunners: "Let the quarter-deck look to the colors, and we will man the guns!"

At this point I would most willingly have died for Captain Hull and the *Constitution*.

The *Hotspur* ran down under our lee and hailed us: "Captain Josceline Percy's compliments, and might he put dispatches aboard for delivery in Boston?"

"He might," Captain Hull made answer.

We waited with tension hanging over the gun deck and a stillness above that boded no good for any insolence that might be offered. But nothing happened. They were meek as lambs. It seemed a great joke to us and we let loose an explosion of jeering laughter as their boat drew away.

Six days later we spoke the 74-gun *Mars*, ship of the line, but she sheered off from our bristling porcupine. Our ship might be a despised "fir-built Yankee frigate," but we left no question of our willingness to fight any who might wish to engage us.

There were no further incidents on this homeward voyage. As we neared home waters, I spent many a sleepless night pondering my lonely problem. With the new spirit abroad, I was proud to be in the Navy, cocking a snoot at the British and at John Meade, wherever he might be. But somewhere in the world was the girl I loved, needing me as I needed her. Without her my life was empty. Rather, it was too full—of pain and a raging bitterness that plagued me without cease. In the Navy I was bound to my ship, the service, and protocol. It was a friendless kind of life, and in view of my deeper preoccupation its satisfactions of belligerence seemed childish. Was I to forget Kirstie and passively accept a blasted manhood for the boyish pleasure of shaking my fist at a British man-o'-war?'

To hell with kings, emperors, and presidents, with their impressments, blockades, and embargoes!

We reached Hampton Roads on February 19. From there I sent to Washington my resignation from the Navy, with Captain Hull's endorsement, and went home to Forbes Landfall.

SIX

My father did not restrain his anger when he learned of my resignation. I matched it with my own. There would have been a serious break between us if my mother had not interposed. "Allen," she said, "remember how it was with us when we thought our son was dead." It was hard for him to curb his temper, but he did—perhaps because he sensed that my own was more dangerous than his.

The Eastern Shore was a narrow community, far more interested in the gossip that Oakes Tichbourne was making weekly visits to Matapeake (and old Mistress Tichbourne scarcely three months in her grave!) than in the news that six Gloucestermen had been haled to Halifax where the British Courts of Admiralty had confiscated ships and cargoes for fishing on Georges Bank off the Newfoundland coast. After my experience on the *Constitution*, I felt that war was at hand. And there was a rumor that the *Constitution* would shortly be sent to sea again. If my resignation had not, by that time, been accepted, I would have to go with her.

I went to Washington to see if I could speed the acceptance. News, rumors, and political intrigue made Washington seethe. There I discovered that our young Warhawks were aprowl. To the British war cry of "Britannia rules the waves" they opposed another: "Freedom of the seas!" But New England's Senator Webster was vocal. New Englanders were openly threatening to secede from the newly formed Union if war were declared against England. West and South cried out as loudly that if war were *not* declared they would form in free companies and march without any formalities.

I was not concerned with war, however. Again I sought Robert Smith, but he had been replaced by Mr. Monroe. But Mrs. Smith was still in Washington and I called upon her. The kind lady let me know that I had been stupid not to have come to her long ago instead of seeing her husband.

"Of course he would not remember you, Mr. Forbes, and how our dear Kirstie was so taken with you when I brought you together. He is only a man. He has forgotten—oh, many things...." She broke off in a rather pretty confusion.

She asked me to give her several days to make inquiry, which I did, meanwhile haunting the offices of the Secretary of the Navy for acceptance of my resignation. When I came to her again, upon receiving a hasty little note, she said that she had learned that secret negotiations were in progress between Denmark and England through the good offices of the American statesmen in France.

"Mr. Barlow," I commented.

"Yes," she said sadly. "We may thank him for it." And she sighed.

Then she saw my puzzlement. "Joel Barlow died in Europe only a few months ago," she said simply.

"Dead!" I cried. "But he can't be dead, ma'am. He promised—he promised to get me word. He was going to find the Baron von Lund for the peace negotiations. He must have succeeded. But he promised to...."

I was babbling. Mrs. Smith stopped me with a hand on my arm.

"We cannot know. Mr. Monroe is close-mouthed. I have been unable to ascertain if the Baron von Lund is engaged upon the peace with Denmark. But never fear. I have friends abroad and will write to them all, every one. I shall work through France as far as possible. Yes. That would be best. The English have long been watching the mails, suppressing letters."

"Why, then," I said suddenly hopeful again, "that means Kirstie must be in England. For I've had no letter from her."

She looked at me sharply. "None at all?"

I was aware of her quick suspicion. Washington had become a different place, charged with hatreds and tensions. The very air seemed bitter. But after all, Mrs. Smith loved Kirstie von Lund and she had only my word for it that we were betrothed. It might very well seem to her that I sought the von Lunds for some other purpose entirely, that I meant them harm.

And so I gave her the letter I had received by way of Nils Knud-Hansen in Saint Thomas. It was worn, almost tattered now, from my constant handling and rereading of it.

Her bosom heaved with emotion when she returned it to me. "I brought you together," she said indignantly, "and I won't have the hateful British separating you like this! I won't have it! Why, it's enough to make a stone weep tears of blood, that it is! Trust me, dear boy. I will find her for you."

Such was her fervor that I went away feeling confident for the first time since I had lost my beloved.

But before I left Washington, war had been declared against England. I was plunged into despair. If Kirstie was in England, how could I get to her. No one could help me now. No one—unless. . . . But even Tom Boyle could not work miracles. I was a fool to think so. Nevertheless I stopped at Baltimore in search of him. I had no doubts of finding him there, for the embargo had unexpectedly been reestablished in April, and I had heard in Annapolis that the *True Love* had been caught in port, the sheriff hopping aboard like a dainty dancing master and tacking his notice to the mainmast.

I did not find Tom but there was much talk of him. The Fountain Inn was abuzz with it. Certain that war was coming Boyle, with the full support of his equally canny owners, had quietly outfitted the schooner with a battery of ten 12-pound carronades and two long 9s. Rechristened the *Comet*—for *True Love* was no fitting name for a warship—Boyle's had been the first of the tall ships to sail from Baltimore. A privateer, she was. Boyle had very likely been in Washington when I was there, for he had sailed all proper with letters of marque, and with a crew of 110 seamen and marines.

Feeling sadly abandoned, I kicked my heels on the water front. All was activity. Other tall ships were readying; there would soon be a veritable fleet of them, the slim strike-and-fly ships, the mosquitoes that would swoop down to bite, and fly to bite again, disrupting British commerce which for so many years had complacently waddled on our seas. I could have joined any one of them. But with Tom Boyle I would be free, as I could not be on any other ship; and being free, I would be that much closer to Kirstie. For Tom would help me if he could.

On my way home I stopped at Annapolis and visited Andrew Callander. He welcomed me warmly, and remarked that 'twas a pity I'd not sailed with Captain Boyle. Never, said he, was there such a captain as that wild romantical Irishman.

"Then you've taken him on again?" I asked.

"I've been fortunate and privileged," he said, "to buy a share in the *Comet*. One leetle share, only one. 'Twill make me a rich man." He rubbed his pale hands, and his stiff white hair stood straight up, seeming electric with excitement.

As I talked to Callander, I began to understand my father's feelings about privateers. They took prizes, of course, bringing home captured ships and cargoes. They might be fighting for their country, but they were also fighting to enrich their owners. I could not love Andrew Callander, sitting comfortably ashore, waiting for a princely return on a small investment— fattening on war. To a Navy man, ready to die without a thought to profit, men such as Callander were little better than carrion crows. Yet they were good, respectable men—and without them the privateers could not sail—and without the privateers how could we hope, with our small fleet, to hold our own against Britannia?

It was confusing.

All the same, the Tom Boyles were very different men from the Callanders. They gambled their lives; the Callanders risked only money. My father damned them all indiscriminately. In that, I knew, he was wrong. Nevertheless, the Secretary of the Navy's acceptance of my resignation burned in my pocket when I saw the *Constitution*, off Annapolis, readying for sea.

On July 5, following a brilliant display of fireworks up and down the Eastern Shore in celebration of our nation's thirty-sixth birthday, the *Constitution* appeared suddenly in the morning off the lower end of Kent Point and stood across the bay almost as if she were coming in to Forbes Inlet. My father and I watched her as she tacked and stood back toward the western shore. I could plainly see, as she turned, that Captain Hull was exercising his crew at the great guns.

I felt as if my heart were being torn in two.

My father watched her through his spyglass until she dropped below Poplar Island and disappeared to the southward. Then he put down his glass, glared at me, and without a word stalked to his study. I remained until dark, staring blindly over the empty water. The moon rose, and in the faint trail of silver on the bay I seemed to see my beloved, stars in her hair and in her eyes. Kirstie!

I stumbled down to the dock, and I must at that point have gone out of my mind. I do not remember anything save that I was going to Kirstie. It was Cato and Virgil, in the skipjack my father had recently purchased to replace the *Ladybug*, who fished me out of the water. I had been crazily swimming out to sea.

A week later on the outrunning tide, soon after dawn, a fleet of tall ships appeared beyond the low loom of Kent Point, running southward together in no semblance of order but tacking this way and that, over and under and across one another's paths, yet never once fouling and quite evidently all together. Privateers they were, playing like porpoises as they put out to sea. I made out the *Nonesuch,* the *Highflyer,* the *Hornet,* the *Globe,* the *Dolphin,* the *Rossie.*

"Damned pirates!" was my father's comment.

The dreary days passed. My father and I scarcely spoke to each other. My mother begged me to be kind, to be patient, to understand.

"I'm afraid for him, Ben," she said.

I too was afraid for him. His hair seemed to be whitening before my eyes and there were deep lines in his face that had not been there before. He rode furiously about the countryside on his great black horse, and Cato told me worriedly that when he brought it back the stallion was lathered with sweat, wild-eyed, and trembling.

I took to going over to Baltimore in a one-man sailing dinghy I purchased. I heard there the great news of the *Constitution's* victory over the *Guerrière.* In the engagement Bill Bush, who commanded the marines, was shot through the head and killed instantly. A ball passed through Charlie Morris's stomach, flinging him into the scuppers whence he rose and, clutching with one hand his oozing intestines, fought through the entire battle.

My father read the accounts in the *Niles Register* and the *National Intelligencer* which I brought back with me. He could not contain himself.

"You might have been there!" he cried.

"Yes, sir," I said dully. "I might have been there."

At Baltimore there was news, too, of the privateers, by way of the British merchantmen they had captured and sent to the home port with a prize crew to sail them there. A specially appointed court sat in judgment upon the captive vessels, declaring them confiscated and turning them over to the owners of the privateers. The British seamen were sent, I believe, to Norfolk, there to await the cartels—the ships by which exchange of prisoners was effected between the United States and Great Britain. Now and again a prize came in from the *Comet.* In the taverns and counting houses, I heard Tom Boyle spoken of as the Demon Captain and the Fire-eater.

The *Comet* returned in October and I was there to greet Captain Boyle. So, too, was a good part of the city of Baltimore. Boyle had become famous—or infamous, as my father would have it—for his swift raids and slashing attacks on British shipping in West Indian waters, ranging farther than any of the other privateersmen; they preferred to stay close to home. It was some days before I had Tom to myself. At the Fountain Inn I had a supper laid for us in my room, and happy he was to be rescued from acclamations, speeches, and toasts.

"I swear to ye, Ben me lad," he cried, "I've made no more than six captures, and only burned and sunk as many more. Why, there've been a dozen raids better'n mine, and 'tis meself is blamed for all of 'em. 'Tis fair daft they be, these folk!"

"Tom," I said, grinning, "it's a way you have. Be glad for the black name you're making. If it spreads far and wide, you've only to post it on the bulletin board at Lloyd's in London to put the fear of God—or the devil—into the English."

He shouted with laughter. "By the Prophets, we'll do it one day! Burn me britches if we don't!"

The moment came that I dreaded. "Sure, lad, ye'll be comin' along. The schooner's being refitted and rerigged. 'Twill take no time at all to put out again, and I've more need of ye than when we were tradin'."

"But you've no place for a supercargo now, Tom," I temporized.

"Hah! Begad, there's such a mort of writin' 'tis a regular secretary I'm needin'."

To sail on a tall ship with Tom Boyle, if only to forget, to escape from what now confronted me at Forbes Landfall—my very soul seemed to take wing at this thought which I had been sternly suppressing. Tom sat very quietly while I struggled with myself.

"Then ye'll not be comin'?" he said at last, sorrowfully.

"My father is gravely ill," I explained drearily. "I'm afraid it would kill him, Tom."

There were tears in his eyes when we parted. "I'll be back for ye, Ben," he said, "and then we'll be off together after Mistress Kirstie. 'Tis a promise."

I smiled at him. "And what would your owners say to that, you crazy Irishman?"

He chuckled. "I'll make it so 'twill all be war and good business, and what they don't know won't do 'em no harm."

But there was no place in my heart for hope when I returned to Forbes Landfall.

SEVEN

My father had been struck down by one of the intermittent fevers that plague our shore. But it was more serious than such attacks usually are. Although he had suffered them often enough, as we all did, he had never before taken to his bed. Now he lay helpless and all of Doctor Tilghman's tried and true remedies were having no effect.

My frightened mother sorely needed me, and I tried to conceal my own anxiety in comforting her and in taking on the overseeing of our acres, the marketing, the accounts, and the small but ever-tumultous affairs of our field hands and house servants. But there were many nights when I could not sleep, and I would stand outside my father's half-opened door to listen to his labored breathing until Cassie, who sat beside him, came out to report to me. For I was not permitted to see him. The sight of me raised his fever alarmingly.

It was bitterly hard. I blamed myself for the mysterious persistence and malevolence of his illness. No one knew better than I how he had long burned within himself because of me. Our country was at war and his only son, whom he had reared for the Navy, sat idly at home instead of faring forth to bring honor to the good name of Forbes. I knew his sufferings almost as if they were my own, for was I not part of him? A fever did not kill. But add to it the smoldering rage of a lifelong ambition that has been damnably frustrated! Hell-fire, I saw it. Hell-fire that might only be quenched by death.

As the days and weeks dragged on, Doctor Tilghman became angry. "A man can't feed on his own gall and bile without poisoning himself!" he fumed. He began to spend more and more time in the sick room and from outside I heard furious voices. My father, weakened though he was, seemed to be holding his own against the doctor. From what I could make out they were fighting the first War of Independence against England, Napoleon's wars, the four duels, and the present war. And they were fighting over privateers versus the Navy.

"You'll kill him!" I cried after one such engagement when the doctor came down, red-faced with choler.

"Ben," said Doctor Tilghman, "he's sick with spleen, as Colonel Savage was. I'll have it out of him—if he doesn't kill me first!"

It was in the winter that the letters came, one after another. The first was from the Department of State. It told me, curtly, that among the official papers of the late Joel Barlow a note had been found with my name and address and the message: "Inform him that those he seeks are in London."

A second letter came from Denmark by way of Hamburg. It was written in French by a lady who declared herself a friend of a friend of Mistress Robert Smith, and it said that the Baron von Lund was in Copenhagen.

A third followed, also written by a lady, and sent by way of Antwerp. She must have been a young lady, for it was a long letter and in it I could almost hear the delighted and triumphant squeals and the ecstatic giggles. But in brief it said that the Baron von Lund was in Paris.

And there came a fourth, from Mistress Smith herself, written from New York where she was visiting with friends. "You will find our dear one in London. My heart goes with you."

I was in a turmoil. London—Copenhagen—Paris. I saw myself pursuing Kirstie for all eternity.

Paris—Copenhagen—London. I must go, but where? To France, to England, to Denmark? And how could I go anywhere at all, with my father lying close to death?

Nevertheless, I went to Baltimore to find news of Tom Boyle. He was still cruising in West Indian waters, ranging up as far as the Bermudas. In Annapolis I learned from a gleeful Andrew Callander that Boyle's captured booty on this long voyage was already astronomical. "By the time he's done, 'twill come to more than three million dollars!" Callander exulted.

A month later I went again to Baltimore. I learned that Tom Boyle had come home, but he was in Beaufort, North Carolina, where he was selling the *Comet* at his owners' direction.

I would have gone to Beaufort but that my father's illness was reaching a point of crisis. Not for a moment did I believe that Boyle would be retiring from the sea. I knew him better than I did my own father. He would be getting another ship. I left word for him in Annapolis and Baltimore, reminding him of his promise. If my father lived, I would be sailing with Tom. If he died—but it was better not to think of that.

In the terrible weeks that followed my mother and Doctor Tilghman fought with death while I, filled with dread, could do nothing. I had been through many things, but never through anything so diabolically tormenting as this enforced uselessness.

One day Doctor Tilghman came heavily down the stairs from the sick room and I saw with dull despair that his face, gray with fatigue, had a look of finality. I started up.

"It's all right, Ben," he said. "He'll live—the stubborn old fool!" The next I knew he was pouring brandy down my throat and swearing at me with hearty good will.

It was midsummer and the British were thick as thieves in the bay, when one afternoon I saw a strange schooner swinging around Kent Point and beating across the eastern bay. I watched her with mounting excitement. At the mouth of Forbes Inlet her anchor splashed down raising a fountain of spray. Her great sails settled gracefully in exact folds along the booms. She was a taller ship than any I had seen. I judged her to be about 350 tons, nearly 120 feet long, and almost 30 in the beam. Her hull was long, low, and black with gold tracery across the fantail and above her cutwater. There was a bold gold streak along her strakes. Her masts were set at a rakish tilt that made her look as though she were leaping through the water even as she lay at anchor. I picked out the name gilded across her transom: *Chasseur*.

As I watched, a boat dropped down and came smartly toward the inlet. I ran down to the dock to greet the stocky figure climbing out of the boat. We embraced French style. Then we slapped each other about in every way imaginable.

"Tom," I cried, "I'm ready now. My bag's been packed for months. You'll take me on, won't you? You'll get me over to Europe, won't you, Tom?"

"Avast!" he said, laughing. "Heave to, lad! Aye, I'll get ye there!"

But not another word would he say of that as I took him to the house. He would only talk about his new command. "A beauty, she is. Why, Ben, our *True Love-Comet* was good enough for the old days, but 'twas a waddlin' sow she was beside this fine lady. And we're better armed. With 150 men aboard, she carries a battery of sixteen long 12s and eight short 9s."

I gave a low whistle. "What are you up to?"

But still he would not say.

My mother greeted him graciously, and he bent low over her hand. Then, to my astonishment, she said, "Captain Boyle, my husband requests the pleasure of your company. He has been ill, or he would be down to receive you. Would you be so kind . . .?"

Tom bowed again. "'Tis an honor, ma'am."

She led the way, and I, following behind, had a glimpse of my father sitting among pillows in an armchair by the window. He was pale and thin. My mother did not permit me to enter but closed the door on me. I paced up and down before it, waiting apprehensively for sounds of altercation.

The door opened at last, and Tom bowed himself out. He was smiling.

"Ben," said my mother, motioning me to enter. I looked at her questioningly. She nodded, her eyes misty. I stepped in and the door closed behind me softly.

Slowly I approached my father. "Well, sir?" he said.

With a great rush of joy and love, I said, "Yes, sir. *Very* well, sir!"

He cleared his throat. "Your Captain Boyle," he said, "is almost a gentleman."

"No, sir," I said stoutly, "he is not a gentleman. He is a man!"

"Ben," he said reprovingly, "you've a bad temper and you're obstinate as a mule."

"That's true, sir," I retorted. "I get it from my father."

He laughed then, and I with him.

After a while he said, "She must be a great lady, your bride-to-be. Bring her back, son. We'll have the wedding here. You'll not deny us that pleasure?"

He looked at me pleadingly, almost fearful. "I'll bring her back," I promised him, "for the wedding."

He shook my hand. "God bless you, son."

In my own room I caught up my sea bag and leaped down the stairs making such a clatter that my mother looked up with the little frown she had put on so often, on many another like occasion, when I was a child.

"You see," she confided in Tom, "he's only a baby."

Tom flashed me a wink, but he said gravely, "Yes, ma'am, but we'll get him wed, ma'am. 'Tis Tom Boyle that says it."

"I declare," said my mother in a happy flutter, "I've so much to do. So many new dresses.... Ben, is she very smart? A Baron's daughter.... Ben, how does she dress?"

"She wears clothes, mother," I said with a great hug and kiss. "But sometimes she doesn't."

As I swung down the path with Tom Boyle I heard her shocked voice,

"Ben! Good heavens, whatever do you mean? Ben!"

Laughing, I waved back to her.

"Come along," Tom hurried me. "We've got to be down the bay just outside the Capes by nightfall, for between then and dawn we've the blockade to run, and beyond that the whole ocean waitin'!"

EIGHT

The *Chasseur* was indeed a beauty. She appeared to have been built especially for privateering, for her guns were well mounted—some privateers had blown out their own sides with their makeshift guns—and she had proper quarters for gunners, marines, and crew. She was handy. She answered the slightest touch of her helm, and she soared over the water like a sea gull.

By nightfall we were close by the Wolf Trap and standing across to the little hook-shaped inlet on the Eastern Shore, just where the land begins to curl eastward toward Cape

Charles. We anchored there. Even as we slipped into our anchorage, we could see the British ships far out beyond the Capes, patrolling in the deep water—two frigates and a ship of the line—passing alternately across the gap of water.

At midnight the tide reached full flood and turned. We set out with it. The night was very black, for there was yet no moon. Tom took the wheel himself and I stood beside him as he took the *Chasseur* into the labyrinthine channels that thread across the upper and outer banks. I knew these waters well. It was trick sailing even in broad daylight. By night it did not seem possible. But Tom Boyle did it as easily as if he had spent his entire life among the twisting waterways.

When I complimented him, he only said, "Sure, 'tis a favorite escapeway for privateers in or out."

The blockading vessels carried no lights to betray their position, and as we approached the open water I began to sweat with a new fear—that by accident we might sail directly into one of them. Tom, however, had not only studied their habits but had also timed our dash with the moonrise. For as we cleared the shoals and crowded on sail, the moon's silver edge began to show over the eastern horizon and the ghostly light flowed over the pale ocean, revealing the black hulk of a frigate far to the north and another far to the south. The huge ship of the line was hauled in close between the Capes, in a position to intercept any that might attempt to skip past her in the ordinary lanes. She was a good 2 miles away, and anchored. She spied us, of course, and loosed a gun at us. The water plume spouted, pretty as could be in the moonlight, more than a mile astern. She only had a look at our fantail for her pains. We fairly flew over the sea. As for the frigates, they never had a chance.

Tom was avoiding me. He had presented me to Jack Stansbury, his secretary. Since he had a secretary, there would be little or no duties for me. I seemed to have no place among the lively ship's company. I bombarded Stansbury with questions, but he was as solemn and silent a young man as ever I had seen, so close-mouthed that he might have been well employed as a king's messenger. And my old friends of the *True Love* aboard the *Chasseur,* from the first mate down to the cook, were no better. They seemed to be enjoying a private secret, one too precious to be divulged. Anxiously I watched our course. It appeared to me that we were heading for West Indian waters. At the end of twenty-four hours, however, the *Chasseur* turned and bore northeast by east.

I managed to corner Tom. "Captain Boyle," I demanded, "what are my duties?"

"Mr. Forbes," said he with like formality, "if we come into action I'll be askin' ye to take a musket with the marines. For the rest, till the time comes, ye're a passenger." He lowered his voice confidentially. "I'm readin' straight through the Bible o' nights and Stansbury's no good to me. I tried Samson and Delilah with him, and, Ben, ye'd think he was readin' out an official report. He'd've had Samson interned and the gel put under house arrest!"

"Tom," I said in exasperation, "I swear I'll take a belaying pin and beat it out of you."

He hugged himself as if to keep in laughter. But he said, "Wait, me lad. I wouldn't want ye to be disappointed, so wait a bit until I see what's afloat for our takin'."

And that was all I could get out of him. We read the tale of Samson and Delilah in his cabin at night and agreed that Samson was a dolt and a bully who deserved what he got, but we could not love Delilah, and so we went to Ruth among the alien corn.

We were a month out—it was early in the afternoon of August 16, to be exact—when the man at the masthead called out that a brig was in sight. I followed his hoarse cry—"Sail to leeward, sail to leeward!"—with my eyes. From the cut of her topsails, from that silhouette, there was no mistaking what she was—a British brig.

"Set all sail! Put her before the wind!" It was Boyle's voice, a throaty roar, hoarse with excitement, that boomed out behind me. "Clear for action!"

I turned. Though the mouth had roared like a lion's, the eye held the gleam of a fox. And the eye was turned on me. "Go to quarters, Mr. Forbes, for that musket." It almost seemed that his soft voice was laughing at me, even through his excitement. "Sure, we'll be making more than a messenger boy of ye yet."

As I stumbled below, the steady rhythmic beat of a drum sounded through the ship. Footsteps went racing along the deck, not wildly but purposefully. Groups of men were running to the guns. Breechings were cast off, tampions taken out, rammers and sponges snatched from their racks. All sixteen of our long 12s, of which Tom Boyle was so proud—"Ye can't upset 'em," he'd explained to me, "and they're best for the long shot and the chase"—all sixteen were made ready to blast the brig right out of the water.

My stumbling trip below for the musket was also a voyage into the past. Once again I was standing on the cluttered deck of the *Chesapeake,* transfixed, watching the innocent white mushroom clouds form by the *Leopard's* guns, hearing the ear-splitting crash, feeling the sick lurch of the stricken ship receiving the broadside, then the scream of rending timber, the top of the mainmast falling lazily. . . .

Somehow I got back on deck, shaking the cobwebs of the past from my brain. Boyle had piled on all canvas and the *Chasseur* fairly leapt through the water. He eyed me sharply and smiled as if to say, "You were long in search of that musket, Mr. Forbes." And a glance showed me that indeed I had been. Already we were within easy range of the brig and fast bearing down upon her, though she was making frantic efforts to escape, uselessly piling on more sail and changing course.

The closer we came the larger grew the knot in my guts. I listened for Boyle's order to fire, but it did not come. His face was a study in tense waiting. The men were poised at their guns, the ship cut through the waves straining against her own full sail. Yet with all the speed and motion, the world stood still, waiting upon the word of one man. And as the gap closed between the *Chasseur* and the British brig—she was the *Eclipse;* we could even read her now—no word was forthcoming from Tom Boyle.

It was the hapless prey that, in desperation, struck first. Around the stern chasers of the *Eclipse* I saw the dreaded mushrooms form. But there was no answering lurch, no break in the *Chasseur's* stride. The brig's desperate shots went wild and, as if in pathetic admission of futility, she steadied on a course parallel to the *Chasseur's* as we forged up alongside.

No man will ever know what was in Boyle's mind. I think now, having watched him take so many prizes and knowing his preference for ensnaring an enemy by guile rather than force, that he meant to force the *Eclipse* to haul down her colors without firing a single shot. But before he could give a single order, one of the forward long 12s went off with a bang. Boyle's head turned in the direction of the gun and a savage frown swept his face. I had just enough time to think, "My God, I wouldn't want to stand in that gunner's shoes," when his order to fire swept my mind clean in a single instant.

A crashing, near-simultaneous broadside came from the long 12s. I reached out to steady myself as the *Chasseur* heaved to the recoil and smoke poured upward in a cloud, enclosing me and cutting off the *Eclipse* from view. I braced myself for an answering blast but it did not come. I peered through the smoke, but with the wind directly abaft it was hard to see anything. I looked for Boyle and he was beside me, oddly relaxed, the tension and excitement gone from his face. In its place was an expression I can only describe as a kind of mild regret.

I followed his gaze to the *Eclipse*, or what was left of her. From the deck up she was more of a wreck than I would ever have imagined a ship could be reduced to by a single broadside, had I not myself once stood in the litter and tangle of the *Chesapeake*. Her canvas was in tatters, her mainmast split and hanging, her rigging cut to pieces. Yet only one gaping hole could I see in the brig's side, and as the smoke cleared I looked in vain for the wounded on the decks of the *Eclipse*. Boyle had kept his fire high to disable but not to massacre his prey.

As the two ships wallowed uneasily not a cable length apart, a single cry came from the *Eclipse*, a high shriek that ended in a sigh or was blown away by the wind. Then it was that I saw her colors coming down.

In this way I saw the *Chasseur* take her first of many prizes. I played out my role of spectator, my musket unfired. The *Eclipse*, it turned out, was out of Buenos Aires for Liverpool, with hides, furs, and a small quantity of specie. We took aboard the latter, put a prize crew upon her, and ordered her to the United States.

Three days later we picked up the brig *Commerce*, from Newfoundland for Spain with codfish. She was a new, copperbottomed vessel of no small value. We placed ten men aboard her and sent her home to Baltimore. The next prize was the brig *Antelope*, of Guernsey out of Havana with 900 boxes of sugar. She surrendered without firing a shot, although she carried eight 18-pound carronades and a long gun. Her too we sent home with a prize crew. Tom Boyle, puckishly irritated by her lack of spirit, had Stansbury write a report of the affair to the British Admiralty.

The next day we took the little sloop *Christiana*, of Scottish registry, from the Canaries with a cargo of cork. She was hardly worth sending home. Boyle made her a cartel ship, putting aboard all the prisoners we had taken from our other captures, and also the report to the Admiralty. Entirely manned by British seamen, she sailed off for Plymouth. A privateer cannot afford to crowd herself with prisoners; there is always the danger that they might rise and take over the ship. Further, only a limited number of the crew can be spared to sail a prize to the home port. With growing admiration I watched Tom Boyle carefully dispose of men and prizes.

It was after we rid ourselves of the *Christiana* and our prisoners that Tom took me down to his great cabin to reveal his secret. "We've got British specie now," he said, "and we'll be takin' more cartels, so all goes well. Now, me lad, ye'll be runnin' up to London to do an errand for me—that's if ye've a mind to." He put his head on one side and looked at me almost coyly.

"London!" I cried. "London! Tom, you know I'd give my right arm to get there!"

"So I thought," said he with an air of having arranged the universe to his satisfaction.

"Thought!" I laughed at him. "You knew damn well.... But, Tom, she might not be there. She might be in Paris, or Copenhagen."

"Mistress Kirstie'll be in London," said Boyle with conviction.

"How do you know?" I demanded.

"To tell the truth," he admitted, "I don't. But d'ye see, Ben, I've me heart set on marryin' ye, so she's got to be in London and ye'll bring her aboard and—Ben, sure and ye'll let me do the marryin', won't ye now? Many's the night I've dreamed on it. 'Twould be the grand and glorious moment of all me life."

Deeply moved, I could only nod. Somehow I'd find a way to mollify my mother. He blew his nose vigorously and turned to rummage in his chest. I heard the crackle of papers, and then he thrust into my hands a large, official-looking document. On it was embossed a flying eagle holding in its beak a ribbon with the legend: *E Pluribus Unum.*

Across the top, the imposing letters read:

PROCLAMATION ISSUED BY THOMAS BOYLE, ESQ.,

Commander of the *CHASSEUR*

I glanced up at Tom. Sitting with downcast eyes, he looked as modest as a maiden.

Returning in no little bewilderment to the important document, I read:

Whereas, it has been customary with the Admirals of Great Britain commanding small forces on the Coast of the United States, particularly with Sir John Borlaise

Warren and Sir Alexander Cochrane, to declare the Coast of the said United States in a state of strict and vigorous blockade, without possessing the power to justify such a declaration, or stationing an adequate force to command such a blockade,

I do, therefore, by virtue of the power and authority in me vested (possessing sufficient force) declare all the ports, harbors, bays, creeks, rivers, inlets, outlets, islands, and sea coasts of the United Kingdom of Great Britain and Ireland in a state of strict and rigorous blockade, and I do further declare that I consider the forces under my command adequate to maintain strictly, rigorously and effectually, the said blockade.

And, I do hereby require the respective officers, whether captains, or commanding officers, under my command, employed or to be employed on the coast of England, Ireland, and Scotland, to pay strict attention to this my proclamation.

And, I hereby caution and forbid the ships and vessels of all and every nation, in amity and peace with the United States, from entering or attempting to enter or from coming or attempting to come out of any of the said ports, harbors, bays, creeks, rivers, inlets, outlets, islands, or the sea coasts, on or under any pretense whatsoever; and that no person may plead ignorance of this, my proclamation, I have ordered the same to be made public in England.

Given under my hand on board the Chasseur.

THOMAS BOYLE
By command of the Commanding Officer,
J. J. Stansbury, Sec'y.

Incredulous, I read it twice over, and was beginning a third time.

"Me, I'd of liked some trumpetin' words," said Tom, "but Stansbury's mighty strict with me. Says governments don't read Shakespeare nor even the Bible."

I let out a long breath. "I'm damned!" I said.

"'Tis as sensible as any of their decrees or Orders-in-Council," said Tom defensively. "They don't blockade *me*, do they now? So if they'll have their foolishness, I can have me fun, too. Anyhow, 'twas you that set me to it, Ben."

"What do you think of doing with it?" I asked, fingering the extraordinary document.

"Why, ye'll take it to London, lad, and ye'll post it up at Lloyd's for all England to see. I hear tell they're scared of Tom Boyle. Up go the insurance rates for shipping, which is all to the good. And belike some ships won't sail that would've been settin' out, and owners and merchants'll be screamin' for more convoys. And on our side, 'twill do us good to be pullin' the British lion's whiskers. . . ."

He gave me a worried look. "Ye don't like it, Ben?"

"Like it?" I began to laugh.

"Like it!"

I howled uncontrollably. I heard Tom splutter and then let out a roar. Stansbury came in with reports to be signed, and a look at his sober face sent us off again. The discussion of plans and strategy had to wait until the next day. I laughed in my sleep that night, actually waking myself with the humor of it.

The scheme, when we got down to it, was simple. I would go ashore in a cartel as a British seaman taken on a previous capture and kept aboard the *Chasseur* because of a serious wound. Tom gave me papers that identified me as Benjamin Weld of Cornwall. "I've more'n a score of 'em," he said. "They've been taken from men killed in action on ships we've boarded, or from prisoners who died aboard."

Suddenly anxious, he said, "Ye'll not let yerself be caught, lad. They'll treat ye as a spy."

With more confidence than I felt, I assured him that no Englishman on earth could take me, any more than Tom Boyle could be taken on the seas.

I began my new role at once by submitting to Mr. Osbourne, the ship's surgeon, for a blood-letting in order to acquire the necessary pallor. I was literally bled white by our zealous surgeon, and spent several days in bed, weakly cursing him. I was equipped with a British seaman's bag into which I packed some of my own gear, including my one suit of shore clothes, and provided with a moneybelt of English specie. Jack Stansbury had a map of London which I studied carefully for a week.

We were now close under the mouth of the English Channel. Here we took in rapid succession six more prizes, including the sloop *Favorite* and the brigs *Prudence* and *Marquis of Cornwallis*. Their cargoes and seamen were taken aboard, and all the ships save the *Marquis of Cornwallis* were burned.

It was while Tom Boyle and the marines were boarding the first of the new prizes that Mr. Osbourne took me in hand for the final preparations. Slitting my shirt sleeve to the shoulder, he bound my arm in splints. In bandaging it he rolled the proclamation around my arm so that, when he had done, it was concealed under the dressings. He used a long black silk neckerchief for a sling.

Meanwhile, Jack Stansbury repeated my instructions as if intoning a litany:

"You were wounded in our first encounter, Mr. Weld. The brig *Eclipse*. Your shipmates went forward in our first cartel. We kept you aboard for treatment. Now our surgeon deems you well enough to join the new prisoners and go home. You will do a certain errand in London and have some days for an errand of your own. You will then take the stage for Penzance in Cornwall at Land's End. Four miles eastward of the village and at the bottom of the cliffs, you'll find a stony little shingle well-known to Cornish smugglers. It's called the Lizard. We'll be standing off and on, off the coast, waiting for your lantern signal to send the boat in for you. You've ten days.

"Is all clear, Mr. For- —Weld?"

"Ten days," I said. "Penzance. The Lizard."

He shook my hand and said dryly, "Good luck, Mr. Weld."

"Good luck to the *Chasseur!*" I said fervently. "You're taking a risk standing off the English shore just to pick me up."

"Captain Boyle's orders," he said crisply. And then he startled me by adding wistfully, "Wish it was me that was going."

I laughed to myself when he had gone. Stansbury, for all his staid demeanor, was just as crazy as Tom Boyle. Or myself.

NINE

When the new prisoners came aboard, I was curtly presented to the first of them by Mr. Osbourne. From then on I was one of them. Seaman Benjamin Weld was a morosely silent Cornishman, sickly pale under his tan and with a stubble of beard. His right shoulder drooped slightly—the natural result of my old wounds from the *Chesapeake*—and his right arm was in a sling. When spoken to, he glowered and replied in monosyllables. There was many another like him—men tired to their very souls of long years of war. He was not conspicuous and he was let alone.

It was nightfall when Tom Boyle took the *Marquis of Cornwallis* right in the English Channel—a daring feat that made me sweat with apprehension. Luckily she carried no guns. We were transferred that very night, tumbling down into the heaving boat and being rowed over to her through black seas that swept over us, wetting us through and through. Philosophically accepting their bad luck, the brig's own crew sailed her back to the port from which they had only just set out. The brig wallowed and waddled through the night and all the next day. I was thankful that it was dusk when we came into Portsmouth and a cold rain falling. Nevertheless, a small crowd of honest well-wishers were on the dock to greet us. Annoyingly sympathetic, they wanted to escort me to the naval hospital. With a growl I shook them off, and they were advised by the others, who were swiftly dispersing, to let me be.

The thing was ridiculously easy. There were no officious personages questioning or probing, as Boyle and I had feared there might be. If there were any suspicious authorities in Portsmouth, they were snug in their houses that night. No doubt the captains of the six vessels would be spending the night in some tavern or other, preparing reports to their owners and insurers. Their seamen, however, had nothing to do but to go as quickly as possible to their home ports to look for another ship.

I accepted the proffered services of a lively street urchin. He shouldered my bag, led me into town, and with money I gave him bought passage for me on the stagecoach to London that left within the hour. It was a cold, wet journey of eight hours, for I had a seat outside. Jolted, drenched, my arm cramped, and all of me numb with weariness and hunger, I appeared so wretched a creature that my fellow passengers descended in a body upon me and with a solicitous clamor deposited me in the best room of the posting inn. From the innkeeper's wife they elicited the promise to send forthwith for a doctor before they would go their separate ways.

There was no time to lose.

In breathless haste I removed my sling and the bandages, and changed into my shore clothes. But in this dress I could not go about carrying a sea bag. I must leave it behind. The proclamation presented a sudden problem. It was too large to be hidden on my person. I rolled it up. Holding it in my hand, I walked out with the boldness of desperation, looking neither to right nor to left.

At the door a small man in the very devil of a hurry collided with me, muttered an apology, and darted in. "Here we are!" I heard him call out. "Where is the sick gentleman?"

From the corner of my eye I saw a potboy eying me dubiously.

I took two long strides and the crowds of London surged about me.

A map is only a flat, lifeless sketch, an abstraction. It leaves out the thronging people that make up a great city: the men, women, and children dashing about their business, the street vendors crying their wares, the dickering housewives, the shrill beggars, the hazards of the broken wooden sidewalks, the perils of streets crowded with carts, lumbering wagons, and coaches. I had no idea where I might be. Carried on the bewildering flood of a people intent on the day's work, I walked, it seemed to me, for miles.

I was brought to my senses by a rumbling voice in my ear, "Lookin' for a berth, sailor?" The owner of it was a square, bluff, blue-eyed man who had sea captain written all over him. I was startled but I rallied enough to reply, "No, I'm careening here, scraping off my barnacles." He gave me a humorous, crinkly look and walked on, but after a dozen paces halted to look back at me.

This incident troubled me. It was high time I got out of my sailor's garb and into a suit of London clothes that would render me inconspicuous. A grubby street urchin who had been lingering to listen to this dialogue now drifted up to me, pulled his forelock with mock gravity, and announced, "At your service, capting." I told him I was looking for a clothing store.

"Store? You're an American, hey?"

"Why should I be an American?"

"Americans says 'store' when they means 'shop.'"

"Well, put it down in your book that Canadians also say 'store.'"

He conducted me round a corner, up a side street, and into a Gentlemen's Clothing & Haberdashery.

Half an hour later I issued forth attired as a young gent who might be a club man or an attorney's confidential clerk, and, I hoped, as the sort of person who would be found naturally in the precincts of Lloyd's or the Royal Exchange. My beaver hat gave me a worldly air. My carpetbag held my shaving kit, shirts, stockings, and undergarments. My stylish coat had been chosen for a hidden virtue: pockets deep enough to hold Captain Tom Boyle's dangerous proclamation.

The street arab, having given me the name of an inn near the Exchange and called up "an 'ackney coach," acknowledged my six-penny bit with a good-by pull at his forelock. And so in short order I found myself at the Three Crowns in Cheapside. Washed and shaved, I went down to the coffee house for a belated, hearty breakfast, and gave thought to my next step.

The map I had so carefully studied had become in my mind a jumble of lines and names. If he could have peered into my brain, the methodical Stansbury would have been thoroughly disgusted with me, as I was with myself. I had the shopkeeper's word for it that Cheapside was cheek by jowl with the Royal Exchange, and I knew that Lloyd's rooms were in the Exchange. But when I went out, I could see no edifice that proclaimed itself the Royal Exchange—only crooked lines of grimy houses, offices, and shops pierced by dark passages. The din of London smote upon my ears. As one stunned, I retreated back into the coffee house.

This, I told myself severely, would not do. I was reluctant to call attention to myself as a stranger, yet there was no help for it; I must ask to be directed. Quickly I conjured up for myself a new identity. I was a Canadian, the seagoing son of a merchant of Hamilton in Ontario—this to account for my seaman's look, which cannot be disguised. Inwardly debating what merchandise it was that my assumed father dealt in, I became aware of two gentlemen close beside me who had been engaged in conversation. It was the parting words of one of them that struck me like a bo's'n's pipe calling all hands on deck.

"Well," said he, "I'm for Lloyd's—the auction, y'know."

He was already gone. I sped after him, and it was with profound thankfulness that I caught sight of his hat. Taller and glossier than mine or any other, it bobbed above the throngs. I blessed him and his unknown hatter as I struggled after him. I saw him enter a doorway at one end of a huge building and was at that moment accosted by a whining old woman who carried oddments on a dirty tray slung by a rope around her neck. I thrust her off, but a thought occurred to me and I turned back once more. "Have you a packet of pins, Mother?"

"I've that, son," she replied, suddenly brisk.

I gave her sixpence for the twisted paper. She blessed me as if I had handed her a purse of gold. The pins would probably have been dear had they cost her six packets for a penny.

"Would that be Lloyd's, Mother?" I asked, pointing to the door through which my man had disappeared.

"Son," she said, "it would."

I went up a steep, dark stairway and emerged into a large room in which were so many men raising such a hubbub that I could only stand gaping. It was crowded with tables and benches. At one end rose a chair that looked like a throne, and on the desk before the man who honored it was a tall candle, half burned. At the other end of the room was a long bar from which coffee was being served. Waiters plunged about with steaming coffee cups on perilous duty among the packed assemblage. Every table was occupied, and so too was every inch of space upon which two feet could stand. The man on the throne was droning in a voice that could not be heard in the tumult, but he did not appear at all annoyed by the fact. Now and again someone shouted above the others—a number. "Five!" A little later would come "And a half!" from another place entirely.

Pushed and jostled, I found myself at one end of the bar. Before me on the wall was a notice by which I was informed that the brig *Lucania* was being auctioned by candle. The numbers being called, then, must be pounds—five hundred? Five thousand? "Six and a guinea!" someone called at that moment, and it was apparently amusing for it was followed by a roar of laughter. The man on the throne looked offended at this. He was, I supposed, the auctioneer.

I turned back to read the particulars about the brig that was being auctioned. But I did not read them. For it burst upon me that the notice was not on the wall itself. It was pinned to a large frame of green baize within which were other notices. I was in Lloyd's and here before my eyes was the bulletin board!

Waiters pushed by me, gentlemen crowded me. I planted my feet and stood like a rock, glancing about. Gentlemen stood around me in noisy little groups, being turned and shifted with the stir and movement in the room. The shouts of the bids were coming faster, for the candle was burning low. To the man who raised his bid and his voice with the last flicker of the candle, the brig would be knocked down. Already the auctioneer was holding up his wooden hammer. The uproar in no way diminished, but all heads were turned toward the auctioneer and the candle.

In a moment I had Tom's proclamation out of my pocket, and in another moment it was pinned to the middle of the board, over the notice of the auction. For long seconds I dared not stir, expecting a shout greater than any of the others and a rough hand on my collar. Slowly, very slowly, I turned.

"Seven!" I heard a voice, shrill with excitement.

"And a half!" The second was a cry of triumph, for with it the candle went out and down came the auctioneer's hammer. Then there was such a surging and swirling that I was caught up in it and carried down the stairs. I found myself out in the street face to face with the old woman who had sold me the pins. To her utter astonishment, I bent and kissed her.

"Lord love you, son!" she gasped.

"God bless you, Mother!" I called back to her.

I was off to find Kirstie.

Many hours later I was still wandering through the streets of London. I must have crisscrossed the sprawling city, draped like a vast spider web upon both sides of the humpback bend of the Thames, as often as the ancient ghosts of those who had built it in ages gone. Long since careless of calling attention to myself, I inquired everywhere after the Danish legation, the Danish consul, and even specifically for the Baron von Lund of Denmark. Coach drivers, shopkeepers, innkeepers, errand boys, ladies with kindly faces, gentlemen of portentous bearing—I stopped many in the street and asked. Did they perhaps know of a Danish coffee house, club, restaurant? Or of a neighborhood where Danes resided? Did they know any single subject of Denmark now residing in London?

They did not.

It was a ragged, emaciated little boy, a chimney sweep by the sooty look of him, who told me that the Danish legation was in the neighborhood of Portland Square, which was, said he, close by. He had cleaned its chimneys only two days ago. He took me to the house, an old one it was, with a dead look, for it was closed. It was guarded by a crusty old custodian appointed, he was proud to say, by the Foreign Ministry.

This he told me at once, and then he said, "They an't here."

"Who?" I demanded. "Who is not here?"

"Who was it you was askin' for?" he countered.

"Whoever it was that lived here," I replied confusedly. "I mean—the Danes—the staff of the Danish legation."

"Oh. Them. Interned like as not. It's wot 'appens to 'em all in war time."

"But the peace has just been made with Denmark. There's no war with Denmark, not any more."

"So that's it!" he said darkly. "So that's why I had to let in this 'ere creetur to clean the chimneys." He glowered at me as if I were in some way responsible.

My small sooty friend hereupon let loose a stream of abuse, to which the custodian replied in kind.

I interposed. "If they've had the chimneys cleaned, they'll be coming back," I said. "But when? And where are they now?"

The custodian shrugged. " 'Oo's t's'y?"

I took my chimney sweep aside and questioned him. He could only say that he had been sent with a note by his master to this house. I ordered him to lead me at once to his master.

But he took fright. He wriggled out of my grasp—I had kept him fast by the arm—and shot off like an arrow. I ran after but I was no match for him. In a moment he had disappeared. It was almost like a conjuring trick.

Late that night a hackney coach carried me back to the Three Crowns in Cheapside. Sick at heart, I tossed and turned, unable to sleep. I was oppressed by a sense of urgency. Tom Boyle had given me too little time. They had told me below that it would take a week's traveling to get to Land's End unless I traveled day and night. To find a single Dane in London it seemed that I would have to knock on every door. How many doors would there be in a vast city? At fifty doors a day, how many days? I fell asleep at last and dreamed of doors at which I knocked and knocked, but each was guarded by a crusty old man and a chimney sweep and they would not open.

The next morning I wandered out hopelessly, staring into women's faces. Perhaps I would see Kirstie in the street. It came to me that once before I had walked the streets somewhere, staring at women in much the same way. Philadelphia, it had been. I had been looking for Nancy Savage. So long ago—an eternity. And Nancy had not been there. But Kirstie —Kirstie was different. Kirstie would be here for me. Kirstie. . . .

"I would not say he is a knave," said a woman's voice, a rasping kind of voice.

I looked up—and up. She was uncommonly tall and uncommonly bony. She was swathed in plum-colored velvet, but what the garment was I could not say. On her hat an elegant plume reared skyward. Her face would have been all nose, were it not for her eyes—eyes so sharp that I felt myself impaled, as if on the point of the gold-handled walking stick she leaned upon.

A man came out of a doorway. "Silk-net mittens from France, your ladyship," he said seductively. "Only just arrived. From Paris."

We were standing, I saw, before a glover's shop.

The plum-colored lady paid him no heed. She did not take her eyes from me. "Not a knave, niece," she said decisively.

"No, not a knave, dear aunt."

I looked down then. The second voice belonged to a very small young woman, plain of face and square of form.

"Then what is he about?" milady demanded.

"Young man," said the small square lady to me, "what are you about?"

I said to the tall lady, "I am looking for my betrothed, ma'am, a Danish girl with golden hair and eyes the color of the sea."

"How," said milady, still staring down into my very soul, "did he lose her?"

"Silk mittens," cried the glover desperately. "From France, come this very morning."

The niece said, "Young man, how did you lose her?"

In ten minutes the two ladies between them had my story—all save the fact that I was an American. But perhaps they knew even that.

"Niece," said milady, "take him to Trask, but bring him back. I will examine the mittens."

The niece, on the way, was kind enough to explain that Trask was an important man on the great journal, *The Times* of London, which was close at hand, for we were in Fleet Street. Trask was the son of her ladyship's gardener and her ladyship had been so kind as to set him up. From which I gathered that she had had him educated and had found him employment.

The offices of *The Times* were in great confusion, and I had the feeling that they always were, night and day. The niece moved stolidly to her destination, a dark corner at which a young man with an old face and rumpled hair sat at a small table scratching away with his pen. He leaped up when we appeared beside him, bowed several times, very rapidly, and gave the niece his chair.

"Her ladyship is, I hope, in good health this morning?" he said anxiously.

"She is," replied the niece.

They exchanged a long look which announced to any who might care to see that they were deeply in love.

"Great alarm in the city," said Trask adoringly. "The Americans are blockading England."

"It won't do," said the niece. "You know her ladyship." She gave him a melting look.

"Body of a respectable female, hacked about the middle, discovered in a coal hole in Bloomsbury," said Trask worshipfully.

"Splendid. Splendid." The niece yearned at him and he blinked.

"Billingsgate Molly was hanged yesterday," said Trask rapturously.

"Excellent."

This remarkable exchange went on for some time while I

stood by, marveling at the way these English expressed their devotion.

At last the niece rose. As if from out of a sleep she said "Danes."

"Danes?" Mr. Trask blinked a good many times. "Danes as in Denmark, would it be?"

"Danes here in London. Where do they live?"

"Sinjin's Wood."

He wrote an address on a piece of paper and gave it to her, and in the giving their hands touched. They gazed at each other. They sighed together. Then without further ado she left him, I following in a state of complete bewilderment.

Her ladyship, upon our reappearance, swept out of the glover's, the shopkeeper scurrying to bow her out and being rapped by her stick for his pains. Her ladyship's stick, raised in the street, swept off a gentleman's hat, but it also brought a handsome private coach, apparently her ladyship's own. Having handed up the two ladies, I was ordered in beside them, and off we went.

During the drive the niece entertained her ladyship with the news she had culled from Mr. Trask.

"Good," said her ladyship after each item, or "Very good," or, "Excellent."

"And, dear aunt," the niece reported rather timidly, "there is great alarm in the City. The Americans are blockading England."

Her ladyship frowned. "Niece," she said severely, "I will not be put upon. I'll not hear of the wars. Mittens at five shillings the pair! Indeed!" She was very angry, and her small niece hastened to apologize—for herself, for Mr. Trask, for the price of mittens, for the wars.

St. John's Wood was a countrylike neighborhood of stately homes, each set in its own small acre of garden and surrounded by iron-rail fences. Bushes crowded the lower windows, trees overhung the roofs. We stopped before one of these houses and I leapt out, forgetting the ladies.

An ancient was guarding the gate. He might have been twin brother to the man in Portland Square. " 'Ere, 'ere," he said, stopping me. "Show your pass."

"Why," I demanded, "do I need a pass?"

He did not deign to answer.

"Where does one get this pass?" I asked.

"Foreign Office," he said shortly.

I considered felling him with one blow. He seemed to read my thought for he planted his feet apart and stared at me balefully. I turned away, fearing that in another moment I could not be responsible for my actions but would end up hanging in chains on a gibbet at Tyburn—a murderer.

From the waiting coach I caught her ladyship's commanding eye. I turned back and shouted, there in the quiet street, at the top of my lungs:

"Kirstie! Mistress von Lund! Kirstie!"

I was answered almost immediately by a cry, an exclamation. "Benje? Oh! Benje!"

In the next house but one, bushes and shrubbery threshed. A gate clanged open. A slim, supple figure flew out and into my arms.

As from a long distance, I heard her ladyship's rasping voice. "Splendid! Splendid! Niece, mind what I tell you. Love will be served."

Much later, when I looked about me, there was no sign of the carriage. The street was empty. My benefactress had gone.

TEN

The Baron and Kirstie had been permitted to join their compatriots in London under house arrest. Kirstie had at first written me many letters, but then had stopped. "You see, my dear one, I thought you might have married—Nancy." She looked at me in sudden fear. "Did you, Benje?"

I answered her in a manner better than words.

Breathlessly she said, "Forgive me, but I could not know, and it would not have been right to send words of love to a man who belonged to another. I thought of you sometimes— with her. Ah, my dearest dear, it was very—hard...."

In anguish for her suffering I held her close, murmuring broken endearments, kissing her hair, her eyes. "We must be married at once," I said. "I dare not let you out of my sight until that is done."

"Yes," said the Baron dryly, "I was about to suggest it."

We were in the tiny parlor of his little house, but for all of me he might as well have been a stick of furniture. Half laughing, half crying, Kirstie stumbled into his arms and he smiled at her lovingly.

With sudden dismay I said, "But there is no time—for the banns—for a proper wedding—for any kind of wedding. Kirstie, you must come with me to Land's End, to Boyle's ship. We have no time. Boyle will marry us."

"But Benje," she said, "I cannot be wed without Papa to give me away. I cannot."

"All can be quickly arranged," said the Baron. "The English move slowly but our legation has been officially at work for more than a week. Svenson, our consul, is empowered to wed you."

She flung her arms around his neck. "Papa, how can I leave you!"

He kissed her gently on the forehead. "You and Ben will have Calabasboom, and I will come to you there, and perhaps there will be another Kirstie then, a very little one, to pull my hair and tweak my nose and be a trial to me, as you were."

He pushed her toward me and I saw, with delight, that she was blushing. The Baron gave me an affectionate little shake and clapped me on the shoulder. "I will see to the arrangements."

"Dear heart," I murmured to Kirstie, who was once more safe in my arms, "I love you so much—but I wonder—sometimes I think I love him even more. . . ."

With a low laugh she drew down my head and pressed her lips to mine. "Now," she said. "Now, tell me, who is it you love most?"

I told her.

There were things to be done. I bought Kirstie a wedding ring. Then I repaired to Gray's Inn to arrange for our journey to Penzance. There I did not trouble to substitute a different name for my own. It did occur to me but I laughed at myself for excess of caution. No one knew Benjamin Forbes. What difference did it make?

I turned from the wicket, counting my change and pondering the amount of luggage it would be possible for Kirstie to take with her. I glanced up and looked across the big, busy room to where the boys were sorting out trunks and boxes that had been taken from the stagecoach just arrived from Exeter. I looked straight into the eyes of a tall, dark man. For a moment I froze, and in that moment I saw recognition flare in his face. Instantly I turned and fled, pushing my way through the churning crowd until I found a side door and slipped outside. I hurried across the street and rounded the corner. Flattening my back against the wall, I peered back. He was at the door, looking up and down the street, and there was no mistaking him—Lieutenant John Meade of His Britannic Majesty's Navy.

I daresay I was the color of old paste when I returned to Kirstie, for she took alarm at the sight of me. I explained to her what had occurred. "He saw me buying our passage to Penzance. If we take that stage he is certain to be waiting."

She considered. "Mr. Svenson will help us," she said.

So he did, but it was the Baron who thought of the plan. Mr. Svenson took into his confidence a young married couple of his staff. They would take our places on the coach to Penzance as far as Woking. They were instructed to watch for a man of John Meade's description.

We were married late that afternoon by Mr. Svenson, and the simple ceremony was followed by a fine supper at which all the Danes in the neighborhood were present, and they were many.

That night I carried my bride up the stairs to the little bedroom that had been hers alone for too long. Ah, the shining beauty of her, the sweetness! Fumbling with the fastenings of her dress, I swore under my breath at all the dressmakers in the world. She shook me off, her eyes downcast and her fingers almost as clumsy as my own. She left her garments where they fell, and stood before me in all her loveliness. I cried out. I could not move.

With a shy little smile, she came to me.

Later in the night she stirred beside me and nibbled at my ear. "Ah, Benje," she breathed. "It is sweet to wait, but it is sweeter when the waiting is done."

My lips sought hers. "Dear heart," I said, "we have lost so much time. Your father has given us a large order."

She laughed and snuggled close. "Benje," she said. "Benje, my own, don't your people want grandchildren, too?"

Early the next morning we set out in a hired coach for Woking. We were at the posting inn, the Hound and Garter, in time to meet our young Danes who arrived in the stage. They informed us that a man answering John Meade's description had been at Gray's Inn, but had made no move to stop or question them.

Vastly relieved, Kirstie and I took their places in the stagecoach, and went on with it. It was a long journey, but while every mile of it seemed beautiful to me, a sense of urgency hung over us and the fear of pursuit. On the road beyond Exeter a two-wheeled chaise overtook us and spun past, the horses at a gallop. The driver was half hidden in a cloud of dust. Nevertheless, I could have sworn him to be John Meade. I prepared to be intercepted at Plymouth, but he did not appear. I began to breathe more easily. After all, I must not assume that every man who passed the stagecoach at a gallop on horse or in a light, swift turnout was after me.

We reached Penzance in the afternoon of the tenth day. I

had no time to explore the terrain over which we were to pass
or to search out the cove where the *Chasseur's* longboat would
be coming in to take us off. I found a little inn near the eastward road along the coast, at the top of the cliffs overlooking
the sea. There I settled Kirstie for a much-needed rest, taking
rooms as if we meant to stay for some time.

I went out to find a guide. This did not prove difficult. It
might well have been, if I had had the time to pursue inquiries
discreetly. As it was, I approached the first likely fellow—a
dark-visaged, wizened old man who was plodding along the
road leading a shaggy pony.

"Do you know the Lizard?" I asked.

He winked and nodded.

"Will you take me there tonight—and my wife?"

Again he winked and nodded.

"I'll need your pony," I said, "and a lantern." I added, "And
your silence."

"Ten shillings," he said. "Name's Fiddler."

"Yours?"

"Not *his*." He jerked his head at the pony.

"You'll not fail me, Fiddler?" I begged him.

He shook his head and with that I had to be content.

A little before midnight Kirstie and I slipped down the back
stairs and met our man a little distance from the inn. He
strapped Kirstie's luggage on the shaggy pony and I swung
her up to sit atop the load. The night was black, and in her
dark-hooded cloak she was all but invisible. Now and again as
we went along, I called to her softly, to hear her dear voice.

In about an hour's time the track ended. I lit Fiddler's
lantern. We were on a high barren moor sparsely covered
with bracken that ended abruptly at the sheer cliffs. A cold
sea wind made me shiver, and I called to Kirstie to ask if she
were warm enough. She reassured me. Her voice was gay, but
my sense of uneasiness was heightened. This place which I had
never seen before was somehow strangely familiar.

We went on, to the cliffs. I thought I heard the click of hoofs
upon the stones behind us in the darkness, and all at once an
eerie, apprehensive feeling settled down upon me, like a gently
tumbling, wind-torn spider web.

"Fiddler," I said softly, "what was that?"

"Wot was wot?"

I listened again, but heard nothing, only the sea breaking
on the rocks far below.

" 'Ere we are," said Fiddler abruptly. "Down we goes."

293

We were at the edge of the cliffs and the lantern revealed a stony path. I helped Kirstie from her perch on the pony and held her for a moment very tightly.

"Benje," she said, "it is the dream. No?"

"Shall we turn back?" I asked her.

"Never!"

Fiddler demanded to be paid. I gave him one-half the sum agreed upon and told him he'd be damned for the rest if he did not see us down to the Lizard. I gave Kirstie the lantern and we started down. Kirstie stumbled and I helped her up. "Fiddler," I called, "lend Mistress Forbes a hand here— Fiddler?" There was no sound. "Fiddler!"

Kirstie swung the lantern. "He has gone, Benje," she said lightly. "That is well. I did not like him."

"But the pony. . . ."

"Look." The lantern showed me the shaggy little beast— its hindquarters, rather—plunging down, already far below. "He knows the way," Kirstie laughed. "He is our guide."

I took the lantern and held her hand as we picked our way through the blackness and the long dancing shadows cast by our smoky, golden light. The path had been well worn by the feet of countless smugglers, but it was in places treacherously steep. We slipped and slithered downward, twisting and winding with it. I had never been here, yet I could almost tell where the next bend was going to be and where the stony rubble lay over which we must slide; and even the dank smell of the undergrowth was eerily familiar to me.

Suddenly, from above, a rock rolled down, chuckling through the brush. That, too, I had expected. "Hurry!" I said to Kirstie.

We scrambled down into a gully. The way was a little less steep now. All at once I had the certain feeling that whoever had been behind us was now very near, and on our flank. I hissed to Kirstie and we stopped abruptly. We stood very still, listening. But if anyone was there, he, too, had stopped, for not even the rustling scamper of a field mouse disturbed the silence of the night.

"Hurry!" I said again to Kirstie, urgently. "In God's name! It's our only chance!"

We went on. The sound of the sea grew louder in our ears. Below, I heard the pony nicker, as in welcome. Someone was on the little beach. What should I do? There was no going back, not now. But why not? For if someone was there, I dared not signal to Tom Boyle and draw him into a trap. For an instant I knew the sinking, wrenching feeling of panic. But Kirstie's hand was warm and firm in mine, and she drew me on. They would not harm her, I thought to myself. And as for me, I would sell my life dearly. I would not again be parted from her—not in life.

For the most part we carried our hooded lantern shuttered because the shadows were confusing. But now and again we had to open it to see our way. At these times the strange feeling of familiarity was so strong that I began to feel I could almost follow the path with my eyes closed.

We clambered over the shoulder of a rocky wall at the mouth of the little ravine we were following and started down the last sharp pitch to the stony beach, slipping and sliding over the rubble. We came out at last on a level stretch. Tide-washed boulders loomed like black monsters on either hand.

It was there that it happened. A ghostly figure detached itself from the side of a boulder and barred the way. Kirstie uttered a little scream and shrank back. From the darkness came a voice I knew too well.

"Good evening, Mr. Forbes."

"God damn you, John Meade!" I raged. "I knew it would be you!" I launched myself upon him. Under my fierce onslaught he went down, and I with him, raining savage blows upon his body and expecting at any moment to be set upon from all sides.

Then, as from far away, I heard Kirstie: "Benje, stop! He does not fight! You will kill him! Oh, Benje, if you love me ...!"

I awakened as from a nightmare. I leapt up and back, ready for whatever might come. But there were no shouts or shots, no clatter of feet, no gleaming muskets. Nothing but the sound of the sea. Kirstie had opened the shield on the bull's-eye, and in the light I saw John Meade lying on the shingle, staring up at me in pained reproach. Behind him was Fiddler sitting stolidly on a rock, and over Fiddler's shoulder I saw the innocent face of the little pony, as blandly peaceful as Fiddler himself. I looked stupidly from one to the other— Meade, Fiddler, and the pony.

John Meade raised himself on one elbow. It was to Kirstie he spoke, and what he said was very strange. "I do not thank you, madam."

I thought him quite mad.

"Where are your men?" I cried.

"Men?" He looked puzzled. "Ah, you think I've been pursuing you in the King's name! But of course you could not know. I resigned my commission long ago, after Nancy and I were married.... Forbes, by your leave I will get up. It is deucedly uncomfortable on these wet stones."

He rose painfully. I watched him, for I did not dare to trust him. He bowed toward Kirstie. "I am sorry to have alarmed the lady. I would have called upon you at the inn, but Fiddler...." He gave that worthy a look that boded no good. "You see, I had Fiddler watching for you, but having made the arrangements with you, he stopped at the tavern. He is overfond of drink. So it was not until very late that he told me, and I did not wish to delay you."

A thousand questions clamored at my mind, but still I watched him, and I listened. He tidied his disordered clothing, wincing a little as he touched the bruises I had raised. And nothing stirred in the night.

"We live here, you know, Nancy and I," he said.

I said with deliberation, "There is a ship out yonder, waiting for my signal to send a boat to take us off."

"But of course," he said. "We Cornishmen know well the meaning of an appointment on the Lizard."

I hesitated, but Kirstie said, "Benje, I believe Mr. Meade intends us no harm."

I flashed the lantern out to sea, five times opening and closing its shutter. Meade did not stir.

"Now," said Kirstie as charmingly as if we were in her little parlor in St. John's Wood, or on the veranda at Calabasboom, or in Joel Barlow's mansion in Washington. "We have a mystery. Mr. Meade, you have given us much trouble."

"Trouble!" John Meade laughed rather wildly. "Madam, this man—your husband ...?"

She nodded, smiling at him, and her beauty made him catch his breath.

"And you, sir," she said, "you are married to the lovely Nancy. And you are not happy?"

"Madam," he said savagely, "I am a haunted man. Benjamin Forbes stands between my wife and me."

I started forward. "It is a lie!"

"I beg your pardon," he said quickly. "I must explain. You see, I told Nancy that you were dead and so she accepted me. When I came aboard the *Chesapeake* I thought that we had killed you in an action that was a disgrace to Great Britain. Then before my eyes you rose from the dead, off Saint John. Oh, you were real enough; I had a broken arm to prove it. But in a sense I killed you a second time. I wrote to Nancy that you were dead. But I knew in my heart that you were hidden in the cellar in the house of the Baron von Lund. It was a dishonorable thing to do. And so I have been waiting, knowing we must meet again and hoping that you would kill me."

He sighed. "But it seems I must live on with my shameful secret."

I had a vision of Nancy at crumbling Holly Hall, a creature to be feared, and again in the spinster's parlor in Brookline— every word that had passed between us there came back to me.

"But Nancy loves you!" I said. "She as much as told me so."

"Told you so?" he said slowly.

" 'Twas in Boston," I said. "She refused me. 'A true man,' she said of you, and she was very happy. She hated me!"

He stared from me to Kirstie.

"Poor Nancy," said Kirstie gently. "Must she forever be tormented by misunderstandings?"

"She makes them herself," I said. "It's her way."

"By the Lord," cried John Meade, "I'll not have you speak against my wife! The fault is mine, sir; never hers. I've been a fool!"

At the edge of the rim of light, Fiddler spoke. "Aye," he said.

John Meade began to laugh. He laughed so hard that he had to sit down on a rock.

Kirstie smiled down at him, then raised her eyes to me, and they were misty in the golden glow. I took her into my arms and a great peace descended upon me. All that had passed was like a storm that one remembers only to relate to one's children before the warm fireside when the wind blows outside and all is snug and safe within.

We heard the dip of oars.

John Meade rose and looked at me uncertainly. "Forbes," he said, "will you honor me by being my friend?"

I gave him my hand.

There came a low "Hallooo!" We went down together to where the boat waited on the shingle. John Meade shoved us off, splashing in the water. "My kindest regards to Mistress Meade," I called to him.

"God bless you!" came his voice.

We clambered over the rail into a darkness half-lit by the binnacle. Shadowy figures gave us a hoarse, whispered huzzah. Tom Boyle greeted us as if determined to cave in our sides and led us to his cabin. Jack Stransbury was there, grave as a deacon, and Mr. Osbourne, equally solemn.

"Now!" cried Tom. He was dressed in his best coat with

the gilt buttons, and a fine white-ruffled shirt. He was in a veritable fever of beaming. He picked up the Bible from the table and opened it to a marked place.

Kirstie looked at me, puzzled, and I at her.

"Be ye ready?" asked Tom.

Light dawned on me. I whispered to Kirstie and then said to Tom, "The bride begs to be excused for a moment, if the parson will permit. It's rather sudden for her."

"Of course, of course!" cried Tom, fussed.

Stansbury conducted us to our cabin and left us. I told Kirstie of Tom's eagerness to wed us, and how if he knew we were already married he would be sorely hurt. She laughed. "I enjoy marrying you," she said, and kissed me and gave me back her ring.

So we were remarried amid the creaking tackles, the groaning blocks, and the slatting sails of a tall ship getting under way. The Captain claimed his right to kiss the bride, a liberty which was also accorded his two side boys. A bottle of champagne was broached. Now that we had our breaths we saw how Tom had gone to the trouble of festooning the cabin. There was a board stuck up with homely lettering on it: "God Bless Our Bride and Groom!"

When we came up on deck Tom flung formality to the winds and bawled, "They're spliced, boys!" And they gave us three times three.

All hands were so intent on this ceremonial that we did not see the towering loom of the mighty seventy-four until we were almost upon her. I think our own appearance upon her weather beam came as an equal surprise, for there was a sudden barking of orders and a clatter of running feet that we heard plainly across the intervening water.

"Luff! Luff!" Tom shouted. "Show 'em our fantail, and let's be running for it!"

Beside me Kirstie laughed excitedly.

We swung on a pivot scarcely larger than a golden guinea, and went squattering away into the enveloping dark. Behind us a gun boomed. The ball whistled over our heads. In splendid defiance Captain Boyle threw back a reply from one of our own long 12s. We heard the crash and thud of it as it struck —our good-by kiss for England. Then we were away, swallowed up in the sheltering night, the *Chasseur* flying fast as the wind itself.

Long afterward, when Kirstie and I lay abed, a thought struck me. "Dear heart," I began, but couldn't think how to go on.

"Say it, Benje," she murmured. "What are you thinking of?"

"Of my father and mother. Kirstie, would you mind very much being married still a third time? I promised them."

She began to laugh. "Oh, Benje, you are so wholehearted, you never do things by halves. You pursued two women over a good part of the globe. You fought four duels in one afternoon. And now you insist on marrying the same woman three times!"

I could think of no retort to this indictment. I did better. I took her into an embrace which had now become doubly lawful. And the *Chasseur* sped through the glorious night toward home waters and Forbes Landfall.

ABOUT THE AUTHOR

With almost twenty books to his credit in as many years, John Jennings, author of such vigorous adventure stories as *Next to Valour, Gentleman Ranker,* and *The Salem Frigate,* brings to his newest novel, *The Tall Ships,* a wealth of experience in dealing with historical material together with the spontaneity and energy of the born yarn-spinner. From his youthful travels in the merchant marine and his wartime service in the U.S. Navy, where he was for a time officer in charge of the Naval Aviation History Unit, Mr. Jennings gained a personal knowledge of the sea and seamen; this, with years of painstaking historical researches, provides him with both the invaluable store of firsthand impressions and the authority in his field that combine to give his novels their sense of authenticity and reality. In *The Tall Ships* John Jennings has constructed his story around the American privateers that, virtually unaided, took 1344 British ships during the War of 1812, and around Tom Boyle, whose exploits included the daring "blockade" of the English coast.